"You can figh...
but we *will* m...

Theo didn't seem ab...
pulled Sadie against...
beneath his. After a...
the edge of her sweatshirt...
"I promised myself that I wasn't going to touch you
again tonight."

Sadie nipped his ear playfully. "Ah, but I promised
myself that I'd *definitely* be touching you."

"I like your promise better." He laughed.

"You know, if your conscience is bothering
you, you could just let me do the touching," she
quipped.

"Good idea." His hands found her breasts and she
arched towards him. "I'll hold you to it next time."
Then he kissed her again.

Desperation built immediately. She could feel his
hunger when his heart thundered against her palm,
taste it when his tongue aggressively met hers. The
heat of his response fuelled her own. Would the
pleasure he gave her always be this sharp? This
necessary?

He dragged his mouth away. "Why do you have to
look so damn sexy in my sweatshirt?"

"You could always take it off…"

"Brilliant suggestion." He held her tight against
him as his breathing slowed. "If I had any blood
left – in my brain, that is – I'd have thought of it…"

Wicked, wicked thoughts raced through his mind.

Bill stared at Ellie, trying not to think how drop-dead sexy that fishnet cover thing was over her red bikini. Very teasing. Very exciting. She was all grown-up and hot and sexy in that get-up. Enough to make a man howl at the moon.

"What're you thinking about?" she asked.

With another woman, that question would have stopped him cold. But with Ellie… well, it was different. He was tempted to detail his lusty thoughts to see if she was as keen to get busy as he was.

"Something about you, Ellie," he said instead.

The heat from the sun poured down on them. But it had nothing on the sizzle between them. Her expression encouraged him, told him to go for it, to seduce her into indulging in the kind of no-regrets wickedness dominating his mind.

With that kind of invitation, who was he to refuse?

THE DEFENDER

BY
CARA SUMMERS

&

SHOCK WAVES

BY
COLLEEN COLLINS

◉™ MILLS & BOON®
Pure reading pleasure™

All the characters in this book have no existence outside the imagination of the author, and have no relation whatsoever to anyone bearing the same name or names. They are not even distantly inspired by any individual known or unknown to the author, and all the incidents are pure invention.

First published in Great Britain 2008
by Harlequin Mills & Boon Limited,
Eton House, 18-24 Paradise Road, Richmond, Surrey TW9 1SR

The Defender © Carolyn Hanlon 2007
Shock Waves © Colleen Collins 2007

ISBN: 978 0 263 86717 6

14-0708

Harlequin Mills & Boon policy is to use papers that are natural, renewable and recyclable products and made from wood grown in sustainable forests. The logging and manufacturing processes conform to the legal environmental regulations of the country of origin.

Printed and bound in Spain
by Litografia Rosés S.A., Barcelona

THE DEFENDER

BY
CARA SUMMERS

Dear Reader,

Writing about TALL, DARK…AND DANGEROUSLY HOT! men has been a challenge and a delight! I really hate to see it come to an end. Kit may have been my first love and Nik my favourite, but I have to admit that it's Theo who will remain in my mind and heart the longest.

In the courtroom hotshot defence lawyer Theo Angelis has a winning reputation, but outside the courtroom he's lost his edge. An incident with a stalker has him doubting his instincts. He's even stopped dating! So the last thing he needs right now is a damsel in distress – especially one as sexy as fellow lawyer Sadie Oliver.

Sadie's in *big* trouble. Her sister has disappeared, her brother is seriously injured *and* the prime suspect in a murder…and Sadie's libido has just shot into overdrive, thanks to Theo Angelis. Professionally, Sadie needs Theo's help to find her sister and prove her brother's innocence. Personally, however, she has other needs she'd like Theo to take care of…

I hope you'll come along for the ride as Theo and Sadie discover just what the Fates have in store for them. And enjoyed meeting the other Angelis brothers in *The PI* (May) and *The Cop* (June).

For more information about the Angelis brothers and their family, including excerpts from all three books, visit www.carasummers.com.

Happy reading!

Cara Summers

CARA SUMMERS

Award-winning author Cara Summers loves creating memorable characters. And for her, the best thing about writing for Mills & Boon® Blaze® is that the series allows her to bring to life strong women and seriously sexy men – like the Angelis brothers. "They're smart, they're kind, they're hot and they each have a great sense of humour. What's not to like?" She hopes that her readers have as much fun reading about Kit, Nik and Theo as she had writing about them. When Cara isn't busy with her characters, she spends time with her students at Syracuse University in New York state and travels south as often as she can to play with her grandchildren.

To my son Kevin. Thanks for your advice
(which I don't always take), your unfailing
support and your pride in my work. You make
the writing life a bit easier. Thanks, too, for
being my biggest fan! I love you.

Prologue

TWILIGHT WAS ONE OF THOSE special times of the day when Cassandra Angelis' power to see into the future sharpened; this evening she needed all the help she could get. A sense of urgency propelled her along the garden path until she caught her first glimpse of the sun still hanging above the Pacific. Only the faintest shades of pink and blue streaked the sky. So there was still time.

Deliberately slowing her pace, Cass let the scent of the flowers and the songs of insects and birds fill her senses. It wouldn't do any good to rush. She knew from experience that she couldn't force her visions. She had to just let them come.

Psychic abilities ran strong in her family and she'd never denied or run away from her special gift. Over the years, she'd established a reputation as a psychic in the San Francisco area.

This evening, Cass had no client. She'd known for almost a month that this weekend would be a pivotal one in the lives of her family members, but it hadn't been until midnight and again this morning at dawn that her feelings had begun to clarify into visions. She now knew the Fates would bring two of her nephews, Kit and Nik, mortal danger. And love, if they chose to open their hearts to it.

She paused near a patch of white flowers. The delicate blossoms always reminded her of the wildflowers that grew near the seashore in Greece where she'd first met her husband, Demetrius. She could still recall that moment of knowing that there was no one else, would never be anyone else, for her.

It had been the same for her sister Penelope and Demetrius' brother Spiro. None of them had thought twice about grabbing what the Fates had offered them. She'd never regretted choosing Demetrius even though they'd only had little more than a dozen years together before he and her sister had been killed in a boating accident. In the intervening years, she'd raised Penelope's children, her nephews Nik, Theo and Kit, and her niece Philly, coming to look on them as much her own as her son, Dino.

Leaning down, Cass picked one of the flowers and inhaled its scent as she continued along the path. Eighteen years had passed so quickly. Her children were all grown up and making their own way in the world. But it was her sister's middle son, Theo, who'd been slipping into her mind all day.

As she thought of him, her lips curved in a smile. Even as a child, Theo had always been a bit more of a risk taker than his two brothers, trusting his luck to get him out of scrapes. Now that he was older, Theo had put those characteristics to good use as a criminal defense attorney. In fact, his reputation for winning high stakes cases had garnered him some attention from the press.

A couple of months back, he'd even made a list of the ten most eligible bachelors in San Francisco and there'd been a photo of him in the Sunday paper. That photo had earned him quite a bit of razzing from his brothers. It had also earned him a spot on the invitation lists of several prominent party givers. However, there'd been a downside to his sudden fame. Theo had also picked up a stalker.

On the surface, one would never have suspected that the situation bothered him. But little by little, Cass had seen Theo withdraw into himself. Eventually, he'd even withdrawn from his family by taking what he termed a "temporary" apartment in town. Of course, he'd done it to protect them—that was Theo's way—but in the end his efforts had failed. In spite of his precautions, the woman who'd been stalking him had followed him to his father's restaurant one night and pulled a gun. He'd managed to talk her outside before she'd injured anyone, but in the process of getting the gun away, he'd gotten shot. Then in a move that was so typically Theo, he'd arranged for a good attorney to represent her.

Cass frowned as she watched the sun edge lower toward the water. The family had expected that Theo would move back home once his stalker had been arrested. But he hadn't. And he'd stopped coming to The Poseidon altogether. She thought she knew what was bothering him. All the Angelis children had some latent psychic ability, but Theo's was the strongest. He didn't have visions, but sometimes he just *knew* things. As a child he'd called the ability luck. But since the incident with his stalker, he was doubting his "lucky feelings."

She knew what he was going through. She hadn't

foreseen the boating accident that had taken both her
husband and her sister, Penelope. The guilt that she
hadn't seen it, hadn't been able to prevent it, had caused
her problems for a time, but she'd finally learned to
trust in her powers again. Theo would have to learn that
lesson, too.

With a sigh, Cass sank onto a bench and looked out
at the ocean in the darkening light. Overhead, a bird
sang its heart out. Cass listened and, keeping her gaze
fixed on the distant waves, emptied her mind. In front
of her, the evening shadows shifted, blending together
and separating, then blending again until they formed a
thin mist. Through it she saw the image of a woman—
tall with short, dark hair and dark, intelligent eyes.

Yes, she thought, Theo would want intelligence. The
mists darkened. As if through a glass darkly, she saw
Theo and the woman someplace high with the lights of
the city spread out beneath them. She felt the sharpness
of their fear, but she also sensed the emotions of the
other person with them. The coldness of anger and the
irrationality of greed sliced through her with an intensity that took her breath away. Then the image faded and
she was once more alone in the garden.

The evening was warm, but Cass felt cold right to her
bones. Of her three nephews, Theo would face the
greatest danger. But he would also find love—if he had
the courage to take it. And that love would teach him to
trust in his instincts again.

1

ST. PETER'S CHURCH looked deserted. When Sadie Oliver had driven by a few seconds ago, there'd been no one on the steps. Her sister Juliana's note had said to come at seven, but the only indication that there was anything going on was a dark van she'd spotted blocking the entrance to the little parking area behind the church.

There'd been something vaguely familiar about the man behind the wheel but she hadn't been able to draw up the memory. Sadie was debating whether or not to swing back and ask him to move so that she could park behind the church when she finally spotted a space just big enough to squeeze her Miata into.

She hated being late, but a glance at her watch told her she'd slipped into the tardy zone by almost ten minutes. Grabbing her purse, Sadie scrambled out of her car, locked the door and slipped her key into her pocket. She also hated feeling guilty. Maybe if she wasn't so obsessive-compulsive, she'd have been willing to leave some unfinished work on her desk over the weekend. But she *was* obsessive-compulsive *and* late *and* feeling guilty.

Spotting her reflection in the driver's window of her

car, she added *dowdy* to her list. Just the cherry she needed to top off a very depressing sundae.

Sadie narrowed her eyes as she studied her image in the glass. Her long, dark hair was pulled back in a braid because she didn't like to fuss with it. Her earrings and suit were definitely conservative and work oriented. She'd taken great care in the selection because she wanted to represent her family well. But the ensemble reflected in the glass didn't make the transition to after-five easily. Not that she was an after-five kind of girl, or had been, well, ever. It wasn't until she'd begun to work at Oliver Enterprises that she'd bought a couple of basic black dresses appropriate for the social functions that she was expected to attend as part of the Oliver family.

Finally, she glanced down at her shoes and winced. They were…well…serviceable was the best word she could come up with. *Dowdy* repeated the little voice in the back of her mind.

Annoyed, she turned and hurried up the street. A few months ago, she wouldn't have given a second thought to the way she looked. Her baby sister Juliana, who'd taken after their mother, had always been the girlie-girl. Since Sadie had tried to do everything her older brother Roman could do, she'd become a bit of a tomboy. Being a *woman,* fussing with her clothes and her hair had always made her…uncomfortable. But she'd been satisfied with herself. Hadn't she?

Sadie frowned. It had only been since Theo Angelis had stopped to talk to her in the courthouse two months ago that she'd caught herself glancing in the mirror more frequently and…what? Seeing herself the way Theo would see her? *Dowdy,* insisted the little voice.

"Stop being ridiculous," she scolded herself as she picked up her pace. Theo Angelis didn't see her as a woman. He saw her as a colleague. He'd sought her out to congratulate her on the way she'd handled a case, a case that she'd been surprised to learn he'd sent her way. Sandra Linton, the woman she'd defended that day, had stalked him and pulled a gun on him in his family's restaurant. And Theo had actually been pleased that she'd gotten the woman psychiatric treatment instead of jail time. He'd said that he'd admired her work, a great compliment since she felt the same way about his work.

Just thinking about the encounter shouldn't have her recalling his scent…soap and something a little earthier. She was tall, but he'd been taller so that she'd had to look up to meet his eyes. Dark eyes with just a hint of danger in them. Just talking to him shouldn't have made her knees grow weak. And shaking his hand—she could still recall the way her mind had fuzzed over, as if her brain had been replaced by a vat of cotton candy. It had been hot in the courtroom. *That* was why she'd felt heat shoot right down to her toes; *that* was why her throat had gone dry.

What she'd experienced in that moment of contact had to have been some kind of aberration, no doubt due to that rush of adrenaline she experienced at the end of every trial. And that was probably the reason she'd developed a sort of schoolgirl crush on Theo Angelis— totally one-sided and very self-indulgent.

And *safe,* nagged the little voice. Ignoring the voice, Sadie lifted her chin. It was just a handshake, for heaven's sake. She'd better get over it. She knew from experience that she didn't have the…know-how or the…equipment to attract a man like Theo Angelis. The kind of man she evidently appealed to was the practical, steady kind. Someone like Michael Dano, who headed up the legal department at Oliver Enterprises. The kind of man she thought of as a mentor and a friend. Michael had waited almost six months to make a move on her…and then she'd felt nothing. Theo had made her feel more with one look. It was just her fate to only be able to feel things with a man who could have any woman he wanted.

And she'd do well to put him out of her mind. The whole San Francisco legal community was buzzing with the fact that Jason Sangerfeld, defense attorney to the stars, had offered him a job in Los Angeles.

Glancing at her watch again, Sadie broke into a run. Her sister Juliana hadn't given her much notice. The invitation hadn't arrived until shortly after four o'clock, and she hadn't had time to go home and change. Not that she knew what she was changing for. Her younger sister's note hadn't been very specific. All it had said was: *Come to St. Peter's Church at seven tonight. Please. Juliana.* And she hadn't been able to reach her cell.

As Sadie reached the foot of the steps, she felt another wave of guilt wash over her. Juliana and she weren't close. Part of that was due to the fact that her sister was eighteen and she was twenty-six. The eight-year difference in their ages had seemed even greater when they were kids. Juliana had still been playing with Barbie dolls when Sadie had gone East for college and law school. And when Sadie had come back home to work in the legal department at Oliver Enterprises a year ago, Juliana had been away at boarding school.

When her sister had come home three months ago, Sadie's goal had been to get to know Juliana better. But she'd let her work and perhaps her current frustration with it interfere.

Frowning, Sadie hurried up the last steps. For the last five months, ever since the kiss, Michael Dano had seemed intent on keeping her buried in busywork—real estate deed and title searches. And when she wasn't doing that, her father and brother were insisting on her presence at various social functions.

No, Sadie gave herself a mental shake. She was not going to blame Michael Dano or her father or brother for the fact that she hadn't taken the time to get closer to her sister. There was no one to blame for that except herself.

Pulling the door open, she stepped into the gloom of the vestibule and felt the silence of the church envelop her. Then she heard two gunshots in rapid succession.

AFTER LEAVING A MESSAGE on Nik's cell, Theo dialed Kit and left the same one. Then he turned his cell phone off for the weekend, strolled onto the porch of the cabin and took his first look at the sea. The tide was coming in, but the water in the little inlet was relatively calm.

The position of the sun in the sky told him that there was about a half an hour left before sunset. Still plenty of time to sit and relax and enjoy the view.

It didn't surprise Theo that his brothers hadn't picked up when he'd called them. They would have known the minute they checked the caller ID what he was calling about. He'd made it to their grandfather's fishing cabin first, so it was his brotherly duty to gloat.

From the time they'd been kids, they'd always raced from their father's car to the cabin. The winner got the first pick of the lures and poles.

Well, he'd won the race this weekend, but it hadn't been for the choice of fishing equipment that he'd left his office early. He'd set out to beat the weekend traffic because he'd wanted some time alone before anyone joined him. There was something about being near the sea that helped him to sort things out. Perhaps it would even settle the restlessness that had been plaguing him lately. No— it was more than restlessness. For the first time in his life, he was doubting himself. In the courtroom he was hanging back, second-guessing his instincts.

A joyful bark had him shifting his gaze away from the water. Bob, a neighbor's dog, was bounding happily toward the cabin. No one was quite sure what Bob's actual lineage was, but Theo had always suspected that there'd been a Saint Bernard among his ancestors. He opened the door and Bob shot into the cabin. Theo heard his toenails clicking on the floorboards as he raced from room to room.

A moment later, Bob returned to the porch and Theo could have sworn that his expression held reproach.

"Ari is coming with Kit," he said. "He'll be here in another couple of hours." Over the years, Bob and Ari, Kit's dog, had become friends. Reminding himself that he wanted to have time alone before that joyful canine reunion, Theo strolled into the kitchen. He stored the whole grain bread he'd brought in the pantry and put the selection of cheeses into the refrigerator. When he turned, Bob stepped into his path, sat down and thumped expectantly his tail on the floor.

"Kit's bringing the stuff you like," Theo said as he reached into the refrigerator and broke off a chunk of cheese for the dog. His youngest brother always provided the more basic essentials—eggs, bacon, rolls and enough deli meat for an army. Nik, whose cupboard in his apartment was always bare, would bring what he considered essential—beer and junk food.

While Bob made short work of the hunk of cheddar, Theo unpacked the wine he'd brought. There were two dry Italian whites from different regions, a German white and a French chardonnay. All would go well with the fish they would catch this weekend.

Kit was the real fisherman of the family. Even as a kid he'd had their father's patience and ability. Nik and Theo would throw in their lines, of course; but Nik would spend the majority of the weekend on his boat testing his skills against the wind and waves and what Theo enjoyed most about the cabin was simply being near the water and being with his family.

Bob padded after him into the bedroom and sat ever hopeful as Theo stripped out of his city clothes and hung them neatly on hangers. Noticing the way that Bob was eyeing his Italian loafers, he rescued them and placed them on the closet's top shelf. After pulling on the well-worn jeans and T-shirt that he kept at the cabin, he strolled barefoot back to the refrigerator, poured a glass of the Italian white and carried it to the porch.

Theo sank into a chair, put his feet up on the railing and crossed his ankles. As he sipped his wine, he reached absently down and ran a hand over Bob's head.

A gull cried out as it swooped close to the water's surface before soaring into the sky. Far out in the distance, an outboard motor thrummed as a boat moved slowly into the center of the inlet. The driver already had his running lights on in anticipation of the sunset. At Theo's side, Bob sighed.

Theo could second the sigh. He had a decision to make this weekend. The fact that he wasn't looking forward to it didn't mean that he could avoid it any longer. Taking a slow sip of wine, he gazed out at the water. He wasn't usually indecisive.

His Aunt Cass believed that psychic powers ran in the family and she'd told him once that his own gift was particularly strong. He didn't see visions the way she did, but from the time he'd been a child, there'd often been occasions when he just knew things. Most of his success in the courtroom had been due to the fact that he'd had a hunch about which strategies to implement. And when it came to making choices, he was usually pretty sure which one to make.

But that had all changed since Sandra Linton. It was that damn most-eligible-bachelor list that had started it all. After that splash of publicity, Sandra had been among the women who'd started attending his trials. His brothers had called them his groupies. Then he'd made the mistake of agreeing to have coffee with her. Why hadn't he sensed that simple choice would lead to tragedy? For that matter, why hadn't he sensed that she was disturbed?

For two months the woman had followed him everywhere. Reasoning with her hadn't helped. Neither had a restraining order. He'd rented a small apartment in town to keep her away from his family and he'd taken to sneaking out the delivery entrance of his office building. He'd even changed his parking lots. Still, she'd eventually tracked him down at his father's restaurant.

Panic slithered up his spine even now when he thought of it. They'd been in the small lobby of The Poseidon when she'd pulled the gun. His sister, Philly, had been only a few feet away and there'd been customers waiting for tables. He hadn't needed psychic powers to know what she'd intended to do—the violence, the fury and the despair had been there in her eyes. If he hadn't been able to convince her to leave…

Taking a sip of his wine, Theo shoved the fear of what might have been out of his mind and focused on the now. Watching the rippling surface of the sea, he repeated the little lecture he'd been giving himself for the last two months. It was high time he put Sandra Linton out of his mind. It was more than time for him to get his balance back.

Perhaps taking the position with Jason Sangerfeld would help him do that. The high-power defense attorney had called him a month ago and offered him a job—a dream job, one that any defense attorney would jump at. If Theo accepted, he would be working second chair with Jason on high-profile cases. The experience would be incredible, the money…well, it would be a lot more than he was making now. The catch was that he'd have to give up his own practice and move to Los Angeles.

Theo knew exactly what his Aunt Cass would say— the Fates were offering him a choice and his decision would make all the difference in his life. The truth was, he'd be a lot quicker about making his decision if he just had some inkling which choice was the right one. But his lucky hunches were leaving him high and dry. He wasn't sure anymore what the right thing to do was. And he couldn't help but wonder if this was due to doubting his instincts.

When Bob sighed again, Theo lifted his feet off the railing, rose and started moving toward the shoreline. One thing he did know: he should have put Sandra Linton behind him once she'd been arrested and he'd contacted the public defender's office to request that they assign the case to Sadie Oliver.

Theo strolled out onto the dock and sat down. Bob stretched out beside him. For a moment, he let his mind empty and fill with nothing more than the soft sound of the waves and the sight of the sky turning red in the west. Behind him, insects murmured in the grass.

Watching the sun sink into the water, his thoughts returned to Sadie Oliver. She'd been on his mind a lot lately. His brother Kit's best friend, Roman Oliver, had mentioned both of his sisters on occasion. He was very proud of the fact that Sadie had gone east to college and had edited the law review at Harvard Law School. His other sister, Juliana, who was twelve years his junior, had been sent away to a boarding school for high school. Theo had been aware through Kit that both sisters were back in town and that Sadie worked in the legal department of Oliver Enterprises, a multimillion dollar real estate development company that her father and her brother Roman ran.

Theo set his wineglass down on the dock beside him. His curiosity had been piqued when Kit had mentioned that Sadie was also doing some pro bono work for the public defender's office and he'd been intrigued enough to sit in on one of her trials. She was very good. His mouth curved slightly. Her style was more conservative than his, but she had a logical mind and a cool, unflappable manner that played well with a jury. An aloof, controlled ice princess was the way he'd summed her up in his mind. Not his type. Then he'd seen her address the jury and for the first time he caught a hint of the passion that lay beneath the cool exterior. The next time he'd seen her name on the docket, he'd gone back to watch her again. It was only natural that when his stalker was arrested, he'd thought of Sadie.

Theo frowned as he picked up his glass and sipped his wine again. Something had happened when he'd talked to her after that trial. Actually, a few things had happened and they'd given him pause. As the bottom edge of the sun disappeared into the Pacific, he let his mind drift back to that meeting…

When he'd approached her, the courtroom had already emptied and Sadie was packing papers quickly and efficiently into her briefcase. He'd had plenty of time during the trial to take in the details of her appearance. She was taller than average and she always wore a conservatively tailored suit and plain black pumps. Her long, dark hair was pulled back into a neat braid that fell below her shoulders.

There was nothing in her appearance to hint at the passion he sensed when she was pleading a client's case. For some reason, the contrast appealed to him.

He was about to speak to her when his gaze came to rest on her hands and he felt that first inexplicable tug of attraction. Her fingers were long and slender, the nails short and painted with a clear polish. They moved competently. Theo could imagine them pouring tea into delicate china cups. He could also imagine them moving over his skin. With no more warning than that, desire had snaked up his spine and settled in his gut. Where in hell had it come from?

Her cell phone rang and as she took the call, Theo took the opportunity to gather his thoughts.

"Yes?"

Even though he could only see her face in profile, he noted the frown and the way her grip tightened on the phone.

"Michael, I told you I had a trial today." She glanced at the watch on her wrist. "I'll be back in half an hour and I plan on working late. You'll have my report on your desk first thing in the morning."

Her shoulders had tensed and one of her feet had begun to tap. Whoever this Michael was, she wasn't happy with him. Still, she kept her tone cool. He wondered what it would take to chip through her control. What would he find beneath the surface? There was definitely passion there. He could see it in that tapping foot. A man couldn't help but wonder what it would be like when it was released.

"I'm sure that you and Daddy and Roman can mingle at the mayor's fundraiser without me. The Olivers will be well represented." Then she snapped the phone shut and stuffed it into her purse. Sadie was reaching for her briefcase when he said, "Ms. Oliver."

She jumped and turned to face him.

Theo looked into her eyes and for a moment his mind went totally blank. All he thought of was her. He took in the fact that her skin was a golden shade, her scent something floral. But it was those almond-shaped eyes in a deep shade of chocolate brown that he felt he was sinking into.

"Mr. Angelis, I'm…surprised to see you here." She secured her purse on her shoulder and reached for her briefcase.

Theo reined in his wandering thoughts and took a step to the side so that he blocked the aisle that led to the door. "You know me?"

"I've seen your picture."

Theo thought with embarrassment of the most-eligible-bachelor article. Was he never going to be free of that? "The one in the paper?"

"Well, yes, I did see that one. But I was thinking of the one Roman has in his office. In it, he's just beaten you at tennis."

Theo winced. "He's the best I've ever been up against. So far he hasn't agreed to a rematch."

"When he does, take advantage of his backhand. That's what I do. It's his Achilles' heel."

Fascinated, Theo eased his hip onto the edge of the railing that separated the lawyer's tables from the rest of the courtroom and studied her for a moment. "You've beaten him then?"

She smiled at him. "Once. Just a few weeks ago. And I intend to do it again."

It was the first time he'd seen her smile. In the slanted light pouring in through the narrow courtroom windows, Theo realized she was beautiful. Desire struck again like a punch low in his gut.

He had to put some effort into speaking. "Aren't

you betraying family secrets by telling me something like that?"

"Perhaps, but I figure I owe you one."

"Why?"

She met his eyes very steadily. "I know that you recommended me for this case. But you can't be pleased about the way it's ended."

"Because you got the woman who was stalking me psychiatric treatment instead of jail time? I was hoping that you would do just that."

It was Sadie's turn to study him. "She shot you."

Theo shrugged. "It wasn't a fatal wound and she's a very sick woman." If he'd sensed the problem in time, he might have prevented it. "Jail time won't help her. Mind if I ask a question?"

"Go ahead."

"Why are you doing pro bono work for the public defender's office? Don't they keep you busy enough at Oliver Enterprises?" He thought he saw a shadow flicker into those brown eyes and he recalled the conversation she'd just had with this Michael.

"I want the trial experience." Then she extended her hand. "I have to go, but I want to thank you for the recommendation."

He took her hand in his. In that first instant of contact, they both went perfectly still. Theo was glad that he was still half-sitting on the railing because his knees went weak. It was at that moment he knew—the way he knew a lot of things—his path and Sadie's were going to cross again.

Theo drained the last of his glass and watched the sun disappear into the ocean. He'd been very careful not to go back and watch her in court again, but he hadn't been able to get her out of his mind. Was it Sadie Oliver who was interfering with his ability to make a decision about the Los Angeles job? he wondered. Was she the cause of the restlessness that had been plaguing him lately?

It was a long time before he got up from the dock and went back into the cabin.

2

GUNSHOTS? In a church? Could she have been mistaken? In the dim light of the vestibule, Sadie swallowed hard, reminded herself to breathe and took a cautious step toward the double doors leading into the church. She'd nearly reached them when she heard footsteps pounding in her direction.

A man built like a linebacker exploded into the room. Her heart leaped to her throat and blocked her scream. He was wearing a black T-shirt and jeans; she made out the gun in his hand as he pounded up the circular wrought-iron staircase to the choir loft above. An instant later, another man burst through the doors. She recognized this one.

"Roman?"

When her brother whirled to face her, she saw that he was carrying a gun, too. "What's going—"

He grabbed her by the arm and shoved her into the shadows beneath the staircase. "Stay out of sight. Don't let anyone know you're here."

She'd barely processed the words when more shots sounded from inside the church. Even as terror streamed through her, another gunshot exploded overhead. Her ears were ringing with it as Roman took the stairs two at a time. She wanted to go after him, stop him, but fear had her pressing herself even deeper into the shadows. She did the only thing she could think of. She pulled out her cell phone and dialed 911.

"Juliana, are you all right?" Roman shouted.

Horror paralyzed Sadie, preventing her from speaking to the 911 operator. Had her sister been shot?

Above her, she thought she heard someone—a man—answer, "Yes."

Roman spoke again, but she didn't catch what he said because she was breathlessly giving the 911 operator the location.

Overhead, she heard pounding footsteps and the sounds of a fight—thumps and muffled cries. Peering up through the circle of steps, she saw two figures locked tight in a fierce struggle at the top of the stairs before one of them pitched over the railing.

It happened so fast. One minute he was falling…then she heard the sickening thud as the body smacked against the floor and she felt the shock of the impact beneath her feet. In the dim light, she saw his face. Roman. His eyes were closed, his body so still. Her heart simply stopped.

She wanted to go to him, but her legs refused to work. Footsteps pounded down the steps and hit the floor running. Sadie registered the sounds, the blur of movement. In the light that entered the vestibule as the person pushed through the front doors, she recognized the man Roman had chased up the stairs. Blood streamed from his shoulder.

All of those details registered; still, she couldn't move. She couldn't breathe. All she could do was stare at her brother's body on the ground. There was absolute silence in the church. Then the panic that had frozen her blasted free and galvanized her into action. Lunging out of the shadows, she cried out, "Juliana? Juliana, are you all right?"

No answer.

Her purse dropped unnoticed to the floor as she sank to her knees and pressed two fingers to her brother's throat. There was a pulse—weak but steady. Running her other hand over his head, she felt the wet stickiness of blood. "Roman," she murmured, leaning closer.

His eyes fluttered open.

"It's Sadie. I'm right here." She squeezed his hand. "Don't move."

"Can't…see…"

"It's all right. You fell."

His eyes closed again. "You're in danger…get out."

"Where's Juliana? What's going on?"

"Secret…wedding."

Sadie barely caught the words above the ragged sounds of his breathing. "Juliana…Paulo…Carlucci."

Juliana and Paulo Carlucci? No, that simply couldn't be. The bad blood between the Oliver and Carlucci families went back generations, and the fact that Oliver Enterprises and Carlucci Ltd. were currently competing over a lucrative land deal involving a strip of Orange County coastline had brought that blood to the boiling point.

If her baby sister had indeed planned a secret wedding to Paulo Carlucci and the news had leaked out… Fear knotted hard in her stomach. It *had* leaked out, hadn't it? Roman had certainly gotten wind of it.

And there'd been that man he'd been chasing. And those gunshots from inside the church.

Another possibility had her blood going cold. Had her father found out about the wedding plans, too? Mario Oliver had a reputation for knowing everything. *And who knows what he would have done to prevent his youngest daughter from marrying his enemy's son.*

"…Wanted…to stop it…"

She could all too easily imagine that Roman would have wanted to stop the wedding. They knew from watching their father that marriage was not an easy path, even in the best of circumstances. Their mother had died shortly after Juliana's birth; Mario Oliver was on his third marriage. Sadie had a suspicion that Deanna Mancuso Oliver would not be his last. And Juliana was barely eighteen, Paulo perhaps a year or two older. They were babies. She squeezed her brother's hand. "Don't try to talk."

"Shot…Paulo."

Sadie's stomach sank. Roman had shot Paulo? Had he come here to stop the wedding and…? No. Violence was not Roman's way. He didn't have their father's ruthlessness. She couldn't have heard him right. She lowered her head so that his lips were nearly brushing her ear.

"Make sure…Juliana's…safe." Roman tightened his grip on her fingers. "Trust…no one…go…to…Kit." He paused to let out a breath. Panic threatened to swamp her. Not his last breath. Please. His fingers went lax in hers. No. *Please.*

Fear knifed through her as she checked his pulse again. It was still there, and the rise and fall of his chest told her he was breathing.

For a second, she sat there, her mind numb. Think, she told herself. Do something. She pressed her fingers to her temples. Roman had said to trust no one. To go to Kit. Taking her cell from her purse, she scrolled to Kit Angelis's number and pressed it in. Kit and Roman had been best friends since college. Maybe he could…

She heard the sound of a siren just as Kit's answering machine picked up. Leaving her name and number, she dropped her phone back in her purse and struggled to gather her thoughts again. A new fear had her jumping to her feet. Roman had also said to make sure Juliana was safe. She recalled that shot she'd heard from the choir loft. What if Juliana…?

Sadie hit the stairs at a run, stumbling and coming down hard on the third rung. Pushing herself to her feet, she raced up the rest of the steps. One glance told her the choir loft was empty, but there was an open door directly in front of her. Heart pounding, she stepped into a small, windowless room. There was enough light for her to see that it, too, was empty. Her relief was short-lived as she took in dark stains on two walls. Blood? Then she saw the bouquet of white flowers lying on the floor.

Sadie drew in a deep breath and fought back the terror that had been dominating her actions so far. A good attorney never let emotions rule. She looked at the facts. And the fact she was staring at right now was a wedding bouquet.

Evidence of a secret wedding? Her sister and Paulo Carlucci's? Sadie was still trying to get her mind around that. Roman's words came back to her. "…Wanted to stop it…shot Paulo." She stared again at the dark stains on the wall. Who had shot Paulo? Roman? This time, she ruthlessly shoved the rising hysteria down. Roman would not have shot Paulo. Yes, he would have been upset to learn about the wedding plans. Yes, he would have tried to talk Juliana out of it. So would she if she'd gotten here in time.

But she'd heard those two gunshots when she'd first entered the church, hadn't she? She'd seen the gun in Roman's hand. He could have fired them.

The siren was drawing closer and Sadie could hear more in the distance. Turning, she stepped back into the choir loft and hurried to a window in time to see a red convertible with a flashing blue light on its hood careen around a corner and pull into the parking lot at the back of the church. After sending up a prayer that one of the other sirens belonged to an ambulance, Sadie reminded herself to think. The church was an old-fashioned one where the choir loft extended along both sides, as well as the back. She shifted her gaze to the exit signs marking the far ends of the loft and forced her mind back over the facts.

She'd heard Roman call out, "Juliana, are you all right?"

And she'd heard someone answer, "Yes."

Then the fight had broken out and she'd heard running footsteps. So while Roman was fighting with someone—the man in the black T-shirt with the gun—whoever was in that small room could have run along the side of the choir loft and exited through the back of the church.

The siren was close now and when she shifted her gaze to the street, she saw a police car slow as it crossed the intersection near the front of the church, passing a dark van. She was turning, intending to go back down the stairs and back to Roman, when suddenly, she blinked and leaned closer to the window. If she hadn't been standing right there peering through the glass at that particular minute, she would have missed it.

Two blocks down, a taxi had stopped at the curb and three people had crowded around its open passenger door.

One of them was Juliana. Even at this distance, Sadie was sure of it. Her sister's long, straight, dark hair was unmistakable. A second woman, a petite blonde carrying a dress bag and a tote, climbed into the taxi. A moment later, the taxi pulled away from the curb, leaving Juliana and the man standing on the curb. Sadie got a look at him in profile before he took Juliana's arm and disappeared around the corner. Paulo Carlucci. She also saw the dark stain on his upper arm. Blood?

Below her, the church doors opened and she hurried to the loft railing in time to see two policemen kneeling over Roman.

"The pulse is steady," one man said. "Blood on the back of his head."

"Look's like he fell," the other said. "Be careful not to move him until the EMTs get here."

Sadie hesitated, torn between her desire to go down the stairs to be with her brother and her fear for her sister's safety. Roman was in safe hands now, she told herself. It was Juliana who needed her.

With that one thought in mind, she rushed quietly along the side of the choir loft and hurried down the stairs. The room at the bottom was small. At its center stood a marble fountain in the middle of a shallow rectangular pool where baptisms would be performed. Sadie skirted it and raced for the exit. Once out on the street, she sprinted toward the corner where she'd last seen Juliana.

An ambulance rushed past, but she paid it no heed. The police on the scene would make sure the medics took care of Roman. She had to get to Juliana, make sure she was safe. She was half a block away from the corner when she saw the dark van pull through the intersection. She might not have paid it any heed if the driver's window hadn't been open. But it was—she recognized the driver and the van as the one that had been blocking the parking lot entrance when she'd first arrived.

Possibilities raced through her mind and she didn't like any of them. She thought of the man Roman had chased into the choir loft, the one who'd left through the front door with blood running down his arm. Had the man in the van been waiting for him? Were they, too, looking for Juliana?

Heart pounding, she put all her energy into reaching the corner. But when she turned it, there was no sign of Juliana or Paulo.

And no sign of the dark van.

3

BY THE TIME SADIE MADE it back to St. Peter's Church, there were four squad cars blocking off both Skylar Avenue and Bellevue. She'd run a few blocks trying to catch sight of Paulo and Juliana, but she hadn't even glimpsed them and she hadn't seen the van again, either. A glance at her watch told her that it was 7:30, roughly fifteen minutes since she'd heard those first shots and seen Roman fall over that railing.

A shudder moved through her as the image filled her mind. She couldn't let herself dwell on it. She had to hold it together. Roman was depending on her.

Two ambulances were now parked in front of the church, and uniformed policemen were stationed at intervals by the tape that had been strung along the sidewalks to keep the curious at a distance. She would have to get past them to get back into the vestibule and check on Roman.

As she made her way through the small crowd that had gathered on the sidewalk across from the church, someone tugged on her arm. Turning, she glanced down to find a tiny woman with bright blue eyes and a mass of curly white hair smiling excitedly up at her. The thought that popped into her mind was that this was what little orphan Annie might look like at seventy.

"Did you hear the shots, dear?"

"No, I didn't," Sadie lied, looking for an opening in the police barricade.

"I heard the shots. I live in the house right next to the rectory. At first I wasn't sure. I thought it might be a car backfiring. But altogether I counted six of them. Way too many for a car. Figured they had to be gunshots."

Six, Sadie thought. That roughly tallied with the number she'd heard. Two when she'd first come in, three from inside the church, then one overhead. "Did you see anything?"

The woman shook her head. "Not while the shooting was going on. I'd looked through the window earlier and I knew that a wedding was happening the minute that catering truck pulled into the rectory parking lot. Father Mike is hitching up a lot of couples lately. He has a way with young people and St. Peter's is turning out to be the in place for weddings. He's brought new life to the neighborhood."

There was pride in her voice.

"But there was something odd about this one," the woman continued.

"What?" Sadie asked.

"Very few guests. Usually, the cars fill that little parking lot behind the church, guests hang out on the front steps before the ceremony and they cover the front steps with a long white cloth—to protect the bride's dress, I guess—and the bride arrives in one of those big stretch limousines. But not tonight. I saw her come in a taxi with a little blond woman and I think the wedding dress was in the bag the blond was carrying."

Juliana had arrived in a taxi with a blond woman. The

woman she'd seen get into the taxi had been carrying a dress bag. Sadie felt a little stab of guilt. She had no idea who the woman was, no idea who any of her sister's friends were.

"A young man had arrived a bit before that with a big bruiser of a fellow. Figured one of them had to be the groom until the other man arrived. Handsome as sin, that one. I was thinking the bride was one lucky gal if she was tying the knot with him. He looked a bit familiar, too, but I couldn't place him. I will, though. It will come to me when I'm not expecting it. After the handsome one went inside, I went downstairs to catch *Wheel of Fortune.*"

As "Annie" continued to talk, Sadie glanced at the front of the church. Nothing was happening. She started forward again.

"Figured it must be one of those hush-hush affairs," Annie was saying. "Maybe a pair of celebrities or something like that. Whatever it was, someone got wind of it and put a stop to it. I just hope that it wasn't Father Mike who got killed. Of course, I wouldn't want it to be the bride or the groom, either."

Sadie turned back to the tiny woman. "Someone got killed?"

"I heard the cops talking a few minutes ago. I've got pretty good ears." She leaned close to Sadie and spoke in a tone only she could hear. "They said one dead and two injured. Someone in there definitely bought it."

Not Roman. Sadie glanced back at the church doors. Please, not Roman. "I have to get in there." She lifted the tape.

Annie laid a hand on her arm. "They won't let you past this point."

"But I have to—" She broke off when a young uniformed officer blocked her path.

"Miss, I have to ask you to lower the tape and step back from it," the officer said.

"You don't understand. I was here earlier," she said. "I need to talk to someone who's in charge."

An older man in his late forties moved toward them. "Problem, Jerry?"

"She wants to talk to someone who's in charge."

The older man turned to Sadie. He was on the short side but he had a solid, muscular build and eyes that gave away nothing. "Right now, that would be Officer Carter here and me, and our orders are to keep everyone out. The only people allowed in the church are the crime-scene team and the medics."

"You don't—" Sadie began. But she stopped when the doors of the church opened and two medics carried out a stretcher.

"Oh, thank heavens," Annie said. "That's Father Mike. I was so worried about him."

"How do you know he's alive?" Sadie asked, unable to tear her gaze away from the stretcher.

"They're putting him in the ambulance," Annie explained. "The coroner's van will pick up the dead one."

Sadie's stomach clenched. Was that why they hadn't brought Roman out yet? She was about to step forward again, when the doors opened and another stretcher emerged. Relief streamed through her when she saw that it was Roman.

"They're taking special care of him," Annie commented. "They're using what looks like a back brace. And see how they've got his neck protected?"

Sadie did see and her stomach sank. "How do you know all this?"

"I watch a lot of TV and there's all those crime shows. Beats watching that junk they call reality TV."

As soon as they'd loaded Roman's stretcher into the ambulance, a uniformed policeman climbed in behind him and another one climbed in the passenger seat.

"They're sending cops with him," Annie said. "They didn't send any with Father Mike."

No, they hadn't, Sadie thought. The fact that two policemen were accompanying her brother wasn't a good sign.

"He must have been involved in the shootings," Annie echoed Sadie's thoughts.

As Sadie reached to lift the tape again, she recalled Roman's words—"…shot…Paulo." If he had, he hadn't killed him. The moment she closed her hand around the tape, Officer Carter said, "Ma'am, you have to step back."

"But that's my—"

Sadie found herself gripped firmly by the arms. "You have to stay here," Carter said. "Otherwise, I'm going to have to take you into custody and put you in one of the patrol cars."

Sadie could see in his eyes that he meant it. And beyond his shoulder, she could see the first ambulance pulling away from the curb.

"Jerry?" the older officer called.

Jerry turned his head. "Uh-oh."

Sadie followed the direction of his gaze to where a truck with Channel Five painted on the side had pulled up to one of the patrol cars blocking the intersection.

Both Carter and his partner moved quickly toward the truck as an attractive woman climbed out.

"Good heavens," Annie said. "That's Carla Mitchell from Channel Five News."

As the elderly woman hurried toward the TV truck, Sadie moved through the crowd in the opposite direction. She'd just go down to the middle of the block, cross the street and circle back. She had to get to that ambulance.

She'd reached the edge of the crowd when Roman's ambulance pulled away from the curb. Sadie broke into a run. If she could just beat it to the corner…

As she sprinted toward the intersection, she thanked her lucky stars for her practical shoes. Dowdy they might be, but at least she could run in them. Out of the corner of her eye, she saw the ambulance increase speed. It was gaining on her as she reached the corner. Without stopping, without thinking, she careened into the intersection, waving her arms.

The siren sounded once, but when Sadie didn't move, it pulled to a stop. The officer in the passenger seat rolled down the window. "Lady, get out of our way."

Panting, she moved quickly to the side of the ambulance and placed her palms flat against the door. "You've got my brother in there. I want to ride along to the hospital."

"That's not possible," the officer said. "He's a suspect in a possible homicide."

Homicide? Sadie's heart lurched. "At least tell me where you're taking him. He's my brother."

The officer hesitated, then said, "You got some ID?"

Realizing that she didn't have her purse, Sadie shook her head. "No, I—"

"Then I can't help you." Even as he rolled up the window, the ambulance shot forward, its siren piercing the night air.

Time for plan B. Sadie spotted her car half a block away and ran toward it. Thank heavens she'd developed a habit of carrying her keys in her pocket because of all the time she'd wasted plowing through her purse for them.

Her purse. She thought briefly about it as she slipped behind the wheel. She'd dropped it when she'd raced up those stairs to look for Juliana. There was no time to go back and get it now, not if she wanted to keep that ambulance in sight. The police probably had it tucked away all nice and safe in an evidence bag.

As she shot away from the curb, she recalled the policeman's words. "He's a suspect in a homicide." She had to find out exactly what had gone on in that church.

IT WAS NEARLY TEN O'CLOCK when Theo slipped out of the cabin and nearly stumbled over Bob.

The dog rose and wagged its tail.

"Ari's still not here."

Bob merely looked hopeful.

"Okay." Theo opened the door. "You can go in, but no more treats until I get back from my swim."

Sleep had been eluding him. At the end of the dock, Theo paused. The moon was bright and full, the water black and fairly calm. His grandfather's cabin had been built in the center of a little inlet. A half mile to his right, he could see the clear outline of a row of rocks that jutted out into the ocean. When they were younger, he and his brothers had frequently raced to it and back. If he managed a couple of laps, he ought to be able to catch a good five hours of sleep before sunup. There was nothing he knew of that could drain away his tension more easily than a swim.

Theo stretched his arms skyward, tucking his head between them. Then, bending his knees, he bowed his body slightly forward and shot cleanly into the water. The shock of cold sang through his body. He swam underwater for as long as he could hold his breath, then surfaced and struck out for the rocks. Within minutes, he sank into the rhythm of it, keeping his kick steady and strong, pulling with his arm, turning, breathing and pulling again.

He wondered if Sadie Oliver was a swimmer. She had the sleek, lean body for it. He could almost picture her swimming beside him, matching the rhythm of her strokes to his, kicking those long legs as they sliced through the water together. He imagined their legs scissoring, their bodies stretching, flexing almost as if they were making love.

The water no longer felt cold, Theo noticed. He wasn't sure whether it was the exercise that had raised his temperature or the thoughts of swimming with Sadie Oliver.

He picked up his pace. It wasn't just his career path that he was going to have to make a decision about. He was going to have to make a decision about Sadie Oliver, too. And he was beginning to think that the two choices were related.

4

IT WAS CLOSE TO ELEVEN when Sadie parked her car next to a silver SUV that was a couple of shades darker than her Miata. The small parking area was exactly where Kit Angelis's Aunt Cass had said it would be, a little ways in from the road. But she'd expected three cars.

When she'd tried to reach Kit from the pay phone at the hospital, she'd gotten his office answering machine again. Then when she'd called his house, his aunt had picked up and told her that Kit was joining his brothers for a weekend of fishing at their grandfather's cabin.

That meant that Theo would be here, too.

The fact that she'd thought of that more than once on the drive annoyed her. She was twenty-six years old— way beyond the age of silly crushes. And she had far more pressing concerns. Her brother was injured and a suspect in a homicide and she didn't know where her sister was. When she reached to open the glove compartment, Sadie saw that her hands were shaking. Reaction was setting in. She couldn't, she wouldn't, fall apart yet. Closing her eyes, she drew in a deep breath and willed the shaking to stop. This time her hand was steady as she pulled the flashlight out and climbed from the car.

According to the directions she'd received from Cass

Angelis, the last half mile to the Angelis family's fishing cabin had to be traveled by foot. She located a path on the far side of the SUV. It was narrow, but appeared to be well used when she shone the light over it. The full moon was bright overhead and there were all those stars. Still, she hesitated. Leaves rustled in the wind and she thought she heard the sounds of some small animal scurrying through the brush. At least, it sounded small. Were there bears in this part of California?

Suppressing a shudder, Sadie gave herself a mental shake. Walking down a strange path through the woods at night might not be her cup of tea, but this was no time to be having second thoughts. She could have turned back at any point during the hour's drive from San Francisco and she hadn't. Because she wasn't going to let her brother down. She'd made her decision even before she'd seen her father and stepmother and Michael Dano arrive at the hospital. She'd made it the moment that Roman was being wheeled away on that gurney. Ever since she'd been little, her big brother always seemed so strong, so capable. But as they were taking him away for tests, he'd looked so…vulnerable.

She felt her throat tighten. She'd wanted so much to stay at the hospital, to be with him. But when she'd waylaid one of the attending physicians and asked if she could see Roman, he'd told her that her brother's condition was currently listed as stable, but that they were concerned about a skull fracture and would be doing tests for some time. If she'd stayed at the hospital, all she could have done was wait.

If Roman weren't injured, he'd be moving heaven and earth to find out what had happened to Juliana and what had gone on at that church. So she was going to step into his shoes.

Drawing in a deep breath, Sadie started down the path, shining the light back and forth across it. Thank heavens the ambulance had brought Roman to St. Jude's. Her father had donated the new trauma center there and as soon as the head nurse had found out who Roman was, she'd called in their top specialists.

She'd made herself scarce at the hospital because she hadn't wanted to draw the attention of the two cops who'd accompanied Roman. After all, she'd left her purse in the vestibule of the church. Sooner or later, someone was going to figure out that she'd been there. She might be suspected of having something to do with whatever had gone on.

So she'd slipped away without talking to Michael Dano or her father. She was going to follow her brother's advice and trust only Kit Angelis.

No. That wasn't completely true. Sadie drew in a deep breath and let it out. It wasn't just because of Roman's words that she was walking down this dark path near the midnight hour. Deep in her heart, she knew that she'd come here to ask Kit for his help because her deepest fear was that her own father had something to do with what had happened at St. Peter's church. Her sister Juliana was the apple of Mario Oliver's eye. If he had learned that she planned a secret wedding to Paulo Carlucci…

Sadie had had plenty of time to think while she'd been waiting at the hospital and while she'd been driving. Roman might have tried to stop the wedding, but someone had sent another man to prevent it, too. And if it was their father who'd sent that man Roman was chasing? Well, it would have been just like Roman to take their sister's side. Of course, there was also the possibility that Paulo's father had gotten wind of the wedding, too.

Something shot across the path about ten feet in front of her, and Sadie jumped and nearly screamed. Pressing a hand against her chest, she tried to keep her heart from pounding right out of her body. Then she felt foolish when she realized that the animal she'd seen had been tiny, probably a field mouse or a chipmunk. When her heartbeat settled, she moved forward.

The woods seemed darker now and the trees on either side pressed more closely to the path. The wind seemed to have picked up and over the rustling of overhead branches she heard a noise. One animal calling to another? Wolves traveled in packs, didn't they? Bobcats and coyotes also crossed her mind. She had no idea what kinds of wildlife lived here.

Nerves knotted in her stomach. Perhaps ignorance was best in this instance. Sadie gave herself a mental shake. Think positive. A half a mile wasn't very long. She had to be at least halfway there. It would take her just as long to get back to the car as it would to reach the cabin. But the pep talk she was giving herself didn't prevent her from picking up her pace and, after a few strides, she broke into a flat-out run. She'd been on the track team in high school and college, but her shoes, however serviceable, were not designed for running over rough terrain. She stumbled, managed to keep herself from falling to her knees and slowed to a fast walk.

She wasn't going to panic. She'd kept her nerve at

the church and again at the hospital and she wasn't going to lose it now. Still, when the path opened up into a clearing, relief streamed through Sadie. For just a moment, she stood there, forcing herself to take in air for a count of ten so that her breathing would level. The breeze coming in from the sea was brisk. The moon was full and bright and the dark water reflected even more light. The scene and the sound of the waves pushing into the shore immediately began to calm her.

A wooden dock jutted out from the shore for about forty feet and she could make out the dark outline of a small boathouse at the far end. She could also see the cabin. It was a compact one-story structure with a wide screened-in porch at its front. Light glowed from one of the windows.

Hopefully, someone was up. Sadie strode forward and when she reached the screened porch door, she knocked. The sound seemed loud to her ears and was immediately answered by movement inside the cabin. She had her face pressed close to the screen when a figure rushed through the door and hurled itself against the mesh. Barely suppressing a scream, she stumbled backward and nearly fell down on her backside. The huge creature barked once, backed up and made another lunge at the screen.

A dog. But Sadie didn't feel relieved. It was a very big dog and it was doing its best to get through that screen. Deciding not to wait until it succeeded, she moved quickly around the side of the cabin to the window that was spilling light out into the night. It was open and the ledge was just above her eye level. Rising to her toes, she peered into the room.

Empty. But the bed showed signs of having been used. The patchwork quilt was turned back, the pillows had been propped against the headboard and there was a paperback book lying on the nightstand. Perhaps the occupant had heard the racket the dog had made and was even now on his way to the porch. Circling back around to the front of the cabin, she caught sight of the dog through the screen. He raced down to meet her and kept pace with her as she walked toward the door. He didn't lunge this time. The animal looked even bigger standing on all fours but at least he wasn't barking. She waited for about ten beats. When no one appeared, she approached the screen door and knocked again. The dog whined. She let another ten beats pass, then drummed up her courage and tried the door.

It opened with a loud creak, but she still hesitated. The dog was wagging its tail and managing to look friendly. With a quick prayer that the creature wasn't sandbagging her, Sadie stepped onto the porch.

THEO WAS LYING ON HIS back in the water, enjoying the gentle movement of the waves. He'd lost track of the number of laps he'd swum, but his muscles were weak, his mind finally relaxed. He was about to climb onto the dock when the silence was broken by a sharp, staccato knocking sound. Then he heard Bob hit the screen door. Grabbing the dock with one hand, he glanced toward the shore. He couldn't imagine either Kit or Nik knocking on the cabin door. A tree was blocking his view, but he clearly heard Bob bark and launch himself at the door again.

Bob was not the best watchdog. In spite of his size, he had the people-loving instincts of a golden retriever and viewed any stranger as a possible source of either petting or food, hopefully both.

Staying very still in the water, Theo waited and a moment later saw a figure move around the side of the cabin. He had a quick impression of height. But the build was more slender than either of his brothers. He'd left the light on in his bedroom, and when the figure turned to face the window, he had a clear view of a profile. Female, he thought. The light wasn't strong enough for him to see her features, but he made out that she was wearing a skirt.

Annoyance and frustration streamed through him. Following the arrest of his stalker, he'd convinced his little fan club—the women who'd been attending his trials for the past few months—to stop. And they had. One of them had even confessed to being embarrassed by her behavior and apologized. For the past two months, he'd thought he'd gotten his life back to normal.

But he couldn't think of another reason why a woman would have come all this way in the middle of the night. He wasn't currently dating anyone. He hadn't dated anyone since Sandra Linton had begun to stalk him. And this woman was too tall to be his sister. Besides, Philly would have walked right in. She and Bob were old friends.

The figure had moved back toward the front of the cabin. Her knock was louder this time. Theo thought of calling out to her, but didn't. Instead, moving quietly, he swam toward shore and, once he got his feet beneath him, he walked slowly out of the water. He was still twenty yards away when he saw her open the screened door and walk in. He had to give her points for courage. Bob might be a pushover, but he did have that size thing going for him. To his surprise, he saw her crouch down and speak to the dog, but the sound of the waves behind him muffled her words. Okay, so she had guts and she liked big dogs. She was still in a place she had no business being. Technically, she was breaking and entering.

She'd already gone into the cabin by the time he reached it. Carefully, he opened the porch door and turned sideways to slip in before the hinge creaked. She'd left the inner door to the cabin open. In the darkness of the kitchen, he could only make out her silhouette as she stood peering out the window in the direction of the lake.

Annoyance streamed through him again. Bold as brass, he thought. Not only had she followed him out here to a place that he'd always considered a refuge, but she'd walked right in. It didn't help his mood one bit that Bob was sitting at her feet, beating his tail against the floor, evidently pleased as punch at the new visitor. At the very least, Theo figured he owed her a good scare.

He flipped on the light. "What the hell do you think—"

She whirled and her scream blocked the rest of his sentence.

"Sadie?" His first thought was that he'd conjured her up. His second was that in another moment she was going to slip right to the floor. Cursing himself, he strode to her. She'd gone pale as the moonlight on the water. "Are you all right?" Stupid question when he could see that she was anything but. Taking her arm, he eased her into one of the chairs at the table. Then he moved to the refrigerator, retrieved the bottle of wine he'd opened

earlier and filled a glass. She was still trembling when
he set it in front of her, so he took the chair next to hers
and covered her hand with his to help her lift the glass.

She took a sip and swallowed. Then their eyes met
and held over the rim of the glass. He was touching only
her hand and yet there was that intensity, that same connection he'd felt when he'd clasped her hand in the
courtroom. Suddenly, Theo knew. Not merely that their
paths would cross again, but that she was the *one,* the
one woman for him.

No. Panic shot up his spine and nerves knotted in his
abdomen. He wasn't ready. He forced himself to take a
deep breath as he reminded himself that he still had a
choice. The Fates only presented choices.

But as Sadie lifted the glass for another sip, he didn't
remove his hand from hers and he couldn't seem to take
his eyes off of her. Her lips were parted and moist from
the wine. He very badly wanted to taste that mouth.
Even as lust curled into a tight, hot fist in his stomach,
he let his hand drop and eased back in his chair. He had
to get away before…

Rising, he strode toward the adjoining hallway.
"Drink the wine while I change. Then you can tell me
why you're here."

5

SADIE LET OUT THE breath she hadn't even been aware she was holding and barely kept the wineglass from slipping out of her hand. Very carefully, she set it on the table. Her head was still foggy, still spinning. And it wasn't merely because he'd scared her. It was because he'd touched her again. All he'd meant to do was to help her steady the wineglass, just as all he'd done in that courtroom was shake her hand.

How was it that each time he put a hand on her, even in the most casual of ways, it was as if he'd touched her all over?

She pressed her fingers to her temples, willing her mind to clear and her thoughts to settle. When she'd whirled to see him standing in the doorway, he hadn't looked like the Theo Angelis she'd seen in court. He'd looked larger than life, like some god from the sea—his dark hair slicked back, his darker eyes with that dangerous gleam. And all that damp, tanned skin. Even now she was astonished at just how much she'd wanted to touch him, wanted to taste him. No, more than that—she'd wanted to devour him.

No man had ever affected her this way. With hands that were still trembling, Sadie reached for her wine and took another swallow.

She was overreacting. There were too many emotions pounding at her—Roman, Juliana, the walk through the woods. She had to get a grip. She'd come here to ask Kit Angelis to help her. She couldn't afford to fall apart.

"I'm sorry I gave you a scare."

Startled, she whirled in her chair to watch Theo pour himself a glass of wine. Then he reached into the refrigerator and pulled out a plate of cheese. He was wearing old jeans that had faded at the seams and hem and an equally ancient T-shirt. She could barely make out the word Stanford across his chest. The casualness and general rattiness of the clothes surprised her. Theo had always been so impeccably and fashionably dressed in his court appearances.

"These are my lucky fishing clothes."

Sadie's gaze flew to his face and she saw a gleam of humor there. Could the man read her mind? Was she that transparent to him?

His lips curved as he moved to the table and set the plate of cheese between them. Then he sank into his chair. "I'm not the best fisherman in the family, but I've been wearing this outfit ever since I was in college and I never fail to catch the biggest fish on these weekends with my brothers. Nik has his special pole and Kit has a lucky hat, but neither has ever beaten this outfit. My brothers are hoping that one day soon the cloth will just disintegrate and fall off of me."

In her mind, she pictured them doing just that—first the T-shirt, then the jeans. Was he wearing any briefs beneath them? As heat pooled in her center, Sadie ruthlessly focused her attention back to what had brought her here. She was not going to get anywhere if she continued to imagine him naked.

What in the world was wrong with her? She had to get away from him. Rising, she said, "I have to find Kit. Where is he?"

Theo took a sip of his wine while he met her gaze steadily. "Are you dating my brother?"

"What?"

"It's a pretty straightforward question, counselor. Are you dating my brother Kit? Is that why you're here?"

"No." Puzzled, she narrowed her eyes on him. "Why would you think that? I've only met him a few times. And why are you asking?"

"Curiosity. You came all the way out here in the middle of the night and you want to know where he is."

"I need his help. It's about Roman."

"Roman?" Theo straightened. "What is it?"

"I have to find Kit."

"Why don't you sit back down tell me what's wrong?"

"Roman told me to go to Kit."

His brows rose. "There's an expression that sailors use—*any port in a storm*. You said it was urgent and since Kit isn't here and I am, why don't you tell me what made you drive up here at this time of night?"

He was right. She was letting his effect on her and the difficulty she had handling it interfere with what she needed to do to help Roman and Juliana. She had to tell someone what had happened and figure out what to do next.

In spite of Roman's advice to trust no one but Kit, she trusted Theo Angelis. Sadie sat back down at the table and told him everything she knew.

WHEN SHE WAS FINISHED, Theo leaned back in his chair and studied her for a moment. She was bearing up very well considering the kind of day she'd put in. No wonder she'd nearly slid to the floor in a dead faint when he'd scared her. He was still kicking himself for that. He'd promised himself while he was changing out of his bathing suit that he wasn't going to upset her again. And his resolve had only grown stronger now that he knew what she'd been through.

She had an attorney's mind and laid the facts of her case in a logical order. He'd only stopped her once to take her back over the sequence of gunshots that had been fired and the locations of each of them. She'd heard two when she'd first entered the church.

"So Roman could have fired those before he burst through the vestibule doors in pursuit of the guy he chased up the stairs into the choir loft."

She clasped her hands together in front of her on the table and her knuckles went white. "Yes. Roman could have fired those shots."

"And the lady you met outside, she said that she'd heard the cops talking about one dead person."

"Yes, but—" She cut herself off and met his eyes. "Yes. And you're going to say that Roman could have killed that person. That could be why he's the suspect in a homicide. But the man he was chasing could be the killer, too. He had a gun, and there was more gunfire from inside the church after Roman and that man came out. So neither of them fired those shots."

Theo nodded. He had to give her points for control. He wondered if he would have done as well if she were cross-examining him about the possibility that one of *his* brothers might have killed someone. "From what you've described, more than one person came to that church prepared to stop your sister's wedding and prepared to use force to do so. That could include Roman. He did bring his gun."

Sadie leaned forward. "Roman always carries a gun. My father insists that all his executives be armed because his father had always insisted on it. Even Michael Dano who heads up the legal department has a gun. I think it goes back to a time when my family wasn't so…let's say legitimately connected."

"Do you carry a gun?"

"No. I'm not employed on the executive level at Oliver Enterprises."

There was something in her tone that caught his attention. Was it disappointment? Hurt? Resentment? Before he could pursue it, she hurried on. "I've never known Roman to use his gun."

"Perhaps the need never arose before."

Temper flared into her eyes, turning them almost black. But she reined it in. Here was the passion he'd glimpsed in the courtroom. And Theo knew that he wasn't going to be able to walk away from it easily.

"You're right. That's exactly how the police will see it. He's—" She broke off and her knuckles turned even whiter.

"Roman's in trouble on two fronts," he continued for her. "He may have serious injuries from the fall he took, but he also may be the prime suspect for what went on at that church. That's what you want to see Kit for. You want him to investigate and find out."

"I also want Kit to help me find Juliana. Roman thought she was in danger."

Theo studied her for a moment. "From what you've said, she's with the man she loves, Paulo Carlucci. Don't you trust him?"

"I don't know. I'm not even sure that Paulo and Juliana got away. That van may have been following them. Maybe they got her. If the Carluccis learned of the wedding plans, they'd want to stop it as badly as—"

"Your father and Roman would."

Her chin lifted and she drew back a little in her chair. "If I had gotten to the church on time, I would have tried to talk Juliana out of getting married, too."

"The difference being that you didn't bring a gun."

"Yes." She met his eyes. "But as I said before, Roman wasn't the only one who came to the church armed. And I had some time to think on the drive up here. I received my invitation to come to the church at around four o'clock. It was signed: 'Please, Juliana.' What if Roman received a similar note? I had no idea that the invitation was to a wedding, let alone that Juliana intended to marry Paulo Carlucci. What if Roman was in the same situation? I'm not saying that he wouldn't try to stop the wedding. But he would only have used his gun in self-defense."

Theo didn't know Roman Oliver as well as Kit did. But ever since Roman and Kit had roomed together in college, he had been a frequent visitor at both their home and the restaurant his father ran, and Theo was inclined to agree with Sadie. Roman, like his sister, had a temper, but he knew how to control it. Keeping his eyes on Sadie's, Theo sipped his wine. "Let's bottom-

line it. You suspect your father sent some men to stop
the wedding, don't you?"

Her chin lifted. "Did I say that?"

"You didn't have to. Actions speak louder than words.
You avoided your father when you were at the hospital."

Temper flashed in her eyes as she slammed a hand
down on the table. "What was I supposed to do? Go up
to him and ask him if he'd sent men to shoot up the
church and stop the wedding? Not that he would have
answered any of my questions—my father plays his
cards very close to his chest. Sometimes he doesn't
even let Roman know what he's doing. Roman never
knew about it when he—" Stopping, Sadie reached for
her wine and took a sip.

"When he what?" Theo prompted.

"It happened a long time ago. I haven't thought about
it in years. Perhaps it's because the circumstances are
so similar."

Theo raised a brow. "Did your father stop you from
marrying someone?"

"No." She ran her finger around the rim of the wineglass. "I was a year younger than Juliana is now. I'd
begged to come home from boarding school and finish
my senior year here in San Francisco. I took a theater
class and ended up playing Rosalind in *As You Like It*.
The male lead was Jackson Rayburn, and we started
seeing each other. The short version of the story is that
I fell in love the way that you do when you're that young
and you think that everything is possible."

"Were you lovers?"

"No." Her chin lifted. "But we would have become
lovers. We'd already made plans for the future. I was

going to apply to the same college that he was going to so that we could be together. Then I made the mistake of bringing him home to meet my family and my father took immediate action."

Theo poured more wine into both their glasses. "What did he do?"

"Nothing violent. Nothing even illegal. He simply approached Jackson's father and gave him a business offer that Mr. Rayburn couldn't refuse. It all happened in a matter of days. Jackson and I were supposed to meet the following weekend. When he didn't show up, I went to his house and discovered from neighbors that the family had moved away. Just like that." She snapped her fingers. "Poof! I was so angry. When I confronted my father and he refused to tell me where, I got even angrier. I cried. I screamed."

A part of Theo wished he could have been there just to see the real Sadie, without her carefully controlled facade. Another part was much too aware of the hurt in her eyes and wanted to just pull her onto his lap and hold her.

"Temper is never the way to handle my father. It's cool logic that impresses him. I never saw Jackson again. He never called. He never even sent me an e-mail, a letter. Nothing. My father is nothing if not thorough." She picked up her wineglass and took a careful sip.

"Your father bought him off."

"Yes. He acted the same way he does in a business deal. When he wants to eliminate a potential problem, he does it with the efficiency and skill of a surgeon. And Jackson let himself be bought. That's when I decided to go east for college. I wanted to be somewhere far away where my father couldn't interfere with my life."

"Did it work?"

"I thought so until—" She cut herself off with a wave of her hand. "That doesn't really matter now." She leaned forward a little. "I know that my past relationship with my father could be affecting my objectivity here, but there's something else that's been bothering me. The man driving the van—the one that was blocking the driveway and later might have been following Paulo and Juliana—there was something familiar about him. I just haven't been able to place where I saw him before. I can't help but wonder if it was at my family's estate or at Oliver Enterprises."

For a moment, neither of them spoke. Theo angled his chair so that he could stretch his legs out and cross them at the ankles. "If your suspicion is right and your father did get wind of the planned wedding, does what happened at the church tonight seem like his work?"

When Sadie met his eyes this time, hers were clear and focused. "You're thinking it's messy."

"Not only that, but from the way you've described him and the way Roman has talked about him, sending armed gunmen to stop his daughter's wedding—that just doesn't seem to be Mario Oliver's style. Of course, I don't know him as well as you do."

Theo continued to study her as she thought about what he'd just said. He could almost hear her mind working. Her face and her eyes were so expressive that he could tell the moment that some of her tension began to ease.

Finally, she let out the breath she was holding. "I think you know my father very well. Because you're right. If he'd sent someone there to stop my sister's wedding, he wouldn't have failed. And he wouldn't have sent men with guns to handle the situation. He would have come in person and he would have stopped the wedding. He probably would have brought Roman with him. I should have seen it before. I'm not thinking straight. I—"

Theo covered her clasped hands with his. "It's always hard to think objectively about people we love."

For a moment neither one of them spoke and Theo knew that he'd made a big mistake. He shouldn't have touched her again because he was feeling that same intense connection again. It was like nothing he'd ever experienced and this time it seemed to reach deeper into him. How much longer was he going to be able to resist it? Or her?

Hands off, Theo, he ordered himself. Very carefully, he released his grip and leaned back in his chair.

HER BRAIN HAD FOGGED again. Every time the man touched her even in the most casual way, she couldn't seem to think. All she could do was feel. And there was something inside of her that desperately wanted more.

"How do you think Angelo Carlucci would have acted if he'd learned that his only son was planning to marry his enemy's daughter?"

Sadie blinked. His lips had moved. "Sorry?"

"I was asking about Angelo Carlucci. How do you think he would have reacted if he'd learned that his only son was planning to marry his enemy's daughter?"

"I've never met the man personally, but based on what I've heard…" Rising, she began to pace. If she kept her distance, maybe her brain cells would work. "Angelo Carlucci is much more likely to have an emotional reaction than my father is. Roman has said frequently that in business dealings—including in this major land deal that we're engaged in now—the one advantage we have is that Angelo Carlucci is quick on the draw and likely to promise more than he can deliver. My father is much more methodical."

She turned to face him only when she was some distance away. *Better.* "My father is a bit like you—he waits, plans, then makes a move that will bring him victory. You have a tendency to take more risks, I think. What you pulled off in the Laura Wenger murder trial was nothing short of miraculous. No one expected you to put her on the stand. I would never have risked it. She'd been abused by her husband for twelve years. How did you know that the prosecution wouldn't break her down completely during cross-examination?"

"I just had a feeling that they wouldn't." But the feelings weren't always there, he couldn't depend on them. He just wished he knew how to interpret and act on the feeling he had about the woman walking toward him now. Knowing that she was feeling at least part of what he was gave him some satisfaction. But it was also making it more difficult to stick to his resolve. As a kid he'd always been tempted to play with fire.

Sadie pressed fingers to her temples and then dropped her hands and reseated herself at the table. "Thank you so much. I've been such a fool. I've been so focused on my family, suspecting them, worrying about them, I haven't been able to see the forest for the trees."

"That's natural." Knowing that it was another mistake, Theo covered one of her hands with his. "You've had one hell of a day and from what you've told me, you've managed to keep your cool."

She didn't withdraw her hand. Neither did he. Desire, lust, yearning—suddenly, he was damn tired of dancing around them. Risky as it might be, he wanted to taste her just once. Maybe then he'd be free. Her mouth was so close, all he had to do was close the distance and take what he was dying for. Perhaps then this gnawing need inside of him would stop.

As he saw her eyes darken, watched the pulse at her throat beat fast and hard, Theo knew that he wouldn't be able to stop with a taste. He'd want it all. He wanted it all right now. Perhaps it was the only way to free himself of this hold she seemed to have on him.

But it wasn't what Sadie needed right now. For an endless thirty seconds desire warred with duty. And it was with great reluctance that he rose and moved to the counter where he'd left his cell phone.

"I'm going to see if I can reach Kit on his cell. We need to fill him in so he can get started on this. And there's one thing we haven't touched on yet."

At her raised brow, he said, "Since you left your purse at the church, the police know that you were there. My guess is that they're going to think you're involved in this somehow."

6

"KIT? WHERE ARE YOU?" Theo asked.

Sadie sat very still because her head had gone into a little spin again. The way he'd been looking at her just a moment ago had made her forget everything else but him. He'd been about to kiss her. The thrill of that knowledge was still inside of her. Just the anticipation of his mouth moving over hers had set hot little licks of flame springing to life in her stomach.

She would have kissed him back. And why not? When was the last time she'd done anything just because she wanted it? Law school, her work at Oliver Enterprises—all of that was to please her father and fit in with her family.

"How is Roman?"

She shifted her gaze to Theo's face as she realized that he was actually talking to Kit and not merely leaving a message on his cell phone.

"So they'll know more in the morning, but in the meantime he's still stable."

How had Kit learned about Roman? Had her father called him? Sadie felt a little stab of guilt when she thought of her earlier suspicions about her father. She'd let her own prejudices influence her and she couldn't afford to let her judgment be clouded that way again if she was going to help Roman and Juliana.

Theo met her eyes. "Did you talk to Roman?" He gave her a negative signal with his head and it was only then she realized that he hadn't told Kit yet that she was here with him.

She should really gather her thoughts. What was she going to do about Theo Angelis? There was a part of her that already knew what she wanted to do. But what must he think of her? She'd practically poured out her whole life's story to him, reacting to the quiet, intent way he listened as if it were a truth serum. And he had to know how she was responding to him, to his touch. The man seemed to be able to read her like a book.

Bob whined. When she saw that he was standing in the open doorway leading to the porch, she rose and let him out of the cottage, then watched as he ambled off across the lawn. Through the trees she saw a light wink on and a deep voice called, "Bob, it's time to come home."

Bob picked up the pace and Sadie waited until the light winked off again. She returned to the kitchen in time to see Theo set his cell phone down on the counter.

He didn't touch her. He merely gestured her into a chair, and when they were both seated, he stated, "You'll want to know about Roman first. They've learned that he has a skull fracture. But the doctors are more concerned about some swelling around the base of his spine. They're keeping him sedated to make sure that he remains immobile. No visitors. If the swelling doesn't go down by tomorrow, they're going to operate and relieve it that way."

Sadie had to clear her throat to get out the question. "Will he be…do they know if he'll be…"

"Paralyzed?" Theo kept his gaze steady on hers. "Kit says they don't know. Right now, it's better to concentrate on the good news, Sadie. He didn't break either his neck or his back in that fall. And he's receiving the best possible care."

"Yes—you're right, of course."

"And from a defense attorney's point of view, the upside of his being sedated is that the police can't question him yet. The more we know before that happens, the better."

She drew in a deep breath and let it out. Theo was right. Roman was in good hands. "What else did Kit tell you? Give me all the bad news first."

SADIE WAS CLEARLY BRACED for the worst. More than anything, Theo wanted to reach out and take her hand. But this time he didn't. "What your friend overheard was correct. Someone was shot and killed in the sacristy. A witness—the caterer who was setting up a small reception in the rectory dining room—claims the man who was killed arrived with the man she believed was the groom. Later, your brother arrived and just before shots were fired, this caterer heard your brother arguing with another man, most likely Paulo Carlucci. Then she heard a voice cry out, 'Roman, no!' Then there were two gunshots. They could have been the ones you heard. Kit says Roman is the prime suspect in the death of that man."

She nodded. "What about the priest, Father Mike? I saw him carried out to an ambulance."

A mix of emotions raced through Theo. Relief was foremost. This was the Sadie Oliver he'd seen in the courtroom, focused and tough. She was going to need both of those qualities. Laced through the relief was admiration. "Yes, he was shot. He's at St. Jude's and he's going to make it. The caterer can identify his shooter. It wasn't Roman."

"It could have been the man I saw Roman chase up the stairs to the choir loft," Sadie said.

"True. Or there could have been someone else— those may have been the shots you heard that came from inside the church while Roman and the other man were fighting. Nevertheless, it's just as I feared. The police are favoring Roman for being behind the whole incident. They speculate that he came to stop the wedding and brought some help with him."

He saw temper flare in her eyes. "'Some help' who pushed him down the stairs?"

"According to Kit, they're speculating that he struggled with Paulo and Paulo either pushed him or Roman fell."

"That's not true."

"Stick to the facts, Sadie. Did you actually see who it was that Roman was fighting with at the top of the stairs?"

"No, but—"

"Then it could have been Paulo?"

"I suppose." She sighed. "And I suppose that they're going to think I was working with Roman on whatever plot he'd hatched to stop our sister's wedding."

"That's what Kit expects."

Sadie said in a wry tone, "If Kit gave you any good news, this would be an excellent time for it."

"First, I have a question. The caterer saw a woman arrive at the church in a taxi with your sister. She was blond, petite, and well dressed. Does she sound familiar?"

"It has to be the same woman I saw Paulo and Juliana put into that taxi."

"You didn't recognize her?"

"No." Theo saw emotion flood her eyes again. "I should know who it is. If she arrived with Juliana, she must be a friend and I don't even know her. If I'd been closer to my sister—"

"Sadie…" But even as he said her name, he watched her shove down what she was feeling and regain her focus.

"I know. I have to keep my emotions under control if I'm going to help Roman and Juliana. And I will."

He didn't doubt it for a moment. Keeping his eyes on hers, Theo finally did what he'd wanted to do from the moment they'd sat down at the table. He took her hand in his and pressed his mouth to her fingers. "You're doing remarkably well, I'd say. And there *is* some good news. Kit's already involved in trying to find out what happened. He's spoken to your father and filled him in on what the police aren't telling him yet. And my brother Nik is heading up the investigation. So you've got a cop in charge who's not going to be inclined to railroad your brother."

As she absorbed that information, Theo watched some of the tension ease out of Sadie's expression. He wanted to erase all of it. He'd kissed her fingers to offer comfort— at least that had been his intention—but he'd seen her eyes darken and still, just as they did each time he touched her. And he'd known that he'd wanted more, too. He was tired of waiting, tired of being cautious. Most of all he was tired of second-guessing himself. He didn't have to make any choices right now except for this one.

Keeping his eyes on hers, he slipped a hand around

the back of her neck and slowly drew her forward until his mouth was pressed to hers.

He'd expected shock, perhaps some resistance; instead, she eagerly parted those soft, soft lips and invited him in. Then she strained toward him, digging her fingers into his shoulders to pull him closer. Yes, she had the right idea. Keeping his mouth fused to hers, Theo dragged her up from the chair and pressed that long, lean body to his. He had a second to absorb the sensation of softness against hardness, another to recognize the perfect fit before he could have sworn the ground shifted beneath his feet.

One taste? Good lord, he would never get enough. She was so sweet. That was all he could think of as the flavor of sun-warmed honey seeped into him and fueled his burning hunger, ripe and huge. Oh, yes, he was going to have more and more of this.

Fast and greedy, as if he was afraid she might slip away, he ran his hands over her—the curve of her shoulder, the soft swell of her breast, the length of that torso.

Her, at last. Sadie. He wasn't sure if he spoke the words or if he only thought them.

On a muffled moan, Sadie threaded her fingers into his hair and tried to get closer. Heat, glorious waves of it, poured through her. Her heart was beating so fast. Still, she had to have more. When he drew away for an instant, she fisted her hands in his hair and dragged his mouth back to hers.

She couldn't think. It was glorious not to have to. All her worries and fears vanished. There was no room for them as need battered her, pushing her into a world where there was only Theo and the pleasure he could bring her.

Her back was against the wall, and she had no knowledge of how it had gotten there. Sadie dropped her arms so that he could slide her jacket off, then slipped her hands beneath his T-shirt so that she could explore that smooth skin stretched tight over hard muscles. This was what she'd wanted from the first time she'd seen him. This was what had been waiting for her. And she could have it right now.

They worked together to drag off his T-shirt. Their fingers were tangled, fumbling with the hook on her skirt when the phone rang. Their hands stilled together.

"It could be Kit. He may have news," Theo said.

Slowly, reluctantly, they untangled their fingers and Theo backed up a few steps to lift his cell phone off the table.

"Yes?"

There was a pause and Sadie watched Theo's face change. "Yes, Mr. Oliver, this is Theo Angelis. What can I do for you?"

7

SAVED BY THE BELL. The cliché hummed through Theo's mind even as he ruthlessly focused on what Mario Oliver was saying.

"You're a hard man to reach."

The man might be soft-spoken, but Theo didn't miss the authority in his tone.

"I just turned my cell phone on a few minutes ago, sir." Theo's gaze dropped to the floor where his T-shirt lay tangled with Sadie's suit jacket. If he'd shut the phone off after calling Kit, he and Sadie would be making love right now. Right there.

Lifting his gaze, Theo met Sadie's eyes and saw that she was thinking the same thing. It would have been wild and wonderful, but perhaps not the best thing for her. The timing sucked. He hadn't been thinking about that. His mind had been too filled with her. Even now he wanted to make love to her until they both couldn't breathe. He didn't understand it, but whatever kind of hold she had on him seemed to be grow stronger each time he touched her.

"Theo?"

Mario's voice in his ear made him focus again. "Yes, sir. I'm still here."

"You've talked to your brother Kit."

"Yes, sir. He filled me in on what happened at the church and on Roman's condition. Has anything changed?"

"No."

At Sadie's questioning glance, he shook his head, then motioned her closer and angled the phone so that she could hear, too. "Have you talked to Roman yet?"

There was a beat of silence before Mario replied, "The doctors aren't allowing anyone to talk to him. They don't want him moving or becoming agitated until the swelling on his spine goes down so they're keeping him sedated."

"I think that's for the best," Theo said slowly. He didn't doubt for a minute that Mario Oliver had done what he could to influence the doctors' position. The longer he could keep his son from the police, the better. "Roman should have an attorney present when he's questioned. Have you been able to locate your daughter Sadie yet?"

"No."

If Mario Oliver was worried about his daughter's absence, he gave no sign of it in his tone. But then, hadn't Sadie described her father as a man who played his cards close to his chest?

"When she contacts you, she'll know exactly what to do. I've sat in on a few of her trials. She's a good strategist."

"What's your opinion of Jason Sangerfeld?" Mario asked.

The abrupt change of topic surprised him, but Theo managed to keep his tone even. "In my opinion, Sangerfeld's the best defense attorney in the country, sir."

"He said something similar about you when I spoke with him a few minutes ago. He told me that he's offered you a job and he's expecting you to join him in Los Angeles. He also thinks that at this stage, because you're local, you'll have access to more information than he would. He advised me to hire you."

"I'm flattered, sir. I imagine he told you that if you bring in a celebrity lawyer, the media might twist things to make Roman appear guilty."

"Hmmph. He said something like that. What I want to know is—are you good enough to get my son out of this mess?"

Sadie's fingers gripped his wrist, pulling the phone closer to her mouth. "Yes, he is. I think you should hire him, Dad."

"Sadie? What are you—? Are you all right?"

"I'm fine."

"Angelis?"

"She's fine, sir," Theo said. "Are you on a phone that's secure?"

There was a beat of silence. Then Mario said, "I'll call you right back."

Theo clicked off his cell. "It would be safer if no one knew you were here with me."

"I thought we decided that my father didn't have anything to do with what happened at the church."

"We did, but—"

When the cell phone rang, Theo opened it and once more held it so that Sadie could hear.

"Where are you?" Mario asked.

"We're at my grandfather's fishing cabin," Theo said. "Sadie drove up here to find Kit."

"Give me the directions and I'll send someone for her."

"No, you won't," Sadie said.

"Don't be foolish. Your sister is missing, your brother is seriously injured. I want you back here where I can protect you."

"Dad, we don't know who's behind what went on at the church."

There was a beat of silence before Mario spoke. "The Carluccis are behind it. They tried to kill my son and now they have Juliana."

"Is that what Roman says?" she asked.

"I haven't talked to Roman," Mario replied. "Now, tell me exactly where—"

"Dad, you have to listen to me."

"I know what's best," Mario said. "Angelis, tell me where my daughter is."

Sadie's fingers dug into his flesh where she gripped his wrist. Meeting her eyes, Theo said, "It's her decision, sir. I think you ought to listen to her."

"Please," Sadie added. "I talked to Roman right after he fell, and he told me to trust no one and to go to Kit."

Mario said nothing.

"There might be more going on here than we know," Sadie continued. "I thought at first that you might be involved, but Theo convinced me you wouldn't have botched the job."

This time the silence stretched so long that Theo thought perhaps his cell had cut off.

"Tell me everything," Mario instructed.

Theo had to hand it to Mario. He didn't interrupt even once as Sadie related the same story that she'd told him earlier.

"You're not sure where you saw the driver of the van?" he asked when she'd finished.

"No. But I can't help thinking that I might have seen him at Oliver Enterprises."

"There's something else we have to consider, sir," Theo said. "My mind keeps going back to the invitation Sadie received this afternoon. There's a possibility that Roman received a last-minute invitation also."

"Go on," Mario said.

"The timing bothers me. What if it didn't come from Juliana?"

Silence descended again and Sadie met his eyes. "Theo could be right. I can't swear that it was her handwriting. And if she was smart enough to arrange this whole secret wedding, she's also smart enough to know that Roman or I would have at least tried to talk her out of it. So why take that chance?"

More silence.

Finally, Mario said, "You make a good case." Another pause. "You're hired, Angelis. And, Sadie, I'll have someone there to pick you up within the hour."

"I won't be here," Sadie said.

Her voice had risen and Theo watched in admiration as she took a deep breath and reined her emotions in. When she spoke again, her voice was as soft and controlled as her father's. "This is the way it's going to work. You've hired Theo to defend Roman and I'm going to work with him."

"Sadie—"

"You aren't going to stop me. Roman is my brother. Juliana is my sister. I'm not going to sit idly by and do nothing just because you think I'll be safer."

"Sir," Theo interjected. "She means what she says. I could suggest a compromise."

"I'm listening."

"I could use her help and I'll guarantee her safety." Theo waited a beat before he continued, "I don't like the fact that all three of your children were at that church when the shooting started. So it might be best for now if Sadie's whereabouts remain unknown. That's why I asked earlier if you were on a secure phone."

Once more the silence stretched. Sadie opened her mouth, but Theo signaled her to remain quiet. He didn't envy the position Mario was in, but Sadie's father was an astute businessman and Theo was banking on the fact that he would recognize the value of coming to terms with his daughter.

"I don't like this," Mario said.

"No, sir. In your shoes, I wouldn't like it, either."

"I'll go along for now. But I'm going to hold you responsible for her safety and I want to see you here at the hospital in the morning. If the swelling on Roman's spine has gone down by then, the police will be pushing to question him."

"Yes, sir. I'll be there."

"What about Sadie?"

"She won't be there."

"Fine."

Sadie waited only long enough for Theo to disconnect the call before she fisted her hands on her hips. "I meant what I said to my father. I'm going to work with you on this. And I'm going to be at the hospital when you talk to Roman."

He studied her for a minute. There was a lot he didn't

know about Sadie Oliver yet, but if he didn't miss his guess, she was used to pitting herself against the men in her life. All that passion he'd tasted was now radiating off her in waves. Fighting with her might be nearly as enjoyable as kissing her again, but his best strategy in dealing with her was to pick his battles. Propping his hip against the counter, he said, "You handled your father very well."

"No, *you* handled him." She pointed a finger at him. "You convinced him that I've got a big strong man to take care of me."

"It worked, didn't it?"

This time she jabbed a finger into his chest, and Theo nearly grinned.

"Of course it worked," she went on. "My father has very old-fashioned ideas about women. He thinks they're fragile creatures that need to be protected. Ever since I came back to San Francisco, he's had Michael Dano hovering over me like a guardian angel. My dream has always been to work at Oliver Enterprises. I got a law degree to get my father to take me seriously. But then I discovered he put me in my present position in the legal department because he was hoping that Michael and I would—" she raised both hands and waved them "—get to know one another and make a match of it. He wasn't taking me seriously at all. He just wanted to marry me off safely to someone he approved of."

"You and Michael are dating?" Theo found that he didn't like the idea of that at all.

"No…well, I didn't think it was dating. It was all so casual. I enjoyed working with Michael. He's very smart and easy to talk to. I ended up sitting next to him when he would come to family dinners. And because we often worked late, he would escort me to social functions. The next thing I knew, there was some speculation in the society columns."

With a frown, she turned and began to pace. "But I still thought we were just friends. That is, until he kissed me one night." Turning, Sadie met his eyes. "I didn't handle it very well."

"What did he do?"

"Nothing. It was my fault. I'm not really good at handling men." She raised her hands and dropped them. "I just didn't respond. Not the way he seemed to expect me to. And I felt I had to be honest with him, so I told him that I didn't think of him that way, that I thought of him as a friend."

"What was his reaction?"

She fisted her hands on her hips again. "Oh, he acted the perfect gentleman on the surface. He apologized for acting too soon on the attraction he felt for me and assured me that he was willing to take things slowly. But he was angry." Even now when she thought of what she'd seen for a moment in his eyes, she had to suppress a shudder. "That was when I began to see things more clearly. My father had set me up. He'd set Michael up, too. He's an ambitious man and my father probably led him to believe that a match between the two of us would have his blessing. And Michael really thought he could change my mind. I mean, he's very attractive and he's probably used to getting any woman he wants. It took me almost another month before I could convince Michael of how we'd both been manipulated. He finally listened to me when I told him that I was not going to ever feel that way about him."

"He didn't take it well," Theo said.

The look she gave him held surprise. "How did you know?"

"I wouldn't have taken it well."

For a moment she said nothing, but their gazes held and Theo felt the air in the room become heavy. He couldn't help wondering what it might be like to want Sadie Oliver, to know that he could never have her and still have to work with her every day. He felt a sudden wave of sympathy for Michael Dano. "It has to have affected your working relationship."

She nodded. "I think his ego was hurt. Now, he gives me tedious work that I could have handled after my first semester in law school. And I haven't decided how to handle it. One of the reasons I was late arriving at St. Peter's was because I was determined to clear my desk."

"Have you told him how you feel about the work?"

"Oh, yes. And he accused me of being paranoid. That's one of the reasons I started to volunteer at the public defender's office—because I'm bored at Oliver Enterprises."

Fate, Theo thought. If she hadn't been bored at work and wanted some trial experience, would he have accepted the L.A. job offer and left without ever meeting her?

Sadie strode toward him. "I'm going with you to the hospital tomorrow. You're not going to talk me out of it."

Her braid was lying on her shoulder. Theo picked it up and tested its weight. "Agreed."

She stared at him. "You're not going to argue with me?"

"No." He tugged on her braid. "I'm not lying to you,

Sadie. Until this is all sorted out and I'm sure that you're safe, I'm not going to let you out of my sight."

She frowned. "You told my father that I wouldn't be there at the hospital."

"Sadie Oliver *won't* be with me. Someone would be bound to recognize you." He met her eyes then. "How are you at taking risks?"

"I…" She lifted her chin. "I think I'm up for one. What do you have in mind?"

"We're going to turn you into a man."

8

"A MAN? YOU'RE TALKING about a disguise?"

Theo watched the little line appear on her forehead as she turned the idea over in her mind. "You mentioned playing Rosalind in *As You Like It*. The character pretends to be a boy, right?"

"Yes, but that was a long time ago. Do you think I can pull it off?"

As the plan became more detailed in his mind, he smiled slowly. "It will be risky. But I think you can do just about anything you set your mind to."

"What do I have to do?"

He waved a hand in a circle. "Turn around. You're tall enough and you've got the long, lean lines of a swimmer."

"I was on the swim team in college," she added. He nodded. He'd run his hands over those long lines and the desire to do so again was building. It surprised him how much he wanted to pick up right where they'd left off when Mario Oliver had interrupted them. His conversation with her father should have changed things. He'd promised to keep her safe and he intended to keep that promise. Beyond that, he'd promised to help her brother.

Even as he told himself that he shouldn't touch her again, he took her hand. Theo forced himself to keep his gaze just on the hand that was lying in his. "You don't have a man's hands." The fingers were too narrow. He recalled in vivid detail what they'd felt like on his skin and desire twisted painfully in his gut.

"How about I keep them in my pockets?"

"Yes. Good idea." He'd do well to keep his own hands in his pockets. "In fact, you'll have to keep a low profile in general, especially at the hospital." He shifted his gaze to her face. "Your father will be the hardest to fool. But people usually see what they expect to see."

"And they won't be expecting me."

There was a gleam of excitement in her eyes now that he'd never seen before. It delighted him, intrigued him.

"Exactly." He lifted her braid again and tested the weight in his hand. Perhaps if she dressed as a man, looked like a man, he'd be able to gather more control. "We'll have to cut your hair."

"What?"

"And change the color, I think. I'll say you're an intern, a prelaw student from Stanford, working with me for a few weeks. I take one on every so often to help me with research. The younger we make you the better, I think."

Theo gave the braid another tug, and as he stared down at it, he had a sudden feeling—the same kind of feeling he often got during a trial—that the sooner he changed her appearance, the better, for both their sakes. Maybe then they'd both be able to think more clearly.

SADIE'S THROAT HAD GONE completely dry. Whatever he was saying had faded into a buzz in her ears and all she was aware of were his hands—one holding hers, the other fingering her hair. He looked so intent on his plan to transform her right now. Couldn't he tell that her bones had melted just because he was touching her? While she'd been talking to her father, she'd regained her focus. But now, he was so close....

"Sadie?"

"Hmm?'

"Is cutting your hair going to be a problem?"

"No." He was the problem.

"Good girl." He released her and moved away. "Let's get started."

Sadie reached out a hand to brace herself against the counter. She had to gather her thoughts. Evidently, Theo had. He seemed to have completely forgotten what had gone on between them just before her father had called. Turning, she looked at where her jacket lay beneath his T-shirt on the floor just a few feet away from where she stood. If her father hadn't called, she might be lying beneath Theo right now. He might be buried deep within her, moving...

Gripping the counter tightly, Sadie took a deep breath. She'd never thought of being with a man in such graphic terms before. With Theo she couldn't seem to help herself. Every time he touched her, she wanted. It was that simple. That basic.

"Sadie, come here."

Gathering her scattered thoughts, Sadie moved into a short hallway and through an open door. She recognized the bedroom she'd glimpsed through the window earlier. The bedside lamp was still on and Theo stood in the doorway to the bathroom, holding scissors in his hands. "I want to get you looking different, and then I've got a feeling that we should get back to San Francisco."

"You've got a *feeling?* Are you psychic like your aunt?"

"You know about Aunt Cass?"

"Roman's talked about her."

"I'm not what she is. I do get feelings once in a while, but mine aren't always right. Hers are."

She studied him. "That's how you knew to put Laura Wenger on the stand, isn't it?"

Theo frowned. "Maybe. Yes. But it's always a risk. You can't always depend on getting a feeling."

"No, I suppose not. It's probably like any other talent or natural ability. You have to practice it and keep developing it."

He stared at her for a minute. "I suppose you're right."

"But as far as my being here, who would know? Even my father doesn't know the directions."

"I'm probably overreacting, but I'd rather be safe." He extended the scissors to her. "Do you want to do the honors, or should I?"

"You can do it." Sadie walked toward him. If he could be businesslike and focused, so could she. But the moment she stepped through the bathroom door, her resolve melted. The room was tiny, forcing them to face each other in front of the sink.

"Turn and look in the mirror," Theo said.

As they jockeyed for position, her arm brushed against him, and the contact sent a flame racing along her skin. The heat spread deeper as he tugged the elastic off of her braid. She could see their images in the mirror, him behind her, taller, bigger. They were standing so close that she could feel the heat of his body.

"I've been thinking…" Theo began to loosen her braid. She should be thinking, too, but her mind could only seem to focus on the sensation of his fingers running through her hair.

"I've been trying to put myself in Paulo's shoes. It might be good if you tried to put yourself in Juliana's."

Sadie drew in a deep breath. She had two choices here. She could either pull herself together enough to participate in the conversation or she could turn around and jump Theo Angelis, something she didn't have much experience in doing. Plus, if she chose the latter, Theo might change his mind about letting her work with him.

"I don't know her that well."

"She's your sister and she's in love with a man her father wouldn't approve of. Trust your instincts."

"Okay." She could do it, Sadie told herself as she studied herself in the mirror. Perhaps she and Juliana were more alike than she'd thought. Except that her sister had had the courage to take a huge risk and go against her father's wishes. Sadie had yet to take a risk like that. She shifted her gaze to Theo's in the mirror.

"Brace yourself. I'm going to start cutting."

Sadie met his eyes steadily. "Go ahead. I'm ready for a change."

The snip of the scissors cutting through the strands of her hair sounded loud in the small space. Sadie was aware of each movement of Theo's hands as he released one section of hair and lifted another from the nape of her neck.

"It's not going to be stylish. I've got an actor friend in San Francisco who can style it. He'll have some clothes to dress you in, too."

The scissors sounded again and Theo's fingers moved along her neck to select another piece. Little ripples of ice and fire raced along her skin every time he made contact. Gradually, the anticipation of his touch became nearly as torturous as the reality.

"My guess is that Paulo didn't get in that taxi with Juliana because he isn't willing to trust anyone in either family right now, not while Juliana's safety is in question. Your turn."

"Hmm?" Her brain had become foggy again. She wasn't sure she could clear it.

"Think like Juliana," Theo prompted as he continued to cut.

Sadie put her hands on the sink to steady herself. "Juliana wouldn't trust anyone, either. And if you're right and she didn't send those invitations, she must have been horrified when Roman arrived and argued with Paulo."

"Yeah. That's the way I see it, too. I have a strong feeling they went underground."

Her brain cleared as hope leaped in her heart. "You don't think the man in the van got them?"

"No. They were smart enough to plan a secret wedding—I think they'll be savvy enough to hide out until the dust settles. Isn't that what you would do?"

"Yes," Sadie said. At least that's what she'd like to think she'd do. She'd like to think that she was as much of a risk taker as her sister was, that she had Juliana's guts.

"Turn around and face me now. I need to finish the front."

Sadie did as he asked and found herself just inches away from his bare chest. And she recalled just how it had gotten bare, how they'd practically ripped the T-shirt off of him. She could smell the scent of the sea on him—and something else that was darker, more male. Her mouth watered and the room, which had seemed warm before, turned hot. The air was suddenly charged.

She was vaguely aware of the snipping sound and the little shower of hair that grazed her cheeks, but she couldn't think anymore, couldn't even remember why she wanted to. All she was aware of was Theo and the huge need growing inside of her.

"There." He placed his hands on her shoulders and turned her so that she could see herself in the mirror. She blinked and stared. The woman looking back at her *wasn't* Sadie Oliver. Her hair was bluntly chopped around her face, making her cheekbones look more pronounced and her eyes huge. The dowdiness was gone; more than that, the person looking back at her looked as if she had guts.

Taking in a deep breath, she met Theo's eyes in the mirror. "I want you to kiss me again." Then, turning, Sadie threaded her fingers through his hair and dragged his mouth to hers. "This time, don't stop."

HE WASN'T GOING TO BE able to. That was the one clear thought that Theo had as he felt himself sinking into her flavor, her scent. In seconds his blood was teeming with her and his pulse went wild. Her lips were so hot, her taste so…necessary. Desperation clawed through him. Oh, no, he wouldn't be able to stop this time, not until he had everything. Her.

One stray thought did surface as he ran teeth and tongue along her jawline to nip her earlobe. "Protection. I don't have any here."

On a low moan, she dragged his mouth back and murmured the words against his lips. "On the pill."

"Good. That's…good." He wanted to go slowly, but his hands were no longer taking orders from his brain. The need that had been simmering in his veins ever since she stepped into the bathroom with him had exploded into a fast boil. Those low, desperate sounds she was making in her throat shot fire right to his groin. He had to get his hands on her. When her blouse ripped, the sound only urged him to go faster.

Turning, he braced her against the doorjamb and let his hands feast on the slim lines of her body. Soft skin, hard muscle. The contrast made him dizzy. Greedy for more, he tore her blouse off, then her skirt. In some far corner of his mind, he registered the creamy silk and lace of her bra before he got her out of it. Then, gripping her hips, he raised her and took his mouth on the same fast journey his hands had taken. Each sound she made, each shudder that wracked her drove him to take more. To need more. All.

When his mouth covered her breast, Sadie cried out his name. Then she braced her hands on his shoulders and wound her legs around him to feel the hard length of his penis press against her core. Sensations battered her, heat threatened to consume her. In desperation, she sank her teeth into his shoulder, dug her nails into his back. And she still needed more. She began to move against him, arching and straining for something.

"Wait." Swearing, Theo pulled away, then drew her with him to the floor. They struggled in the cramped space, jockeying for position as they fought with his jeans. When he was free, they were both panting. Then he reared up to his knees and lifted her so that she could wrap her legs around his waist.

"Now." He lifted and filled her.

For seconds neither moved. Sadie could feel their hearts pounding together. Even their breathing seemed to be in synch. She wanted to hold on to the moment. Finally, she had to shift to adjust to his length. When a fresh wave of pleasure swamped her, she cried out.

Theo covered her mouth with his and they moved in unison, each racing faster and faster until they both plummeted over the edge together.

9

THEO WASN'T SURE how long they lay there side by side on the floor before sanity returned. Even then, he couldn't talk. He wasn't sure that the oxygen he was dragging in was making it to his lungs. His head was still spinning and his thoughts were sluggish.

"You all right?" The question came out in a hoarse whisper.

"Mmmph," was her muffled reply.

He couldn't get his mind around what had just happened. He'd never made love to a woman like that before. He'd always prided himself on being a considerate and gentle lover. What had she done to him? What could she still do?

"That was...like nothing I've ever experienced," Sadie finally said.

He found her hand and linked their fingers. "Ditto." His voice had moved from a whisper to a croak. Things were looking up. He might even walk again someday.

"What would you have done if I hadn't been on the pill?"

Surprised, he turned his head, opened an eye and found her studying him. "Something more creative."

She traced a finger along his jaw. "Maybe I should go off the pill and see what you can come up with."

The glint of amusement in her eyes gave him the energy to smile. "Not necessary. I'll be happy to demonstrate. Just give me a few minutes. I'm going to need a little recuperation time." But already, a fresh ripple of desire moved through him. Incredible.

He had his hand at the back of her neck intending to kiss her again when a series of sharp, staccato barks pierced the silence. Theo immediately froze.

"What?" Sadie asked.

"Bob doesn't sound friendly. That's not like him."

As if to agree, Bob growled, then let out another series of barks.

"Grab your shoes." Theo kept his tone hushed as he rose and dragged on his jeans. Moving quickly, he retrieved his loafers from the closet shelf and tossed a pair of sweats at Sadie. "You'll have to roll these up."

To his relief, Sadie did what she was told, moving with admirable speed as he slipped his loafers on and found a T-shirt.

Bob's barking had changed to a low, menacing growl. Theo figured his neighbor was trying to settle his dog. But he had a very bad feeling about what had disturbed Bob. He'd had the feeling earlier that he should have gotten Sadie out of here. But he'd delayed. Yeah, he'd wanted to cut her hair, but mostly he'd wanted his hands on her again.

Cursing himself silently, he moved back to the closet and removed a revolver and a box of ammunition. His grandfather had been a mix of the old school and the new. A man had a right to have a gun, but he damn well better keep it in a safe place and unloaded. And he'd made sure that all of the Angelis men knew how to shoot and care for the weapon.

After tucking the gun and box into the waistband of his jeans, he took Sadie's hand and led her out of the bedroom. Avoiding the lights in the kitchen, he steered her down the hall to a bedroom at the back of the house. Thankfully, the woods pressed close to the cabin here. Saying a quick prayer that the window wouldn't protest too much, he raised it.

Bending close to her ear, Theo whispered, "If Bob spotted them, they're probably at the front of the cabin. Since the door's open, I'm hoping they'll use it."

"You think there's more than one?"

"I think it's best to plan for the worst-case scenario. You go first and get into the woods. I'll be right behind you."

Another woman might have argued and he wanted to hug her when she simply threw one leg over the windowsill, wiggled the other one over and dropped to the ground. By the time he followed suit, she'd disappeared into the line of trees. In a low crouch, Theo made his way around the cabin to the window that looked into the kitchen. Then pressing himself flat against the shingled exterior, he risked a quick glance into the room. There were two of them. Both were carrying guns and built like linebackers. If there'd been only one, he might have tried to take him by surprise. But his wisest course was to get Sadie away pronto.

SADIE STOPPED THE MOMENT she was far enough into the woods that she knew she couldn't be seen. Then she waited, peering into the darkness to look for Theo. As seconds ticked by, she realized that he hadn't followed her. Above the sound of her breathing, she began to hear the sounds of the night again. A skittering noise to her right had her pressing a hand against her chest. The animals were just as scared of her as she was of them, she reminded herself.

Where was Theo? Surely he hadn't stayed behind to confront whoever it was who'd upset Bob. But that was exactly the kind of thing her brother Roman might have attempted. Men. She was about to retrace her steps when a darker shadow separated itself from the trees.

"Theo," she whispered.

A second later, he took her hand. "No talking," he whispered. "The water magnifies every sound."

Together they moved deeper into the woods. Though her legs were long, every so often Sadie had to stop to roll the sweats up again. Theo kept their pace so brisk that in spite of the fact that the length of her stride nearly matched his, she had to put some effort into keeping up with him. Her sense was that they were giving wide berth to the path she'd used on the way in. A good strategy since whoever it was they were running from would probably use that path once they realized that the cabin was empty.

Theo stopped and together they listened.

An owl hooted, the leaves above them moved in the breeze, and an animal scurried through dried leaves to their left. But there was no sound of human pursuit. Yet.

They hurried on and a few minutes later, they reached a road. Sadie was surprised to see the shadowy outlines of the silver SUV and the smaller ones of her Miata. The woods were so dark that she hadn't noticed when Theo had angled back toward the path leading to the cabin.

Idling near the two vehicles was a large, black SUV. It had its headlights on, thankfully in the other direction, but she could see the silhouette of a man behind the wheel.

Motioning her to crouch down, Theo leaned close to whisper in her ear. "Since they've got our cars blocked, we'll have to move theirs."

She whispered back, "What about the driver?"

He shot her a quick grin. "We'll have to persuade him." He pulled the revolver and the box of bullets out of the back of his jeans and proceeded to load the gun. "Speed is essential. I spotted two men at the cabin and they were both armed. Once they're sure we're not there, they'll head back this way."

"What can I do?" she asked.

"You up to a little playacting?"

"Yes. Tell me what to do."

He pulled up the hood of her sweatshirt, then leaned close to her ear again and told her.

THEO CROUCHED LOW BEHIND the vehicle and held his breath as Sadie approached the SUV. He didn't like sending her out there as the front man, but it was the lesser of two evils. There was no telling when the other two men would step out of those woods, and he preferred to play backup.

Sadie was smart, she had guts, he reminded himself. And the Fates had been with them so far. He just had to bank on the fact that they could pull this off in time. Thank heavens he'd followed his gut instinct and cut her hair. He had no doubt that whoever these thugs were, they had an accurate description of Sadie Oliver. And the tall figure in the baggy sweats who'd just raised her hand to bang on the driver's side door didn't look anything like her.

The moment the driver turned his head, Theo moved toward the passenger door. He was banking on the fact that it would have been left open by the man's partners. And it was. Sadie was still spinning her story of a flat tire, when he yanked it open, leapt into the passenger seat and pressed the barrel of his gun to the startled driver's temple.

"Don't move and you won't die," he said softly. "And don't even think of sounding the horn."

Sadie opened the driver's door right on cue.

"Now, get out," Theo said. "And start walking up the road. If you turn around before you're out of my sight, I'll pull this trigger."

Without a word, the man got out of the car and Sadie, bless her heart, was already heading to his car and unlocking it. By the time he'd disabled the black SUV, she'd started the engine and opened the driver's door for him.

"Hang on." Theo backed up, executed a U-turn and floored the gas pedal.

They were still picking up speed when Sadie said, "We did it."

"We did indeed, partner. You played your part very well."

"I've never done anything like that before. Never."

Out of the corner of his eye, he could see that she was beaming, pleased with herself. He figured that he'd want to put that expression on her face again—but not this way. "Did you recognize that guy?"

"No." Her smile faded. "But I never did get a good look at the face of the man who chased Roman up the stairs. I want to know who sent them and how did they find us so quickly?"

Those were the key questions all right, and they'd been spinning through Theo's mind ever since he'd followed her out of that window. So far he hadn't liked any of the answers he'd come up with.

"Your father knew we were at the cabin."

"He agreed to let me work with you," she pointed out. "He doesn't go back on his word."

Theo considered that as he eased the speedometer up past seventy. "Okay. Second on my list is anyone who might have overheard him when he talked to us."

"They don't allow the use of cell phones in the hospital," Sadie said, "but there was a courtesy phone in the waiting room. My stepmother, her son, Eddie and Michael Dano were there with my father when I left the hospital. One of them could have overheard him."

"They could have easily figured out that he was talking to me. That was no big secret. I only asked about the security of the phone after he said your name. So anyone within hearing distance could have deduced that you were with me."

Theo braked at a traffic light on the outskirts of Sausalito and glanced in the rearview mirror. If the thugs at the cabin were willing to leave someone behind, there was a chance they might be able to hotwire Sadie's Miata. Just in case, he wanted to get back to San Francisco as quickly as possible.

"The timing's wrong," Sadie said. "No one at the hospital could have driven all the way here from San Francisco since we talked to my father."

"I agree." The light turned green and he shot the car through the intersection. "Even without the weekend traffic, it usually takes a good forty-five minutes to get here once you're over the Golden Gate Bridge. My brother Nik can make it in half an hour, but since he's a cop, he doesn't have to worry about a traffic ticket. And they would have had to stop somewhere around here to get specific directions to the Angelis cabin. The gas station where we turned onto the main road is used to giving directions to our place."

Theo glanced sideways at her and saw she was frowning in concentration.

"Someone could have followed me from the hospital," she finally said.

"True. Your Miata is pretty distinctive. They could have located it in the parking lot at the hospital and waited for you to leave."

She glanced at him. "But why didn't they follow me into the cabin right away? Why wait for so long?"

Once again, she was asking the same questions he was asking himself. "Maybe you lost them. That turn into the cabin is pretty easy to miss."

Sadie nodded. "So they would have contacted someone who overheard my father talking to you."

"Makes sense. I really admire the way your mind works, counselor."

"If we're right that I was followed from the hospital, none of our suspects can be eliminated. Angelo Carlucci could have had someone checking the hospitals."

"But he wouldn't have known you were at the cabin—unless, he has someone at the hospital feeding him information. And if it was someone associated with Oliver Enterprises who sent you that note to come to the wedding, he or she might have assumed that you'd eventually show up at the hospital to check on your brother's condition. So they followed you, lost you, and then someone who overheard your father talking to me put it together that you were with me and tipped them off."

"That narrows it down to the people who were near my father when he called you. Deanna, Eddie and Michael were probably in the waiting room, if that's where he called from. But there were probably plenty of other people there, too." She sighed in frustration. "We don't seem to be getting anywhere."

He reached over to cover her clasped hands with one of his. "We'll ask your father who was near him when he made the call. In the meantime, let's try another tack. Juliana and Paulo were very clever and very careful to get as far as they did with their wedding plans. But in light of what happened at the church, one or both of them must have confided their plans to someone. Who might Juliana have talked to?"

Sadie thought for a moment. "I don't know. I haven't had that much contact with her except for when Dad holds his big family dinners on Sundays."

"Who would know?"

"Eddie or Deanna might know something. Perhaps the housekeeper."

"Then we'll ask them." Theo linked his fingers with hers. "We're going to figure this out, Sadie."

As they left Sausalito, Theo once more glanced in the rearview mirror and then he floored the gas pedal.

"What do we do first?" Sadie asked.

"Since the doctors currently aren't allowing Roman to see anyone, there's nothing more that we can do tonight. So we're going to get a good night's sleep." He glanced at her again. She was still tense, still running on an adrenaline high. She was going to crash, he thought.

And he needed to get a handle on just what had happened back there at the cabin. "First thing in the morning, we'll finish turning you into a man and then we'll go to the hospital. We'll ask your family those questions we've been discussing and we'll talk to Roman. I have a feeling that he can shed quite a bit of light on what actually went down at that church."

10

SADIE OPENED HER EYES, then shot up in her seat and blinked in surprise. They were on a residential street in a neighborhood that boasted rows of the lovely Painted Ladies that San Francisco was famous for. "How long did I sleep?"

"Not long. You dozed off shortly before we crossed the Golden Gate Bridge," Theo said.

She struggled to orient herself. "We were talking about the security setup at the house, weren't we?"

"Yes."

It was coming back to her. They had been talking about who might have known about Juliana and Paulo's affair, and Theo had been questioning her about the Oliver estate—who lived there and who didn't and how difficult it would have been for Juliana to meet secretly with Paulo Carlucci. Though she and Roman had apartments in the city, Juliana still lived at home with Mario, Deanna and Eddie—home just happened to be a huge sprawling house with extensive gardens, a pool and tennis courts. But since the office complex that housed Oliver Enterprises was also located on the estate grounds, the security staff that her father maintained for business also looked after the house and manned the

gate at the entrance to the estate, making it very difficult for Juliana to have secret meetings of any kind. "I'm
sorry I faded out on you."

"You needed sleep. And we're here now."

It wasn't until he squeezed her hand and released it
that she realized she'd probably been holding his the
whole time she'd been asleep. Something moved
through her then. Not the heat that she'd experienced
from his touch before, but something warm and sweet.

He turned into the driveway of one of the largest
houses on the block and she caught a glimpse of twin
turrets and a wide porch before he pulled in behind the
house and parked the SUV so that it couldn't be seen
from the street.

"Where are we? Is this your house?"

"No, it belongs to that actor friend of mine I told you
about, Franco. He's going to finish your transformation."

Before she could pump him further, Theo slipped out
of the car and circled around to open her door.

A glance at the clock on the dashboard told her that
it was nearly one in the morning. "Isn't it a little late to
be paying your friend a visit?"

Placing his hands at her waist, Theo helped her out
of the seat. Then he guided her up the porch steps. "Currently, Franco has an acting gig at the local repertory
theatre. He has a lot of theater experience from New
York, and since he moved out here, he's picked up character parts now and then. On weekends, he usually hits
the club scene after the play, so he's probably still out."

"We're going to wait for him?"

Opening the door, he ushered her into a small foyer.
"Franco can work his magic on you in the morning. I've

brought you here tonight so that you can crash." He turned to her then. "You've had a rough day and I'm afraid I just added to it by making love to you back in the cabin. That shouldn't have happened."

Something squeezed her heart. "I wanted that to—"

He placed his fingers over her lips. "No. Let me finish. I should have had more consideration. More control. There's something about you…" He raised a hand, then dropped it to his side. "I had a feeling that I should get you out of there, and I let my desire for you interfere. That's not going to happen again. You'll be safe here. You'll be safe with me. And a good night's sleep is what we both need."

The little band around Sadie's heart tightened. Was he regretting what had happened between them at the cabin? She might have asked him if she wasn't afraid to hear the answer. She wanted to tell him that in the midst of the nightmare her life had turned into, making love with him had felt so…right. But what if he didn't feel the same way?

Theo guided her toward a staircase at the end of the hall. "I signed a year's lease for this apartment on the third floor six months ago, once I realized that Sandra Linton was turning into a problem. Only my family knows that I have this place and even they don't know where it is."

She said nothing, but she was intensely aware of him just behind her as they climbed upward.

Theo went on talking, but her mind was fogging over again. He was too close, the staircase too narrow. Sadie wished fervently that she had more experience with men. She'd certainly misread Michael Dano. Maybe

Theo hadn't found what she'd found in their lovemaking. The one thing she was sure of was her own body's reaction to him.

Focus, she told herself. Say something. Anything. "I never realized how hard being stalked must have been for you. There aren't many men who would have wanted their stalker to have treatment instead of jail time."

"Justice doesn't always equal revenge."

As they reached the narrow landing at the top of the staircase, Sadie felt her heart racing and it wasn't because of the steep climb.

"There were some side benefits to the whole Sandra Linton thing." His body brushed fully against her back as he reached around her to open the door. The contact was brief, an accident, but it was enough to have lust curling in her stomach. Suddenly, she was being bombarded by the same feelings, the same cravings that she'd felt when he'd cut her hair.

Not trusting herself to speak or to keep her hands off of Theo, Sadie focused all her efforts on moving through the open door. The separation brought some relief and she tried to concentrate on the small, round room. It was one of the turrets. Through a circle of narrow windows, she caught a brief glimpse of city lights before Theo flipped a switch and the room was bathed in a rosy glow of light from a Tiffany-style lamp. Glancing around, she took in the details and found herself immediately and completely charmed.

The room was furnished sparsely but well. There was a Victorian settee covered in burgundy brocade and a generously sized antique desk with brass fittings. She moved toward it and ran her fingers along the intricately carved edge. "Where on earth did you find this?"

"Right here—courtesy of my landlord. He came into the place as part of a palimony settlement with his ex-partner. The man had an aunt who loved antiques and Franco got the house plus the furnishings. Most of it is in storage, but when the need arises, as it did in my case, he provides a furnished space."

Sadie was finding it easier to concentrate if she just didn't look at him, so she continued taking an inventory of the room. Thick files were stacked neatly on a corner of the desk. The Tiffany-style lamp sat on another corner, flanked by framed photos. Shelves lined with books filled one wall and there was even a fireplace. In her mind, she pictured flames burning brightly, the smell of wood in the air, how the wind would sound as it rattled the windows. She could easily imagine making love to someone with the fire hissing and moonlight splashed across the floor.

Someone? Who was she kidding? She was thinking of making love to Theo again. Reining in her thoughts, she forced herself to concentrate on the rest of the space. Through an archway to her left, she caught a glimpse of cabinets and a stainless steel stove. Beyond an open door to her right, she could see the corner of a bed. She glanced quickly away, after realizing that Theo was at her side again. It wasn't just her wandering thoughts that she was having trouble with. The fact that they'd been physically intimate had only intensified her body's sensitivity to him and now she was fighting and losing a battle on two fronts.

"This place is really lovely." Her voice sounded thready,

but she managed to walk pretty steadily to the windows. The house was perched on one of San Francisco's many hills and the turret offered a breathtaking view.

"I envy you. It must be easy to work here," Sadie said turning back to him.

He smiled at her. "I think so. I find myself coming here instead of going home when I'm in trial. During the day, the windows offer a view of the bay and I always seem to be able to think better when I'm near water."

"Me, too. When I was in law school, I had an apartment with a view of the Charles. It's what got me through my criminal law class and tortes."

"You said you were on the swim team in high school. Do you still swim?" Theo asked.

"Only during the summer. There's a pool on the estate."

"I use a club downtown. If you'd like I'll get you a guest pass."

"Thanks." It suddenly occurred to Sadie that they were talking as if they were just becoming acquainted. Which they were—in spite of what they'd shared at the cabin.

"Well," Theo said and then paused.

For a moment, neither of them spoke. They were standing about ten feet apart and Sadie badly wanted to close the distance. If she just took her fate in her hands and moved…

"YOU NEED SOME REST." It was happening again, Theo realized. When she'd fallen asleep in the car, he'd promised himself that he wasn't going to touch her again. But he was finding that his grasp on those good intentions was slippery at best. Seeing her in this place, watching her run her hands over his things, stirred feelings in him that went deeper than mere desire. And if she continued to look at him in just that way, he was going to act on those feelings.

Turning, he strode into the kitchen. "First, I'm going to fix you something to eat." That would keep his hands busy at least. "I stocked the refrigerator before I left town because I intended to come back here and work on Sunday evening."

"You don't have to bother. I'm not really hungry."

"Yes, I do." He pulled meat and bread from the refrigerator. "You probably haven't eaten since lunch and you barely picked at that cheese I offered you at the cabin. Your body needs fuel."

Theo heard the lecturing note that had crept into his voice and tried to soften his tone. "The need to feed people runs in my family. My father is a restaurateur and he's very disappointed that none of his sons have followed in his footsteps. There's still my sister, Philly, of course. Or maybe my cousin Dino will decide to work there when he finishes his tour of duty in the Navy." Now he was starting to babble.

"You're talking about The Poseidon?"

"Yes." He sent her a glance over his shoulder. "Have you been there?"

"No."

He wanted to see her there, he realized. And he hadn't taken a woman to The Poseidon in a very long time, not since high school. There were a few charged seconds of silence as he tried to concentrate on assembling the sandwiches. He wasn't aware of what he'd slapped on the slices of bread, but he knew that she'd moved closer. He could feel her. Smell her. He could all but taste her.

"Can I do something to help?"

Images of just what she could do filled his mind. "Why don't you open some wine?" He gestured vaguely toward the refrigerator. He had to get out of the kitchen. Avoiding her eyes, he moved carefully around her. "I'll go fix a spot for us to eat in the other room."

Swearing silently, Theo strode to a small closet and pulled out a tablecloth and napkins. He had to get a grip. How in the world could he keep her safe when all he could do was think of touching her again, of having her again? She wanted his help and he had a growing feeling he needed hers.

After she'd fallen asleep in the car, he'd reviewed what they'd surmised so far, and the evidence pointed to the fact that even if Angelo Carlucci was behind what had happened at St. Peter's Church, there was someone inside Oliver Enterprises who was working with him. Sadie held the key to discovering who that was.

Ruthlessly shaking out the tablecloth, he spread it on the floor and wished it was just as easy to keep his libido in line. Their lovemaking at the cabin should have at least taken the edge off the desire that had been building in him since he'd touched her that first time in the courtroom. But instead of setting him free, making love to her had created an ache inside of him that he couldn't seem to shake loose.

After placing the napkins on the cloth, he returned to the closet and located two tapered candles. Franco thought Theo had rented the apartment to use as a little love nest, and so he'd provided what he believed were essential amenities. Theo fumbled with a match, swore silently then managed to light the candles.

Why the hell did she have to look so sexy in his sweats? For a moment there, when he'd offered to get her a guest pass at his club, he'd thought of how it might be to swim with her in the early morning with no one else in the pool. He doubted they'd get through more than five or six laps before they wouldn't be swimming anymore.

Dammit, Theo thought as he rose. He seemed to have a one-track mind where Sadie was concerned. They were going to eat. After he fed her, he'd send her to bed. He glanced around the room. And he'd somehow make do on the floor.

He surveyed the candlelit dining space he'd just created in the circle of windows, and he ran a frustrated hand through his hair. Who the hell was he kidding? He'd just set the scene for a romantic seduction.

Theo glanced at the archway to the kitchen. The more he tried to convince himself that he had choices where Sadie Oliver was concerned, the narrower they became.

OPENING THE REFRIGERATOR door, Sadie grabbed a bottle of wine. Clearly, she was misreading Theo. For a moment there, when they'd been standing together in the turret, she'd thought she'd seen something in his eyes— a reflection of what she was feeling. Then he went to make sandwiches.

What was the matter with her?

Answer: she was obsessed with Theo Angelis. He was trying to feed her and make sure she got a good night's rest. That was practical, kind, logical. She certainly needed rest. They both would if they were going to be of any help to Roman in the morning.

But all she could think of was having sex with him again.

Closing the refrigerator door, she faced her distorted image in the stainless steel door and frowned. She might look different than the dowdy woman who'd found Theo Angelis at that cabin, but she was still acting like that Sadie. Why? Why couldn't she be more like the Sadie she'd been at seventeen, ready to take a risk with Jackson Rayburn? Why was she so willing to go along with what others thought best for her?

Hadn't that been exactly what she'd been doing with her father and Michael Dano? Just going along in the hopes that the situation at work would resolve itself?

Now she was doing the same thing with Theo. First she'd delayed acting on her attraction to him for months, even knowing Jason Sangerfeld had offered him a job in L.A., and that her time was running out. She'd almost missed her chance with him completely. Was she now going to let him call all the shots?

Sadie stared at the bottle of wine in her hand, then at the pile of sandwiches he'd fixed. She didn't want to eat. And she didn't want a glass of wine. What she wanted was Theo.

Slamming the bottle down on the counter, she whirled and saw him standing in the archway. "Look." She strode toward him. "Let's just get a few things straight. I'm not going to eat. I'm not hungry. And I don't want to sleep right now." She poked a finger into his chest. "I want to make love with—"

The rest of her sentence faded away when he grabbed her against him and his mouth crushed hers.

"It's been too damn long," he muttered against her

lips. His hands found the edge of her sweatshirt and slipped beneath it. "I promised myself that I wasn't going to touch you again tonight."

"I promised myself that I *was* going to touch you." She ran kisses along his jawline, nipped his earlobe.

"I like your promise better. But I wasn't gentle with you back at the cabin."

Together they sank to the floor. "If your conscience is bothering you, you could just let me do the touching."

"Good idea." His hands found her breasts and she arched toward him. "For next time." Then he crushed her mouth again.

Desperation built immediately. She could feel his hunger where his heart thundered against her palm, taste it when his tongue aggressively met hers. The heat of his response fueled her own. Would the pleasure he gave her always be this sharp? This painful? This necessary?

When he finally dragged his mouth away to bury it at her throat, she said, "This gets better every time."

"I know," Theo murmured as he skimmed those wonderfully hard hands up her back.

"Incredible."

He nibbled kisses along her jaw. "I'm with you there. And it's all your fault. Why do you have to look so damn sexy in sweats?"

"You could take them off…"

"Brilliant suggestion. If I had any blood left…in my brain, I'd have thought of it."

Together they struggled, their fingers tangling as they pulled the sweatshirt over her head and tossed it away.

He drew back enough to run his eyes down her. "If that was supposed to make you look less sexy, it's not working." Then, gripping her waist, he lifted her and covered one breast with his mouth, the other with his hand.

Sadie arched back with a moan. No one had ever made her heart beat this fast. No one had ever sent these sharp shocks of pleasure shooting through her system. But even as his hands raced up her body in one hard possessive stroke, it wasn't enough.

More. Hurry. She wasn't sure if she'd said the words aloud or if he could read her mind. But his hands raced over her again. She slid her own beneath his T-shirt, grazing his skin with her nails as she tugged the shirt over his head. Then, overcome with her own hunger, she sank her teeth into his shoulder. She barely kept herself from biting him again when she heard his moan.

Instead, she licked the spot she'd bitten. "I'm sorry."

"For what?" He slid his hand beneath the elastic at her waist.

His fingers set off little flash fires as they moved over her buttocks and between her legs. As pleasure and anticipation streamed through her, she nipped his earlobe. "I can't seem to stop biting you."

"Not a problem. Bite me again if you want to."

But that wasn't what she wanted. His fingers were right there, brushing along her folds. She tried to sink onto them, but couldn't. "Theo?"

"What?"

His breath made the barest touch against her ear, but she felt it right to her center. "Please." She pressed down hard against his hand and when he finally slipped two fingers into her, the climax ripped through her with a force that had her crying out his name.

She barely had time to ride it out before he eased her to the floor.

"Let's get rid of these, too." Theo slipped his hands into the waistband of her pants and yanked them down her legs. Then he knelt between them and looked at her. He touched her only with his gaze, but she could feel a shudder start in the soles of her feet and move through her.

HER EYES WERE heavy-lidded and locked on his. Her body was slim, naked, and as he watched the tremor move through her, Theo knew she was his. The last tight thread he had on his control began to slip.

He needed a moment, just a moment. That was why he'd eased her onto the floor. But his hands were already reaching for her. And hers were reaching for him.

She levered herself up enough to grip his shoulders. "I want you, Theo. Now."

He thought he could hear his control snap as together they struggled to unfasten his jeans. When she shoved his hands away to deal with the zipper, he framed her face with them and crushed his mouth to hers. She found him with her hands and pleasure shot through him with an intensity that bordered on pain.

With her scent clouding his mind, her taste drugging him, he dragged her back to the floor. He touched her now, her throat, her breasts…the soft damp skin on her stomach. He wanted to linger, to savor. He wanted to use his mouth on her, but he simply couldn't wait.

And neither, it seemed, could she. If they were racing, the end result was a tie. Her hands were as fast and aggressive as his, her mouth just as hot, just as demanding. And her desire only fueled his as they grappled for position, rolling through patches of moonlight on the floor.

He'd wanted women before, but not like this. He'd felt need before, but it had never been this unmanageable. This consuming.

Then she was rising over him, straddling him. And taking him in.

They raced again. His fingers dug into his hips to force her to match his rhythm. Her eyes locked on his as she lured him into hers. Then he lost track of who was winning, who was losing. All he knew was Sadie as they drove each other faster and higher until they shattered. And fell.

11

"THERE. I THINK YOU'RE almost ready." Franco helped her into a navy blazer, then stepped away from her.

"Stand the way I told you to," he said.

Sadie did as he asked, widening her stance.

"Now make a quarter turn to your right." Franco stood to her left, wearing an embroidered red kimono, his bleached-white hair standing up in perfect spikes. As for the expression on his face, Sadie figured it was exactly how Cinderella's fairy godmother must have looked right after she'd waved her magic wand at Cindy.

So far he hadn't let her look in the full-length mirror, a gilt-framed monstrosity that seemed to blend perfectly with the rest of the decor in his bedroom. The huge brass bed and red brocade drapes reminded Sadie a bit of a Victorian bordello.

Franco motioned with his hand. "Another quarter turn."

Theo hadn't seen her, either. Franco had wanted full artistic control until the transformation was complete. In Franco's words, "Henry Higgins didn't take Eliza out until he was absolutely sure she could pass muster."

"All the way around," Franco ordered. When she was

facing him again, he stepped forward and adjusted the shoulders of her jacket. "You're ready. And just in the nick of time. Our mutual friend is wearing a hole pacing back and forth on my Persian carpet." He smoothed her lapels and stepped back. "I've never known him to be nervous before. You're good for him."

"Why do you say that?"

"Ever since he made—" Franco used both hands to make little quote signs in the air "—the 'ten-most-eligible-bachelors list,' he's built a shell around himself. He rented that little love nest upstairs from me six months ago and you're the first woman he's brought here."

"He didn't rent it as a love nest," Sadie said.

"Exactly my point." Franco lifted a mug of coffee from his dresser and took a swallow. "He rented it to hide away. Shortly after he moved in, I started going to his family's restaurant, at his suggestion. The food there is fabulous, by the way. And when the place really gets hopping at night, there's Greek music and dancing. I haven't had as much fun since I was in the chorus of *Zorba*. Have you been there yet?"

"No."

"My point is that *he* hasn't been back there since the shooting. His family is worried. But he'll take you there. He'll want his family to meet you."

"I don't think so," Sadie said. "We've only just met, really, and we're just—" what were they? she wondered "—friends."

"Right." Franco picked a piece of lint off her sleeve. "I've noticed the way he looks at you. He's not thinking of you as a friend. Now practice your walk again."

Sadie strolled the length of the room. The truth was,

she didn't really know what she and Theo were, except very attracted to one another. But last night after they'd made love, he'd insisted that they sit cross-legged on a tablecloth in the turret and have a picnic by candlelight. It had overwhelmed her that in the midst of everything else, he'd given her romance. There was no doubt that she'd felt her heart take a little tumble. Pressing a hand against her chest, she turned and walked back to Franco. They'd talked about…all sorts of things. Silly things like the scrapes they'd both gotten into as children. And they'd discovered that they both had a secret fondness for Gilbert and Sullivan, of all things.

Pausing, she rubbed at her chest. For a moment, she'd just felt right—as if she somehow had found the correct slot and slid perfectly in. And when Theo had taken her to bed, that had felt right, too.

When she'd woken up this morning, he'd already left the bed. And though she'd told herself it was ridiculous, she couldn't shake the feeling that he was slipping away from her. When she'd joined him in the kitchen, he'd already showered, dressed and was sipping coffee. He'd even called the hospital and spoken with her father.

Roman's condition hadn't changed and they'd scheduled the surgery to relieve the swelling on his spine for later that morning. Somehow, the fact that Theo was several steps ahead of her and operating on all cylinders had made her feel even more lonely.

That was just ridiculous, she told herself with a little frown. Last night had been wonderful, but today they had work to do.

"You've really got it bad," Franco said.

"What?"

Franco shook his head. "You've been standing there staring into space for two solid minutes. He's been out there pacing. Theo Angelis never paces. You've definitely taken the fall. You'll just have to get used to it."

"The fall?"

"Into *L-O-V-E*."

"No." A little sliver of panic raced up her spine and Sadie raised a hand in denial. "No. What Theo and I have is temporary. Jason Sangerfeld has made him a job offer."

Franco gave a long low whistle. "That's the big time."

"He'll have to move to L.A." She felt a little band of pain tighten around her heart.

Franco frowned then. "That will allow him to isolate himself even more. You may have to take matters into your own hands."

"Are you ready yet?"

Theo's voice had the two of them turning toward the door.

"Just a minute," Franco called. Then he took her hand and pulled her toward the mirror. "There." He patted her on the shoulder and stepped back. "You can come in, Theo."

Sadie just stared at her reflection. The transformation that Theo had begun in the bathroom of the cabin, Franco had finished with a vengeance. And a flourish, she felt compelled to add.

"What do you think?" Franco asked.

Sadie spoke first. "I don't recognize myself."

"That's the whole point." Franco turned to Theo. "It's your call. Will he pass?"

"He looks young for a law student," Theo said.

Sadie could see a great deal of Franco's nervousness ease at Theo's use of the masculine pronoun.

"So? He's precocious. Here, try these."

Sadie took the eyeglasses Franco handed her and put them on. The glasses were without prescription, and she stood there, admiring her scholarly look. "With these glasses, I look like this preppy nerd I worked on the *Law Review* with at Harvard. Harry Fitzweiller. He finished his law degree at twenty. We all hated his guts."

"The glasses make you look like Harry Potter," Theo said.

For a second, Sadie thought she saw something in Theo's eyes that she recognized. Desire? It was masked so quickly that she was almost sure she'd been mistaken.

"Puh-leeze." Franco threw up his hands. "Lightning will strike you. That little sorcerer wouldn't be able to afford these. They're Armani frames. One of a kind, never mass-produced. I couldn't afford them, either. They were a gift from the costume designer of the last play I worked on in New York. They once appeared on the cover of *GQ*."

Sadie turned so that her back was to the mirror and she was facing Theo. This time she was sure it was desire she read in his eyes. Just seeing it, just looking at him standing there not only eased the loneliness she was feeling, but also triggered an onslaught of other feelings she couldn't name.

As panic threatened again, she reminded herself that Franco had to be wrong. She and Theo were still exploring, learning things about each other. And she was experienced enough, well-read enough, to know that desire could exist without the four-letter word. The fact that Theo seemed to have his mind strictly on business today was good. She'd better follow his example because her brother and sister were depending on her.

"What do you think, Sam?" Theo asked.

He was talking to her. With a frown, she gathered her thoughts. Sam was the name they'd decided she'd use. Sam Schaeffer. It was the name of a prelaw student Theo had met when he'd guest-lectured at Stanford during the spring and who had applied to do an internship with him. No doubt Theo was calling her that now to test her.

Turning back to the mirror, she studied herself with a critical eye. "I'm taller than Harry Potter, but the nerdy look isn't a bad one."

Franco had shaped the haircut that Theo had given her and done something subtle to the color so that it was lighter and had some golden highlights. Then he'd added enough hair products to create the sort of casual unstyled look that a college student might wear.

She ran her gaze down her clothes. Since she and Franco were about the same size, he'd outfitted her from his own closet with a well-tailored navy blazer and pale blue shirt, khaki slacks and loafers. The shoes were Italian and Franco had winced when she'd had to stuff tissues in the toes. She swept her gaze up to her face again. The truth was, she not only looked different, she felt different. The first haircut and wearing Theo's sweats had started it, but Franco's magic had really done the trick. She felt more confident. More like a man, she supposed. And she liked it. "I think the costume is working."

"So do I," Franco said. "Just remember what I told

you and sink into it. Feel it. Trust it. In the first Batman movie, Jack Nicholson's advice to Michael Keaton was to let the costume do the work. I find it works every time. Just let yourself become *one* with the outfit and pretty soon you will *be* Sam Schaeffer."

Widening her stance, Sadie shoved her hands in her pockets. Immediately she looked and felt more masculine—more like the young man she saw in the mirror.

"That's it. You make a very handsome young man. But remember, the clothes are on loan. If you discover that you're into cross-dressing, I have a friend who runs a great boutique." He flicked a glance at Theo. "There are straight couples who are finding that switching clothes releases their inhibitions. I could give you the name of a boutique, too."

"I don't think so, Franco." Theo's tone was dry.

He shrugged. "Whatever." Then he winked at Sadie in the mirror. "If Mr. Conservative changes his mind, I can also recommend some good nightspots. My new partner's club is one of them."

"Thanks." Sadie couldn't prevent a smile, but she was very much aware that Theo was still studying her with a critical eye and she could almost read his mind. If she didn't pass his inspection, he was going to insist that she keep a very low profile at the hospital.

Perhaps that was why he'd been keeping her at a distance this morning. Maybe he'd already decided that she should try to blend into the background when he'd checked in with her father earlier.

A little flame of anger sprang to life inside of her. Well, Theo Angelis would just have to deal with the fact that she wasn't going to let him or anyone else sideline her.

"Remember to avoid shaking anyone's hand," Franco said. "Yours are a bit too feminine. You've got your notebook to help with that. Just whip it out and ask a question when you're introduced to a man. Where else will you be going besides the hospital?"

"The police station where Theo's brother works." That was something they'd discussed while Theo had French-pressed her first cup of coffee this morning. Business had been at the top of his agenda. He wanted to get his brother Nik's slant on the case and find out what kind of evidence the police had already gathered.

"Then we'll go to the Oliver estate and see what we can learn about who Juliana might have told about her plans," Theo added.

Straightening her shoulders, Sadie turned to view herself in profile. In her opinion, it was the carefully applied makeup that had really completed the transformation. The effect was subtle, but she could have sworn that her jawline and cheekbones both appeared to be more masculine.

"I think you're a genius, Franco," she said.

"I am."

"Walk across the room," Theo said.

Sadie turned away from the mirror. As she moved across the room, the image in her mind was that confident saunter that Theo always used.

"Good. That's good," Franco said. "Our Sam here is a quick study."

"Say something," Theo said.

Sadie lowered her voice the way Franco had coached her. "I'm Sam Schaeffer, Theo's new intern." She remembered to pull out her notebook as she spoke. "And you are?" She was pleased with the husky sound, so she met Theo's eyes and said, "The rain in Spain stays mainly in the plain."

Theo's smile spread slowly. "I think she's got it."

Franco did a little hop and a two-step. "By George, she's got it."

"And not a minute too soon." Theo glanced at his watch. "We're due at the hospital in twenty minutes."

"Wait, wait, wait." Franco set his mug on the dresser and dove for the closet. "I have to pack a bag. He'll need the makeup for touch-ups, and an extra shirt and tie."

While he was tossing things on the bed, Sadie turned to Theo. "You're having second thoughts about this whole masquerade thing, aren't you?" She saw the flicker of surprise in his eyes before he took her hand and raised it to his lips. This was the first time he'd touched her since she'd woken up and found him gone. The small gesture reassured her more than words could have.

"I have some news that isn't good."

"You called the hospital again? Is it Roman?"

"No." He squeezed her hand. "I just got off the phone with a friend of mine who works in the D.A.'s office. The ballistics report is in and the bullet that killed the man in the sacristy came from Roman's gun. They've also identified the dead man as Paulo Carlucci's body-guard, Gino DeLucca."

Sadie's stomach knotted. "He shot Paulo's body-guard. They'll arrest him, won't they?"

"They're still gathering evidence. But when that news leaks to the press—and it will—there will be a lot of pressure brought to bear on the police to make an arrest."

She nodded and made herself swallow through the tightness in her throat. Then she met his eyes. "You haven't answered my question. Are you having second thoughts about my being able to carry this off?"

"I'm not going to go back on my word. I said that we'd work together on this. And the disguise was my idea. But I've had this feeling ever since I woke up this morning that you're going to be in danger at the hospital."

"What kind of danger?"

Theo frowned. "I wish the hell I knew. My feelings are never that explicit."

"You're going to be there and my father will have his own security people in place. Plus, I'm disguised. I should be perfectly safe."

"I can't explain it. But I made your father a promise, too. I intend to keep you safe, so we have to set some ground rules."

She narrowed her eyes. "Ground rules?"

Theo hesitated, then said, "I'm not sure you can fool your father."

"I'm not sure I can, either. So we'll handle that problem when it arises. Agreed?"

Theo's frown deepened. "I think it might be best if you kept a low profile at the hospital. Let me talk to your father alone. But I want you to stay where I can see you. No wandering around on your own."

Sadie withdrew her hand from his. "I could question the others while you talk with my father."

"I don't think that's a good idea."

She studied him for a moment. "You really don't trust me to pull this off, do you?"

Any response Theo might have made was prevented

when Franco joined them and began to chatter. Summoning up a smile for Theo's landlord, she shouldered the black duffel bag he'd packed for her. Franco was still rattling off instructions as Theo drew her out of the apartment.

Even when they were alone, he didn't answer her question. Ignoring the little pain that settled around her heart, Sadie decided that she'd just have to take Franco's advice—she'd take things into her own hands.

12

SADIE WAS UPSET WITH HIM. The fact that she had a right to be didn't help one bit. She hadn't spoken on the drive to the hospital. Now he stood shoulder to shoulder with her in the elevator as it climbed to the fifth floor, but they might as well have been miles apart.

She hadn't asked him again whether or not he trusted her to carry off the masquerade. She didn't have to. Because she no longer trusted him. If there was one thing Theo Angelis was good at it was reading people, and Sadie Oliver was easier for him to read than most. Everything she thought, everything she felt was there on her face, in her eyes.

And it had him scared. *She* had him scared. He knew how to handle women and he knew what he wanted from them. So why was he having so much trouble dealing with her? First, he'd avoided her. That hadn't worked. Last night he'd promised himself he wouldn't touch her, but he had. He'd promised *her* that she could work with him and help. Now she thought he was going back on his word.

The elevator stopped on the third floor, and Sadie moved into the opposite corner to allow an orderly to wheel an empty gurney in. Out of the corner of his eye, he saw that her eyes were fixed on the floor numbers. She did look like a young man. Franco had orchestrated an amazing transformation and he should be confident that she could pull it off. But he wasn't.

Dammit, he'd been the one to suggest that she pretend to be a man. The idea had seemed good at the time. But something had happened during the night. Something that he hadn't expected, hadn't wanted.

He'd lost count of the times they'd made love. She was so responsive, so generous. And no matter how much he'd demanded and taken, he'd wanted more. But what Theo recalled most vividly was the way she'd looked at him when they were sipping wine and talking in the candlelight. And the way he'd felt when he'd awakened to her sleeping beside him, her head on his shoulder, her arm around his waist.

The sweetness, the rightness of just seeing her there, had sent his heart into a very long tumble. In that moment, he'd never wanted her more—not just sex. He wanted *her,* all of her. He wanted to know everything there was to know about her, to share her thoughts, feelings, dreams. And he wanted to share himself with her, too, with no boundaries, no doubts.

And that was when fear had slipped in and sunk its claws into his gut. The depth of what he was feeling scared him. So did his desire to wake her up and tell her. Instead, like a coward, he'd taken a shower, dressed and gone out to the kitchen.

Now he was letting his emotions affect the work that they had to do together. He couldn't afford to let that happen. It hadn't just been a gesture on his part when he'd come up with the idea of her disguise. No one knew the players in this deadly little game better than Sadie Oliver. She was an insider and he *needed* her.

That was the real crux of the matter. He was beginning to need her for a whole lot more than the case. For the first time in his life, his mind and emotions were at war. There was a part of him that wanted to keep her at his side—and another part that wanted to take her back to Franco's and lock her up in his apartment. Right now. Neither one of those options would be acceptable to Sadie.

The icing on the cake was that, because she didn't trust him now, he couldn't predict what she would do. He'd seen the look in her eyes before they'd left Franco's house. It was the same reckless gleam he'd seen when she'd strode out of the kitchen last night and demanded that he make love to her.

Theo studied her as the gurney exited on the fourth floor and left her standing alone in the corner. Isolated. From what she'd told him, that's the way she'd spent most of her life.

Maybe he ought to just trust her. He let her precede him through the door when the elevator stopped on the fifth floor. The glass wall directly in front of them enclosed a small waiting room. Through it he could see Mario Oliver and others, and the feeling that she was in danger struck him again. The sensation was so acute that he strode forward, grabbed her hand and pulled her a few paces down the hallway. He could sense anger radiating from her.

"Problem?" she asked sarcastically.

What could he tell her? That she couldn't go in there? Should he tell her about his feelings or would she think he was using them as an excuse to protect her? She wouldn't believe him. He wasn't sure he could believe in his feelings himself. "No. I just thought you might give me a little preview of who's in there."

"*Everyone* is in there," she bit out. "Why isn't at least one of them with Roman?"

Temper, as well as the recklessness he'd sensed earlier. Not a good combination. Realizing that he was still holding her hand, Theo released it. He wanted to keep it in his to comfort her, but she wasn't Sadie. She was Sam Schaeffer. If he wasn't careful, he'd be the one to blow her masquerade.

"Your father said the doctors want him kept quiet. Even if we get in to see him, he's so sedated that he probably won't even know we're there." Then to take her mind off of that, he said, "I assume the blonde must be your stepmother and the young man sitting next to her is Eddie Mancuso and not Brad Pitt?"

"Yes."

Theo caught the slight twitching of her lips and felt a little of his tension ease.

"The dark-haired man looking at the TV screen is Michael Dano."

Theo studied the trio for a minute. Deanna Mancuso Oliver was a fragile-looking blonde that his sister Philly would have described as a trophy wife. She certainly didn't look old enough to be the mother of the young man sitting next to her.

Eddie Mancuso was handsome in a pretty, movie-star kind of way. His long blond hair nearly grazed his shoulders and he wore a navy blazer and khaki slacks similar in style to the ones Sadie was wearing. Franco definitely knew something about young men's fashion.

"Tell me about Eddie," he said.

"I've sensed that Deanna would like him to have a more secure future at Oliver Enterprises. So far he hasn't found his niche. At one point, I think she entertained thoughts of Eddie and Juliana making a match of it. Right after Juliana came home, Deanna was seating them together at dinner parties, but nothing clicked."

"What's wrong with Eddie?" Theo asked.

"Wrong?"

"He looks like he ought to be in movies. I'm wondering why your sister didn't go along with your stepmother's matchmaking plans."

"I haven't spent much time with him, but I know the type. My guess is that Eddie knows he's pretty. He's probably a player, the kind of man who'll never be satisfied with one woman. Juliana's no dummy."

He sent her a sideways glance. "You know a lot more about your sister than you give yourself credit for. What about Eddie? Is he a dummy?"

She thought about that. "A bit self-centered, yes. But he's smart. If you want to know if he could have orchestrated what happened at the church last night…I'm not sure. I suppose if he got wind of Juliana's plans, he might have been able to hire some thugs. And I suppose his mother might have helped him. She's not dumb, either. But I think she really loves my father."

"What about Michael?" As he spoke, Theo turned his attention to the man standing a little apart from the group on the couch. Slick and tough were the words that came to his mind.

"Michael's very smart. Brilliant, perhaps. And he's good with people."

Theo narrowed his eyes as he studied the man.

"But I can't see him sending armed men to the church. He has a great future at Oliver Enterprises. He's been working closely with Roman in negotiating a major land deal. What would his motive be? Plus, he's incredibly loyal to my father and Roman. If he'd learned of Juliana's plans, he would have told them. He knows which side his bread is buttered on."

Theo continued to study the man who'd hoped one day to marry Sadie Oliver. A little taller than average, Michael had the compact build of a boxer and his clothes hadn't come off any rack. He reminded Theo of the Las Vegas casino owner in *Ocean's Eleven*. Theo was betting that Michael Dano wasn't a man who liked being crossed and he could see why that quality might appeal to Mario Oliver.

His gaze shifted to the TV screen Michael was watching. The set was tuned to a local news station and Theo could see a reporter standing in front of St. Peter's Church. The banner headline running at the bottom of the screen read "Breaking News: Feuding Families Search for Missing Bride and Groom."

"It looks like the press has identified your sister and Paulo Carlucci as the missing bride and groom. I'm surprised that TV crews aren't camped out in the lobby of the hospital already."

"My father has a lot of pull here because he donated the trauma center. I'm sure that the staff has been warned to deny that Roman is here."

That would only work for so long, Theo thought. He wanted to keep Sadie close, but at the same time, he knew that he had to regain her trust. "Look, it's your call. If you want to come in there while I talk with your father, you can."

She faced him then. "Thanks, but it's probably not a good idea. My father has good eyes and even better instincts. If he isn't fooled, everyone in there will know who I am." She gave him a smile. "I'm not sure Franco can top this disguise, so I'd like to make it work for a while. I'll just hang around out here and see what I can learn."

"No." The moment the word was out, Theo could have bitten his tongue. His tone had been too sharp and he didn't miss the hurt that shot into her eyes before she glanced away. "Sorry." Once again he had to stifle the urge to touch her. "Look. Remember our ground rules. Stay where I can see you."

YOUR GROUND RULES, not mine, Sadie thought silently as Theo walked away from her. She'd thought for a few minutes that they'd been on the same wavelength, but they evidently weren't. Sadie Oliver might worry about why, but Sam Schaeffer didn't have the time.

She hesitated only until everyone in the waiting room had their attention focused on Theo before moving down the hall toward the nurse's station. She'd spotted a cop standing sentinel outside a room at the far end of the hallway. There was another, larger man sitting on the other side of the door in a chair. She was betting that was Roman's room.

Once again, she found herself imitating Theo's slow but purposeful saunter. It got her past the nurse's station without so much as a glance.

The cop and the bodyguard might pose more of a problem, and as she drew closer, her heart sank. The large man sitting in the chair was Mason Leone. He'd been in her father's employ since she was ten. Originally, he'd provided security for Roman and her, which had included administering first aid whenever her desire to compete with her brother had resulted in scraped knees and elbows.

As she approached the room, Sadie tried to remember everything that Franco had told her. Keep your voice low and let the costume do the work.

Mason appeared to be asleep, but he opened his eyes the moment she stopped. "I'm Sam Schaeffer, assistant to Theo Angelis who's representing Roman Oliver." She extracted one of Theo's cards from her pocket. "I'd like to see our client."

"Only family is allowed." The young cop frowned at her as Mason took her card.

The older man gave her a quick look up and down, but there was nothing in his eyes or expression that suggested even a hint of recognition. Then he turned to the cop. "I'm pretty sure Mr. Oliver has cleared the attorney with his son's doctors." He pushed some buttons on a hospital phone that had been placed on a small table by his chair. "I'll just check with him."

Shit, Sadie thought. She had no idea if Theo had mentioned Sam Schaeffer to her father when he'd spoken to him earlier.

"What was your name again?" Mason asked.

"Sam Schaeffer." Sadie held her breath while Mason talked to her father.

"Yeah, this is the guy."

Mason had shifted his gaze to a point beyond her and even as she turned, Sadie felt a little chill slide up her spine. Sure enough, her father was on the phone at the nurse's station while Theo stood nearby. Would he recognize her? Would he come down to get a closer look? Would Theo give her away? The questions were still spinning through her mind when the two men turned and walked into a room.

Mason hung up the phone. "You can go in."

Sadie didn't let out the breath she was holding until she was in the room with her brother. And then her heart sank.

13

THEO CLAMPED DOWN his anger as he followed Sadie's father into a spacious, well-appointed office. What he was feeling wasn't rational. Telling himself that there were two guards outside of Roman's room and that Sadie ought to be perfectly safe didn't help much. So instead, he focused on his surroundings. According to Mario, the head of the trauma unit had offered the use of his office while the family waited for Roman's tests and surgery to be completed. The room contained a computer, a fax and a private phone line. With the door shut, even the noise from the nurse's station was blocked out. Not one of the trio in the waiting room had seemed pleased when Mario had suggested he and Theo retire here for some privacy.

Evidently, Mario had listened to what Sadie had told him last night, and at least for the moment he didn't trust anyone close to him. Theo had to give him high marks for that.

Mario seated himself behind the desk and gestured Theo into a chair on the opposite side. Without preamble he said, "You didn't say anything about bringing an intern here."

"No." Theo had known the question would come

eventually, and he had prepared for it. "Sam is prelaw at Stanford and very good at research. I thought I might be able to make use of him. When I spoke to you, I wasn't sure he was available."

"And if I have one of my men do a little research on this Sam Schaeffer, he will check out."

It wasn't a question, but Theo nodded. "Yes."

For a moment the silence stretched in the room as the two men studied each other. What Theo saw was a tall, dapper-looking man, trim and in good shape, his dark hair going stylishly gray. Though he wasn't a large man, Mario Oliver had the kind of magnetism that filled a room and there was no mistaking the shrewdness in his eyes. This was a man who gave orders and was used to having them obeyed. It occurred to Theo that in thirty years, Roman Oliver would look very much like the man he was facing across the desk.

Right now, Theo was more concerned with what Mario Oliver was seeing. The man knew Kit, but they'd never met before. He could only hope that Sadie's father would trust him more than Sadie currently did.

Mario put his arms on the desk and steepled his fingers just below his chin. "We both know that's not Sam Schaeffer in Roman's room. That's my daughter Sadie and you promised that you wouldn't bring her here. Explain yourself."

Theo bit back a smile. He admired a man who laid his cards on the table. And he couldn't fault Sadie's instinct about her father. He'd seen through her disguise at twenty-five feet.

Keeping his eyes steady on Oliver, Theo said, "I didn't bring Sadie. I brought Sam Schaeffer. It's a good disguise—I had some help from a man who works in the theater. How did you see through it, if you don't mind my asking?"

"I know my daughter. I haven't always understood her in the same way that I understand Juliana and Roman. But I heard what was in her voice last night when I spoke to her. I haven't heard that kind of determination, that kind of defiance for a long time, not since she went east to college. I figured that she'd find a way to come with you. She's stubborn." He sighed. "She comes by it naturally."

"She evidently knows you, too. She was pretty sure you'd see through the disguise. That's why she didn't come with me into the waiting room."

Mario's eyes narrowed. "Instead, you let her wander around unattended."

Pushing his own fear about that aside, Theo raised his hands palms out. "If I had my way, she would have stayed right with me. She was concerned that if you recognized her you'd give her away."

"Which means she doesn't trust the people closest to me."

Theo glanced pointedly around the room. "I'd say you have some reservations on that score yourself."

Mario's gaze remained steady on his. "I believe that Angelo Carlucci is behind what happened at St. Peter's Church, make no mistake about that. If…no…*when* he learned about his son's plans to marry my Juliana, sending his men to storm the church with guns is exactly his style."

"Sadie would agree with you there. That doesn't mean he didn't have an inside man."

A little frown appeared on Mario's forehead. "Perhaps." He leaned back in his chair and another silence stretched between them. Then he said. "I'm going to tell you something in confidence. I've told no one, not even the police or the FBI. I want your word that you won't tell anyone."

"I won't tell anyone except for Sadie. I've promised her that she can work with me on this. If I'm going to keep her safe, I can't allow her to have trust issues with me. She already thinks that I want to keep her on too short a leash. And that's not the way to handle her."

After a moment, Mario nodded. "I've received a ransom note for my daughter Juliana's return. It came by special messenger and was left at the nurse's station."

"A ransom note." Theo's eyes narrowed. He'd been so sure that Paulo and Juliana were safe, that they'd gotten away. "You checked with the delivery service."

Mario nodded again. "The description they gave of the man who dropped it off isn't familiar to me. They're asking five million in cash. That's the exact amount that my sources say Angelo Carlucci needs to come up with if he wants to beat me out on this land deal."

"Sadie and I were hoping that Paulo and Juliana had gotten away." And the last thing he wanted to have to do was give her bad news.

"She didn't. Paulo Carlucci may be in on this with his father. This whole thing may have been a plot to make sure that the Carlucci family gets that strip of coastline."

"Interesting that the ransom is for the exact amount. Angelo has a reputation for being smart."

Mario's eyes narrowed. "Yes, he does. Perhaps the son is handling this on his own."

"Or someone wants you to think that. I'm not telling you anything you haven't already thought of. But I still think it's too soon to jump to the conclusion that the Carluccis are acting alone in this. Roman told Sadie to trust no one."

"I don't, when it comes to my children." Mario looked directly at Theo. "Unless circumstances force me to. And it seems that my daughter doesn't completely trust *me,* either."

Theo said nothing. Mario Oliver was a perceptive man, soft-spoken and controlled. The only sign he was affected by what he was saying was the slight tension in the set of his jaw.

"There's something that you may be able to check on," Theo said. "Sadie told you that her invitation to go to St. Peter's came at around four o'clock yesterday afternoon and that we suspect Roman might have received a similar invite. Sadie left hers on her desk. It's possible that Roman did the same."

"I'll have someone check for me."

Theo nodded. "It would show that Roman didn't know that he was being invited to a wedding and we could use it to throw doubt on what I suspect will be the prosecution's theory that Roman brought some hired guns with him to put a stop to the wedding."

Theo saw a flicker of something in Mario's eyes, but it was quickly masked.

"You come with high recommendations. I trust your brother Kit and I might have hired you even without Sangerfeld's urging. However, I don't like the fact that Sadie is here, disguised or not. I'm going along with this little masquerade for now because it's important that she see her brother and I understand her need to be of help. But I may still decide to end it, and as my attorney, I'd expect you to follow my orders."

Theo met the older man's gaze steadily. "As Roman's attorney, I advise against it. There are several pluses to allowing Sadie to continue her masquerade. First of all, Roman and I can use her help. She was at the scene. She told you that the man driving the van seemed familiar to her. I want to be there when she remembers where she saw him. She also has a first-rate legal mind. If Roman is arrested, she's going to be an asset. Finally, she's Juliana's sister. Sadie doesn't think she's that close to her, but I'm hoping that she might have some insight that will help us find Juliana."

Mario studied him for a moment. "How long have you known Sadie?"

"We met after one of her trials two months ago. But I'd already seen her in court several times before that. She's an excellent attorney."

Mario said nothing.

"I also want Sadie safe," Theo continued. "Until this is sorted out, I want her where I can keep an eye on her."

"That's the only reason I'm going along with her disguise. Right now, allowing you to take responsibility for her safety is the lesser of two evils. But I may still change my mind. Have I made myself clear?"

Theo nodded. "Completely. You should know that someone came after her at my grandfather's fishing cabin."

There was a beat of silence and Theo watched Mario Oliver go absolutely still. This was not a man he would elect to cross swords with.

Mario's voice was even softer when he finally spoke. "Tell me exactly what happened."

When he'd finished, Mario asked, "So you believe that in order to trace her to the cabin, someone would have had to know that she was with you?"

Theo nodded. "My mind keeps coming back to that. If those men simply followed her from the hospital to the cabin, why not come after her right away? I think they lost her, then got a name from someone who'd figured out who she was with, then got directions to the cabin. The attendants at the gas station on the highway all know where it is. Who was with you when you called me?"

"I was in the waiting room. Deanna, Eddie and Michael were all there. So were a policeman and two other men. I don't know who they were. They're not here today." He frowned. "I moved in here as soon as you asked about a secure phone."

They were quiet for a moment, then Theo said, "On another topic—do you have any idea who Juliana might have confided in about her relationship with Paulo? Anyone she might have spent time with?"

"She's a quiet girl. Keeps to herself. But there might be something in her diary. She was always writing in it."

SADIE'S THROAT TIGHTENED as she looked at Roman. His head was bandaged and he looked so pale and still that for one awful moment, she was afraid that he might be dead. The steady rhythm of the beeping noises from the machines he was hooked up to gradually erased that first horrible impression. She'd seen enough TV hospital shows to recognize a normal heartbeat when she spotted one on a screen. Still, she was relieved to feel the warmth of his skin when she tucked her hand into his.

He was alive. That was what was important.

Leaning down very close to his face, she said, "Roman?" She spoke very softly, not sure how sound-proof the door was. "It's me, Sadie."

He probably couldn't hear her, but she felt compelled to tell him. "I'm working with Theo Angelis and we're going to find Juliana. I think she and Paulo got away. Kit's working on the case, too. And so is their brother Nik, the cop. I don't want you to worry about me. I'm disguised as a man, so I'm safe. You should see me. I kind of like the clothes. But I want you to know every-thing is being taken care of. All you have to do is to con-centrate on getting better. Okay?"

Later, Sadie thought that she'd felt Roman's fingers tighten on hers for an instant, but at the moment it happened, her attention was distracted by the sound of the door opening.

"Who are you and what are you doing in here?"

Sadie recognized the voice of Eddie Mancuso even before she slowly straightened and turned. Behind him, Mason leaned against the doorjamb and her nerves steadied a little. "I'm Sam Schaeffer. I'm working with Theo Angelis, Mr. Oliver's attorney."

Eddie looked her up and down. "You have any ID?"

"I already checked it, Mr. Eddie," Mason spoke softly from the doorway. "And if you don't keep your voice down, you'll have to leave."

Eddie immediately lowered his voice to a whisper. "Yeah. Okay. Does Mr. Oliver know that this guy is in here?"

"No one gets in here unless Mr. Oliver permits it."

Sadie slipped her hand from Roman's and pulled a pen and a small notebook out of her pocket. Then she moved beyond where Eddie was standing to a corner of the room and waited for him to join her. "What are you doing in here?"

"I'm Eddie Mancuso." Crossing his arms, he leaned a shoulder against the wall. "Your client's stepbrother. The doctor allows family to come in and my mother thought that one of us should check on him. See if he's come to. The doctors are trying to keep him sedated."

Sadie scribbled something in her notebook.

"Did he say anything to you? He's been out like a light ever since they brought him in," Eddie continued.

"No." Eddie didn't sound very concerned, but she'd always sensed that he was rarely concerned about anyone except himself. "I have a few questions for you."

"And if I refuse to answer?"

Sadie met his eyes but kept her tone pleasant. "Well, then I'll have to tell Mario Oliver that you're being uncooperative."

Eddie's brows shot up, but he spoke without heat. "Anyone ever tell you that you're a prick?"

"All the time. How well do you know Juliana Oliver?"

"Well enough."

"Sam" sent him a long cool look.

Palms raised, Eddie smiled and said, "All right, I'll cooperate. I don't want Tony Soprano breathing down my neck."

She arched a brow. "Tony Soprano?"

Eddie laughed softly. "You know. Mario Oliver. I give everyone nicknames and that's what I call him behind his back. It drives my mom nuts. But it's only a joke. You won't rat me out, will you?"

She kept her gaze steady. "Not if you give me something I can use."

His grin faded. "You can't bluff me. You're a lawyer. Anything I tell you is privileged. You tattle to the big guy on me and I'll sue."

Sadie decided not to educate him on what constituted attorney-client privilege. Instead, she repeated, "How well do you know Juliana Oliver?"

"We've lived in the same house for the last three months. She's quiet, shy, reads a lot." He wrinkled his nose. "Shakespeare, poetry. Not really my type."

"Did you know anything about Juliana seeing Paulo Carlucci?"

He frowned then. "Hell, no. I would have told her father if I'd gotten wind of it. The big guy would have been in my debt."

Sadie bit back her temper. "Do you have any idea when they might have met?"

Eddie smiled again. "Now, there's something that I might be able to help you with. I've been giving it some thought and I think they may have met when the trauma center at this very hospital was dedicated. My mother commented on the fact that there were so many political bigwigs at that party that the Carluccis couldn't afford to boycott it the way they usually do when the Olivers are involved. Angelo didn't come, but his brother Frankie was here with his wife and Paulo."

He was right, Sadie thought, and mentally congratulated Eddie for remembering something that she'd forgotten. The event had been held about three months ago, right after Juliana had returned home from boarding school.

"Can you think of anyone Juliana might have confided in about her relationship with Paulo Carlucci?"

"Maybe." His smile widened. "Can you make it worth my while?"

Maybe I won't punch you in the face, she thought. "I'm sure that Mario Oliver will be very generous when I tell him how helpful you've been."

"I was thinking that maybe later we could meet somewhere and have a drink."

Sadie was so surprised that for a moment she couldn't speak. She simply stared at him.

Eddie lifted a hand and fingered the lapel of her jacket. "C'mon. Surely you can sneak away from the Greek attorney and join me later? I noticed you the moment you stepped off the elevator and I saw the big guy take your hand."

She wasn't imagining it. Eddie Mancuso was hitting on her. Gathering herself, she said, "I'm sorry. I don't date men."

"I might be able to change your mind."

She met his eyes steadily. "No. You couldn't."

He shrugged and tossed back his hair. "Your loss. What other kind of incentive can you offer me to share what I know?"

"The alternative is that I turn into a prick again and rat you out to the big guy. Who would Juliana have confided in?"

"You are no fun at all."

She merely waited, holding his gaze.

"Okay. As far as I know Juliana Oliver didn't have

any close friends. She's a shy thing, always kept to herself. The most exciting thing she did was taking lessons—golf, Spanish, tennis. My mom was pushing me to date her, but Jule wasn't having any of it."

"Jule?"

He flashed her a grin. "I told you I like to give people nicknames. Want to hear what I'm going to call you?"

"No."

"Too bad." Eddie paused to run his eyes up and down her again. "I'm betting she put everything in that diary of hers."

A diary? Sadie nearly dropped her notebook. Why hadn't she known that?

"She was always scribbling away in it in the library or out in the gardens. And then she'd hide it when anyone approached."

They both turned at the sound of raised voices in the hallway. An instant later, the door swung open and this time a tall, strikingly attractive woman wearing a white coat over a designer suit strode into the room. Her name tag read Dr. Anita Rinaldi and the woman oozed authority and anger. Still, she kept her voice soft as she fisted her hands on her hips. "I do not want my patient disturbed. Get out now. Both of you. And take those people in the hall with you."

Eddie went first. Outside the room, Sadie wasn't at all pleased to see Deanna and Michael Dano standing in the hall. They both stared at her, but it was Deanna who spoke. "Who are you and what are you doing in Roman's room?"

Costume, please do your stuff, Sadie prayed. It helped her confidence to know that it had certainly fooled Eddie. "I'm Sam Schaeffer and I'm assisting Theo Angelis."

"Neither Mr. Oliver nor Mr. Angelis mentioned you," Michael said with a frown.

Because it would have been not only suspicious but cowardly not to, Sadie met his gaze squarely.

Without breaking eye contact, Michael asked, "Mason, aren't you supposed to keep everyone out of Roman's room?"

"I cleared him with Mr. Oliver," Mason said. "Mr. Eddie, too."

Deanna looked as if a bit of wind had been knocked from her sails. "Eddie is family. He hardly needs to be cleared. This man—" she pointed at Sadie "—is a stranger."

"I have my orders, Ma'am."

Dr. Rinaldi stepped out into the hallway and hissed, "Out! If you don't all go back to the waiting room, I will call hospital security."

Sadie noted that even Michael seemed intimidated by the doctor. He fell into step beside her as her stepmother led the small parade back toward the nurse's station.

"Were you able to speak to Roman?" Michael asked.

"No. Has he been able to talk to anyone?"

"Not yet. They don't want him moving until they're able to take care of the swelling on his spine. I'm Michael Dano, by the way. I head up the legal department at Oliver Enterprises. If I don't get an opportunity, please tell Mr. Angelis that I'd like to help in any way I can. I'll put all the resources we have at Oliver Enterprises at his disposal."

"I'll let him know." Out of the corner of her eye, she noted that he was watching her very closely.

"Do you have any idea of what they'll be charging Roman with? How strong their case is?"

Sadie struggled to keep her voice even. "So far, the police haven't shared any evidence with us."

"I was under the impression that Mr. Angelis worked alone," Michael said.

"He usually does. I feel fortunate that he agreed to take me on as an intern." She shrugged. "He rang me up this morning and I was available. I was asking Eddie if he knew who Juliana might have confided in. Can you think of anyone?"

He shook his head. "She's only been home from boarding school for about three months and I only saw her at family social occasions."

"Do you have any idea when or where she might have met Paulo Carlucci?"

His smile was wry. "Her father asked me that very question. I have no idea. The families never mix."

As they reached the nurse's station, her father and Theo stepped into their path.

"Deanna, I need to speak with you and Eddie," Mario said. "Michael, I'd like you to be there, too. There's been a development." With that he turned and led the way back to the waiting room.

Sadie barely had time to feel relief before Theo said, "I need to speak with you privately, too."

He was angry and Sadie felt her own temper rising in response. He'd told her to stay within sight and she hadn't. Well, tough. He was just going to have to deal with it.

She strode past him, heading toward the elevator, but he grabbed her arm. "Your father said we could use the office. It's private and there's something you need to know."

14

THEO URGED HER INTO the office, then closed the door and leaned back against it. He watched her stride to the window and fist her hands on her hips. She was angry and he thought he knew why. He needed to calm down himself. When he'd first stepped into the hallway with Mario and seen her surrounded by Deanna, Eddie and Michael Dano, the feeling that she was in danger struck him like a blow. His first thought was that they'd discovered who she was. If Mario Oliver hadn't put a hand on his arm, he would have rushed down the hospital corridor to rescue her.

"She's handling it," Mario had said. "And if she doesn't, Mason will help her out. He's known her since she was little."

But Sadie had handled it herself. He was going to have to learn to trust her to do that.

They were about to wheel her brother away for a very tricky surgical procedure and he had to tell her about the ransom note her father had received. Then he was going to get her out of the hospital. Rational or irrational, he couldn't rid himself of the feeling that someone or something here posed a threat to her. Maybe he'd been wrong in thinking that Paulo and Juliana had gone underground, but he had no choice but to trust his instinct where Sadie was concerned. Better safe than sorry.

"Sadie," he began.

She whirled to face him, striding toward him. The walk, the stance she took when she reached him, both were very masculine. And when she spoke, it was in her Sam Schaeffer voice. "There's something that you need to know, too. You have no right to think you can be the boss all the time. I may be posing as your intern, but we're working together on this." She met his eyes and the heat in hers very nearly seared his skin. "I'm not going to be sidelined. Not ever again. Not by my father, not by Roman and not by you. So deal with it."

Lord, but she was magnificent. And different. The passion he'd always sensed in her had blossomed beautifully to the surface. And to his surprise, there was something incredibly erotic about the way she was standing and about the huskiness in her voice.

When he realized the direction his thoughts had veered off to, Theo shifted his gaze back to her eyes. Big mistake. Lust curled in his stomach whenever he looked at the glasses—just as it had when Franco had first placed them on her. When his gaze drifted down to her mouth, he saw that those soft, unpainted lips were still moving.

"What?" he managed.

Widening her stance, she frowned at him. "Pay attention, counselor."

He was paying too much attention to that mouth. Her taste was inside of him now. He remembered it. Craved it. But he couldn't help wondering if her flavor had changed as much as the rest of her. Would he prefer "Sam" to Sadie? The direction of his thoughts shocked him and sharpened the desire that was escalating inside of him. He grabbed her arms to drag her closer.

To his surprise and delight, she struggled, throwing his hands off, then giving him a hard shove that sent him stumbling back into the door.

"If you want a fight, you're going to get one," she said in Sam's voice. He watched in astonishment as she fisted her hand and drew back her arm. He stopped the punch inches from its target—his stomach.

"I've got a better idea, Sam." This time he succeeded in dragging her against him. Then he covered her mouth with his.

She struggled for just a moment before she threw her arms around him and sank her teeth into his bottom lip. One lone thought streamed through Theo's mind before he drew back to catch a breath. Sam bit a hell of a lot harder than Sadie.

WHEN THEO'S MOUTH COVERED hers again, Sadie could do nothing but dive into the kiss. His hands were so hard. So was his chest. The result was that in spite of her clothes and all of Franco's work, she felt gloriously feminine pressed against him. The heat between them was building so quickly that she was sure that it would burn everything away—the costume, the walk, the talk, everything that Franco had trained her to do. And then it would consume her….

She wasn't even aware that she needed to breathe until Theo drew back. She dragged in air. Her back was against the door. "This is crazy."

"Agreed." But he didn't release her.

"We shouldn't be doing this." She didn't release him.

"Right with you there. Want to know something that's even crazier?" he asked. "Sam is turning me on."

"Really?" For some reason, his confession had a knot of pure lust tightening in her stomach. She moistened her lips. "Sam wants you, too."

"Say that in Sam's voice and you've got me."

"I want you."

Theo reached around her and locked the door. Then he took two steps back. "First, take your pants off."

There was a recklessness in his eyes that was the perfect match to what she was feeling. She made quick work of the belt and the snap, then fumbled with the zipper.

"Hurry." Closing the distance between them, he gripped her by the waist, turned her around and pushed her against the wall. "Brace yourself."

She planted her palms on the wall. As he finished with the zipper and pulled her slacks down, her breath backed up in her lungs.

He gave a quick muffled groan.

"What?" she asked.

"I've never thought of boxers as being erotic," he murmured. Then he slid his fingers beneath the boxers' waist and shoved them down her hips. One of his hands pressed against her stomach, his other molded itself to her right cheek as he drew her back a little.

"Now bend over a bit." His words were just a breath at her ear. Heat pooled in her center as she heard him draw down his own zipper. She stopped breathing as she felt the head of his penis probe her, then sink in to the hilt.

"Ohhh," she said.

"Shhhh. We have to be very quiet and very quick."

She tried not to moan again when he pulled out of

her. His hands tightened on her hips and when he thrust in again she very nearly lost her balance.

"This won't work," Theo said.

She glanced over her shoulder. "Then find a way that will."

"Aye-aye, sir." Sliding an arm around her waist, he lifted her, holding her close as he carried her to the desk and bent her over it. He kept his hands tight on her hips as he probed her and thrust in again. "Better?"

"Again," she demanded. "And this time don't you dare stop."

"Don't worry. I can't."

This time when he thrust into her, he bent close and sank his teeth into her shoulder. "Told you I'd get even," he murmured.

Sadie felt an arrow of pleasure so sharp that tears pricked her eyes. "Again."

He obliged her. "I'm going to take you hard and fast."

"Promises," she murmured.

He pushed into her, moving one hand around to her stomach and sliding it down so that his fingers touched just the right spot between her legs. Then he kept his word, thrusting harder and faster, driving them both higher and higher. When she felt her own climax beginning, she reached behind and gripped his butt. "Come with me, Theo. Now."

Once more he did exactly what she demanded and she felt him thrust one last time just as she shattered.

WHEN HE FINALLY FOUND the strength to stand, Theo said, "We've got to get ourselves back together." He glanced at the door. "I think we've already pushed our luck."

"You're going to have to help me up. I'm not sure I can get any of my body parts to work."

Theo helped her stand, but she managed to pull her clothes back on by herself. He was still fastening his belt when she said, "Done. I beat you."

"No fair. I had to stop to help you stand up." He looked at her then and his smile spread slowly. "I've never done anything quite like that before."

"Ditto." She glanced at the desk and then back at him. "I can buy boxers in a three pack if that's what turns you on."

Theo threw back his head and laughed. Then he drew her close into a hug. "I'm damned if I can explain it, but when you first put those glasses on this morning, you gave me a hard-on."

She drew her head back and met his eyes. "You know, Franco may know what he's talking about with the cross-dressing stuff. I'm beginning to wonder what you might look like wearing nothing but a black lace garter belt and some fishnet stockings. Maybe some three-inch platform heels."

With a grin, he shook his head. "Not going to happen."

As she snuggled her head against his shoulder and simply held on to him, something stirred inside. Not the hot and driving desire he'd felt only moments ago. This was different, warm and steady and the need to go on holding her just like this grew into an ache. This was what he'd felt when he'd awakened and found her sleeping in his arms, and this time it wasn't a tumble his heart took, but a fall. He was in love with Sadie Oliver.

The panic that had driven him to leave the bed this morning was less intense, not even strong enough to make him step back from her. Along with everything else Sadie Oliver could make him feel, he knew that he was going to have to deal with this, too.

"I owe you an apology," he finally said.

She drew her head back then and met his eyes. "Not for what we just did, I hope, because I think I'm serious about buying those boxers."

"No, I'm not apologizing for what we did just now. I'd like to do that again. Soon. I'm sorry for the way I've been treating you all day. I...I just couldn't seem to help myself."

He lifted one hand and laid it along her cheek. "You make me feel so many things that I'm having a little trouble handling it. But I wasn't fair to you this morning. I led you to believe that we would work as partners, and then I tried to..."

"Sideline me," she offered.

"Yeah. I was worried about your safety. Once we got here I got a very strong feeling that something or someone posed a threat to you. And I think I was also dealing with the fact that I've been lusting after you ever since Franco turned you into Sam Schaeffer."

Smiling, she raised a hand and laid it on his cheek. "All you had to do was ask. Sam is evidently a very easy lay."

Theo found himself returning her smile as some of his tension eased. "He's also very bossy."

With a shrug, she grinned at him. "He's a man. It's in the genes."

"Touché." He ran a finger along her jaw. "I told your father that trying to keep you on too short a leash was a mistake."

Sadie stared at him. "What did my father say to that?"

"Nothing. He knew who you were when he told Mason to let you in to see Roman."

Her eyes widened.

"He said he was expecting you to show up. I've persuaded him to let you continue to work with me by telling him Roman and I both need your help. But in his words, that's only because it's the 'lesser of two evils.'"

"If you convinced him of that, you're nothing less than a miracle worker."

"Don't be too impressed. I also tried to pry him loose from the position that Angelo Carlucci or Paulo is behind everything that went on at the church. I'm not so sure I succeeded on that score."

Her brow knit. "He's suspicious of Paulo? Why?"

Theo eased her into a chair then, keeping her hands in his, he sat down on the edge of the desk. "Your father received a ransom note this morning."

She squeezed his fingers involuntarily. "For Juliana."

He nodded and filled her in on the details of the ransom note. "Your father hasn't informed the police yet or the FBI. He's telling Michael Dano and your family right now. Then he'll call the authorities."

"Then surely Roman won't be a suspect anymore. I mean, no one could believe he would kidnap his sister. But this…this isn't good news for Juliana. I was so hoping that you were right, that she and Paulo had gone underground."

Theo bit back a frustrated sigh. "I was hoping that, too."

"The two men in that van must have gotten them. If I could just remember where I saw the driver before…"

"You will." Theo drew her up from the chair and into his arms again. "There are a lot of very good people who will be looking for your sister. You're going to be one of them."

"Yes."

Theo could feel her struggle to gather her thoughts and to focus. She was so much tougher than she appeared to be.

"I hate to think Paulo is involved."

"It could be involuntary on his part. Suppose the men in the van didn't get them. When the chips were down, perhaps Paulo decided to go to his family for help. There might have been someone he trusted that he shouldn't have."

"That's a possibility, I suppose. Maybe it's just wishful thinking, that I don't want him to be in on this, even inadvertently." She gave him a wry, frustrated smile. "It just doesn't feel right."

He rubbed his hands up and down her arms. "Believe me, I understand. And there's something about dumping this whole thing on the Carluccis that doesn't quite gel with me, either. I can't make it fit with the fact that someone came after you at the cabin last night. That's what I told your father."

"You think someone at Oliver Enterprises is involved."

"Yeah. It would help if I could pinpoint just who, but the feeling that you're in danger gets stronger whenever your family and Michael Dano are around. So I want to get you out of here."

Dropping his hands, Theo stepped away from her. "There's nothing else we can do here for now. They're going to take Roman into surgery, so we won't be able to talk to him until later, perhaps not until tomorrow. In the meantime, I thought we should pay a visit to the Oliver estate. Your father told me that Juliana kept a diary. We might find out who she told about her wedding plans."

Sadie stared at him. "Eddie told me about the diary, too. I'd almost forgotten." She strode with him toward the door. "Before we leave, I think we should talk to Father Mike. I want to find out what he knows about how Juliana and Paulo met and how long they've been going together."

"Good idea." At the door, he turned to her, lifted her chin and kissed her softly. "I'm certainly glad I thought of asking Sam Schaeffer to help me out on this case. So far the only problem with this whole masquerade thing is keeping my hands off of you in public."

She shot him a look as they moved out of the office. "You'll just have to deal with it."

FIFTEEN MINUTES LATER, WHEN they left Father Mike's room, they knew a lot more about how Juliana and Paulo had managed to see each other secretly for three months. Paulo had been tutoring her in Spanish. No one had questioned her lessons with her tutor.

"Your sister is a smart girl," Theo said.

"I feel sorry for Father Mike," Sadie said. "He blames himself for everything. He probably believes that if he hadn't agreed to marry them, Juliana and Paulo would be all right. But I'm convinced they would have found another way to get married."

"It helped that you told him that." Instead of stopping at the elevator, Theo urged her toward the door to the stairs and ushered her through it. "I want to find a back way out of here just as a precaution. Our friends at the cabin last night know you left with me. They might try to pick up my trail in hopes that I'll lead them to you."

As they started down the stairs, she continued, "It's not like Father Mike is anything like that meddling Friar Lawrence in *Romeo and Juliet*. *He* married them because he wanted to end the feud between the two families—a classic case of believing the end justifies the means."

When they reached the first floor, Theo took her arm and urged her down one more flight.

"You know, the more I think about it, the more this whole scenario with Juliana and Paulo smacks of Shakespeare's plays. And not just *Romeo and Juliet*."

"Enlighten me." He pushed through a set of double doors and drew her toward the exit.

"The fact that Paulo became her tutor in Spanish as a ruse for meeting with her. That's right out of *The Taming of the Shrew*. Two of Bianca's suitors disguise themselves to court her secretly while they're waiting for her older sister Kate to be married."

"You may have something there." Once outside, they headed toward the parking lot. "Paulo must have been wearing some sort of disguise. Father Mike says he even came to your house on at least two occasions."

"Gutsy," Sadie said.

"I agree. Gutsy on both their parts. Your sister might be in good hands with Paulo."

"If they're both…"

Theo stopped and putting his hands on her shoulders, turned her towards him. "They're alive. I may have been wrong about them going underground, but I have a very strong feeling that they're both all right. So do you. You just have to trust it."

"Yes. Okay." Sadie fell into step beside him again.

"By the way, I figured out why Juliana never went along with Deanna's attempt to match her up with Eddie."

Slanting her a look, Theo raised his brows.

"Eddie Mancuso hit on me."

Theo stared at her. "That Brad Pitt wannabe hit on you?"

She grinned at him. "Hey, Sam seems to be irresistible—and Eddie didn't even see my boxers."

Theo opened the passenger door, then circled the car and climbed in behind the wheel. It was totally irrational that he was feeling jealous of Eddie Mancuso. But that was just another thing he would have to learn to deal with. He figured that if he was going to continue having a relationship with Sadie, he was going to become more and more familiar with his irrational side.

As they pulled out of the parking lot, Theo glanced in the rearview mirror. The SUV pulling out behind them made the same left turn. Two blocks later, it again turned right behind them. At the next traffic light, the driver drew even with his car and Theo got a good look at Mason Leone before the light changed and the car dropped back.

"Dad has evidently assigned Mason to watch over us."

"That's one of the many things I like about you, Sadie Oliver. You don't miss much." And privately, he was very happy that Mario Oliver was providing a little backup security.

"Eddie evidently bought your disguise. How about his mother and Michael Dano?"

She thought about it for a minute. "I think they both did. Michael seemed to be more interested in pumping me for information—like, did Roman say anything to me. Eddie asked the same question."

"It sounds like they want to know Roman's version of what went on at the church. If any of them was involved in what went down at St. Peter's, the suspense of not knowing what Roman saw or heard must be killing them."

"That would be one explanation of why Eddie burst in on me when I was in Roman's room. He said his mother had sent him."

Theo was about to reach over and take Sadie's hand when his cell phone rang. He dug it out and checked the caller ID. "It's your father."

He listened a moment, then glanced over at Sadie. "Your father called the housekeeper to tell her that we were coming and to ask her to take a look around for Juliana's diary. She just called back to report that your sister's room has been trashed."

15

SADIE SHOT OUT OF THE CAR as soon as Theo parked it in front of the house. He grabbed her hand just as she reached the porch steps. "Slow down," he said. "Let's give Mason a chance to catch up."

She glanced back down the long drive, but there was no sign of Mason. He'd stopped at the gate to speak with the security man on duty. Impatience streamed through her. She wanted to see if the diary was still in her sister's room. They'd discussed it on the way over and it was logical to assume that whoever had trashed Juliana's room had been after the diary. Which meant that there must be something in it, perhaps a name that might incriminate someone. "We should be safe enough in the house. There's a very high-tech security system in place."

"And yet someone must have gotten through it to get to your sister's room," he pointed out. "A few more minutes isn't going to make a difference." Stepping back, Theo let his gaze roam over the house and the grounds. "Nice digs."

If she'd been less tense, Sadie would have whole-heartedly agreed. The house itself was three stories and constructed of marble and stone along the lines of an Italian villa. "When I was little, I thought of it as a castle. It seemed to have everything but a moat. So I always imagined the pond on this side was the moat."

"My aunt's house has a pond, too. Greeks love to live near water and my father keeps it stocked with fish."

Theo's cell phone rang. Glancing at the caller ID, he said, "It's Kit."

Mason's car came into view and Sadie barely kept her foot from tapping impatiently as it moved slowly up the drive. By the time it stopped behind the SUV, Theo had finished his conversation with his brother.

"Kit doesn't have any news that we don't already know. But he wants me to draw up this contract for a client of his. I offered your services."

She turned to him.

"Actually, I offered my intern's services. Just to lay the groundwork for the disguise in case we run into him. He's still working on tracking down the mystery blonde you saw with Paulo and Juliana. My source at the D.A.'s office says no one has been able to identify her yet."

"Mason's got our back now," Sadie said as the older man climbed out of his car. "I think it's safe to go in." She walked up the steps and rang the bell. "If I weren't Sam Schaeffer, I could just put my code into the door. Each member of the family has a different one. It's one way my father still keeps track of our comings and goings."

"Remember to let me do the talking," Theo reminded her. Since the housekeeper had known her since she was a little girl, they'd agreed that she'd keep a low profile.

When the door was opened by a small, round woman with gray curls framing her face, Theo extended his hand. "I'm Theo Angelis and this is my intern, Sam Schaeffer."

"Edith Andreoli," the woman said. "Mr. Oliver called and said to expect you. This is terrible." As they stepped into a large foyer, she wrung her hands. "Mr. Roman hurt. Miss Juliana and Miss Sadie missing. And now this."

Mason shut the door and joined them. "Mr. Oliver wants you to show them Miss Juliana's room."

"Of course." She led the way up the stairs. "I was going to clean it, but Mr. Oliver said to let it be. I'm to call the police and report it after you leave."

"Do you have any idea when it happened?" Theo asked.

"At Mr. Oliver's request, I checked the room early last evening around eight o'clock. He called from the hospital and wanted to see if Miss Juliana had returned yet. She hadn't been at home when they got the call about Roman and they all went to the hospital. The room was in perfect order then."

"You didn't check this morning?"

"Mr. Mancuso and Mrs. Oliver were here for breakfast and they told me that Juliana and Miss Sadie were missing. I only went up there when Mr. Oliver called to tell me that you were on your way and asked if I could find Juliana's diary for you. I called him right back to tell him."

So someone could have searched Juliana's room anytime between eight o'clock last night and this morning, Sadie thought. And that "someone" could easily have been Eddie or Deanna.

"You didn't hear anything?" Theo asked.

"No," Edith replied. "My rooms are in a wing behind the kitchen. It's very disturbing to realize that there was someone in the house. Here we are. This is Miss Juliana's room."

Mason put a comforting arm around her. "You can wait downstairs, Edith."

"One more question, Ms. Andreoli," Sadie said. "Did Juliana by any chance confide in you that she was seeing Paulo Carlucci?"

Shock flickered over the older woman's face. "No. Then it's true what they're saying on TV?"

Sadie didn't answer the question. Instead, she asked, "Can you think of anyone she might have confided in? Anyone she seemed to be spending time with here on the estate?"

"No." Edith shook her head. "I can't believe it."

Mason gave her shoulder another squeeze. "You can go now."

WHEN SHE WAS OUT OF earshot, Theo said, "I thought I was supposed to do the talking."

Sadie met his eyes. "I let you do most of it."

Shaking his head, he opened the door and let his gaze sweep the room. Sadie let out a gasp as she joined him. The room had been thoroughly ransacked. Furniture had been overturned, glass broken. The bedclothes had been stripped off and the mattress lay half-off the bed, its stuffing spilling out from long slashes.

He strode into the room. Through the open closet and bathroom doors, he saw that both of those areas had suffered the same kind of destruction.

As Sadie joined him, Mason gave a long, low whistle from the doorway. "The boss isn't going to like this. I'm going to check and see if any of the other rooms have been damaged. I'm sure that Edith didn't have the stomach for that. You two going to be okay?"

"Yes." Leaning down, Sadie picked up a wilted white rose. "This happened awhile ago. The flower is dead and the carpet underneath is dry."

Theo watched her scan the room, a frown of concentration on her face. Even though Mason no doubt knew that she was Sadie, she'd decided that it was good practice to keep up the masquerade in front of him.

"They had to be looking for the diary," she said. "Maybe they found it."

"I don't think so. There's a lot of frustration and anger here. Looks to me like they got really pissed off because they couldn't find what they were looking for."

Tucking her hands in her pockets, Sadie surveyed the room again. "Maybe you're right. They must have known that the house was empty and that Edith wouldn't hear them. This wasn't a quiet search."

"No," Theo agreed.

"Eddie and Deanna came home last night. There'll be a record of when they arrived."

She was expressing the thought that had already crossed his mind. Either of them would have intimate knowledge about the way the house was run. Either or both of them could have easily searched Juliana's room.

"I've got an idea." She strode to the nightstand. "It's a long shot." She dropped to her knees and plowed through the contents of one of the overturned drawers. "Ah, here it is."

To Theo's surprise she held up a nail file. "That doesn't look like a diary to me."

"It isn't. But I had a secret place for my diary and

Juliana was in my room once when I took it out. I made her swear that she'd never tell anyone. There's a chance that she might have used the same hiding place."

Theo watched as she knee-walked her way to an air conditioning and heat vent and began to loosen the screws with the file.

"I caught Roman in my room once." She shot a look at him. "He was searching for it. Can you believe that?"

Theo could. Brothers were born to tease sisters. He had once put frogs in Philly's bed. But considering the fiery light in Sadie's eyes, he thought it might be better to share his thoughts at a different time.

"If I hadn't caught him going through my bookcase, he might have found it. That's when I decided I needed a better hiding place." Removing the cover on the vent, she took off her jacket and rolled up her sleeves. "After that I always used code words instead of naming names. And I hid my diary in one of these vents." Leaning down, she felt around. "It's not in this one."

Theo moved to the bathroom. "There's another one in here."

He pulled out a penknife and they loosened the vent together. This time when Sadie pulled her arm out, she was holding a volume bound in red leather. Still kneeling on the floor, she placed it on her knees and ran her hand over the cover. "Juliana was tagging after me all the time that summer. I remember being annoyed. I wasn't really close to her then. And I'm still not now."

Theo knelt down, took one of her hands in his and linked their fingers. "You can change that. She admires you. And I think the two of you have a lot more in common than you realize."

Drawing in a deep breath, she opened the diary and began to skim its contents. A few pages in, she raised her eyes to meet his. "She not only stole my hiding place, she also stole my code words. There are no names, just letters. ML is My Love. That's probably Paulo. She met him for Spanish tutoring on Tuesdays at the café in the Westin St. Francis hotel. That's a pretty ritzy venue for a Spanish lesson."

"It's also a very public place," Theo commented. "If someone saw them there, it would look legit. Smart choice."

Sadie skimmed a few more pages. "There's also someone in here that she refers to as MBF. My best friend? Whoever it is, Juliana seems to trust them and talks to them."

This time when she met his eyes, Theo could see a trace of bleakness in hers. "You're wishing the MBF stood for you, that she'd chosen you to confide in."

Temper flared in her eyes. "Of course I am. If she had—"

"You wouldn't have approved. You already said that if you'd gotten to the church on time, you would have tried to talk her out of going through with the wedding. She's smart. She would have sensed that."

"You're right. But I still don't feel good about it."

Mason appeared in the doorway of the bathroom. "I checked all the doors. There's no sign of a break-in and this is the only room that's been disturbed. I've notified the head of security at Oliver Enterprises to check the door codes and see who used them."

Sadie looked at Theo. "The Carluccis couldn't have done this without help from an insider."

"The boss is with you on that," Mason said. "He also wanted you to know, in case you missed it, that Angelo Carlucci did an exclusive interview on Channel Five News about ten minutes ago. He has also received a ransom note, one demanding money for the release of his son. He publicly pleaded with Roman's accomplice to safely return Paulo."

"So both of them were kidnapped." Sadie turned to Theo. "Roman will be a prime suspect again. The police will theorize that the ransom note to his father was just an attempt to avert suspicion."

"There's one way to find out exactly what the police are thinking." Theo drew her to her feet. "We'll go ask Nik."

WITH A FRUSTRATED SIGH, Sadie closed Juliana's diary and slipped it into her duffle bag. She and Theo had been at the police station for more than an hour. From her vantage point at one of the desks in the "bull pen" area, she could see the entire squad room.

In a glass-walled office to her right, J. C. Riley, the woman who'd been hired to cater Juliana's wedding, had finished working with a sketch artist to create an image of the man she'd seen shoot Father Mike. Now she was also waiting for an Angelis—Nik. Directly ahead of her, Theo was huddled with his two brothers in a small room where they were observing an interrogation. An interrogation that just might result in clearing her brother's name.

Nerves knotted in Sadie's stomach. When they'd arrived at the station, the whole place had been buzzing. Nik had taken Theo aside to tell him that their brother

Kit had located the mystery blonde Juliana and Paulo had put into that taxi. From the scraps of conversation she'd overheard, the woman's name was Drew Merriweather. She'd designed Juliana's wedding dress.

Not only had Kit brought Drew in, but he'd also delivered the two men who'd tried to kill her. When Theo had learned that the men had been driving a van, he'd arranged for Sadie to get a look at them. One of them was the man Roman had chased up the stairs and the other was the driver of the van that had chased Juliana and Paulo. But she still couldn't dredge up the memory of where she'd seen him before.

Captain D. C. Parker was questioning Drew right now. More than anything she wanted to be in that room with Theo and his brothers so that she could hear what Drew was saying. Surely, she had to be revealing some evidence that would clear Roman.

The diary hadn't been as helpful as she was hoping it would be. Juliana had indeed had a confidant, MBF, but for the life of her, Sadie couldn't figure out who MBF was. She couldn't even tell if it was a man or a woman. There was only one place where Juliana had given more information by adding the letters EM before the MBF. Were they the person's initials or were they just another code—one that Sadie wasn't familiar with? There was no mention of having to arrange special meetings with MBF as there had been with ML—Paulo. That suggested MBF was someone who either lived on the Oliver estate or who worked at Oliver Enterprises. And who just might have the initials EM.

Of course, the name that had immediately leaped into her mind was Eddie Mancuso. He certainly could have searched Juliana's room. And while she doubted he could have been behind everything, Eddie could be providing Angelo Carlucci with information. But two things bothered her. She was having trouble envisioning her sister confiding in Eddie, but also, what reason would Eddie have for getting into bed with Angelo Carlucci?

Sadie let her gaze stray again to the observation room. Kit stood closest to the window and Sadie sensed that his interest in Drew Merriweather was more than just job related. Nik stood with his hands on his hips, but his attention on the interrogation was just as focused as Kit's. He was shorter than his two brothers, but he radiated a toughness that she thought must suit him admirably in his job. Theo had a hip propped against a table, and though he looked much more relaxed than his two brothers, Sadie knew that he wasn't missing a thing.

Another wave of frustration moved through her. Here she was twiddling her thumbs. Picking up the phone, she dialed St. Jude's hospital. When the operator put her through to the fifth floor, she gave the nurse at the desk her name, the number and extension and asked to have Mario Oliver call her back.

Within sixty seconds the phone on her desk rang. When she lifted the receiver, her father asked, "Can this call be traced?"

Sadie nearly smiled. Right to the point—that was her father all right. "I'm at a police station, speaking from one of the detectives' desks. I think it's a safe line."

"Theo's with you?"

"Yes."

"What is he thinking taking you there? There's an APB out on you."

"Theo is trusting me to be able to carry off this disguise and so far I've succeeded."

There was silence on the other end of the line.

"How's Roman?" she asked.

"He came through the surgery very well and the doctors were able to relieve the swelling on his spine. The prognosis is good. They'll know more when he comes fully out of the anesthesia."

Sadie felt one of the little knots in her stomach loosen. "You haven't been able to talk to him?"

There was a beat of silence on the other end of the line. "No. Dr. Rinaldi is barring all visitors at this time. Once I do talk to him, I'm sure the officer at the door will let his superiors know and then Roman will be arrested."

Sadie's stomach sank even though her father was only giving voice to her own suspicions. "I'm afraid you're right. Angelo Carlucci's TV appearance has increased the pressure on the police. Have you heard anything more from the kidnappers?"

There was another beat of silence and for a moment, Sadie thought that he wasn't going to answer. Finally, he said, "I'm to transfer the five million to an offshore bank account the moment the banks open on Monday morning."

"You're going to do that?"

"If I have no other choice."

She glanced toward the room where Theo was still talking with his brothers. "They've arrested the two men who were in the van I saw following Juliana and Paulo. They're denying any connection to a kidnapping and they've both gotten attorneys. But there may be a development here that will postpone or even prevent Roman's arrest—I can't be sure, though. What I wanted to let you know is that Theo and I found Juliana's diary. She was confiding in someone, someone she trusted. There's a person involved in this who is close to us and who knew about the wedding. Juliana uses a code in her diary so I can't figure out who it is. But I think it has to be whoever wanted to get their hands on that diary. There's one place where she doesn't strictly adhere to her code and she used the initials E.M."

"For Eddie?"

He was right with her there, Sadie thought. "You know him better than I do. Could he be feeding information to the Carluccis?"

"I've already got some people looking into it."

She should have known that he'd be ahead of her. It had to be very hard on him, investigating the people who were so close to him. For the first time in her life, she felt sympathy for her father. "Did you find out who used the code to get into the house last night or early this morning?"

"Deanna used her code at 1:00 a.m. According to the record, someone used Roman's code before that at 11:30 p.m."

Sadie's heart sank. She'd been so hoping that his answer would identify Juliana's MBF. "Then Juliana was confiding in someone who would have access to Roman's code. And he or she must have believed that something in that diary would incriminate them."

"I agree. What else did you find in your sister's diary?"

"As far as I can tell, she and Paulo met at the dedication of St. Jude's trauma center. After that Paulo posed as her Spanish tutor."

Mario muttered something in Italian. Sadie didn't

quite catch all of it, but what she did had the corners of her mouth curving. She didn't believe she'd ever heard her father swear before.

"You have to admit, it was a very clever plan. They met in plain sight in the cafe at the St. Francis."

"Mason followed her there every Tuesday. He would have recognized Paulo Carlucci."

"Paulo might have been wearing a disguise. She says in the diary that he even came to the estate—and he came at least twice. You know how Juliana loves Shakespeare. This is right out of *The Taming of the Shrew*."

Mario muttered more in Italian.

"You have to admit, she's a very clever woman."

"Too clever," Mario said. "We may lose her."

"No, that's not going to happen," Sadie said firmly. "We'll see to that."

There was a beat of silence, then Mario said, "You're right. We'll get her back. Tell Theo that I checked Roman's office and he also received an invitation to be at St. Peter's Church at 7:00."

"So we were right. Is it Juliana's signature?"

"I'm checking on that." There was another beat of silence. "Thank you, Sadie. Mason will stay with you. Keep him informed of anything you learn."

Something tightened around her heart.

"Better still, keep me informed."

"I will," Sadie said softly, but the line had already gone dead.

16

THEO FOLLOWED HIS brothers and Captain Parker out of the narrow observation room. More than once during the time he'd spent listening to D. C. Parker interrogate Drew Merriweather, he'd felt both his eyes and his mind wandering to Sadie. He'd sidelined her again. By necessity. Kit had met her and if her disguise fell apart while they were here in the station, she'd be arrested. While that might keep her safe, he sensed that she would be crucial in saving her brother and finding her sister.

Still, she'd looked so alone sitting there at the desk pouring over that diary. She had looked alone, but she hadn't been entirely alone, and she'd made a phone call to someone. When he reached her, he asked, "Who did you call?"

"My father. The surgery was successful. Roman's prognosis is good. They won't be sure about the paralysis until he wakes up."

"Can we talk to him?"

She shook her head. "Dr. Rinaldi isn't allowing any visitors yet. My father believes that when we do talk to him, the police will insist on access and that might speed Roman's arrest."

"He's probably right. Could be he's putting a bit of pressure on the doctors to delay that as long as possible."

Sadie studied him for a moment. "You're getting to know my father very well."

"Did you find anything in the diary?"

She told him about the initials she'd found and about her conversation with her father. "He's way ahead of us in terms of investigating Eddie, Deanna and Michael, I think. This has to be very hard on him. Roman's injured, Juliana's been kidnapped and he's investigating his wife, her son and a man who's worked very closely with him. Do you have any good news?"

"We can't talk here." He wanted to give her the news in a place where he could take her hands, where he could hold her. "Let's take a little walk. Captain Parker has agreed to see me in twenty minutes, so we'll come back."

As Theo led the way through the arched entrance to the squad room and down a short flight of stairs, they passed another couple. The man had perfectly coiffed hair swept back from his forehead and curling down to his shoulders. He wore a jacket made out of snakeskin, a shirt and pants that Theo was sure were silk, and he guessed that the diamond on the man's pinkie was a good three carats. The woman was a stunner, too, if you liked the Pamela-Anderson type.

Once they'd passed them, Sadie spoke under her breath. "That's Frankie and Gina Carlucci. Frankie is Angelo's much younger stepbrother. Paulo was with them at the dedication party for St. Jude's trauma center, so they were there when Juliana and Paulo met."

"You can bet they're here for one purpose—to put pressure on Parker to arrest your brother," Theo said. They'd reached the entrance to the building and he stopped short when he spotted the reporter and a cameraman from Channel Five News. The reporter's name was Carla Mitchell, and he'd met her a few times when Kit was dating her. Nik had taken her out once, too. After he'd been chosen one of San Francisco's most eligible bachelors, Carla had turned her attention to him and launched a campaign to get an interview. So far he'd avoided it and her.

"I'm not going to get past that reporter." Theo glanced around and spotted a bench at the far end of the hall where they could talk in relative privacy. "This way."

"Drew wasn't able to clear Roman, was she?" Sadie asked.

"No. She actually saw less than you did. She met Juliana and Paulo about a month ago when they walked into a shop that carries her designs. Juliana commissioned her to design a wedding dress. Drew didn't even know their last names. And she says that Juliana invited her on Friday afternoon to the wedding so that she wouldn't be alone."

Sadie narrowed her eyes. "Why would she be worried about being alone if she sent those invitations to Roman and me?"

"My thought exactly, counselor. Someone else definitely sent those last-minute invites to get you and your brother to the church."

"What did Drew see?"

"Drew and Juliana were in that little room in the choir loft when they heard raised voices from the sacristy—your brother arguing with Paulo. Then the shooting started. When Paulo joined them, he'd been shot in the arm and he gave a gun to Drew. She shot the next man who came through the door."

"That must have been the big man Roman chased up the stairs to the choir loft. I saw blood running down his arm when he ran out of the church."

"Yes. And Drew saw him jump Roman when he got to the top of the steps. While Roman and he were struggling, Drew ran with Paulo and Juliana along the side of the choir loft and out the door in the baptismal room."

"That's the exact route that I used after I spotted Paulo and Juliana putting Drew into a cab. So the man Drew shot pushed Roman over the railing then ran right past me to join his buddy in the van."

"Yes," Theo said.

"Then they took off after Paulo and Juliana."

"Presumably. But according to J. C. Riley, the caterer, neither one of them shot Father Mike. So there's someone else involved in this." Theo covered her hand with his. "We're going to sort it out."

"Time is running out. My father has been contacted about the ransom. He only has until Monday morning. What about the men in the van?"

"Nik and Captain Parker believe they were involved in the kidnapping, but the two of them have clammed up and lawyered up. The police will be checking on any connections they might have to the Carlucci or Oliver families. If they find a link, they'll put some pressure on."

"Maybe if I came forward and told them what I saw. They were following Paulo and Juliana."

"No." He took her chin in his hand and tilted it so

that Sadie had to meet his eyes. He'd known that she might consider this option and he had his argument ready. But he wasn't sure if it was the man or the attorney speaking. "You didn't actually see them take your sister. Besides, you'd have to come forward as Sadie Oliver and I'd lose my partner. I think that you can help your sister and brother more if you keep up this masquerade for a while longer."

"What if I can't? If someone figures out who I am and that you've been helping me, you could get into trouble."

"Right now you're only wanted for questioning. I'm willing to risk it. Parker will see us in about ten minutes. I'm hoping I can persuade him to fill me in on what they've got on Roman. Then we'll take a break."

"A break?"

"I think we both need one."

She studied him for a minute. "One thing puzzles me. Why didn't Drew come forward and tell the police her story right away?"

"That's the most interesting part of her story. Paulo and Juliana sent her to Kit, but on the way there, the cab got into an accident and when Drew came to, there she was in the backseat, wearing a bloodstained suit and carrying a wedding dress, $20,000 in cash and a gun, with no memory of who she was or where she was going. The only reason she hooked up with Kit was because she had one of his business cards and she'd given the cabdriver his address. Aunt Cass would call it fate."

"Is she the client that Kit asked you to create a contract for?" Sadie asked.

Theo narrowed his eyes. "I didn't ask, but I'll bet you're right."

"Since you volunteered my services, I'll do it. She was at my sister's wedding. I'd like a chance to get to know her better." Whatever else she would have said was interrupted by the sound of raised voices coming from the squad room.

Theo rose and drew Sadie with him. They reached the arched entrance in time to see Nik grab J. C. Riley to prevent her from launching herself at Frankie Carlucci.

"He's the man I saw! He's Snake Eyes," J.C. shouted. "You're not going to arrest him?"

"Frankie Carlucci shot Father Mike?" Sadie asked in a low voice.

"That seems to be J. C. Riley's opinion." His brother Nik had a tight hold on her now, but she didn't seem to be giving up.

Sadie shook her head. "Frankie is not the brightest light in the Carlucci family. His nickname is Fredo after the dumb son in *The Godfather* trilogy."

"But you said it yourself—he was there the night when we believe your sister first met Paulo. Maybe Frankie knew about their secret meetings. And let's face it, whatever it was that went down at St. Peter's last night was not a very smoothly run operation."

In the squad room, D. C. Parker was talking now and Theo couldn't catch every word. Something about Frankie having an alibi.

Sadie turned to him. "Did you hear that? I think that the captain just provided Frankie Carlucci with an alibi."

It was J.C. that Nik finally led away. No one made any move to arrest Frankie.

"More and more curious," he said as Frankie and Gina Carlucci walked confidently past them. When the couple had exited the building, Sadie turned to him. "What just happened?"

"C'mon. We're going to see Captain Parker and find out."

A HALF HOUR LATER, THEY made their way out the side entrance of the building. Theo hadn't spoken to her since they'd left Parker's office. That was just as well because her head was still reeling. Captain Parker had dropped the bombshell that both Roman's and her own fingerprints had been found on the ransom notes.

They'd also learned that in spite of the fact that J. C. Riley had identified Frankie Carlucci as the man who'd shot Father Mike, Frankie's alibi was rock solid. He and his wife had been at a charity fundraiser in the ballroom of the St. Regis Hotel sitting in plain sight of hundreds of people, including Captain Parker and Police Commissioner Galvin.

"This way," Theo said as they reached the sidewalk. "That reporter is hot on our heels."

A quick glance over her shoulder told Sadie that Theo wasn't exaggerating. Carla Mitchell, star reporter from Channel Five News, was only a few yards behind, her microphone at the ready.

"Theo. Theo Angelis. Just one question. Is it true that you will be representing Roman Oliver when he is charged with murder and double kidnapping?"

Theo ignored her and Sadie nearly had to run to keep up with him as he strode down the block. They hit the traffic light at the corner just as it turned green. Over her shoulder she saw that the Channel Five reporter had given up on catching them, but Theo didn't slow his pace until a full block later when they reached the spot where he'd parked the car.

Mason was leaning against the fender of his SUV, which was idling near a fire hydrant. "Where to next?" he asked.

"We're taking a break. You can follow us to The Poseidon."

Once they had pulled out into traffic, she said, "How can we possibly take a break? Roman's and my prints are on those ransom notes. I'm not just wanted for questioning. I'm wanted for kidnapping."

Theo reached for her hand. "We're going to sort this out."

"I've been trying to. The ransom notes had to have been written on paper that Roman and I touched. So it had to be someone who either works at the house or at Oliver Enterprises. I'm betting it's the same person Juliana trusted enough to confide in and the same person who used Roman's code to get into the house and trash Juliana's room. And probably this same person who sent the wedding invitations to Roman and me."

"The MBF in her diary. That's my theory too. What I'm trying to figure out is how Frankie Carlucci managed to be in two places at once."

"So you believe J.C.?"

He glanced at her as he took a left turn. "Don't you?"

"Yes. Your brother Nik believes her, too."

"Yeah. I'm going to let Nik worry about breaking Frankie's perfect alibi. Once he gets on something, he's like a bulldog with a bone. I'm betting that by tomorrow at the latest, Frankie's alibi will be history."

"We should be working on something. I don't really need a break, you know."

He smiled at her. "Don't worry. It will be a working break. I've prepped for some of my most challenging cases at my family's restaurant. The noise and the atmosphere will allow our subconscious minds to mull things over."

17

AT FIVE O'CLOCK ON a Saturday night, The Poseidon was providing plenty of noise and atmosphere. Sadie's eyes widened as Theo urged her through the glass doors into the small lobby. It was the view that caught her attention first. A large window directly ahead of her framed the San Francisco Bay and the Golden Gate Bridge in the distance. Banquettes lining two walls were filled with people. Up a stairway to her left, she could see tables with white cloths and the gleam of candlelight on silver. But the atmosphere and noise Theo had spoken of seemed to be emanating from the floor below where she caught a glimpse of a busy bar and dining room.

"Theo!"

Sadie's attention was drawn back to the hostess desk as a slender woman with a mop of glossy dark curls stepped out from behind it and launched herself at Theo. "It's so great to see you." She gave him smacking kisses on both cheeks, then announced to the customers sitting on the banquettes, "This is my brother, Theo."

A round of applause went up, and Theo said, "Philly, I'd like you to meet my intern, Sam Schaeffer."

Philly held out her hand and, without thinking, Sadie

shook it. She saw Philly's eyes widen at the contact, but all the other woman said was, "Nice to meet you."

She turned back to Theo. "How is Roman? Kit and Nik were both here at lunchtime. All they could tell me was that he had to have surgery. Was it successful?"

"The doctors were able to relieve the swelling and the prognosis is good," Theo reassured her.

"Good. That's good," Philly said. "And you're handling his defense. So, he'll be fine."

More customers entered just then. As Philly turned to smile at them, Sadie was sure she saw the sheen of tears in her eyes.

"She's really worried about Roman," Sadie murmured to Theo as Philly dealt with the new influx of diners.

"When she was sixteen, Roman saved her life. It happened at the cabin. She wanted to take Nik's sailboat out and Roman insisted on going with her. One of those sudden storms came up and he brought her in safely. She had a crush on him for at least a year."

Sadie studied the young woman behind the hostess desk. If she wasn't mistaken, Philly Angelis still had a crush on her brother.

More people poured in through the door. Sadie spotted Mason in this batch. As if Theo were waiting for that, he said, "Philly, is my regular table still free?"

She laughed. "It's just where you left it. I'll try to join you as soon as things settle a bit. I have a lot to tell you."

Sadie followed Theo down the stairs. Most of the tables were filled and people were standing two and three deep at the bar. Skilled waitresses with laden trays wove their way through the crowd. Music flowed in from the patio. "You prep your most challenging cases *here?*"

"I grew up here," Theo said. "I find it relaxing—it's probably like coming back to the womb or something."

Sadie studied his profile as she recalled what Franco had told her. Theo hadn't been back to The Poseidon since the night that Sandra Linton had shot him six months ago.

"I want you to meet my father." Theo created a path to the bar.

Sadie felt a little flutter of nerves when she recalled that Franco had also predicted that Theo would bring her here to meet his family. But he wasn't, she reminded herself. Not really. He was bringing Sam Schaeffer.

Sadie would have recognized Theo's father anywhere. The resemblance to his sons was striking. He had the same tall, rangy build, the same dark eyes. The only difference was his white hair, which was mussed as if he'd just taken a fast ride in a convertible.

He reached long arms over the bar to give Theo a thumping bear hug. Then he turned his dark eyes on her.

"Do I have you to thank for bringing the prodigal son back to me?"

"You do," Theo said. "Sam Schaeffer, I'd like you to meet Spiro Angelis."

Spiro held out his hand, and she had no choice but to shake it. Philly's eyes had widened, but Spiro's narrowed. "And how do you know my son, Sam Schaeffer?"

"Sam's my intern. We came here to work on Roman's case," Theo explained.

"I see." Spiro's gaze remained on her for a moment longer. Then he smiled. "Welcome to The Poseidon. What'll you have to drink?"

"He'll have a beer. Same as me," Theo said. "I'm going

to my usual table. You can send the drinks over there along with one of your appetizer samplers. Sam's starved."

"I'm pretty sure Philly saw through my disguise," Sadie murmured as they moved toward the patio. "And I think your father may have seen through it, too. Franco was right about not shaking hands."

"Philly may have found you out. But if my dad suspected you were a woman, he would have hit on you. He's flirted with every woman I've ever brought here. Which is why I stopped doing that in high school."

"He was looking at me pretty closely. Maybe he thinks you're gay."

Theo threw his head back and laughed.

"I'm serious."

He picked up her hand and raised it to his lips. "We're in the right city for it. By the time we leave, we might have given my whole family something to talk about."

She narrowed her eyes on him. "I thought you said this would be a working break."

"I did." He nibbled on her knuckles and Sadie felt ice and fire streak along her nerve endings before she snatched her hand away. Then he opened a door to a small storage room. Shelves were piled with linens, glasses, crockery. Stacked chairs lined one of the walls. And right near the door, there was a table set with one chair. Theo pulled it closer to the open door, grabbed a second chair and invited her to sit. Then he sat down and took her hand again.

"You have a regular table in a storage room?"

He smiled at her. "It's always available. When I was in high school, I used to come here to study." He glanced around. "I've grown attached to the ambience.

It's private, but with the door open, I can hear the music and I don't have to worry about being interrupted. If I get bored, I can always go out and join the crowd in the bar."

He raised her hand to his lips, then glanced up to smile at the waitress. "Hi, Sophia."

"Good to see you, Theo. It's been too long."

The waitress was a plump woman in her forties and Sadie noticed the quick little survey she gave her. When Sophia set the glass of beer in front of her she kept her eyes fixed on it as she took a sip.

"Your father sent this to get you started." Sophia set a plate down. "I'll be back with the rest of the platter."

The moment she left, Sadie raised her eyes to Theo's. There was that gleam of recklessness there that she'd seen in the office at the hospital. "She saw you kiss my hand."

"I believe she did."

The fact that she could feel the same sense of recklessness building in her made her frown. "She thinks…"

"So what?"

This time when he reached for her hand, she put it on her lap. "You said a working break."

He sighed. "All right. We'll do some work." He pushed the plate toward her. "First, try one of these. They're spanakopita—spinach, garlic, dill and feta in filo pastry." He lifted one and offered it to her. "They have absolutely no relationship to the ones you can pick up in the freezer section of your grocery store."

She opened her mouth and when Theo popped it in, the flavors exploded on her tongue. "Mmm. I agree," she said around the bite of food. "This is marvelous."

Pushing back his chair, Theo stretched out his legs,

crossed them at the ankles and watched her eat. He hadn't known how much he'd wanted to see her here at his family's restaurant, at his table, until they'd walked through the front door. He'd needed to see her here, he admitted as she bit into another appetizer and licked cheese from her thumb.

Taking a sip of his beer, he glanced around. The Poseidon was just as much his home as his aunt's house was. And this small space, this table was particularly his own. Even Nik and Kit had always known not to disturb him when he sat here.

"Okay, I'm eating. We should be working, too."

"Nag, nag, nag."

At the look in her eyes, he glanced at his watch. "Okay. This is how it goes. We'll work for ten minutes. Then we're going to let it rest and let our minds mull things over."

"Define mull."

"You're tough, Sadie Oliver." Then he raised his hands, palms out. "We'll eat, dance some, and then I'm taking you back to my apartment and we're going to make love again. And again."

He watched her eyes darken and the pulse at her throat quicken.

"Work first," she said in a husky voice.

"Right. I just wanted you to know my full agenda for the evening. He leaned back in his chair. "Instead of re-hashing what we already know or think we know, what is the one question that you'd like the answer to?"

She took a sip of her beer. "What was the real goal at the church last night? To stop the wedding? To kidnap the bride or groom and hold them for ransom?

Or both? Or was the real goal the murder of Roman, Juliana and me?"

"That's at least four or five questions," Theo pointed out.

"Sue me."

"If murdering you, your brother and your sister was the real goal, then the Oliver heirs are all eliminated in one fell swoop."

"If Paulo was a target, too, then that would have taken out the sole Carlucci heir at the same time."

Theo stared at her. "That's a very interesting theory. I hadn't even thought of it from that perspective. It would have been a blow to both families and to both businesses."

"The question is, which family would have the advantage when the dust settled," Sadie mused. "I'd say the Olivers, but I'm prejudiced."

"I don't want to go up against you in court, counselor. I think you've gotten to the core of it. Who comes out with the biggest advantage?"

She gestured with her glass. "If the real goal was to eliminate all the heirs, the kidnapping may be plan B. A sort of I-didn't-get-the-jackpot-so-I'll-take-what-I-can-get." She picked up another spanakopita and popped it into her mouth.

"The question is still who. Frankie Carlucci might benefit with Paulo out of the way."

"But he isn't in it alone. He has someone who's close to or is a part of the Oliver family that he's working with. This is a partnership that has to be mutually beneficial. Except..." She chose another appetizer and bit into it thoughtfully.

Theo waited as she chewed, waited for her to echo his own thought.

"Except what happened at the church did not look like a partnership."

"Exactly." Theo folded his hands behind his head. "So maybe what we're dealing with is two villains. Frankie Carlucci arrives with one plan in mind and Juliana's MBF with another."

Sadie took a sip of her beer. "I like it as a theory. But it doesn't bring us any closer to helping Roman or finding my sister."

"Not yet. So we'll stop talking about it and let our subconscious minds mull it all over."

She studied him for a moment. "This is really how you prepare for a trial?"

"You'll see. Tomorrow, you might wake up with a whole new perspective." He pushed the platter toward her. "Our first priority in the morning is to talk to Roman. But if we can possibly make it, we're going to attend the garden party that the mayor is throwing."

"We're going to a garden party?"

"I want to be there to give Nik some backup. Someone is still after J.C. Since she's the mayor's daughter, she has to attend the party, and Nik is betting that *someone* will make a move on her. He gets feelings, too. We could have the answers to some of our questions before that party ends."

"And in the meantime we can't talk about the case?"

"That's the plan."

"So what do we talk about? The weather?"

Theo straightened in his chair. "I've been wondering, why law school? Besides wanting your father to take you seriously. You could have accomplished that with an MBA."

She gestured with her glass. "I think originally I wanted to learn how to argue well and make cases. Then, I became fascinated with it. How about you?"

"I liked the way it puts everyone on an equal footing. Or at least it attempts to. And defense attorneys are in the best position to ensure that equal treatment. Isn't that why you do your pro bono work for the public defender's office?"

"I suppose." She put down her beer. "Are you going to accept Jason Sangerfeld's offer and move to L.A.?"

"I don't know." The truth was he hadn't thought about Sangerfeld's offer since he'd walked into the cabin and seen Sadie Oliver in the kitchen.

Sadie dropped her gaze to the plate and picked up the last spanakopita. "These are very good. And it's a nice place, too. The table in the storage room is very convenient. That way when you bring a date here, you never have to wait."

"I told you, I haven't brought a woman here in a long time. And I've never brought a date to this table."

Her eyes met his and there was something there he wanted to soothe. He wasn't sure how.

Sophia appeared at the table. "You finished with that?" Sadie stared down at the empty plate sitting in front of her, then, as Sophia whipped it away and replaced it with a second platter, she said to Theo, "Tell me you ate at least *one* of those."

"Sorry."

As Sophia left, Sadie placed a hand against her stomach. "I think I'm falling in love with your father."

"Too late," Theo said. "Six months ago, right after Philly graduated from college, he took a trip back to Greece and brought a woman back with him. Helena's a five-star chef and he convinced her to come back here and open a fine-dining restaurant on the upper level. Philly and Aunt Cass believe that it was a case of love at first sight for both of them, but the course of true love has not run smoothly."

"Until today," Philly said to Sadie as she drew a chair up and sat down. "This has been a day of very high drama here at The Poseidon." Then she turned to Theo. "Don't worry. I can only stay a moment. But I wanted you to know the latest. Helena bought a motorcycle."

"Really?" Theo grinned at Sadie. "My dad bought one about a month ago. Midlife crisis."

"Kit's friend Drew Merriweather put her up to it," Philly explained. "And when Helena told Dad this afternoon, right there at the bar, he tossed her over his shoulder and carried her off—just like a caveman. The whole place broke into applause."

"I wish I'd been here," Theo said.

"That isn't all. They went off for a ride together—in the middle of the lunch-hour rush. I was worried that they might have just ridden off together into the sunset."

"They're businesspeople," Theo pointed out. "The restaurant will always come first."

Philly raised two fingers and crossed them. Then she turned to Sadie. "Now that I've brought Theo up to date, I want to know if you'll dance with me."

SADIE STARED AT HER. "You want to dance with me?"

"That's what the lady said." Theo had that reckless

gleam of laughter in his eyes that he'd had when he'd kissed her hand in front of Sophia. Sadie wanted to hit him—a hard punch right in the belly.

"C'mon." Philly grabbed her hand and pulled her out of the storage room. Short of making a scene, there was nothing Sadie could think to do but comply. There were only a few other couples on the floor when Philly turned to face her and placed a hand on her shoulder. "I figure you'll want to lead."

Sadie felt as if she were about two beats behind. "Lead?"

"In the dance. I'll help, but it would look strange if I led, don't you think? You're the guy."

"Right." Together, they began to move around the dance floor. And Sadie vowed that as soon as she returned to the table she was definitely going to punch Theo.

"I know that you're not Sam Schaeffer," Philly said.

Sadie stumbled. Trying to ignore the skip of panic, she said, "Is everyone in your family psychic? You knew when you shook my hand, right?"

"Partly. But it wasn't the fact that I'm psychic. My gift is strong with animals, not so much with people. It was your eyes. You have Roman's eyes. You're his sister Sadie, right?"

Sadie's step faltered again. "You can't tell. Theo would be in so much trouble."

Looking up, Philly met her eyes steadily. "I would never betray either one of you. I just want to know about Roman. You've seen him? He's going to be okay?"

"We think so."

"You've taken us off the dance floor a bit. We'd better go back."

Glancing around, Sadie realized that they were blocking a waiter from his tables. "Dancing is not one of my strong points."

In reply, Philly guided them back to the floor and took them into a spin.

"Do you think I could visit Roman?"

"Of course," Sadie said. "But not until tomorrow. Dr. Rinaldi—she's a real dragon lady—is not allowing visitors right now. I think my father may be influencing her to keep them away. As soon as they allow anyone to talk to Roman, the police will be knocking at the door."

"They're going to arrest him, aren't they?"

A little band tightened around Sadie's heart. "Not if your brothers and I can prevent it."

Philly guided them into another spin. "Tell me what I can do. I'll do anything."

"You love him, don't you?"

"No, I—he saved my life once. That's all."

Sadie once more glimpsed the sheen of tears before Philly looked away. "It's a silly crush. I thought I might be over it by now. You won't tell him, will you?"

"I would never betray you," Sadie promised. But her heart ached a bit for Philly Angelis.

There was a sudden change in the beat of the music. Relieved, Sadie thought it was a signal that they could return to the table, but Philly gripped her hand again. "It's a Greek dance. Come, I'll show you."

And she did. Sadie stumbled a bit at first, but then suddenly, Theo was on one side of her and Philly was on the other. The dance was surprisingly easy once you let the music tell you what to do. Of course it helped that Theo's hand was guiding her. And it seemed the most natural thing in the world to turn into his arms and let him whirl her around the floor.

There were more Greek dances after that. At one point she found herself dancing between Spiro and a tall, beautiful woman.

"I'm Helena," the woman said. "Spiro is so happy that Theo is back here in the restaurant. I want to thank you for that."

"You don't have to," Sadie said. "I didn't—"

"You brought him back. He hasn't been here since the night that woman shot him. And I want you to know that we can accept whatever makes Theo happy. We can accept you."

Sadie didn't know what to say. Over Helena's shoulder, she saw Theo smiling and she knew that he knew exactly what Helena was saying to her. He was going to pay, she promised herself as she found herself handed off to Spiro.

18

"I COULD HAVE DANCED all night. I could have danced all night."

Theo opened the door of his apartment and eased Sadie through it.

"And still have begged for more." She tried a little twirl and he took her hand to steady her. "Your family liked me."

He guided her into the bedroom and eased her onto the bed.

"Yes. They did." His family had sensed that she was important to him. Before they'd left the restaurant, Spiro had insisted that they make a toast with ouzo welcoming his "long lost son" back to The Poseidon. His father was nothing if not dramatic. Then Spiro had toasted Helena. At his suggestion, Sadie had made her glass of ouzo last for both toasts, but along with the combination of stress and exhaustion, she was a little tipsy.

Easing her onto the bed, he said, "You need some rest."

"Mmm." She snuggled into the pillow and reached for his hand. "You, too."

"I will." He sat down on the edge of the bed.

"They think you're gay. Helena told me it was all right. So did your dad."

"I know." Family. He hadn't realized how much he'd

missed them until today—talking with his brothers while they'd watched Drew Merriweather being interrogated and then dancing with his family at the Poseidon. How had he believed that he could leave them and move to L.A.?

They'd known and accepted even before he had what he was feeling for Sadie. As he watched her lying there, he admitted to himself what he hadn't been ready to before. He loved her. He wasn't quite sure when it had happened. Had it been that first day when he'd seen her in court? Or was it when he'd found her in the kitchen at the cabin? All he knew for sure was that the feelings she'd stirred in him from the beginning had deepened until his heart had become hers.

A part of him wanted to tell her. Another part wasn't quite sure that he could say the words out loud yet. Once he did, the choice would be made. Besides, the timing was off, he told himself. She was drifting off and she needed the rest.

So instead, Theo unfastened her slacks and drew them down her legs. Then he pushed the blazer off her shoulders, eased her onto her stomach and drew it carefully off her.

"I'm okay," she murmured.

"That you are."

"Just need a little nap."

He began to unbutton her shirt. "You're worn out."

"Mmm. I was dreaming of Henry Higgins and Eliza Doolittle. She could have danced all night, too."

"I'll bet she did."

Sadie sighed and tucked her hand under her cheek. "Henry turned her into a lady and then he fell in love with her. Probably would have had a different ending if he'd turned her into a man."

Theo rose from the bed and let his gaze run down the length of her. Maybe not, he thought as he drew the sheet over her and watched her snuggle in again.

"Just need a little nap," she murmured. "You won't leave me."

"No, I won't leave you, Sadie."

HALF AN HOUR LATER, THEO stood in the circle of windows looking out over San Francisco. That's when the feeling came to him—a raw fear deep inside of him. Sometime during the next twenty-four hours Sadie was going to face mortal danger again.

And he couldn't see the outcome. Frustrated, he turned away from the view of the city and began to pace back and forth along the windows. They weren't any closer to knowing who was really behind what happened at the church than they'd been when she'd first arrived at the cabin on Friday night. He ran his hands through his hair. They had theories, yes. But that wasn't enough.

"Theo?"

He turned to see her in the doorway to the bedroom, wearing nothing but the tank top and boxers. He would not let anything happen to her. When the time came he would have to trust that he would know what to do to protect her.

"Aren't you going to make love to me?"

"I wanted to let you sleep."

She narrowed her eyes. "Why?"

The annoyance in her tone nearly made him smile. "Several reasons. You had your first experience with ouzo. You're worn out. We have a big day tomorrow."

"Full of excuses, aren't you?"

She'd changed, Theo thought. This was not the controlled woman he'd first seen in court. Though he had no doubt she could call on that control if she wanted to.

"I didn't drink enough ouzo to forget the promise you made. You said we'd eat, dance a little and then you would bring me back here and make love to me." Sadie held out her hand.

"My intentions were good." He crossed the room.

She smiled when he reached her. "The path to hell is paved with those."

Taking her hand, Theo led her toward the bed. If he couldn't tell her he loved her yet, he could certainly show her. He eased her onto the bed, then took off his clothes and lay down beside her so that they were facing each other.

She nipped at his bottom lip. "It was the boxers. That's what got you, right?"

"What?"

She smiled at him. "If the boxers have lost their charm, then what did the trick?"

He nipped her lips right back. "I promised. And I'm a man of my word."

SADIE BEGAN TO TOUCH HIM. It was almost as if she'd known him forever. The texture of his skin was familiar, soft on the surface, but she could feel his strength as his muscles moved beneath it. She knew where he liked to be touched—just where a stroke would make him sigh—over his nipples, down that hard stomach.

His hands knew her secrets, too. They moved over

her with the skill and knowledge of a longtime lover. The press of those fingers as they traced a pattern on her thigh had the breath catching in her throat. The heat of his palm as it cupped her breast made her release that breath in a gasp.

His mouth was so soft, so warm, and she knew his taste. It seemed to be a part of her—familiar and vital. She ran her hands down his chest, absorbed the hardness. Beneath her fingers, his heartbeat quickened and she felt her own heart skip, then race to keep up. She ran her hands over his shoulders then framed his face and looked into his eyes. She loved him. Here in the darkness it was safe to admit to herself what his family had sensed. Whatever time they had together, she would take.

"Make love to me, Theo," she murmured.

"I will." Turning her onto her back, he moved between her legs and entered her in one slow push. Even then they didn't rush. There was none of the speed they'd brought to their lovemaking before. This was new. Surprising. Addicting.

His thrusts were so slow—in and out, in, then out. Still the pleasure built and as it did, his hands found hers and their fingers linked. He spoke only her name. That was all it took to have her whole world narrowing to this man, this moment. As they continued to move together, pleasure intensified into an ache that bordered on pain.

His eyes burned into hers. "Follow me, Sadie."

"Anywhere." She matched his rhythm perfectly as she increased the pace. Then with fingers joined, their hearts beating as one, he took her with him.

Sunday, August 30th—Late Morning

MARIO WATCHED HIS SON sleep. The machines were gone and though Roman was still pale, still drifting in and out of consciousness, he was going to make a full recovery. Knowing that helped Mario deal with the rage he felt for whoever had done this to his son. And to his daughter Juliana.

Time was running out. Dr. Rinaldi was permitting visitors in the afternoon. When Theo and Sadie had dropped by earlier, he'd given them the news. They'd left to go to Mayor Riley's garden party, but they'd return soon. He knew that Captain Parker had also been informed of the fact that Roman would soon be cleared for visitors. If Roman couldn't shed some light on what had happened at the church, it was highly likely that he would be arrested and charged with murder and kidnapping before the day was out.

Mario sank into the chair beside Roman's bed. He had men working on it, questioning staff, running financial checks. He already knew the name of someone in the Carlucci family who needed money badly. But he also knew that Theo and Sadie were right in their theory that someone in his company or even his family was involved. By the end of the day, he should know if Eddie Mancuso was the EM in Juliana's diary.

Last night he'd sent everyone home. Michael Dano had offered to stay, but he'd ordered him not to. Not only that, but he'd hired someone to follow Michael to make sure that he didn't return to the hospital during the night. Michael, a young man he'd hired himself. A young man he'd hoped Sadie might eventually marry. A man he'd expected to become the father of his grandchildren. Now he didn't want Michael anywhere near Roman. He'd gone home himself with Deanna and Eddie because he didn't want them near Roman, either. He was having them watched. Instinct told him that it was one of those three who'd betrayed him and he was trusting no one until he knew who it was.

It cut him to the quick that he was doubting his wife. In his own way, he loved her. It wasn't the same feeling that he'd had for his children's mother. But he cared for Deanna, and he'd believed that she cared for him.

Even though he'd gone to bed, he hadn't been able to sleep and he'd returned at dawn to be close to his son. As he studied the sleeping Roman, he thought of his two daughters. He'd promised their mother on her deathbed that he would take care of all three of them. He'd always been certain that he knew what was best for them and he'd made plans accordingly. Roman had never been a problem. The boy had always wanted to run Oliver Enterprises one day, and so he would.

It was his daughters who'd always challenged him, Sadie especially. Maybe Theo was right. Maybe she was more like Roman and him. He might not agree with it, but he admired her choice to don a disguise so that she could work at Theo's side. The girl had guts. Maybe it was time that he put her to better use at Oliver Enterprises.

As for Juliana. It was odd, but it wasn't disappointment he felt that she'd fallen in love with Paulo Carlucci and deceived him. In fact, he found it in himself to admire her for her courage and her cleverness. Maybe he'd been underestimating both of his daughters.

He was going to get Juliana back safely. He was not

going to let himself doubt that. And whoever had taken her would pay.

"Dad?"

He rose, moved to the bed and took his son's hand.

"I'm here, Roman. Right here."

"Can you tell me what happened?"

Keeping his son's hand gripped tightly in his, Mario told him.

"MOST OF THE USUAL suspects are here," Sadie said. "And we don't know any more than we did yesterday."

The truth was the truth. More than anything, Theo wanted to take her hand, to offer some kind of reassurance. Instead, he let his gaze sweep the rolling lawns at the back of Mayor Riley's sprawling mansion where guests had gathered to give their support—both personal and monetary—to the mayor. Both the Oliver and the Carlucci families had sent representatives. Twenty-five yards to his left, Frankie and Gina Carlucci were chatting Riley up. Michael Dano, Deanna Oliver and Eddie were helping themselves at a food-laden table.

"Time is running out," Sadie murmured.

It was. Theo sympathized with her frustration, but he sorely wished that frustration was all that he was feeling. The fear that had knifed through him at midnight was back in full force. Whatever it was that would pose a mortal danger to Sadie was going to happen sometime today. And someone at this party was involved. Who? When? Those were the questions he couldn't answer. As he jammed his hands into his pockets, he questioned once again what good it did to have a gift for precognition if it didn't provide more accurate information. If it didn't allow you to protect the ones you loved.

His gaze shifted to Sadie. With each passing hour he was becoming a bit more…if not comfortable, then at least less panicked about what he was feeling for her.

But he'd have been a hell of a lot more at ease if Mason Leone hadn't had to be left with the cars. With members of her family present, there was a chance Mason would be recognized. And if he hung around too close to Sadie, it might blow her disguise.

Theo's gaze shifted to Nik, who stood a few feet to his right. He could sense the same mix of fear and frustration in his brother. Nik was sure that J.C. was in imminent danger. He was watching her like a hawk in spite of the fact that her father, the mayor, had ordered extra security to protect her during the garden party.

"J.C. is holding up well," Sadie said.

Theo slid his gaze to where J.C. stood with her mother on the other side of the lawn talking to Captain Parker, Police Commissioner Galvin and his aunt Cass. Theo had been surprised to see his aunt and had learned that the mayor's wife was one of her clients.

"Frankie and Gina Carlucci have a lot of nerve," Sadie said, "showing up here when they know J.C. believes Frankie shot Father Mike."

"They either have nerve or a plan," Theo murmured.

She turned to him then. "You have a feeling, don't you? That's why you've been so quiet."

"Yeah." He caught the excitement in her voice, but all he felt was a mix of fear and even more frustration. "I wish to hell it was more specific."

She placed the glass of white wine she'd been holding in a death grip on a passing waiter's tray, then put her hands back in her pockets. She was holding up well, too, considering the roller coaster of emotions she'd been on since their visit to the hospital that morning. Roman was going to make a full recovery, but with his improving health, Sadie worried more and more about him being arrested.

And that was a very real possibility, at least according to Parker. As soon as they left the party, Parker was going to go to the hospital and take Roman's statement. And unless there was a break in the case, Theo surmised that Roman would be under arrest before nightfall.

He had some idea of the emotions rolling around inside of Sadie. He knew what he'd be feeling if one of his brothers was about to be arrested. And she had to be very worried about her sister. He still felt that Juliana was all right, but he sensed that time was running out on that score, too. In spite of what she had to be feeling inside, all through the time they'd been at the party, she'd played the role as Sam Schaeffer flawlessly. She'd played it at the hospital, too, since Michael Dano had been talking with Mario when they'd first arrived.

Theo shifted his gaze to Michael now. He had his head thrown back, laughing at something Deanna or Eddie must have said.

"You had an invite to this party, right?" he asked Sadie.

"Sure. Dad would be here, too, if it weren't for Roman."

"Roman and Juliana would be here, also?"

Sadie nodded. "Oliver Enterprises has contributed a lot of money to Mayor Riley's campaigns. He's reasonable and grateful. We want to see him remain in office."

"So Michael, your stepmother and stepbrother have

stepped in to fill the gap. If Juliana, Roman and you had all been killed at St. Peter's, their positions in the company and in the family would have been greatly strengthened in a permanent way. If Eddie *is* the EM your sister mentioned in her diary, maybe he's not in it alone. Maybe they're all in it together."

Sadie didn't speak for a minute. "Any one of them could have sent those ransom notes with Roman's and my fingerprints on them. And any one of them might have been able to forge Juliana's signature to the invitations Roman and I received."

"One or two or all three. They also could probably have gotten hold of Roman's code to get in the house anonymously."

Whatever else they might have said was interrupted when Nik suddenly grabbed Theo's arm.

"I can't see J.C. and Frankie's still talking to the mayor. It would be just like that scumbag to try something when he's in plain sight of everyone. I'm going to check in the house."

Theo scanned the area. Nik was right. There was no sign of J.C. Frankie Carlucci still held the rapt attention of the mayor, but his wife, Gina, was missing.

Nik was already sprinting toward the house when Theo grabbed Sadie's hand and raced after him. As Nik vaulted onto the porch, tires squealed and an engine roared at the front of the house.

"Don't go in," Theo called to Nik. Keeping a firm grip on Sadie's hand, he led the way around the side of the house. They reached the front lawn just in time to hear tires screech again as a dark sedan shot out of the curved drive and onto the street.

Mason Leone raced toward them. "Gina Carlucci came out with a little redhead. She had a gun."

"That bitch has got J.C." Nik sprinted toward his car.

"Wait!" Theo called to him.

"Take your own car," Nik called. "We'll try to box her in."

A man and a woman Theo recognized as two of the extra security people the mayor had hired appeared as Nik climbed into his car. They had cell phones to their ears. He got his own out as Sadie pulled him toward his SUV.

"No," he said, stopping short. "You can't come with me."

"Of course, I can," Sadie insisted.

Theo shot a look at Mason and the man stepped forward to grab Sadie's arms.

"I can't explain now." How could he when he didn't understand it himself? How was he supposed to know whether it was safer to leave her or to take her along on a car chase? But something told him she'd be safer here with Mason. When he saw his aunt appear around the side of the house, the feeling deepened. "Trust me." He grabbed her, kissed her hard and then raced to his SUV.

SHE DID TRUST HIM, but Sadie was still ping-ponging between anger at being left behind and fear for Theo's safety when Theo's Aunt Cass reached her.

Cass took her hand. "He'll be all right."

Sadie looked into the older woman's eyes. "You're sure?"

Cass smiled. "As sure as I can be. Human choice is always involved, but Theo is a smart man. I'm equally sure that he was right to leave you behind."

Somehow, Sadie believed her. "And J.C.? Will she be all right?"

"I think that will all work out. Nik will have a plan. And he has help."

Sadie swallowed hard. "What about my sister?"

Cass put her free hand on Sadie's cheek. "You're going to find the answer to that very soon. You're learning to trust your instincts and that's very good. You'll have to trust your heart, too."

Though Sadie couldn't for the life of her have explained why, she found that looking into Cass's eyes calmed her.

Behind her, Mason said, "Others are coming. I'll have to step away now."

"Oh." Sadie broke her gaze away from Cass and turned to Mason. "This is Theo's Aunt Cass."

Mason extended his hand. "Theo left her in my care, ma'am. But if I stay too close someone may put it together that she's not Theo's intern."

"She'll be safe with me," Cass promised as she shook his hand.

Sadie looked to the end of the driveway and prayed that Theo would return safely.

19

FOR CLOSE TO AN HOUR, Sadie had been watching Parker interrogate Gina Carlucci through a two-way glass, hoping and praying that something in her story would change. Her husband, Frankie, was being questioned in another room, but he'd asked for an attorney. Gina was singing her little heart out, hoping for a deal.

Parker was very good. He had his sleeves rolled up, his arms on the table, his body relaxed as if he had all day to question her. She couldn't fault his techniques. In fact, she was picking up some pointers. But Gina's story remained firm and fear for her sister and brother had become a steady ache right around Sadie's heart.

With the help of Paulo's bodyguard, Gino DeLucca, Gina and Frankie had planned to kidnap Paulo and Juliana, but they'd failed because of Roman. They hadn't expected him to show up.

Theo was a foot or so away, sitting on the corner of a table. She glanced at him. She'd been feeling the need to do that every few minutes or so since he'd been dropped off at the mayor's house. The chase after J.C. and Gina had ended in an accident involving Gina's car and Theo's.

But Theo was all right. Aside from a cut on his

forehead, he'd suffered no other injury when J.C., in an attempt to get the gun away from Gina, had plowed her car into his. The passenger side of his SUV had taken the brunt of the impact. And that, of course, was where she would have been sitting. If he'd allowed her to go with him, she'd be in the hospital now with J.C. So he'd been right about leaving her behind.

She hoped that his feeling that Juliana was all right was just as accurate.

J.C. hadn't been as lucky as Theo. Her injuries were minor, but she was being held overnight at St. Jude's for observation. Nik had gone to the hospital with her. Sadie turned her gaze back to Gina Carlucci. The woman was smarter than her husband, Sadie was betting. Of course, that didn't mean that the blond bombshell was in any danger of being invited to join Mensa.

This was the third time Parker was taking her through her story and it wasn't changing. Gina had seen Paulo and Juliana talking behind one of the clusters of palm trees at the dedication of St. Jude's trauma center. She'd told Frankie and they'd persuaded Paulo's bodyguard, Gino DeLucca, to keep them informed. At first, they'd thought to win Angelo's favor by reporting the trysts of the two young people. Then when Angelo had expected Frankie to come up with five million to close on the land deal, they'd decided that rather than admit they were broke because of Frankie's gambling debts, they'd kidnap the couple. They'd hired a lookalike to stand in for Frankie at the charity ball on Friday night and Frankie had gone off to St. Peter's to kidnap the bride and groom.

It was supposed to be a snap, Gina had said. DeLucca had told them no one was invited. Certainly not Roman

Oliver and definitely not that twerp of a caterer who'd hurled a cell phone at her Frankie's head and made him blow his disguise. First Frankie had wanted to kill J.C. Then when they discovered she was the mayor's daughter, she and Frankie had come up with their second kidnapping plot.

Which had come within a hairbreadth of succeeding, Sadie thought. They'd managed to snatch J.C. right out from beneath everyone's noses. As Gina launched into her third description of the car chase, Sadie turned to Theo. "I believe her."

Theo met her eyes for the first time since they'd started listening to the interrogation. "I do, too." He rose and moved to her. "I know that you were hoping everything would be over. That your brother would be cleared and we'd know where your sister was."

When he held out his arms, she stepped into them and laid her head on his shoulder. She couldn't name all the emotions tumbling through her. All she knew was that it felt like coming home. For one moment, she let herself be held. She didn't want to think about what would happen next.

"We were right about there being two different villains. Frankie and Gino DeLucca are just one piece of the puzzle. That man Drew shot and his partner out in the van—they were working for someone else." Closing her eyes, she drew on the strength Theo was giving her just by holding her. "The police are going to believe those men were working for Roman and that they came there with the same agenda—to kidnap Paulo and Juliana. They're going to arrest him."

Theo said nothing. He didn't have to. For a moment

longer, Sadie allowed herself to lean on him. Then drawing in a deep breath, she stepped back.

"I want to go to the hospital and talk to my brother."

SADIE STOOD AT THE WINDOW in Roman's hospital room, her notebook in hand, trying to ignore the knot of tension in her stomach. The late-afternoon sun slanted across Roman's bed. His head was still bandaged, but his eyes were open and the machines were gone.

Her father sat in a chair next to Roman's bed and Theo and his brothers had taken positions around it. Theo had wanted his brothers there so that they could consolidate what each of them already knew with what Roman was going to tell them. Captain Parker was on his way so they didn't have much time.

She'd had a few minutes alone with Roman before Kit and Nik had stepped into the room, long enough to be satisfied that he was indeed on the road to recovery. He'd moved his legs and wiggled his toes and even teased a smile out of her by commenting on what a handsome man she made.

"We'd better get started," Nik Angelis said with a look at Theo. "I figure Parker will be here in about fifteen minutes."

"I thought it might be good if Roman told us what happened at the church from his point of view," Theo said. "And you two could add what each of you know as we go along. Then maybe we can make some sense of it. Sam will take notes."

The three Angelis brothers had positioned themselves around the bed. Theo leaned against the wall, seemingly at ease. On the other side of the bed, Kit stood next to Mario Oliver's chair, his hands in his pockets, and Nik had stationed himself at the foot of the bed. Of the three of them, the cop had the most direct view of Roman's face.

Theo nodded at Roman. "Why don't you tell us what happened?"

"I received a note by special messenger from my sister Juliana at about four Friday afternoon asking me to please come to St. Peter's Church at seven. When I got there a few minutes before seven, I parked in the back and entered through the open sacristy door. Paulo was shocked to see me and when I realized the wedding was going to take place in a matter of minutes, I tried to talk him out of it. We argued. Then this man entered the room from the altar. He had a gun in his hand and it was aimed directly at me."

"That would have been Gino DeLucca, Paulo's body-guard," Nik said. "J.C. saw him arrive with Paulo."

"Paulo stepped in front of me and told him to put the gun away, that he was making a mistake. Gino said that it was no mistake. He told Paulo that there'd been a change of plan, that he and his bride were going for a little ride as soon as Frankie took care of the priest and he took care of me."

"Paulo cried out, 'Roman? No!' Then he threw himself at the big guy. In the scuffle he was shot in the arm. When this DeLucca pointed his gun at me again, I shot him."

"So you shot him in self-defense," Theo said.

"Yes. He intended to kill me. He would have if Paulo hadn't stepped in front of me. The kid saved my life."

"Then what happened?" Theo prompted.

"Paulo grabbed this leather bag and raced up the back stairs to the loft where Juliana was. I checked the altar. That's where DeLucca had entered from. I was on the lookout for Frankie. But there was no sign of him or the priest. They might have been in the room on the other side of the altar, but before I could check, I spotted another man with a gun standing in the center aisle of the church. He was looking up at Paulo, who was running along the choir loft trying to get to Juliana. When this guy ran down the aisle toward the back of the church, I took off after him. When I reached the vestibule, he was already running up the staircase to the choir loft. I saw my sister Sadie and shoved her out of sight and then I vaulted up those stairs."

"Can you name the guy you chased?" Nik asked.

"No." Roman turned to his father. "But I recognized him. He works security for us. If you'll bring me the personnel files, I can point him out."

"We believe we have him and another man in custody," Nik said. "They both have long criminal records, so the name this guy used at Oliver Enterprises is probably false. Would the personnel files show who hired him?"

"Perhaps," Mario said. "I'll have them here within the hour."

"What happened next, Roman?" Theo prompted.

When Roman reached for water on the stand next to the bed, Kit picked up the glass and handed it to him. After he'd taken a swallow, he continued. "Just as I went up the stairs, there were more shots. I called out Juliana's name and Paulo answered that she was all right. Then the guy I chased stumbled out of this little room and fell to the floor."

"The wedding dress designer, Drew Merriweather, shot him," Kit said. "Since Paulo's right arm was affected, he gave his gun to her."

"I wanted to see Juliana for myself, but before I made it to the door of the room, the guy she shot got up and jumped me. I yelled at Paulo to take Juliana and go to Kit. I figured that was the safest place until we could figure out what the hell was going on. Then I fought with the guy until he pushed me over the railing. He said something interesting before he got the better of me. He said that the Olivers were going to be history. That's all I remember."

"You don't know what happened to Sadie?" Nik asked.

"No." Roman met Nik's eyes steadily.

"Then for all you know," Nik continued, "she could have taken your sister and Paulo Carlucci from the church?"

"If she did, it was to keep them safe," Roman said. "My sister is not behind this kidnapping and neither am I."

"It doesn't make sense that she has anything to do with this. If that thug was telling the truth and his job was to eliminate all of the Olivers, then Sadie could be a victim here as much as Juliana," Kit said.

Silence filled the room.

Finally, Theo spoke, "Roman, that's the story I want you to tell Captain Parker. No embellishments. Just answer his questions. Then I'll make my case. He already knows Frankie Carlucci was working with Paulo's bodyguard and they intended to kidnap the bride and groom and eliminate witnesses. Someone else had a different plan. They invited you and Sadie to the church and I believe the two thugs the police have in custody, the one who threw you over the railing and his driver, were hired to kill you, Sadie, Juliana and Paulo, too. That would certainly end the Oliver family and perhaps the Carluccis, too. All they'd have to do was to arrange the scene afterward so it looked as if you'd all died in some kind of tragic shootout when you failed to stop the wedding."

"Two villains or two sets of villains," Roman murmured. "It makes sense." He met his father's eyes. "And one of them is very close to us."

"They're being watched," Mario said.

"And neither set of villains," Theo continued, "expected there to be a caterer or a dress designer there. Those women threw a monkey wrench into their plans."

"J.C. literally threw her cell phone at Frankie and kept him from killing Father Mike," Nik said.

"And Drew shot the guy you fought with," Kit added.

"Of course, you did your part," Theo said. "Taking out DeLucca helped even the odds for everyone."

Roman was still looking at his father. "And this bastard, whoever he is, has Juliana."

Sadie heard the anger and the pain in her brother's voice. It was the perfect match to what she was feeling and to what she was sure her father was feeling, too.

"We're working on it," Theo said.

Nik planted one hand on his hip and ran the other one through his hair. "Parker may want to buy your story, but with the kind of pressure he's under, he's going to charge you unless we can come up with something more concrete."

"Theo?" Mario said.

"I agree. But we're going to come up with something. Those personnel files could point the finger at whoever is behind this. Parker may wait until you look at them. Even if they don't give us a name, they should allow the police to put pressure on the man who assaulted Roman."

"I'll let Parker know we're finished," Nik said.

Once Nik and Kit had left the room, Theo moved to Sadie. "I want you to leave now."

"No, I—"

"You've held up very well so far, but if Parker arrests Roman, I'm not going to take the chance that you'll give yourself away." He took her hands and raised them to his lips. "J.C.'s room is just down the hall. Drew's with her. Why don't you wait with them. You can even question them and see if they can throw any new light on what we already know."

"He's right." Roman nodded.

"Go," Mario said.

Sadie met each one of their eyes in turn. She was being sidelined again. She moved toward the door, turning when she reached it. "I'm going. But only because I agree with you."

20

A HALF HOUR LATER, Sadie stepped out of J.C.'s room. Nik was with her now and Kit had picked up Drew a few minutes ago.

Theo was right to have worried that she would let down her guard. That's exactly what she'd done in the time that she'd spent with J.C. and Drew. Pepper Rossi, a member of the security team J.C.'s father had hired had been there, too. As much as she'd enjoyed masquerading as a man, it had been good to just be with other women. At some point, talking with them had cleared her mind.

When she walked by Roman's room, she saw that Mason was once again sitting outside the door reading a book. Through the small pane of glass, she noted that Theo and her father were still with Roman.

Deciding against interrupting them, she said to Mason, "I think I'll take a walk down to the waiting room."

Once she reached the nurse's station, she could see through the glass wall of the waiting room. There was no sign of Michael Dano or Deanna, but Eddie was stretched out on a couch watching TV. On the screen, Channel Five was running clips of Gina and Frankie Carlucci being taken into the precinct. The banner headline read: Frankie Carlucci Involved in Wedding Shoot-out.

It had to be fate, she decided as she walked into the room. It was the perfect opportunity to question Eddie Mancuso.

"Eddie, I have a few questions for you if you don't mind."

Eddie smiled as he rose and walked toward her. "Sammy. I have something to tell you, too."

"Sammy?"

"I told you I give people I like nicknames." Reaching her, he ran a finger down her lapel and let it linger.

She glanced at his hand, then glared at him. "If you like that hand, you'll keep it off me."

Eddie threw back his head and laughed. "I like a man with spirit."

"I'll show you spirit," she said. Placing both hands on his chest, she gave him a good shove, then followed him when he took a step back. "Maybe it's time you came clean about your involvement with Juliana Oliver's disappearance."

"Whoa!" Eddie took two steps back this time. "I don't know what you're talking about."

"You lied to me. Juliana was confiding in you, wasn't she? She told you all about her wedding plans."

"No way. She didn't tell me anything. My mother was pushing me at her, so I kept my distance and so did she."

Sadie studied him for a minute. What he said gelled with their behavior whenever she'd seen them together. But that didn't mean that they hadn't met secretly. Her sister was evidently very good at secret meetings.

"She used your initials in her diary—EM. How do you explain that?"

Eddie's brows shot up. "I can't. But I was *not* the

person the little bride was pouring out her secrets to. That was the very topic I wanted to talk to you about. I remembered something."

"What?"

"Sammy, I was hoping for a little quid pro quo here."

"Eddie, you better spill it before I tell the big guy you're holding back something that might help him find his daughter."

Eddie threw up both hands. "Okay, okay. If you're looking for someone Juliana was telling all her troubles to, talk to Michael Dano."

"Michael Dano?"

"He was teaching her how to sink a put a couple of times a week on those greens the big guy built last spring behind the pool house. I got to thinking it over and she would have had plenty of time to pour her little heart out during those lessons."

Sadie narrowed her eyes. Would Juliana have actually confided in Michael Dano? The man was a good fifteen years older than she was. True, he did have a kind of personal charm that drew both men and women. Roman liked him and so did her father. Sadie had liked him, too. She'd found him easy to talk to. And hadn't she been convinced that he'd been her friend until he'd tried to take their relationship that one step further?

It had only been after she'd straightened him out about what their relationship was going to be that he'd changed. And even then the change had been so subtle. He always had a rational explanation for the increase in her workload. And she'd only seen a flash of temper in his eyes once—on the night she'd finally convinced him that they would never have a romantic relationship.

Juliana must have needed *someone* to talk to. Her baby sister had found herself falling in love with the last man in the world she ever should have been attracted to. During that time, Roman had been busy with the big land deal and she'd been buried in work. Juliana might have found Michael Dano a very easy person to confide in. Especially if he went out of his way to make himself available.

"He might even be your E.M., you know. His first name is Elliot."

She stared at him. "How do you know that?"

Eddie shrugged. "He uses the initial on his business cards and I asked him about it one day. Elliot's a family name, and he doesn't like it."

Sadie felt her anger start deep and spread quickly as she checked items off a mental list. Michael could have easily sent the invitations—particularly if Juliana had told him the time and place for the wedding. And he could have forged her signature. He also could have seen to it that the driver of the van and his buddy were hired at Oliver Enterprises. It would have been even easier for him to obtain stationary with Roman's and her fingerprints on it for the ransom notes.

As for motive—Theo might have hit the nail on the head earlier at the garden party. If she and Roman and Juliana had all been killed on Friday night, Michael Dano would have been in a position to become her father's right-hand man. And with the Oliver dynasty eliminated, he would have been in an excellent position to start one of his own. Why hadn't she seen it sooner? Had she felt so guilty for refusing to date him that she'd worn blinders where he was concerned?

"Elliot Michael." She spoke the name aloud. Clever

Juliana. Using the initial of a name he didn't use was a perfect way to disguise his identity. The more she thought about it the more convinced she became that this man had her sister. Sadie's stomach sank. Unless he'd already gotten rid of her.

"You can ask him now," Eddie said. "He just stepped off the elevator."

Sadie whirled in time to see Michael push through the door of the waiting room. The best way to rattle a witness was to surprise him.

Striding to him, she grabbed his arm. "We know that you've got Juliana. She names you in her diary. If you tell me where she is right now, I'll try to get Mario Oliver to go easy on you."

There was no surprise on Michael's face and all she saw in his eyes was that flash of anger she'd seen only once before. Her breath caught in her throat the same way it had the first time she'd seen it.

"Sadie."

His voice was soft when he spoke—almost tender. Ice slithered down her spine.

"Sadie?" Eddie said.

She felt Eddie's eyes on her, but she couldn't drag her gaze from Michael's, who ignored him. "I wondered when you would finally come to me. I knew you would eventually."

"You saw through my disguise?"

"Not until today at the garden party. By that time, I'd put in a very uncomfortable day and night trying to figure out where you were and what you were doing. When you slipped away from the men who followed you to that cabin, I knew that sooner or later you'd come

and see your brother. Then today, when I saw Theo
Angelis grab your hand when all hell broke loose at that
garden party, I realized that you already had. You were
just hiding in plain sight. Very clever."

"Dammit," Eddie swore. "I didn't see it."

"We would have made a great team, Sadie."

"Where is my sister?"

Michael took her arm. "We can't talk about that here.
Let's take a little walk." Then he pulled out a gun.

Sadie swallowed hard. She'd forgotten that all Oliver
Enterprises executives had them.

"You too, Eddie." Michael motioned with the gun.
"You're going to lead our little parade across the hall
and into the elevator. Try anything—either one of you—
and I'll shoot."

She considered resisting, but Michael seemed to
sense it. "If you want to see your sister alive again, I
suggest you come with me quietly."

In two seconds they'd crossed the hall, entered a
waiting elevator and Michael had punched the top floor.
She could only pray that Mason had happened to glance
up from his book.

"What the hell is going on?" Eddie asked.

"A little revenge," Michael said in that same calm and
friendly tone. "It's just too bad that you were in the
wrong place at the wrong time."

"You're not going to get away with this," Sadie said.

"Yes, I will. I have to."

The hint of desperation in his tone had another chill
moving through her.

"I've put too much time and energy into this to give
up now. I only have to wait until tomorrow morning for

your father to transfer the funds. You're not going to ruin this plan for me the way you ruined my first one."

"Your first one?"

"You were supposed to marry me," he explained in a friendly tone. "And one day we would have run Oliver Enterprises together." The smile he gave her frightened her more than the gun. "Eventually, Roman would have had to meet with an accident, but I think I would have kept you around. I would have made a perfect husband, you know—just what you were looking for. I did my research. I knew what you needed, all the things you weren't getting from your father and your brother. I would have given you equal footing in our marriage. We would have worked together side by side at Oliver Enterprises. We would have made a perfect match. But you were too stupid to see that."

His voice tightened on the last sentence and Sadie saw that flash of anger again. Irrational and uncontrollable. This was a facet that Michael had kept well hidden from everyone.

"You're crazy," Eddie exclaimed.

"Speak again and I'll shoot you right here."

Michael's tone was so cold that Sadie shivered. Eddie was right. There was something...missing from Michael's eyes.

"If you'd married me, I wouldn't have been forced to change my plans. And you wouldn't have to pay for it now."

When the doors slid open, he motioned to Eddie with the gun again. "Lead the way. We're going to the roof. And don't make a sound. I would prefer not to shoot you."

Eddie found the stairwell and they climbed to the roof.

"I didn't want to hurt anyone," Michael said. "But it's all your fault that I have to do this, so you deserve to be punished."

Panic. Sadie could feel it bubbling up and fought it down. She had to think. She had to figure out a way to talk him out of what he planned to do.

When they stepped out onto the roof, the sun had just set, and the lights of the city were winking on.

"Don't hurt him," she pleaded. "He isn't involved in any of this."

Without warning, Michael raised the gun and struck Eddie on the back of the head. Sadie watched in horror as the young man's body crumpled.

"That was just in case you don't think I mean business. Move," he ordered.

With her heart in her throat, Sadie walked toward the edge of the roof.

21

THEO WAS JUST STEPPING out of Roman's room when fear hit him like a punch in the stomach. It was the same feeling that he'd gotten at midnight when he'd stood in the turret room at Franco's house and again when Sadie had wanted to go with him to chase J.C. and Gina Carlucci. Sadie was in mortal danger.

"Where's Sam?" Theo asked.

Mason put down his book and rose from his chair. "He went down to the waiting room."

Theo sprinted down the hall and Mason ran after him. The room was empty. Shoving down panic, Theo turned to Mason. "Who was in here?"

"Mr. Eddie and Mr. Dano were in there the last time I checked."

"Dammit." She'd confronted one or both of them, he knew it. It was exactly what he'd been thinking of doing himself.

"Where would they go?" He murmured the question to himself as much as to Mason.

"If either Mr. Dano or Mr. Eddie went to their cars, they'd be followed." Mason pulled out his cell phone. "I'll check."

A minute later, Mason shook his head. "Neither of them has gone anywhere near their cars."

Theo shut his eyes as the fear roiled through him. Why the hell didn't he know? Why couldn't he feel something when it really mattered? Trust, he told himself. Open yourself. And suddenly, he knew. "It's Michael, and I think he's taken her to the roof."

They ran to the elevator together and Mason punched the button for the top floor. "Michael has a gun. All the executives carry them." Mason pulled out his own. When the doors opened on the tenth floor, Theo ran to the nearest stairwell. The feeling inside of him was escalating. Panic swamped him as they raced up the stairs.

DON'T PANIC. DON'T PANIC. The words formed a little mantra in her mind as Sadie walked toward the edge of the roof. She had to keep her head. A few feet short of the edge, she stopped and turned around to face Michael. He looked calmer now, but she wasn't sure if that was a good or a bad sign.

All she had to do was stall him for a few minutes, give Theo time to get here. And the man had an ego. He'd want to talk and she'd learned how to lead a witness on the stand. "You sent those invitations to Roman and me, didn't you? You forged Juliana's signature."

"Yes, I did. She has the handwriting of a schoolgirl, very easy to copy."

"You were going to kill us all at the church?"

"That was my plan."

The matter-of-fact way he said it had Sadie once more fighting back the panic. "Why?"

"I wanted to run Oliver Enterprises one day. Eliminating all three of you was a perfect plan—even better than my original one of marrying you. In his grief, your father would have turned to me. I would have become indispensable to him. And everything should have gone perfectly." His voice tightened. "Juliana assured me that no one knew about the wedding. But Paulo had told his bodyguard, she had invited a dress designer and the priest had hired a caterer. Still, my men could have handled it if Frankie Carlucci hadn't arrived with his half-assed kidnapping plan. Now, thanks to you, I have to settle for ten million and start over somewhere else."

"What have you done with Juliana?" she asked.

The irrational anger once more flashed into his eyes. "She's with her lover and I have no idea where they are. The little brat wouldn't tell me when she called. She said Paulo didn't want her to tell anyone. Something about Romeo and Juliet's biggest mistake was that they trusted people. Luckily, I was able to persuade her that she and Paulo were in mortal danger and that they must stay in hiding. That was easy. I told them that you were probably dead and that Roman might not make it. Then I sent the ransom notes with your fingerprints on them. She called again after Angelo Carlucci appeared on TV, but I convinced her that the Carluccis were behind the kidnapping notes, that they were a ploy to make her and Paulo appear, and that they'd risk their lives if they did. I'm sure sweet little Juliana will call me again when she hears about your suicide."

Sadie swallowed hard. Don't panic. Just keep him talking. "No one will believe that I committed suicide."

With a smile, he shook his head. "Sadie, Sadie, Sadie. Of course they will. Your brother has been arrested and the police are convinced that you're his accomplice. Your kidnapping plot failed and you couldn't stand the scandal or the idea of going to jail. It's the perfect solution. Besides—" he motioned her closer to the edge of the roof with the gun "—I only need everyone to believe it until tomorrow morning."

Sadie stood her ground. A siren sounded and out of the corner of her eye she saw the lights of an ambulance turning into the entrance drive below them. For a moment there was no other sound.

Michael just might pull it off. It was that thought that had her anger pushing through the terror and panic. Then beyond his shoulder, Sadie saw Theo step out onto the roof and she was frightened all over again. But not for herself. Whatever she did, she couldn't let Michael know that Theo was there.

THEY WERE FACING EACH other, silhouetted against the darkening sky and standing much too close to the edge of the roof. The image was seared in Theo's brain and fear hit him like a blow to the stomach. He must have made some kind of move because Mason gripped his arm.

He had to think. The fading sound of the siren had masked any noise they'd made as they'd stepped onto the roof, but there was silence now. He spotted Eddie Mancuso's body and fear sliced deeper.

Mason raised his gun.

"No." Theo barely breathed the word. They were too close to the edge. Michael could take her with him.

Mason seemed to realize that, too, because he didn't fire.

"Check on Eddie." Theo breathed the sentence, then watched Mason squat and press two fingers to the young man's throat.

"Steady pulse," Mason whispered back.

Then Sadie spoke, her voice clear and steady. "You don't have to do this, Michael. There's still time. You haven't killed anyone yet. You only hit Eddie on the head. The goons you hired haven't killed anyone, either."

"I want that money," Michael stated dispassionately.

Stall. Theo willed the word across the distance to her. If she could just keep him talking until the next siren sounded, he and Mason could make a move and take Michael unaware.

"But there's a very good chance you won't get the money. It's a long time until tomorrow morning. Juliana and Paulo could come out of hiding at any time. And Roman recognized the man who shoved him over the railing. Turns out he works security for us. But you know that. Roman and my father are going through the personnel files right now. They'll either figure out that you got those two men their jobs or they'll find something that will give the police leverage while interrogating them. They're in jail, you know."

"You're lying," Michael said, grabbing her arm.

Theo had to use all of his control not to move. But Sadie's voice was calm when she spoke again.

"No. I'm not lying. They've been in jail since yesterday afternoon. When was the last time they called to report?"

"I figured they decided to cut and run."

"Not true. How long do you think it will be before they decide to make a deal?"

She wasn't just stalling, Theo realized. She was trying to talk him out of his plan, just as she might handle a reluctant witness on the stand. And Michael was beginning to listen. Admiration streamed through him.

STOP THINKING ABOUT THEO, Sadie told herself. Focus. Focus on the argument. "You're an attorney, Michael. A good one." Keep talking. Just pretend he's a jury. "You know the law. What can they charge you with right now? You haven't even kidnapped anyone. Not me and not Juliana. So the Feds won't be involved."

Michael's eyes narrowed on hers. "You're suggesting I give myself up?"

He was listening now. She raised her brows. "Isn't that what you'd advise a client to do? It will count a lot if the case gets to court."

He didn't speak for a moment. But he was thinking it over and the anger had disappeared from his eyes. For the moment.

"There might be an extortion charge. You did send the ransom notes." She didn't want to paint too rosy a picture. He was far too sharp to buy it. "I could talk to my father. You didn't throw Roman over that railing and you didn't kidnap Juliana." She paused, giving him a chance to mull that over.

"I don't want to go to jail."

Sadie nearly let out a sigh of relief when he released her arm and took a step back. Drawing in a deep breath, she played her trump card. "With a good defense attorney…" She let the sentence trail off. "This is a very high-profile case. You'll probably attract someone who'll defend you just for the publicity."

DAMNED IF SHE WASN'T RIGHT, Theo thought. A publicity-seeking, high-profile defense attorney would snap the case up. Jason Sangerfeld might even be interested in it.

"I want the money." Michael Dano's tone had become almost petulant. He sounded a little like a kid who knew he wasn't going to be allowed a treat.

"Do you want to spend the rest of your life in jail?"

There was a stretch of silence, then the sound of a distant siren. As it grew closer, Mason whispered, "I'm going to make my move."

Theo put a hand on Mason's arm. "Wait."

Suddenly, Michael dropped the hand that was holding the gun. "All right. I'll turn myself in. You're a fine attorney, Sadie. We would have made a great team."

"Put the gun all the way down on the roof, Michael," Theo called as he and Mason moved forward.

When Michael had done that, Mason said, "I'll take care of Michael. Ms. Oliver needs you."

Banking down the urge to get his hands on Michael, Theo strode to Sadie and took her into his arms. She was safe. Whatever he was feeling about Michael, holding Sadie, feeling her body pressed against his, was more important. She was safe. And it was going to take a minute or two for that to sink in.

"C'mon, Michael. We'll just go back down to the fifth floor and wait for the police."

"I'm turning myself in," Michael said.

"You bet your ass you are." As he moved Michael past them, Mason said, "I'll send someone up to attend to Mr. Eddie and I'll inform Mr. Oliver."

Theo waited until he heard the door to the roof close before he drew back just far enough to brush his lips over Sadie's. She was here in his arms. He kissed her again. "Good work, counselor."

"I was so afraid."

"Ditto."

"My knees…I need to sit down for a minute."

Theo sank with her to the rooftop and then shifted her onto his lap. When she snuggled closer and laid her head on his shoulder, he finally felt some of his tension ease. "How did you decide it was Michael?"

"Eddie was alone in the waiting room, and when I accused him, he told me that Michael could be EM. His first name is really Elliot and he'd been giving Juliana putting lessons on the greens behind the pool house. Suddenly, I just knew. When Michael walked in, I confronted him, too."

"You shouldn't have faced him alone."

She raised a hand to his cheek. "I know, but he was there. And I thought if I took him by surprise, I could crack him. And I did. He's crazy."

As she told him everything, Theo held her, the night air cooling around them, knowing that he didn't ever want to let her go.

"We're going to have to go down and tell Roman and my dad," she said finally.

Theo kissed her forehead. "You know, I have this feeling. They're not always accurate, but…"

"Spill it," she ordered.

"I don't think your father and your brother are ever going to want to sideline you again."

He felt her lips curve. "I'm not going to ever let them sideline me again."

Still, Theo didn't let her go. It wasn't the right time,

it wasn't the right place, but the feeling inside of him was so strong. He'd nearly lost her. And he simply couldn't let another minute go by. "There's something I have to tell you, Sadie."

She stiffened in his arms. "I know. You're going to take Jason Sangerfeld's offer."

"No." He cupped her chin, tilting it so that she had to meet his eyes. "As a matter of fact, I'm not taking his offer. But that's not what I want to tell you."

She frowned at him. "Why not? You'd be great and it's the opportunity of a lifetime."

"That's what I've been telling myself for months. And I've been wondering why I didn't just snap up his offer. But it didn't feel right. I didn't know why, not until you came to the cabin Friday night."

"What do you mean?"

"I think I was supposed to wait for you." He took her hand and raised it to his lips. "Because *you* feel right to me, Sadie. Admitting that scared the hell out of me at first. But I also think this is why I can't keep my hands off of you. I love you, Sadie."

The shock that came into her eyes didn't do much for his ego.

"I…I wasn't expecting this."

"I can see that."

"I thought we were having a fling, that you were going to move to L.A. I had no idea that you felt…"

Impatience streamed through Theo. "Well, you know now."

Sadie looked into his eyes and suddenly she did. She raised her hands to frame his face. "I had myself convinced that when all this was over, you'd walk away from me."

Theo gripped her shoulders. "I'm not walking away. I'm not going to let you walk away, either. I'm not a seer, Sadie. I don't know what the future holds, but will you explore it with me—at my side?"

Emotions prevented her from speaking, and she recalled what Cass had said to her at the garden party. "You have to trust your heart."

"I love you, too, Theo Angelis. And yes, I do want to explore the future with you."

He kissed her then and poured everything he felt into the kiss. It was a long time before he drew away and she snuggled her head on his shoulder again.

"When did you first know that you loved me?" Theo asked.

She lifted her head and kissed his cheek. "Maybe the first time I saw you in court." She kissed his nose. "Or it could have been when I turned and saw you in the kitchen of the cabin, nearly naked and so angry." She kissed his chin. "I'm not sure. How about you?"

"I think it was the morning that I woke with you beside me in bed. What I felt scared me so much that I left you there alone and practically ran out to the kitchen."

She met his eyes then. "Theo, I think I love you even more than I did a few seconds ago." She kissed him on the mouth.

"Well."

The sound of her father's voice had them both springing apart.

Mario looked first at his daughter and then at Theo. "Mason tells me I owe you my daughter's life."

"You owe me nothing." Theo rose and helped Sadie to her feet. "Your daughter talked him down. She convinced him that with a good defense attorney, he'd probably get off scot-free. You should have heard her."

Mario shifted his gaze back to Sadie. "I wish I had. He denies kidnapping Juliana. Says he doesn't know where she is."

"He doesn't," Sadie said. "But I think I do."

"Where?" Mario asked, startled.

Sadie was already striding toward the door. "I could be wrong, but when Juliana called Michael, she made reference to the whole Romeo and Juliet thing again. It's just a hunch, but it's worth a shot."

AN HOUR LATER, SADIE settled on the window seat in the dining room in Father Mike's rectory and slipped her hand into Theo's. A short distance away, her father, Paulo and Juliana sat in a circle of chairs, deep in conversation.

"I thought you did a good job convincing Michael Dano, but Paulo is running neck and neck in his bid to convince your father. Do you think he's won your dad over yet?""

"He has an edge. He saved Roman's life and he kept Juliana safe. He'll have a tougher time convincing *his* father." Mario had already called Angelo Carlucci to tell him the good news and Paulo's father was on his way.

"How did you figure out that they were here?" Theo asked.

"They've been taking their leads from Shakespeare all along—the secret wedding, the tutoring. I suppose you'd argue that my subconscious mind was mulling it over."

He raised her hand and brushed a kiss over her

knuckles. "I told you that it works. And sometimes the ouzo helps it along."

Ignoring the comment, she continued, "The last time I saw them they were on that corner just a couple of blocks away and they'd sent their money with Drew. Your brother Kit was supposed to make arrangements for them. They just needed a place to stay until Kit contacted them. I started thinking of Romeo and Juliet. When the chips were down, Romeo turned to the friar for help. That's where he hid out after he killed Juliet's cousin. So…what better place to stay for a night than Father Mike's rectory? There was food, they didn't have to use a credit card that could be traced and no one would think to look for them here."

"Only you."

Only me, she thought as she met his eyes steadily. "You know I have a little confession to make."

"Go for it."

"If you had decided to take Sangerfeld's offer and moved to L.A., I was going to follow you."

Theo studied her and saw the truth in her eyes. "You were."

"And I was bringing the boxers. You never stood a chance."

They were both still laughing when Angelo Carlucci walked into the room.

Epilogue

"THREE BEERS," THEO called out to the overworked bartender. The Poseidon was packed for a private party celebrating Spiro and Helena's wedding and Nik and J.C.'s engagement, and it looked to him as though half of San Francisco was in attendance. Guests were standing three deep at the bar and there seemed to be an unending stream of people coming down the stairs. Nudging his way to the bar, he grabbed the bottles and passed two of them off to his brothers.

"This is a real bash." Nik took a swallow of beer. "All the movers and shakers in San Francisco are here."

"That's what happens when you get yourself engaged to the mayor's daughter," Kit pointed out.

Nik jabbed a finger in Theo's direction. "Hey, I'm not the reason why we've got the Olivers and Carluccis here. It's *his* lady who invited them."

Theo's gaze shifted to the table a few feet away where his very sexy Sadie sat huddled with J.C., Drew, Philly and Juliana. The five women were pouring over sketches of wedding dresses that Drew had made for J.C. But Theo's gaze remained on Sadie. She was still changing, he thought, and she continued to fascinate him. The only trace of Sam Schaeffer was the haircut. Franco was giving her some fashion advice, and the little black dress she was wearing was a sharp right turn from those little conservative suits she'd always worn in court. From the moment he'd seen her in it, he'd been fantasizing about getting her out of it.

The look she sent him every now and then told him that she knew exactly what he was thinking.

"Not only are the Olivers and the Carluccis here, but they're sitting at the same table," Kit mused. "That's not to say that they're relaxed with one another or that they even look happy about it."

Theo glanced over to where Roman sat next to Paulo and across from his father and Angelo Carlucci. It was Roman's first outing since his release from the hospital and he was starting to resemble his old self. "Sadie's optimistic. Roman's backing the wedding plans. And it was his idea that the families go into partnership on that big land deal they were fighting over."

"A week ago Friday, when I was standing in St. Peter's Church, I couldn't imagine anything good coming out of that mess," Nik said.

"Love can certainly change things," Kit agreed.

The three brothers exchanged looks and raised their bottles in a toast.

"Not only the big things but little things, as well," Kit added. "According to Philly, the restaurant is running much more smoothly now that Dad and Helena have tied the knot. But I'll bet we don't get any more brothers-only fishing weekends at the cabin."

"I wouldn't be so sure," Theo said, nodding in the direction of the table where the five women sat. "They seem to be hitting it off. They're probably going to want some girls-only weekends."

Kit's expression brightened.

"Don't get too happy. I intend to take J.C. up to the cabin and teach her how to sail." Nik handed him his empty bottle.

"Excuse me, but I promised J.C. a dance."

Theo and Kit watched as Nik extricated J.C. from the circle of women.

"Twenty bucks says he doesn't plan on dancing with her," Kit said.

Theo shook his head. "No bet."

Kit grinned. "It was worth a shot. I like making easy money, and I personally like the way my oldest brother's mind is working." He handed his empty bottle to Theo. "But don't tell him I said that."

Theo watched as Kit led Drew away. Choices, he thought. You made them and they changed your life. In fact, they gave you a whole new life. Setting the bottles down on a passing waiter's tray, he walked to Sadie.

"Care to dance?" he asked.

Sadie glanced at Philly and Juliana.

"Go ahead." Philly waved a hand. "Juliana and I are going to go over and talk to Roman, Paulo and the dads."

"In that case, I'd love to." Sadie gave him her hand as she rose and Theo led her out across the patio and into his special storeroom. Then he flipped on the light and closed and locked the door.

"I take it we're not dancing."

"Not right now. I need to get my hands on you." The need had been building since he'd picked her up. He thought it might always be that way.

Sadie glanced around the room. "I think I'm beginning to understand the real purpose of your private space."

He raised her hand and pressed his mouth to her fingers. "I told you that I've never brought another woman here." Then he smiled at her. "That's not to say that my brothers haven't."

Her brows shot up. "You probably just used the spaces that they're using now. You Angelis men are a dangerous bunch."

"Believe it." Theo ran his hands down over her hips. "Are you wearing anything at all under this dress?"

"Of course not." Laughing, she drew his mouth to hers and whispered against his lips. "What makes you think you're the only dangerous one in this relationship?"

CASS ANGELIS STOOD IN THE entrance lobby of The Poseidon and saw only the present. She watched as, one by one, Nik, Kit and Theo wandered off with the women they'd chosen.

The Fates had offered choices and her nephews had chosen bravely and well. Hopefully her son Dino and her niece Philly would be faced with similar choices one day. A little tingle of awareness moved through Cass as she glanced toward the bar and saw Mason watching her. And she'd experienced the same tingle when she'd shaken his hand at Mayor Riley's party. Cass shifted her gaze to Commissioner Galvin. Charlie. He'd asked her out for dinner. She pressed a hand against her stomach. Perhaps there might be a choice for her to make, too…

But that was for the future.

Tonight was for the *now*. The present had always

been her favorite time, one she'd learned to cherish and savor before it slipped into memory. With joy in her heart, she started down the stairs to join the celebration.

* * * * *

SHOCK WAVES

BY
COLLEEN COLLINS

Dear Reader,

I had a challenge with this book – to develop a glam-goth character who's made over into a Malibu beach babe. The latter I understood, having grown up in sunny Southern California and spent time frolicking on its beaches. It was a summer ritual during high school for a bunch of us to rent beach houses (with a few brave-hearted teachers as chaperones) and "hang" in bikinis for a week of flirting, swimming and catching some rays.

But glam-goth? I was clueless. I did research on YouTube watching Marilyn Manson and Siouxsie Sioux videos, watched an entire series on Lou Reed, read up on glam-goth makeup and clothes, but it all felt too remote, too distant. Then I found GiGi-D L'Amour, a glam-goth diva extraordinaire, artist and disc jockey who took me under her gothic wing and patiently answered my many questions. Thank you, GiGi!

Also, big thank-yous to two of my favourite authors and good friends, Dawn Atkins and Cindi Myers. Dawn and Cindi are not only talented, but fun to work with! A big thank-you to my editor, Wanda Ottewell, whose guidance and good humour always keep me on track, and to Shaun Kaufman, who diligently read all six story drafts – including the wrong one I gave him accidentally.

So get ready to read about a glam-goth chick in a beach-babe world as she not only experiences a few shock waves, but starts a few of her own…

Happy reading!

Colleen Collins

PS Check out my upcoming books at www.colleencollins.net.

COLLEEN COLLINS

Deep into the writing, while Colleen Collins was weaving threads of glam-rock and glam-goth into the story, she heard in an old Lou Reed song the name of someone she once knew – Jackie in "Walk on the Wild Side." Jackie Curtis had been her neighbour back in Hollywood, and they used to talk about life and writing and what they wanted to be someday. He was so low-key and easygoing and funny, she had no idea he'd been one of Andy Warhol's superstars until someone told her. And she didn't know he was in "Walk on the Wild Side" until she wrote this book. A tip of the hat to you, Jackie, all these years later.

To GiGi-D L'Amour, who graciously shared her glam-goth world so I could better develop *Shock Waves'* heroine, Ellie. Any inaccuracies are the author's, not GiGi's.

1

COME JOIN the hot, hot, hot Sin on the Beach festival! That's right, beach babes and beach dudes, we're talking hot games, hot competitions, hot bodies to help us kick off the second-season launch of the hottest TV show this season!

Twenty-nine-year-old Ellie Rockwell—glam goth girl, coffee shop owner and serious Lou Reed fan—read the announcement on the kiosk again, certain she was suffering from heatstroke. Or having a heart attack. Or both. Hardly what a woman on her first vacation in five years should be having.

"Sin on the Beach," she murmured, glancing over at the people setting up booths and tents along this stretch of Malibu Beach. It was one thing to read about this festival at her coffee shop, Dark Gothic Roast, located twenty miles inland in fast-paced, hyperstressed Los Angeles, quite another to be standing on the very sand where the TV show was *filmed*.

Everybody and anybody knew better than to call Ellie on Thursday nights between 9:00 and 10:00 p.m. when *Sin on the Beach* aired. She got teased a lot for loving this show, as though goths were narrow-minded enough not to like anything that wasn't black and morbid and reeking of Edgar Allan Poe. Okay, she could do without all the sunshine and tanned bodies on the show, but she dug the buffed actors in Speedos. Especially when they starred in the occasional mystery story line full of shadows and danger. Plus, the night scenes were to die for—moonlight gilding the water, the ocean spilling its secrets and the occasional body onto the shore, the rhythmic tumble of distant, dark waves.

She continued reading. The festival promised games such as Truth or Bare and Hot Shot Photo Scavenger Hunt, surfing competitions, limbo contests, something called Good Vibrations. Even nearby bars were getting into the festival mood by holding karaoke sin-alongs, and…

Her heart stilled.

What was this?

She leaned forward, clutching her black silk top while reading the fine print at the bottom of the poster.

Hey, you! Want to be an extra on Sin on the Beach *and earn beaucoup festival points doing so? Then come to the open audition the first morning of the festival! If you're 18-30, act wicked, dress cool and have a rockin' bod, meet here on Tuesday, August 15, 7:00 a.m. sharp. Be hot, be sinful, be ready!*

For a wild, giddy moment, Ellie imagined herself as an extra on *Sin on the Beach,* looking killer in a black bikini, cavorting in the waves, maybe being the one who found the dead body in a mystery plot and getting to rip loose a bloodcurdling scream. How groovy would that be?

She scanned the ad again. *Wicked, dress cool and have a rockin' bod...*

Her short black hair was wickedly spiked, but she seriously doubted that's the kind of wicked they had in mind. Dress cool? Unless they were into the Mistress of the Dark look, she doubted they'd use that word for her wardrobe, most of it custom-designed by yours truly. Although, lifting everything from cappuccino machines to bags of coffee beans kept her in shape, so humility aside, she could probably pull off the rockin' body.

Wicked. Cool. Rockin'.

She blew out a sigh.

One out of three wouldn't cut it.

Just as well. She expected to hear any day that her business loan had been approved, which meant starting next week she'd begin the expansion of Dark Gothic Roast into the remodeled former warehouse in East L.A. The space was so large, she'd decided to try selling her clothes designs in one of the commercial spaces while overseeing the rental of the others. The enormity of her plans excited and scared the crap out of her. Rather than fret and worry until she got the news, she'd opted to adopt the pragmatic "what happens, happens" attitude.

Until then, she'd chill, do her caretaking thing.

Which meant she needed to ensure her brother, Matt, crossed paths as often as possible with her friend Candy and encourage her other friend Sara to occasionally pry herself off her laptop.

Speaking of which, time to call the mother ship and see how things were going. She flipped open her cell phone and punched in the speed-dial for Sara.

"Hello?"

"It's El. Expecting it was your uncle calling again, hmm? Everything going okay?" She nudged her sunglasses up the bridge of her nose. "Hey, guess who's looking for hot-bodied extras?"

"Johnny Depp?"

"I wish. Seriously, *Sin on the Beach*."

"Cool!"

"Yeah, remember that festival we read about? Well, *Sin* is holding an open audition for extras. Better yet, everybody who gets hired also wins a scad of festival points."

"Ellie Rockwell, I see your name in lights."

"I'm not wicked and cool enough," she muttered.

"What?"

"Nothing. Hey, I'll bring one of these flyers back to the house. There are all kind of games and competitions." And she knew just the people to sign up, too—Matt and Candy.

"Gotta go," Sara suddenly said. "Someone's waiting."

"Tell your Uncle Spence it's your first day on vacation! Girlfriend, you *deserve* a day off."

"Yeah, like you ever close Dark Gothic Roast. Anyway, it's not Uncle Spence."

"Who is it?"

Pause. "Ellie, your goal is to matchmake Candy, not me."

A pause could only mean one thing….

"Sara Montgomery, you wanton mortgage broker you. You landed a guy! While sitting *alone* at the beach house! You rule."

Sara laughed and signed off.

Ellie shook her head. And here she'd been pondering how to help Sara relax, have some fun. Appeared Sara was a lot more resourceful than Ellie had given her credit for.

She started to slip her cell into her shorts' pocket, hesitated, then punched in the speed-dial for Dark Gothic Roast. Overhead, seagulls squawked and circled as a little boy tossed pieces of bread from a bag. Nearby, construction workers hammered, drilled, called out to each other as they worked on the festival site.

"Dark Gothic Roast," answered a female voice.

"Hey!" yelled a male voice. "That your Benz?"

Ellie looked around. "Tish, El. How's it going?"

A groan. "Kiefer called in sick and I ended up handling the morning rush by myself."

"Hey," boomed the male voice again. "I'm talking to you. Miss Spiky Black Hair."

As if that left any doubt who he meant. As Tish droned on about the espresso machine making a "funny sound," Ellie scanned the area. None of the construction workers seemed interested in her. Nor did the nearby jocks tossing a Frisbee.

Wait.

There.

The guy in the Hawaiian shirt, unbuttoned to reveal a buffed, brown and extremely hairy chest, was staring directly at her.

"It sounds kind of like keee-keee klunk," continued Tish, "and it only does it if I'm steaming milk longer than twenty seconds…."

Ellie stared at the man. Something about him looked familiar.

"I suppose I could stop steaming sooner," said Tish, "but then there'd be no froth and you know how some customers would get if their lattes were flat…."

The man smiled, and Ellie's heart ratcheted in her chest.

Only one man in the world had a smile like that.

Impossible…and yet…it was him.

Bill Romero.

He was older—seventeen years to be exact—bigger and *hotter* than the boy she remembered. The rough-around-the-edges guy had morphed into a body like The Rock, with the too-cool aura of a Lenny Kravitz. He leaned against a palm tree, the breezes billowing open his shirt whose bright yellow flowers looked like pats of melting butter on his choca-mocha-latte skin.

"El, what should I do about the espresso machine?"

Ellie cleared her suddenly parched throat. "Turn up the steam," she rasped before terminating the call.

"That your Benz?" he called out again.

Ah, the voice. It hadn't really changed. That deep, rumbling tone and clipped rhythm, so familiar it made her insides squeeze. How many nights had she lain in her childhood bed, her window open on the off chance she'd overhear Bill talking with a pal or family member. The summer she turned twelve, when he was eighteen, she must have written more journals than Anais Nin. Page after page filled with fantasies of her first kiss—her first everything—with him.

"Benz," he repeated, mistaking her silence for not hearing him clearly. "Over there!" He pointed.

Ellie stared at his raised arm. So big, so brown, two-thirds of it covered with a massive tattoo. She couldn't really see the details this far away, but could tell it was colorful, bold and elaborate.

Unlike her tattoos, which were hidden, secretive.

Sea breezes brushed and stroked her, making her realize all the areas of her skin that were bare. In the distance, she heard waves crashing, the fading away of a girl's laughter.

Finally remembering to breathe, Ellie looked to where he was pointing. At the far end of the patch of tarmac sat a gleaming silver Mercedes. She had the momentary urge to laugh—did she really look like the kind of woman who drove a *Benz?* She looked back at him, wondering if, behind those dark shades, his eyes still looked like melted pools of chocolate.

"No," she called out, her voice breathy, unrecognizable. "Not mine."

He pushed himself off the palm tree—did his biceps ripple when he moved?—and stared at her. The sun glinted off an earring. That was new, too. And for a crazy moment, she wondered if he remembered her. No, no way. Back then, she'd been freckled and mousy-haired. Hardly the goth chick he was talking to right now.

Besides, they'd only really spoken once, that memorable summer night she'd worked up the nerve to ask if what she'd heard was true, was he was really moving far away? Her girl's heart had shattered into a million pieces when he'd said yes, he was moving to New York to start film school.

"Just my luck," he murmured, his voice rippling through the air like a heat wave. "Need it moved, hoped it might be yours."

She wiped a trickle of sweat off her brow, wishing she could say something, anything, to prolong this encounter. She was a whiz at chatting, did it all the time with her customers. Asked them about their jobs, their kids. Helped them figure out their love problems. But she couldn't summon one reasonably intelligent thing to ask Bill. Yeah, good ol' helpful Ellie was resourceful when it came to others' needs, but a tongue-tied, sweat-laden mass of messed-up hormones when it came to her own.

She took a few halting steps across the sand, imagining how she'd introduce herself. "Hey, remember me? That scrawny kid next door who wore pigtails?" No, skip the scrawny part. "The girl next door who…" loved, adored, idolized you. No, forget that. Although Bill had been a few years older than Matt, he'd probably remember her brother. Yeah, she'd bring up Matt. "Hey, remember me? Matt Rockwell's kid sister?"

She stopped.

Too late.

Bill was talking to several women, one dressed in Benz-worthy clothes, undoubtedly wicked and cool. And flirting unabashedly with Bill. Jeez, her effusive giggle could be heard over the construction workers' incessant hammering, even over a low-flying airplane towing a bright blue banner with the words Wolfman Pizza 1-800-555-9844 We're Howling Good!

And I've howlingly lost my chance.

She stopped, stared down at her purple-painted toenails, white legs, black shorts, black silk top. Then back up at the giggling babe with the white short-shorts, long bronzed legs and skimpy pink halter top.

They obviously weren't talking about the Benz or she'd be moving it.

I'm standing here, looking like a black dot in the middle of the sand. The anti-beach babe. The kind of woman he'd ask to move her car, but nothing more.

With a sinking feeling, Ellie turned and started heading back to the beach house. It was for the best. She needed to see how Candy and Matt were doing. Catch the story about Sara and this mystery male. Follow up with Tish, make sure the espresso machine wasn't getting the better of her. What had she said it sounded like? *Keee-keee klunk?*

Funny, that's exactly how Ellie felt at the moment. As though something inside her had jarred loose and was rattling around. And she knew what that something was. A piece of her past named Bill. And here she was, walking away for a second time from him, just as she had that long-ago summer night when she was twelve.

Seventeen years and hundreds of life changes later, walking away today felt every bit as hard.

THREE HOURS, two Bomb Pops and one Candy-Sara-Ellie girl-talk fest later, Ellie stood in the cosmetics aisle at Walgreens with Sara, perusing the hair color section.

"I can't believe I agreed to be made over into a beach babe," muttered Ellie, looking at the boxes of color with names like Bombshell Blond, Golden Sunset and Strawberry Vanilla.

Sara, switching their plastic shopping basket from one hand to the other, snorted a laugh. "Gotta look like one if you want to wow them at the audition tomorrow morning. Plus, if—no, *when*—you get hired, think of all those points Team Java Mammas will get toward the grand prize!"

Team Java Mammas. The team name she, Candy and Sara had given themselves in their quest to win the festival grand prize, a free beach bungalow rental every summer for the next ten years. "Just wish I could wow them with black spiky hair," Ellie muttered.

"I'll pretend I didn't hear that." Sara scanned the boxes, all decorated with smiling models sporting luxurious, shiny hair in more shades than a color wheel.

For a surreal moment, everything looked too light, too blond, too perfect. Too anti-Ellie. What was she doing here? Not just here at the store, but here at the beach, too! She wasn't some sixteen-year-old starring in *Beach Blanket Babettes*—she was a businesswoman turning *thirty* in a few months! She shouldn't be here. She should be back at Dark Gothic Roast, getting ready for the big move.

"I don't know, Sara—" she gestured toward the sea of models' faces "—I'll never look like them."

"Hon, even *they* don't look like that. They've been airbrushed and streamlined and photo-enhanced down to their very roots."

It wasn't the words as much as the lilt in her pal's voice that shook Ellie out of her funk. She looked at Sara more closely, realizing her telltale lines of stress had all but disappeared. As corny as it sounded, she even had a *twinkle* in her eye.

And Ellie knew why. She'd just forgotten why's name.

"What was that surfer hunk's name?"

"Drew." The way Sara said his name, it sounded like a piece of delectable candy. "And yours…"

Mine. Oh, man, that was *so* far from the truth.

"Bill." Ellie heaved a small sigh. Crazy how just saying his name sent small shivers all over her. And to think she'd just told herself she wasn't some goofy sixteen-year-old. Truth was, saying his name turned her insides all gooey, like some besotted, crushed-out teenager.

"How long were you two neighbors?"

"Years. I remember first seeing him when I was six, the year my dad left. Bill was twelve, and already a stud-in-the-making."

"You had a crush on him at *six?*"

Ellie nodded slowly. "Crazy, huh? I still remember the first time I saw him. He was standing on his porch, staring out at nothing, lost in thought. I thought he looked like a fairy-tale prince. After that, my heart did a sonic boom every time I saw him, right up to the day he moved to New York to go to film school."

"How old were you when he moved?"

"Twelve."

"You must have been so sad."

"Sad? That was the year the movie *When Harry Met Sally* came out. I saw it at least ten times. I'd sit in the back, drowning my sorrow in popcorn, fantasizing about Bill and how, despite our tumultuous parting, we were destined to be together." She pointed at the box Sara was holding. "Honey blond, no way."

"But, El—"

"Too Reese Witherspoon. I need a bad-girl blond color."

"No, I meant…" Sara hesitated, then set the box back on the shelf. "I was still feeling sad about your childhood heartache."

Ellie didn't want to admit some of that sadness had come back today. She couldn't blame Bill for not recognizing her, but something about his lack of attention had made her feel again like that broken-hearted twelve-year-old.

"So," said Sara, "what's a bad-girl blond? The color of Madonna's hair?"

Ellie felt relieved to be back on topic. "She's not so bad anymore, is she?"

"Cameron Diaz?"

"Maybe."

"Jennifer Aniston?"

Elle gave her friend a look. "Girlfriend, you need to unchain yourself more often from that laptop because obviously you have *no* idea what bad is."

They laughed.

"El," Sara said, turning serious, "I know you're not the type to easily talk about what's on your heart, but I have to add one thing. Maybe it wasn't a coincidence that you saw Bill today. I bet you're going to run into him again."

See Bill *again?* Ellie didn't know if her heart, mind or soul could handle it. What had happened this morning was enough to haunt her for months as it was. But no way did she want Sara to know that. Ellie Rockwell was so much better than some ancient crushed-out angst.

She hoped.

"As much as I've always wanted to have a real supernatural experience," she said in her best breezy voice, "I doubt you've suddenly turned clairvoyant."

Before Sara could follow up with something else serious and heartfelt, Ellie pointed toward the end of the aisle. "Hey, down there are some awesome black hair colors."

Sara made a stopping gesture. "You promised to go blond, and I'm holding you to it. This one—" she grabbed a hair color labeled Lightning Blond "—is perfect. After we wash out your black rinse, this color will give you that Gwen Stefani bad-girl blond you want."

"Okay, we're starting to talk bad."

Grinning, Sara picked up a second container. "Then we'll add some gold highlights, which will give you that sunny, sparkling beach babe look."

Ellie looked over at a couple of sunny, sparkling beachettes. The type who'd snagged Bill's attention today. Here she thought she'd so smoothly avoided further discussion of Bill, but she'd forgotten the nonstop banter in her own head.

One of the beachettes laughed, reminding her of the bimbo Bill had chortled with earlier today. What did those types have that Ellie didn't? Hell, if she could make herself over into the Mistress of the

Dark, she could certainly make herself into a Gidget type, too. Not the sunny, sparkling variety, but definitely a Gidget on the Edge.

"Bad-girl with gold streaks it is," she said, turning back to Sara. "Sold."

"That's my girl! Hey, El, this is fun taking care of you for a change. Oh, look at these yummy pastel lipsticks…"

"Huhhhh." Blond was one thing, but *pastel* make-up?

Sara tossed a peachy lipstick into the basket. "I told you I bought several new bikinis for the trip, right? We're about the same size, so let's have you try a few on when we get back."

"What colors are they?" Not pastel, please God.

"Pink, tangerine…oh, and black."

Ellie's mood lifted. "Black. Cool."

"Okay, next—spray-on tan."

This time Ellie willingly followed her friend to the fake bake aisle, as Sara called it.

Sara held up something called TechnoTan. "What about—"

"Put it in, baby."

Sara, looking surprised but pleased, added it to the basket. "I won't spray over your tattoos, but use one of my makeup brushes to paint the skin around them."

Ellie listened, sort of, but her attention had again been diverted by the beachettes who were giggling in front of the body cream section. It brought back how she'd felt earlier, Miss Black Spiked Hair Can You Move Your Benz, standing in the background, out of place and out of time, wearing her big, broken childhood heart on her sleeve. Okay, so she'd wanted to be better than ancient angst, but the truth was, she wasn't.

Suddenly, it felt as though all the years of caring and yearning and dreaming about Bill had crowded against her heart, squeezing it, constricting the memories into a throbbing lump of ache. Today, her world had stopped when she'd recognized Bill, but his didn't even pause. *He wasn't interested in me.* And as much as she told herself it didn't matter, she felt rejected. Unacceptable.

She picked up a box of something and pretended to read, as though focusing on random words might impose logic on her pain. On her heart. But the letters danced and swam, refusing to make sense.

Maybe that's how she should view the past. Make it blurry, indistinguishable, unimportant. Do what she came to do this week—chill, play matchmaker, audition to be an extra and screw the rest.

"Hey!" enthused Sara, holding up a plastic case. "This will look fantastic with your turquoise eyes. Ghost Silver eye shadow!"

Ghost…exactly how she should view Bill. A ghost from her past, nothing more.

She took the container from Ellie and tossed it into the basket. "Sold."

2

BILL, SITTING in the first row of the audience, shook his head at Mandy, the hyperefficient fortyish principal casting director sitting at the foot of the stage. She nodded, understanding his message that the girl who just auditioned was a no.

"You didn't like her?" asked Jimmie, Bill's best pal and *Sin on the Beach*'s key grip.

"Not hot enough," Bill said, shifting. He tipped his coffee mug, which caused brown liquid to slosh down the front of his white polo shirt.

"Shit."

He set the cup on the sand beneath their folding chairs and pulled the shirt away from his skin. "I'm used to easing into Monday mornings with 9:00 a.m. read-throughs, not getting up when the rooster crows to audition hundreds of extras for some publicity gig." He flapped the shirt to cool the spilled liquid.

"I won't ask if *that* was hot enough," quipped Jimmie.

Bill shot him a look.

"Sorry. But speaking of things that *could* be

hot…have you given any more thought to you and I starting our own indie company?"

Bill nodded. "Sure. Problem is, making big bucks with an independent film production company is a long shot."

"Who's talking big bucks?"

"Me. You know my take on the movie business. Dream big, make it big. No offense, but an indie company is too small for this boy."

Jimmie shook his head. "You're letting your hard-luck roots get the better of you, pal. Producing our own films gives us control, which is big in a better way. Did I tell you *Edge of the Universe* placed first in its category at the WorldFest competition?"

He and Jimmie had known each other from their first day at New York University film school, given each other a lot of support while they crawled up the dog-eat-dog success ladder of L.A. film and television work. Jimmie's first love was screenwrit-ing, but until he started making sales, he worked on film crews.

Bill balled his hand into a fist, knocked it against Jimmie's fist. "*Edge of the Universe* will be your breakthrough sale, no doubt about it."

Jimmie had spent the last few years writing this screenplay, about three friends from East L.A. whose lives take dramatically different paths. He'd loosely based the protagonist on Bill's own coming of age story in East L.A.'s gangland. Bill hadn't minded sharing most aspects of what it'd been like growing up in the barrio but there was one thing he never shared with anyone, and never would.

"It could be our first script, Bill. With a hot screenwriter and a hot up-and-coming director…" He jabbed his thumb at himself, Bill. "My parents are willing to be our first investors, although we'd need to raise the rest. I think we can do it."

Bill paused. "You're my best friend, Jimmie, but I gotta say no. It took years to nail this first AD spot. Gordon's still the director on this week's shoot, but he's stepping aside and letting me take the reins for a few days. If I pull it off, I'll be bagging my first directing gig with *Sin*."

First AD—Assistant Director—was the number two spot on the set, right below director. As such, Bill was basically the jack-of-all-trades on the set, but that wasn't good enough. He wanted to call the shots, be number one. Being the oldest of five kids, as well the man of the house after his dad split, Bill had decided early on that the world belonged to those who stayed strong and focused.

And his focus was to make his mark as a film director.

Which meant he said no to anything that got in his way, even his best pal's business idea.

"Look," he said, lowering his voice, "if I hear of anyone wanting to start up an indie, I'll put them in touch with you, okay?"

"Not that I don't appreciate that, but my first choice will always be you."

Bill groaned. "Is this the part where I say 'We'll always have Paris'?"

Jimmie laughed, gave his pal a friendly slap on the back. "I'll stop laying on the guilt. Besides, you have better things to do. Do you know how many guys would *kill* to fill in for the director on a cattle call for babes in bikinis?"

Bill caught Mandy's wave. Next audition was ready.

"Yeah, it's a burden, but somebody's gotta do it."

He gave a go-ahead nod to Mandy, a small gesture toward a big career. People like Jim just didn't get it.

IN THE BACKSTAGE TENT provided for those auditioning to be extras, Ellie checked herself out in a mirror, amazed yet again at her transformation from a goth chick to this bad-girl blonde in a good-time bikini. Most of it thanks to Sara, who'd woken Ellie up at the crack of dawn and helped wrangle her into beach babe shape.

Ellie looked around at the other extra wannabes hanging out in the small blue tent. They'd all shown up at 7:00 a.m. to sign up, and in the hour since, they'd spent their time primping, talking and drinking the free coffee from one of several urns. Free, but disgustingly *bad*-tasting coffee, although no one except Ellie seemed to notice.

Which was the only bad thing—besides her bad-girl blond hair—about this whole adventure. Now that she was here, she was psyched to audition. It felt silly but fun to try out for a walk-on part on *Sin on the Beach*. And although it felt a little odd, it was nice to do something for herself instead of everybody else.

"Ellie Rockwell?" asked a harried teenage boy wearing a *Sin on the Beach* festival T-shirt and khaki shorts. He looked around the tent while speaking in low tones into his headset.

"Yes?"

"You're next. Follow me." He hurried away, reporting his movements to whoever was on the other end of the headset. "She's here. Yes. Ellie Rockwell. Maybe."

Maybe? What did that mean?

He held open the flap to the tent for Ellie to follow. She grabbed her bag of makeup in one hand, her bag containing her killer stilettos in the other, and followed.

They sprinted across a patch of hot sand and into another tent, this one huge, white and air-conditioned. Ellie paused, relishing the blast of cool air. The area was buzzing with people, props, equipment. In the far corner, next to a table set with rolls, fruit and drinks, a man sporting a handlebar mustache, lime-green turban and a gaudy Hawaiian shirt was pouring himself a big glass of iced tea. He looked up at Ellie and winked.

Oh, hold me back.

"You're up," the boy said, motioning toward an opening in the tent. "Walk onto the stage, head to the microphone and answer their questions. Afterward, exit stage left."

"Who's they?"

"Assistant director, casting director, maybe one of the producers."

Her stomach flip-flopped. These were the big-wigs, the muckety-mucks, the top dogs who ran her favorite show. Okay, sitting with all the extra wanna-bes, it had been easy to think this was fun and silly. But knowing who she'd be auditioning in front of, suddenly this felt freaking scary.

"Stage left?" she rasped, kicking off her sandals. She cleared her throat. "Where's that?"

"The far side of the stage."

She slipped on a stiletto. "Did you say there's a *microphone?*"

But he was already engrossed in another conversation over his headset. Catching Ellie's gaze, he impatiently pointed toward the stage and mouthed an emphatic "Go!" before zipping away.

She quickly stepped into the second stiletto, trying to ignore the little voice in her head telling her to run away, she'd only make a fool of herself, people might laugh, she could fall on her face....

Straightening, she sucked in a shaky breath. *If I can't tackle one silly audition, how do I expect to tackle a new business venture?*

She walked onto the stage.

BILL WATCHED the next girl walk hesitantly out onto the stage. She walked stiff-kneed, staring wide-eyed at the audience that was mostly made up of friends of those auditioning, some crew, a few hungover partiers. When she reached the microphone, she stopped and smiled awkwardly.

She was pretty, in a Kirsten Dunst kind of way, with her short, fluffy blond hair, dimpled smile and pert nose. The kind of girl one saw a hundred times a day in L.A.

And yet…not.

Something about her was different, but he couldn't put his finger on it. Something provocative, simmering just below the surface…

"Look at those *shoes,* man," muttered Jimmie, sitting taller in his seat.

Bill's gaze dropped down the nicely filled black bikini, down long, coltish legs to a pair of black patent stilettos with silver chains. *Whoa.* That something different was hardly below the surface, it was just below the shapely calves.

"Tell us your name, where you're from and something special about yourself," prompted Peter, the casting assistant in charge of extras, into his hand-held mike. Nearby sat Mandy, talking on her cell phone while eating a doughnut.

The young woman leaned forward, at which point Bill noticed the edge of a tattoo peeking over the top of her bikini top. A spiderweb?

She spoke so closely to the mike, it sounded like a thunderous whisper. "Ellie Rockwell."

"Step back and say your name again, please," instructed Peter.

She did. Bill liked the cadence of her voice. Soft, rhythmic like the waves.

And familiar.

She shifted from one spiked heel to the other. "I'm an L.A. girl—grew up in East L.A., currently living and working in West L.A."

A sense of déjà vu prickled his skin. He knew her. But from where? With the long hours he put in on the set these days, his only social outlet was Gold's Gym, and he'd have recalled if their paths had crossed there. Maybe it was her voice, someone he'd conversed with in the course of his too-many business calls every day.

Wait a minute.

Rockwell?

East L.A.?

Hadn't he had neighbors there, years ago, with that name? Right, now he remembered. Mrs. Rockwell, one of those fragile blondes who looked as though she'd crumble if you looked at her the wrong way, and her kids Mark—no, Matt—and a daughter. Yeah, had to be Ellie. He blew out a puff of air. That freckled, knobby-kneed girl had grown up to be this dom-shoed doll on the stage?

"Four stars," murmured Jimmie.

But ever since Jimmie tied the knot last year, he'd been irritatingly intent on setting Bill up for wedded bliss, too. Every potential Mrs. Romero got a star-rating from one—forget it—to four—go for it.

"You and your damn numbers," Bill muttered,

tapping the pencil against his clipboard. But four was dead-on as his gaze raked up past that cleavage-spilling black top to that heart-shaped face to those eyes….

He flashed on a memory from years ago. Ellie, auburn hair barely restrained in pigtails, those big questioning eyes. It had been long past midnight. He'd been sitting on the porch, contemplating his life changes to come, when suddenly he looked down and saw his young neighbor standing on the lawn in front of him. In a soft voice, she'd asked if what she'd heard was true—was he moving to New York?

She'd sounded so anxious, so sad, which had confused him. But with younger siblings, he knew how a kid's unresolved worries could be triggered by a seemingly unrelated event. If he remembered correctly, Ellie's dad had split around this time five or so years before. Another adult figure leaving probably reminded her of that all over again.

Bill had answered her yes, he was moving to New York to go to film school, and that little girls shouldn't be out so late. He'd walked her back to her house where she'd lingered in the front doorway, those big eyes staring at him, before going inside.

Those same eyes stared at him now, reeling him back to the present, and he offered a small smile of recognition. She smiled back, and he swore something in her look shifted, darkened, sparked. For a long moment, they held each other's gaze and suddenly all he was aware of was a churning tension between them, not unlike the distant crashing waves.

He'd at first observed a woman in a black bikini, but now all he saw were glistening limbs, full breasts, bare skin. Lust had fogged his brain and whatever memories he had of the girl evaporated, replaced by this hot woman.

Jimmie coughed. "Five."

"Five what?"

"That eye-lock, as though you two are the only people in this place, just bumped her from four to five stars."

"You've never given a five."

"Yeah, well, I've never seen you go brain-dead so quickly, either."

Bill broke the eye-lock and glanced at his buddy. "It's an *audition*, Jimbo, nothing more."

"Bill-o, sell *that* bridge somewhere else."

Peter lit a cigarette, blowing out a puff of smoke as he said into his mike, "You have one minute to share something special about yourself."

Ellie blinked, straightened, released a shaky breath. Over the speakers, the sound reverberated over the crowd like a throaty sigh, nearly bringing Bill to his knees.

She zeroed in on him again. Later, he pondered if he'd imagined the look she gave him, one filled with a yearning that bordered on defiance. But he didn't imagine her next words.

"I want to share this with you."

Slowly, she turned so her back was to the audience. God. Those heels worked magic on a great ass and a pair of killer legs.

"You're gnawing on your pencil," whispered Jimmie.

Bill released the eraser tip from his teeth. "Oh, shut up."

Ellie slipped her thumbs underneath the waistband of her bikini bottoms and lowered them, slowly, an inch or so. Bill ground his teeth, his entire body on edge, as he read the black-scripted tattoo at the base of her spine.

"Queen of Evil?" he rasped.

"Yeah," murmured Jimmie, "that's what it says all right."

Bill groaned.

Jimmie leaned closer. "So, is she a five?"

Bill returned his gaze to her, gave his head a slow shake. "She's more than a number, Jimmie. I share a past with her."

"ELLIE ROCKWELL."

Standing at the food table in the backstage tent quaffing a blueberry muffin, she froze. Even with her back to him, she'd know that voice anywhere. Swallowing her bite, she set down the muffin and turned.

A shiver passed through her.

Bill was even hotter up close.

His skin, naturally mocha, was darker from the sun. His full, natural hair looked like a deliciously dark aura. Stubble coarsened his jaw, making her think he'd probably rolled out of bed and come straight here for today's audition without shaving. She shouldn't have thought about him rolling out of bed, because she started wondering if he was one of those men who slept in his shorts or pajama bottoms.

Or naked.

She sucked in a shaky breath. *He's only said my name and I already have him naked in bed.*

A hint of a smile raised a corner of his mouth. She hadn't noticed before that he sported a soul patch, neatly trimmed, underneath his full bottom lip.

"Ellie Rockwell, right?"

"Bill Romero," she whispered, then cleared her throat. "I saw you in the audience."

"I thought you noticed me." He looked her up and down. "You've…changed."

"You don't know the half of it," she murmured, her gaze sliding down to the colorful tattoo that trailed from underneath his sleeve down to his elbow. Appeared to be the tail of something.

"It's a dragon," he explained.

Her gaze traveled back up the green and burnished gold scales that disappeared underneath his sleeve.

"The rest," he murmured, "goes up my arm. One claw's on my back, and its head falls across my chest."

She stared at his chest, imagining the head of the beast permanently inked on his molded pec.

"A fire-breathing, ice-breathing or acid-spitting dragon?"

"Fire." He looked surprised. "No one's ever asked me that before."

Being a good glam goth chick, she knew her dragon basics, but no way she'd admit that. Usually her attitude was if somebody didn't like her style, tough. But this was different. This was Bill Romero. He'd obviously come backstage to see the beach babe Ellie, and no way she'd let on he'd fallen for a look that was the antithesis of the real her. This was Cinderella at the ball time. The prince was flirting with her, and she was going to run with it.

"I think I saw some of those dragons when I got my Queen of Evil tattoo," she lied.

Bill made a murmur of approval. "Now *that's* a tattoo I'd like to hear more about." He glanced over her shoulder at the half-eaten muffin. "Looks like I interrupted your snack?"

She made a dismissive gesture toward it. "I'd skipped breakfast, so…"

"I skipped breakfast, too." His gaze held hers for a moment. "If I didn't have to get back, I'd suggest we grab a bite. Catch up."

Get back? She flashed back to yesterday when he'd asked if that was her car. He hadn't been dressed up either day…could he be making money parking cars? She wouldn't ask, didn't want to embarrass him. What had happened to his dreams?

"Last we saw each other," she said nonchalantly, "you were leaving for film school."

"Yeah, went to New York University." He cocked that half smile again. "Surprised you remember."

She shrugged as though, oh, sure, just one of those things that popped up from some distant memory instead of something she'd thought about a lot these past seventeen years. Everything about that night he'd told her he was moving away was burned indelibly into her brain. The moon had been full, yellow and waxy in a smoggy sky. Lavender scented the air. Down the block a radio blasted a popular Ice-T rap song.

She waited for Bill to say more, but nothing. Had he come back to L.A., armed with his degree, only to find nobody wanted to hire another starry-eyed wannabe? She'd seen a lot of people lose their dreams in the city of dreams. Actresses who thought they'd be the next Meryl Streep, writers who thought they'd be the next Eszterhas, directors who thought they'd be the next Scorsese. All of them waiting for their big breaks while serving tables or working on construction sites or...

Parking cars.

She dropped her gaze, caught the splatter of brown on his shirt. "Spill something?"

He looked down, back up with a sheepish smile. "Coffee. Actually, I took a break from my casting duties to see if I can get it out. My buddy's covering for me."

She blinked. "Casting duties?"

"Yeah." He raked a hand through his thick, full hair. "I'm just helping out, for today only."

"Part-time job?"

"More like a favor."

So things hadn't gone well. She'd get off the topic, help him save face. "I'd suggest dabbing that with soda water. If you can't find that, cold water." She smiled. "I run a coffee shop so I deal with stuff like this all the time."

"Coffee shop, eh? I'll definitely take your advice, then." But he didn't do a thing except stand there and stare at her. Was her bad-girl blonde makeover working?

"I should be getting back," he murmured.

"Sure." *Do something! Invite him to the beach house, ask him out for another cup of coffee to make up for the one he sloshed, ask his zodiac sign,* something. "Nice seeing you." *Good one, El. Your big moment and you wuss out.*

"Nice seeing you, too." He started walking away, paused. "Going to the festival later?"

"I'm entering some of the events. My girlfriends and I want to win the grand prize. You can enter as a group, you know, so that's what we're doing." *I'm babbling.* "Except for this audition. Not a group thing, obviously. We figured after I was done over as a beach babe…" *Not good. Overbabble.*

"Done over?"

She smiled shakily. "Girl talk for getting fixed up." She'd never lied this much. "I probably wouldn't have auditioned if they hadn't made me do it." At least that was the truth.

He looked her down, back up, making a zillion goose pimples skitter across her skin.

"I'm an idiot," he mumbled. He hit the palm of his hand against his forehead. "I got so caught up seeing you again, I forgot to tell you something." He smiled warmly. "It's a good thing your girlfriends talked you into auditioning, because Ellie Rockwell, you're hired."

She blinked. "I am?"

He nodded.

"*You* get to pick people?"

"Just for today. See Peter, the casting assistant who's sitting in the front row, and tell him I said you're hired. He'll explain how you're paid, where to report, stuff like that."

"Great. Thanks."

They stared at each other for another long moment.

"I need to get out there," Bill finally said.

"Right. You don't want to blow this opportunity."

He frowned.

She gestured lamely toward the audience out there. "You know, doing this casting gig you're doing as a favor could lead to another job."

He looked surprised, then sputtered a laugh. "I already have a job on *Sin on the Beach*. I'm the first assistant director."

Her body felt as though a shock wave had passed through it. Not unlike how she'd felt years ago at a high-decibel, sensory-overload Marilyn Manson concert. Bill wasn't some dreamy-eyed wannabe, he was the first assistant *director*. Of *Sin on the Beach*.

A Big Man on the Set. He probably had bikini-clad chicky-babes hanging all over him 24/7.

So what if he came backstage to tell her she was hired, tell her he remembered her, there was no way such a hotshot would want anything more to do with an extra.

Bill scrubbed his knuckle over his chin. "A lot of those festival competitions require two people to compete."

She nodded.

"Might be a little awkward to enter some of those with your girlfriends…unless you're into that sort of thing."

It took her a moment to get his drift.

"You think I'm— Oh, no." She laughed at the thought of her being lesbo with Candy or Sara. "Not that they aren't attractive and fascinating women, but I'm not into that. Anyway, they both appear to have guys they're entering the contests with."

"And you don't?"

"No."

"How terrible." He gave her a look that made her kneecaps go soft.

"Yes," she murmured, "downright horrible."

He grinned, glanced at his watch. "After auditions, I'll have the rest of the day off. Meet me backstage, same spot, at two o'clock and I'll be your partner."

It took a moment for the adrenaline rush to subside before she remembered how to nod yes. *Partner.* That had to be on par with "date," right?

She was having a date with Bill Romero.

Bill take-my-heart-and-do-me-all-night-long Romero.

As long as she got home before her carriage turned into a pumpkin, and her bikini into her glam goth T-shirt, this could be a fairy-tale date to die for.

"Two it is," she whispered.

3

ELLIE WAS TOO PUNCTUAL for her own good. Not that being on time was a bad thing, but it was when you were overly anxious to see the guy of your childhood dreams, who happened to *not* be punctual. Back-stage again at the food table, she nibbled on grapes and hoped she looked okay in her red bikini, fishnet cover-up, retro polka-dot wedges and over-the-shoulder mini brocade purse. When she'd left the beach house, she'd felt fine, but after passing dozens of girls in Easter-egg color bikinis and nondescript sandals, she was starting to wonder if she looked too over-the-top.

That she, a glam goth diva, was actually *fretting* about looking over-the-top suddenly made her laugh. Back at her apartment, her entire wardrobe was a swirl of purple, black and red satins and laces. This beach babe makeover was frying her brain. Next she'd be buying frosted pink lipstick, eating granola and saying "dude."

"Hey, how's my Ellie?" said a familiar, deep voice. Bill.

Her heart thumped a wanton, pagan beat.

My Ellie. She lost the ability to speak for a moment. "Great." *My Bill.*

He looked effing incredible. That mocha skin, those brown eyes, that windblown black 'fro—colors so rich and dark, they made her insides quiver.

Maybe it was because of the canvas tent, but the light seemed pale and ephemeral. Summer heat shimmered in the air, hot and intangible. And in the midst of it all stood Bill, like a chocolatey, rough-edged hip-hop prince. Wild on the outside, in control on the inside.

The moment was broken when a girl, who looked to be around nineteen, bounded up and tapped Bill on the arm. She wore short-shorts, a halter top, her shiny blond hair tied back in a ponytail. Daisy Mae's long-lost twin, no doubt.

The girl looked up at Bill with round liquid-blue eyes and smiled.

"Curtiss is having some problems with the boom mike for tomorrow morning's shoot," she said in a baby-doll voice. "He wanted me to tell you he's picking up a new one today as backup."

"Thanks." Bill nodded, turned his attention back to Ellie.

But Daisy Baby-Doll didn't leave. "I'm the new PA. Name's Phoebe."

Bill looked at her. "Hi, Phoebe."

"Actually, my name's Diane, but that's so boring, so a few years ago I started calling myself Phoebe, and now everybody remembers me!"

Ellie had a feeling she knew why.

"Well, Phoebe," said Bill, "nice meeting you—"

"If you ever need anything…" she said, her voice trailing off.

Like it was so hard to guess what that *anything* might be. To stop herself from saying something she might regret, Ellie stuffed a grape into her mouth.

Of course, women had always loved Bill, and he'd loved his share back. She had many memories watching him from her living room window while he laughed and flirted with the girls on the block. Even back then, he had that certain something that attracted the opposite sex in droves. Call it confidence, charm or being blessed with more than his share of pheromones, but the guy had *it*.

Bill glanced at Ellie, back to Phoebe. "Look, I'm taking a meeting here…."

Taking a meeting? This wasn't a date? Ellie shoved another grape in her mouth.

Phoebe rolled back her shoulders, which made her breasts stick out even more, and plastered on a smile. "Well, Bill, see you around the set."

She'd barely bounced away before a tall, preppie-looking guy sidled up to Bill. "Man, you should be bottled."

"Behave." Bill turned to Ellie. "This is my main man, Jimmie," he said. "We met on our first day at NYU. I was the tough guy from East L.A. Jimmie was the class act from Connecticut. I decided to like him anyway."

She smiled while swallowing the grape, which felt like a chunk of lead going down her throat. "Nice to meet you, Jimmie."

"This is Ellie Belle," said Bill. He slung his arm around his friend's shoulders. "He taught me how to order wine, and I taught him how to siphon gas."

But she was still back at Ellie Belle. Nobody had called her that in years. It had been her dad's nickname for her, one her mom had occasionally used after her dad left, but nobody had used it since. Not even Matt. Had Bill overheard one of her parents and, all these years later, remembered?

Jimmie extended his hand, which she took. "And after that eloquent introduction, let me say it's very nice to meet you."

"Nice to meet you, too." They shook hands.

"Heard you two were next-door neighbors years ago."

"That's right."

"No offense, but you sure don't look like someone from the hood."

"Well, we don't normally wear bikinis with fish-net cover-ups there."

Jimmie looked surprised, then laughed. "I, uh, didn't mean that."

"Sorry, I knew what you meant." She'd heard comments like that plenty of times, mostly from people who'd rarely, if ever, been to the hood. She used to take offense, then realized what mattered more than a person's question was the intention behind it. Jimmie, despite his Brooks Brothers appearance and precise diction, had a sincere streak.

"Actually, when my mom and her mother moved there in the late fifties, there were families in that neighborhood straight out of *Father Knows Best.* The melting pot started getting stirred more during the seventies." She'd skip over what everyone knew—that the area grew economically depressed, gangs arrived, street crime mushroomed and that's when things could get dicey if you didn't already have your friends and community in place, which the Rockwells did. "The hood's changing for the better these days, though."

Bill made a disgruntled noise.

"It's true. Homes are being renovated, new businesses are moving in—"

"C'mon, Ellie, nobody *really* cares about our old stomping ground. The powers that be wrote off that part of L.A. a long time ago. I, for one, will never go back."

"Can't turn your back on your roots," Jimmie said to Bill. "Don't you still have family there?"

"Those who stayed deserved what they got."

Ellie bit the inside of her lip. She didn't like hearing his negativity, but she had to remember how Bill, like Matt, had taken on the role of man of the house at an early age. Except Bill had had four younger siblings, which hadn't been easy.

Jimmie, obviously picking up on the heavy vibes, changed the subject. "Those are some shoes." He nudged his head toward her feet.

"They're retro sling back wedgies," she said,

tipping the toe of red-and-white polka-dot sandals this way, then that. "Got them at Sinister Shoes."

Bill gave her a funny look. "Sinister Shoes?"

"I've heard of that place," said Jimmie. "It's down on Melrose. All the goths go there to shop."

"Goths." Bill shook his head. "Elvira's cool, but I don't get that whole vampire thing. They all seem depressed or something."

Her insides shrank a little. Made her feel like a fake and a liar pretending not to be one of those into *that whole vampire thing.* It was really about loving the darkness, the mystery in life, but she didn't want to explain.

All she wanted was this day, this experience with Bill, and for that she was willing to pretend she was somebody she wasn't.

She angled her leg, showing off. "These shoes are really more of a retro pinup look," she said a little too gaily. "Similar to what Betty Grable wore in those World War II posters."

Bill and Jimmie stared at her.

"Betty Grable?" Bill finally said. "She was a movie star *way* before your time."

"I've always loved the Golden Age of Hollywood, even as a little kid. I sometimes envision the stars like Audrey Hepburn, Veronica Lake, Betty Grable when I design some of my clothes." When they looked at her black fishnet cover-up over her red bikini, she added drolly, "These aren't my designs. I bought them at Target."

A grin sauntered across Bill's lips. "You did a lot of sewing as a kid, didn't you? I think my mom said something about it once."

She nodded, feeling a little giddy that he'd remembered something else about her as a child. Maybe she'd been more memorable than she'd given herself credit for.

"Hollywood's Golden Era is one of my favorites," he continued. "It spawned dozens of classic westerns, comedies and thrillers. Plus, it was the birthplace of film noir."

"Watch out, Bill," Jimmie teased, "your cinematic-nerd side's showing." He glanced at his flashy gold watch. "Gotta split. Told Bev I'd take her to the festival, play some of those games. She's hot about trying to win some grand prize cabin."

"Beach bungalow," corrected Ellie.

Jimmie nodded. "Yeah, that's right. I guess the winner gets a free rental there for the next two years."

"Ten," she corrected again. She hadn't realized she'd been so into it until this moment. Sure, she'd been willing to be Team Java Mammas with the girls, but she hadn't been *personally* driven to win anything other than the audition until this moment. Had to be the thought of hanging out with Bill for the rest of the afternoon, doing fun, wild things in some of those hot games.

And, if all went well, even more wild things afterward.

What Happens in Malibu Stays in Malibu.

"Ten, eh?" Jimmie gave a low whistle. "Now I'm glad I gave in and said yes to Bev." He snagged a cookie off the food table. "What time does the shoot start tomorrow?" he asked Bill.

"Five a.m. sharp. We need the rising sun in the background for that first shot."

Jimmie groaned. "Whoever said showbiz is glamorous needs their head checked." He pointed at his pal. "Watch out for that guy," he said to Ellie as he headed toward the tent opening.

Wouldn't Bill be surprised to know she'd been watching out for him for a long, long time.

After Jimmie left, Bill stared at Ellie, trying not to think how drop-dead sexy that fishnet cover-thing was over that red bikini. Very teasing. Very exciting.

Both of which were Ellie right now. All grown-up and hot and retro sexy in that peekaboo red bikini and matching shoes. Enough to make a man howl at the moon.

"What're you thinking about?" she asked.

With another woman, he might have said. But with Ellie…well, it was different. He wasn't exactly sure why, just knew he felt more protective. Of her, certainly. But also of their past. As though that bubble of time so long ago was more fragile than he'd realized.

"Hungry?" he asked.

"Famished."

"Me, too." He guided her toward the tent opening, his arm comfortably around her shoulders, their steps in sync. "Let's go to the festival and get some chow."

Ellie felt as though they'd walked this way a hundred times. His arm rested so easily around her, the side of his body seemed to fit perfectly against her. Muscles against curves, hard into soft.

When he leaned his head down, she caught a whiff of his cologne—cinnamon and musk—and nearly swooned at the rich, dark scent. Someone had once told her cinnamon was an aphrodisiac, and if she didn't believe it before, she sure did now.

"Something about you, Ellie," he murmured, his breath hot against her cheek.

She waited, but he didn't finish the thought. Even if he had, she doubted she'd have been able to stay focused and hear the words because she was caught up in sensations. His breath caressing her cheek, his thigh rubbing seductively against hers as they walked, that cinnamon scent shooting straight to the pleasure center of her brain.

They headed out into the blinding sunshine. The sand sank underneath her feet and she stumbled slightly.

"It's those sinister shoes," teased Bill, helping her regain her balance.

"I wasn't sure what to wear at the beach," she murmured.

"Coulda fooled me." He gave her an appreciative once-over, which gave her no small thrill.

She plastered on her best beach-babe smile, although she felt like a total fake. Except for the shoes. And the fishnet. And the tattoos, of course.

And how she felt every time she was near him. Those feelings were as deep and real as they'd been when she was a girl.

They faced each other, the heat from the sun pouring down on them. In the distance, waves thundered against the shoreline. A couple of teenagers walked past, carrying umbrellas, towels and a radio that was blasting Sheryl Crow singing how she just wanted to have some fun.

So did Ellie. She'd started out telling herself this week was about chilling, then about winning points and being on her favorite show. But now all that paled to what she really wanted—to be with Bill and have fun. The kind of no-regrets, go-for-it fun she never allowed herself. Now was the perfect time to indulge herself.

And he was the perfect man to indulge herself with.

Everything would be great, too, as long as she kept up the facade, never let on that she lived in that depressing vampire world where he assumed goths resided. From what she'd gleaned, this was his only afternoon off, so she didn't have to keep that facade up for long anyway. A few hours, hopefully more. Not a daunting task.

Although the thought of saying goodbye again was.

"Something wrong?" he asked, concern filling his eyes.

She glanced at the coffee stain. "It's probably set by now. Too late to get it out."

"Now, now, Ellie, so pessimistic," he kidded, lightly rubbing her back.

She could feel the heat from his hand through the open spaces in the fishnet, warm and liquid against the bareness of her back. His touch was light, confident, exciting.

"We have bigger things to worry about than a coffee stain." He took her hand and started walking toward the festival. "Like what should we order for lunch?"

It'd been seventeen years since her maddening childhood crush. Seventeen years of remembering and fantasizing about Bill, and now all those memories and dreams and girlish yearnings coalesced into this single afternoon. If she ever had the opportunity to live in the moment, this was it. To revel in each moment, each minute, each hour.

Even if what happened in Malibu stayed in Malibu, she'd have the memories of this afternoon for the rest of her life.

4

GOING TO THE FESTIVAL was one thing.

Getting inside was another.

Ellie stood on the beach, the afternoon sun hot on her skin, her sweaty hand in Bill's, staring down the imposing-looking man blocking the festival side entrance. His size put him in the sumo wrestler league, and that patch over his eye gave him a Captain Barbossa in *Pirates of the Caribbean* look. If that combo wasn't bad enough, the words "You Lookin' at Me?" emblazoned on his tank top indicated either he had a rampant paranoia streak, or she would any moment.

"Go on in," murmured Bill, giving her hand a tug.

Digging her wedgies into the sand, she rasped, "Yeah, right, I've always wanted to die in Malibu."

"C'mon, Ellie. Thought you were hungry."

She averted her gaze in case Captain Sumo thought she was lookin' at him. "Can't we go in the main entrance?"

His eyebrows pressed together. "What's wrong with this one?"

"Like you need to ask."

With a low, throaty chuckle, he leaned his face close to hers. "I refuse to believe," he murmured, "that anyone who wears a Queen of Evil tattoo is afraid of walking past one itty-bitty security guard."

"Itty-bitty?" She blinked. "You've obviously been out in the sun too long."

He squeezed her hand. "Trust me on this, Ellie."

When they reached the guard, Bill paused, nodded a greeting. "How's it going, Sam?"

"It's cool, Bill."

"Mind if we go in?"

"You're the man." Sam stepped aside, motioned for them to enter.

They stepped inside a small tented area, the air cooled with the help of several rotating fans. Ellie stopped, brushed a strand of damp hair off her forehead. "So you two know each other."

"He's one of the security guys on the *Sin on the Beach* set."

"And you couldn't have shared that while I was freaking out?"

A rakish grin spread across his face. "Maybe I wanted to look big and bad in your eyes."

"Aren't you the macho one," she said with dry sarcasm.

"And you love it."

God help her, she did, even if she didn't want to give him the satisfaction of admitting it. She looked around the area, set up with folding chairs, coolers packed with ice and drinks, tables on which sat several monitors projecting black-and-white images of the festival. A buffed guy in shorts and a tank top with the word Security on its back sat viewing one of the monitors. He nodded hello to Bill, went back to his work.

"I feel like I'm with the in crowd," Ellie said, watching a group of people playing volleyball on one of the monitors. Maybe it was her imagination, but that brunette woman spiking the ball looked a lot like Candy.

"I know these guys from the *Sin on the Beach* set, where they work our security. I didn't know that was their special entrance, though." He looked over at the cooler. "Want a soda?"

"Should we—" But he was already heading over. Just like Bill to do what he wanted, screw the rules.

Watching him walk away made *her* forget any rules, too, as she admired the view. Broad, muscled back that narrowed to a fit waist. Great buns that shifted and moved under those khaki shorts. He had a bit of a bowlegged walk, like a cowboy, which made her smile. Unlike a cowboy, his legs were bare so she could see how compact and muscled they were.

She imagined gliding her palms down that muscled back, over that hard behind, around to his front where she'd dawdle…tease…explore….

He turned and she jerked her gaze up to his.

A slow, knowing grin danced across his face.

Caught. Well, so what? He'd probably seen plenty of women doing the same thing.

"Here you go," he said a moment later as he handed her a cold can of pop. "And dig this. Meat loaf sandwiches. I helped us to one." He handed a half to her. "Have a seat, relax." He leaned against a table and started munching.

She looked over her shoulder. "Should we—"

He motioned for her to sit, giving her a knowing nod as he ate.

She did, realizing she was doing that good-girl, what-are-the-rules thing again, which would never go over with a guy like Bill, who claimed his territory on the fly. Reminded her of the boys back in the hood and their power plays over turf—be it a porch, a street corner, a park. She wondered if Bill realized how, despite his so-called new life, he was still a boy in the hood.

For the next few minutes, they ate and drank in silence.

"This is delicious," she said, finishing a bite.

"You make meat loaf?"

She rolled her eyes. "Too busy. The only thing I make is coffee. You?"

"I make the best sandwiches this side of New York."

"Humble, aren't you?"

He grinned. "I prefer to call it truthful."

The guy watching the monitors had flipped on a portable radio to an oldies but goodies station. The upbeat, sexy song, "Walk on the Wild Side," started playing. Same tune she'd downloaded for her ringtone. Perfect background music for sneaking glances at Bill's mouth as he nibbled and chewed, at his tongue as it flicked against his drink. She had no doubt he could do incredible things with that mouth in bed, too....

He lowered his soda. "Who's singing this song?"

"Lou Reed."

"That glam rock, punk guy?"

She heard the disdain in his voice, which put her off a bit. Not that Bill should like the things she liked, it was that he sounded so judgmental.

"That's old news," she said, not meaning to say it so sharply, or maybe she did. "These days, he's respected for his songwriting, electronic music, even his style of rock and roll."

He tapped his finger against the side of his drink. "I offended you."

"Yes." She shrugged. "You sounded critical."

He stuffed the last bite of his sandwich into his mouth. After finishing, he said, "You're honest. I like that. I'm honest, too, sometimes to a fault, but I like to be a man of my word, you know?"

Great. He revered honesty, and before him sat a woman whose very appearance was a lie. She took a sip of her drink, avoiding his eyes.

"I'm also a music dunce," he continued. "I'll listen to tunes when I want to quiet my mind or relax, but—" he shook his head "—it irritates me otherwise. Probably because I heard rap day and night back in the hood. It was like crackling static that never went away. Songs about violence and sex and killing cops. I hated it. Ruined my appreciation for other kinds of music, I guess."

She remembered hearing rap when she was outside, but her world inside her bedroom was a sanctuary of what she liked—be it books or listening to Lou Reed or painting lyrics on her ceiling to her mother's annoyance. "Shame that happened. Music has often been my greatest solace."

"Lucky you."

For a moment they stared at each other, the sounds of the festival receding into the background, leaving the two of them suspended in a time capsule that encompassed the past and the present. She still saw the boy she'd been so crazy about, dark and handsome with a head full of dreams. But she also saw the man he'd become. Tougher, more cynical. A man who'd lost an appreciation of something as sweet and healing as music because he couldn't get past the grating static of his past.

She'd never imagined being with him again wouldn't be perfect. Of course, she was pitting her girlhood fantasies—which were always perfect—against the woman's newfound reality. And what she was learning was that for all the glowing feelings she experienced around Bill, there were also the darker ones.

Were they so dark she didn't want to stay? Because it'd be easy to make a lame excuse, walk away, dust her hands of the childhood fantasy.

She watched as he picked up their trash and tossed it in a receptacle, called out a thanks to Sam, patted the back of the guy who was still watching the monitors. Funny. For all his toughness, he was a caretaker. Just like her.

"Ready?" he said.

"For what?"

"For whatever's out there, of course." He gestured toward the tent opening that led to the festival.

Whoever said life had no guarantees should have added it would always have its fair share of confusion, too. Sometimes all that mattered was making a choice and hoping you made the right one. Okay, so he wasn't the boy of her childhood dreams; she wasn't the girl who'd dreamed them, either.

She took his hand, ready for whatever happened next.

A FEW MOMENTS LATER, they were walking down the midway. It was midafternoon, but the sun was still broiling as though it were high noon. Girls in bikinis and guys in shorts roamed the midway. Coconut-scented suntan lotion competed with the tangy salt air. Barkers and carnies pitched rides and games against a background of calliopes.

Bill interlaced his fingers with hers as he steered her through the crowd. Maybe because she typically dated more artistic types, or because she was accustomed to running her own business, she wasn't used to a guy taking the lead. She had to admit, though, that she liked his take-control attitude as he wove through the crowd, sometimes sheltering her past groups of partiers, other times hugging her close for no apparent reason.

Like she needed one.

"Hey you! Ms. Smoke and Fire! Black fishnet over the red bikini!"

"Is somebody talking to me?" asked Ellie, slowing down.

"That's right, I'm talking to you and that guy with the gravy stain on his shirt."

Bill laughed. "Talking to both of us, it appears."

They looked over at a small stage, on which stood the fellow in lime-green turban and loud Hawaiian shirt she'd seen earlier backstage at the audition.

"Yes, I'm talking to you." He eagerly waved them over. "Step this way."

Bill looked at Ellie. "You game?"

She looked at the sign over the stage. Magellan the All-Knowing. Although she'd always wanted to have a real supernatural experience, she'd never envisioned that might happen with a loudmouthed carnie at a beach festival.

"I don't know," she murmured.

"Maybe we'll win something."

"Don't be afraid," the man, who had to be Magellan, called out. "All that stands between fear and outcome is courage, my friends, courage!" He looked at the audience. "Right?"

The crowd started whistling and yelling.

"Courage, dudes, courage!"

"Don't be afraid!"

"Show your game!"

"We could have a mob scene if we don't do this," muttered Bill, taking Ellie's hand. "You down for this?"

"No tricks, nothing up my sleeve," continued Magellan, lifting the short sleeve of his shirt. He gestured to his turban. "Just the insights of my mind into your lives, and the mysteries I will foretell."

She squeezed Bill's hand. "What the hell? Let's go."

As they approached, people started whistling, slapping high-fives into the air. One guy, who looked as though he'd spent the better part of the day imbibing, gave a loud whoop.

"Wonderful, wonderful!" called out Magellan, welcoming them with open arms. "Come up here and stand next to me so I can read your vibes. Everyone, give these brave people a hand."

As the audience applauded, Magellan fumbled with the clip on the microphone, finally releasing it from his shirt. He held it toward Ellie. "Your name?"

"Ellie."

"Here on vacation?" This close, she noticed his handlebar mustache jiggled as he spoke.

"Yes."

"Funny, that's exactly what I was going to say!" People laughed. "Here with your husband?"

She felt heat crawl up her neck. "No."

Magellan gave the crowd a sly look. "Don't worry, your secret's safe with us." He looked back at Ellie, stared intently into her eyes. "With friends?"

"Yes."

"One of them is sweet like candy on—" he closed his eyes, then reopened them "—your cousin?"

Not cousin, her brother...but close enough to make her wonder if this guy might be the real thing. Maybe he really could tap into another dimension, understand secrets hidden from the ordinary eye....

Or Candy had already been up here today and blabbed about Ellie or Matt.

So much for other dimensions and hidden secrets.

"Something like that," Ellie said.

Magellan turned to Bill. "Your name?"

"Bill."

"Exactly what I was going to say!" The crowd laughed again, obviously enjoying the pretense of Magellan knowing all.

"So, tell us, Ellie and Bill, are you enjoying the festival?"

"Yes."

He stepped closer and peered into her face, as though reading her. Feeling a tad uncomfortable, she averted her gaze to his hands and a sparkling blue ring on his pinkie. Sapphire, she guessed.

"Yes," he whispered, "it's the stone of destiny."

Had he heard her thoughts?

She looked up, but Magellan was busy talking to the audience again, the blue stone sparkling with his gestures. He'd probably seen her looking at it, passed on the tidbit that it was the stone of destiny. Hardly a supernatural experience.

"So, Bill," Magellan said, "are you ready to play our game?"

"Depends."

"Ah!" Magellan made a swirling motion with his fingers again, reminiscent of an actor in a melodrama. "You're not one to believe in life's mysteries, and yet, deep down, you're curious if what is mystical and unseen might in fact be real."

"Not really."

The crowd laughed again.

"We'll see about that," said Magellan, taking a few steps away in his flip-flops. The guy was a mix of Jimmy Buffett and the Wizard of Oz. Too much.

"Time to play Truth or…Bare!" he announced to the crowd. "Which is a variation of Truth or Dare in honor of this very sexy *Sin on the Beach* festival."

Bill squeezed Ellie's hand. "Fasten your seat belt," he murmured, "'cause we're on the ride now."

"Ready?" Magellan asked them.

"Ready," they answered in unison.

"Wonderful." He closed his eyes, although she swore he was peeking out of one of them, and raised a forefinger to his turban as though summoning his powers. "I'm now calling on my spirit guides to reveal a secret about each of you. If I'm wrong—I mean, if my guides have erred—"

The crowd laughed.

"As I was saying, if my guides have erred, you earn fifty festival points as well as free tickets for rides." He reached into the air and—presto!—a string of tickets appeared.

Gasps from the crowd.

"However, if my spirit guides are right, which they usually are—" he looked over at Ellie and Bill "—that person must remove an item of clothing. Not a necklace, earring, ring, hat, belt, shoestring, sock or contact lens, but something major. We're talking the *bare* part of Truth or Bare, my brave friends."

Whoops and clapping.

She glanced at Bill, imagining what she'd like him to take off, first. Considering they were in public, his shirt would do.

But if they were alone...

"Ahem," Magellan said loudly into his microphone.

She looked over at him.

"The spirit guides say 'naughty, naughty'!"

Even she had to laugh. Psychic insight? Nah. He'd caught her checking out Bill, every wanton little thought written all over her face.

Magellan turned dramatically solemn. "It's time for the spirits to speak."

As he put his palms together at his heart level, a flutter of flutes and harps swelled. She figured he'd touched some wireless remote hidden in his breast pocket that triggered the music. She wondered what other buttons he had hidden on his body, and what those might do.

Magellan nodded as though listening to someone speaking. Finally, he opened his eyes and put a hand on each of their shoulders. The music rose, the notes twirling higher and higher…

Then abruptly stopped.

"They've spoken," Magellan said dramatically. "To you, Bill."

A woman in the crowd shrieked.

"She's not my spirit guide, by the way," Magellan said under his breath, the aside accidentally on purpose muttered directly into the microphone. The crowd ate it up, laughing and clapping.

"The spirits have a riddle for you, Bill. Listen carefully. What has roots nobody sees, is taller than trees, its virtues it sows and yet never grows?"

Bill's eyebrows shot up in surprise. "They said all that?"

Magellan shrugged. "They're a little wordy sometimes. They say when you find the answer, you'll also find your destiny. But so you can play Truth or Bare, they also told me a secret. Yes or no. Your friend, they say, based a character in a story on you?"

Bill blinked, nodded. "That's right. No way you could have checked that on the Internet. Awesome trick, man."

"No trick, my friend. I'm merely a vessel for the spirit guides. So, what item of clothing will it be, Bill?"

He tapped the stain on his shirt. "I've been meaning to take this off ever since I spilled coffee on it this morning, so…" He grabbed the end of the polo shirt and tugged it over his head.

A thrill zigzagged through Ellie as she stared at his chest. His muscled, brown and deliciously hairy chest.

But it was the tattoo that made her blood run molten.

The dragon's mighty torso, a marvel of blues and greens, crested over Bill's shoulder, its reptilian head lying seductively across the pec, flames of fire shooting across his breastbone.

Women in the audience went nuts. Ellie hadn't heard that much screaming since her girlfriend's bachelorette party, the night she lost fifty dollars tipping a male stripper named Robby Rawhide.

"Your turn," said Magellan, facing her.

With some difficulty, she tore her gaze off Bill. "Shoot," she rasped.

"The spirits say your age is twenty-nine."

Pause. "That's it? A number?"

Magellan nodded.

She felt slighted. Bill got the riddle, then the insight about being the model for a character. And the spirits only guessed her age?

Which was correct, but too easy. Oh, yeah, definitely the work of Candy, the marketing whiz. She'd probably left a few tidbits about Ellie and Sara with Magellan to boost Team Java Mamma's chance of winning. Maybe someone on *Sin on the Beach* had

done something similar—left a cheat sheet with
Magellan, giving names, descriptions, a few planted
facts about people who worked on the show. It made
Magellan look good, boosted attendance at his performances, which in turn raked in money for *Sin on
the Beach.* A win-win all the way around.

Darn. She'd so hoped for something really supernatural, but it appeared Magellan was just a carnie
with connections.

"Yes, I'm twenty-nine."

Applause.

Magellan made a grand flourish. "Choose a piece
of clothing."

A no-brainer. Her fishnet cover-up. She slipped it
off to much clapping and whistles. She caught Bill's
approving look, which pleased her.

She glanced at his shorts, he glanced at her top.
Those would be the next pieces to go. An idea she
liked. A lot. Just not *here.*

"I'm getting another message from the guides,"
announced Magellan.

"Uh," said Ellie, not wanting to hang here any
longer, "tell them thanks but no thanks?"

Bill chuckled. "C'mon, Ellie. We don't want to
hurt their feelings."

Magellan, his forefinger pressed against his turban like some kind of divining rod, closed his eyes.
"They're speaking…. Okay, here's the message. Cinderella doesn't make it home before midnight, but
that's not the end of her story."

The hairs tingled on the back of her neck. She'd thought of Cinderella and her prince an hour or so ago…one of those funny thoughts that flits in and out of one's head…but how odd to hear Magellan reference Cinderella, too.

"Is that my riddle?" she asked quietly.

Magellan gave her such a focused look, she swore he could read every thought she'd ever had.

"No," he finally said, "it's more of an insight. But because it wasn't a question that can be answered, you win the prize and the points." A festival ride ticket materialized in his hand, which he handed to Ellie along with a voucher for points.

As they walked back into the crowd, Bill hugged her close against his side. "Way to go, Ellie. You've won points at the audition, and now Truth or Bare!"

"Yeah, it's great." But she didn't feel as exuberant as she sounded because now she had Cinderella on the brain. Everybody knew it wasn't until the very end of the story that Cinderella didn't make it home by midnight….

Didn't the story pretty much end there?

5

SEVERAL HOURS LATER, Ellie and Bill had ridden the merry-go-round, gotten dizzy on the Tilt-A-Whirl, slipped and laughed down the gigantic blow-up slide. They'd watched people play volleyball, bowl with coconuts and jiggle and bounce on a community-size trampoline. Ellie had tried her luck at the ring toss and Bill had tested his strength swinging the mallet at the Hi-Striker.

After all that, they were content to simply walk hand in hand down the midway, sipping their lemonades. Bill wore his shirt tied around his waist, Ellie's fishnet cover-up draped over his shoulder, items of clothing they hadn't put back on since Truth or Bare.

He stopped and looked at her. "You'll probably think this sounds crazy, because I see bodies in bikinis all day long." He pulled her cover-up off his shoulder and held it up. "But seeing yours through a sexy fishnet..." He blew out a pent-up breath. "Well, it makes it extra sexy."

"Hold my drink," she said, handing hers to him.

The speed with which she took the fishnet out of his hands made him laugh.

"You want it," she said with a smile, "you got it." She slithered into it, wriggling this way and that, which only added to the heat he'd been feeling ever since she strolled onto the stage this morning.

Those big turquoise eyes glistened as she looked at him, and suddenly he recalled those same big eyes from many years ago as a much younger Ellie asked if it was true…was he really moving away to New York?

He remembered how he'd felt that summer when he was eighteen, so damn anxious to move away and be on his own, it was all he could do to stay put. Once he'd landed in New York, he'd sworn never to go back. And he'd kept his word. His mom and sisters had occasionally visited him, but he'd never returned. In fact, until today, he'd rarely thought of the hood.

Yet spending time with Ellie had brought back memories—too many memories—of where they'd grown up. It brought back the memories of gunshots and kids dealing drugs and rap music and…

Then there was the resurrected memory of a young girl who'd lived next door, all gangly and wide-eyed and interested in the fate of a boy she barely knew.

That girl had been sweet, but the rest of the memories were sour. Getting closer to her didn't mean getting closer to the rest of his past. Or did it?

"What is it?" Ellie asked.

He played with the fishnet, slipping his fingers

through the diamond-shaped knit, feeling as tangled up in his emotions as he did in the threads. He dug her, was more drawn to and excited by her than he'd been to a woman in a long time, and yet...

She frowned slightly as she studied his face. "Are you feeling ill?"

He almost laughed, more at his own mishmash of thoughts than her question. He looked around at the crowd of people, some laughing, some eating, others kissing....

"This isn't the place," he said quietly.

"For what?"

He knew what he was about to say would come out sounding harsh, but he didn't have a choice. Better to say it now, before things went further.

"This afternoon's been great, but..."

"But..."

"I can't do this."

"This meaning...*me?*"

He nodded. Emotion filled her eyes and he went from feeling like a jerk to feeling like a rat.

"You can't spend any more time with me," she clarified, keeping her voice level.

He released a slow breath. "Right."

Her chin quivered, but just when he thought she might crumble, she gave him such a long, judicious look, he realized he was dealing with a woman who might look soft, but could be tough-minded when necessary.

"I was confused about you, too," she said simply.

In the distance, wheezy calliope music and the clang, clang, clang of a bell scraped against his nerves.

"Want to share why?" he finally asked, hearing his defensiveness and telling himself it wasn't because his male ego had just been dinged.

"You first."

He puffed out a breath. "Great, put me on the spot."

"You started it."

"I did." He belatedly realized his fingers were still enmeshed in her fishnet cover-up. He looked down the peekaboo crisscross pattern, past it at her plump breasts, the taut tummy, those nicely shaped legs. "Oh, yes, I did start this, didn't I…."

He dragged his gaze back to hers. In a low, rough voice, he murmured, "It's not that you're not so hot I couldn't lay you right here."

Her eyes widened, the pupils dark. "Wow," she murmured, "you'd like to do me right here and now, but you can't spend any more time with me."

"I'm not *that* callous, Ellie."

"No, just full of yourself."

He looked behind them at a bench next to a taco truck. "Look, this conversation is weird enough without us standing in the midway surrounded by dozens of beach partygoers. Want to sit down?"

"Sure."

A few moments later, they sat next to each other on the bench. Scents of fried onions and spices saturated the air. Across the way, people were lining up for a limbo contest.

"It's been such a nice day," Ellie finally said, "how about we bypass the heavy conversation, agree we can't do this, and enjoy the next few minutes."

He suddenly felt hollow. "All right," he said quietly.

She gestured at the noisy, crowded midway. "Reminds me of that old movie *Carnival Story.*"

"Anne Baxter, nineteen-fifty-four. Not too many people remember that film."

He'd never dated a woman who liked the Golden Age of Hollywood, not with any depth anyway. Most actresses equated those years with Marilyn Monroe, not with films or lesser-known actors of substance.

"Look at that guy." Ellie pointed at a middle-aged, round-faced man walking down the midway with a tray loaded with baked items. "Reminds me of the bakers who'd bring their pastries to the festivals on Olvera Street, near where we lived. Oh, I can almost taste them now—what were they called?"

In East L.A., Olvera, with its cobblestone, pedestrian-only street, was famous for its multicultural festivals and celebrations, from Cinco de Mayo to Christmas to the Chinese New Year.

"*Pan dulce,*" he said, the memory of the Mexican sweet breads making his mouth water. "Remember how they'd stick to the roof of your mouth?

"Yes. Remember the Christmas Eve procession?" asked Ellie. "Afterward, there'd be several hundred kids breaking piñatas and scrambling for candy."

He nodded, remembering his siblings laughing

and grabbing candy while he, big brother and man of the house, watched over them. He didn't want to be lured into the memories, didn't want to look back, but that was like not wanting to swim with the tide. The pull was too strong.

"I especially liked the Ferris wheel. Even though I got kicked off it more than I got to actually ride it." He shook his head, remembering some of the dumb stunts he pulled. "It's been years since I've been on one."

"Sometimes people would wear costumes, too."

"A lot of those people just *looked* like they were wearing costumes." He made a disapproving noise. "Some of the girls wore so much makeup and tats, they looked like they should be in the band KISS!" He laughed.

"My favorite celebration," said Ellie, "was the Dia de Los Muertos. That's how it's pronounced, right?"

"You said it just like a homie, *chiquita.*" Dia de Los Muertos. Day of the Dead. The Mexican celebration to honor those no longer living.

For a moment, the crush of people and sounds and scents were almost like the festivals of years ago... almost. Some people in his past were no longer living, and even though he thought of them, he'd done little to honor them. An old shame bubbled up that he'd tried to bury so many times.

"So," Ellie said, "what is it you wanted to talk about?"

"Bill!" squealed a female voice.

Phoebe, aka Diane, wiggled up to them wearing a white bikini that was barely legal.

"Fiona," said Bill.

Her smiled drooped. "Phoebe."

"Right," he muttered, scratching a spot on his chin.

Ellie wished she and Bill were standing because from their seated perspective, they had a ringside seat to Phoebe's bodacious mounds that threatened to spill right out of her top.

Phoebe glanced at Ellie, back to Bill. "Having another meeting?"

"No."

"Good," she said, batting her eyes. "Because I have a problem and was hoping you could help me."

Ellie couldn't believe her eyes. She thought this kind of big-man-can-you-save-me act only happened in the movies. Really bad, cheesy movies.

Bill shifted, cleared his throat. "Uh, what's the problem?"

To Ellie's shock and wonder, Phoebe-Diane leaned over just enough to give Bill a dead-on cleavage shot.

He glanced down, back up to Phoebe's face. And said…nothing.

Ellie had to remind herself that men were made of flesh and blood. Offer a man a boob-flash and he'd look. Shame Phoebe wasn't a rap song.

"I was supposed to enter the Hot Shot Photo Scavenger Hunt with a friend," Phoebe said in a baby-talk singsong voice, "but he couldn't make it." She put on a sad look, which consisted of sticking out her bottom lip and making a noise like a pigeon cooing.

Unbelievable. No goth chick in her right mind would pull that stunt.

"Everyone's signing up for the Hot Shot Photo Scavenger Hunt in an hour," continued Phoebe, as though someone had asked for details. "That's when they give everyone the text number where to send their photos. One category is tattoos, another tan lines—" she ran her finger along the edge of her bikini top "—stuff like that. And the photos are flashed on the screens." She leveled a look at Bill. "Want to be my partner?"

Ellie took a big sip of her lemonade, making a loud slurping noise. When Bill looked at her, she gave a couldn't-help-it shrug.

"Sorry, Phoebe," he said, turning back to her. "But I made other plans."

"Later, then?"

"Look," Bill said, gesturing to the crowds of people, "there's at least two guys for every woman here. Just hold up a sign, and you'll have a partner within seconds."

"But…" She pouted. "I wanted *you* to be my partner."

Bill took Ellie's hand. "I already have one."

Ellie's very breath scattered and for a moment she couldn't breathe, couldn't move, couldn't think. Well, not for long. A coherent thought finally took shape in her mind. *Wasn't this the confused guy who'd decided he couldn't do this with me?*

Yeah, and she was the confused girl who hadn't been too sure about giving this a chance, either.

She interlaced her fingers with his and smiled to herself. Maybe two wrongs didn't make a right, but two confused people could certainly make a go of it.

A SHORT WHILE LATER, Ellie and Bill stood in front of a ticket booth. The sun was hovering low in the early evening sky. Neon lights were coming to life along the midway.

Ellie looked up at the Ferris wheel then back to Bill. "Think you can behave so we don't get kicked off?"

"I'll do my best." He grinned. "Can't make any promises, though."

"Candy and Sara are expecting us at the Hot Shot game in thirty minutes, so let's try not to be escorted out of the festival, okay?"

"Hey, look on the bright side. If we get kicked off, who will be escorting us out of the festival? Our pals at Security." He winked. "So all we need to do is put on a good show, pretend we're really leaving, then turn around and sneak back in."

She gave him a teasing look. "And you claim to be such an honest man."

"Ellie," he said, lifting her hand, "I'm always honest when it comes to you." He placed a kiss on the back of her fingers.

She closed her eyes and shuddered a release of

breath, liking the feel of his lips against her skin even as she didn't like her own deceit. *Wait a minute—how bad am I really being? Lots of women, and men, dress or act a certain way to attract the opposite sex.*

The justification, however, felt hollow. In a way, she felt more manipulative than Phoebe, whose dress and behavior were an extension of herself, whereas Ellie was being something she wasn't.

"You okay?"

"Huh? Oh, sure." Not.

"We don't have to go on the Ferris wheel."

"No, I want to." *The longer we're together, the greater the chances he'll figure out my deceit.*

Neither moved. He gave her a quizzical look. "Something's wrong, I can tell. Do you want to talk about it?"

"Stop," she said softly, pressing her finger to his lips.

He liked the soft feel of her touch against his mouth. He imagined nibbling a little on her finger, slowly sucking it into his mouth, running his tongue around it.

He grew hard again just thinking about where else she could put her hands…where else he could put his mouth.

She must have picked up on his thoughts because she slowly ran her finger along his top lip, trailing along the cushion of his bottom lip, down to his soul patch.

"I like this," she said, lightly feathering the patch.

"I like you touching it."

Her fingers trailed to his jaw. "The reason I'm acting oddly is…this will be over soon."

"Who said?"

"Me." She dropped her hand. "Our crossing paths in Malibu was total serendipity."

"So?"

She took a breath. "So, considering how busy we are the rest of this week—well, you more than me—it's sheer luck we have the rest of today to spend together. I mean, sure, we'll probably see each other on the set, but from a distance. Then the week will end, we'll return to our routines, and that's that."

He raised his eyebrows. "Gee, Ellie, your romantic streak is showing."

She laughed softly. "I'm being realistic. Like Cinderella at the ball, midnight will strike and it will all be over."

"So, this ends at midnight?"

She shrugged, nodded.

"But I thought Magellan said Cinderella doesn't make it home before midnight."

"Yeah, but Magellan is nothing more than a Jimmy Buffett character in a turban."

One could never say Ellie was an easy-to-read woman, which appealed to Bill even if it had its frustrating moments. He'd always liked a challenge, and Ellie certainly gave him that.

Amazing, she was offering him a tidy ending. No strings. What he would have given for other women to have offered him the same deal. Problem was, with Ellie, he wanted more. He never thought he'd admit this to himself, but he'd enjoyed their reminiscences about Olvera Street, down to how the *pan dulce* stuck to the roofs of their mouths.

What other memories would they share? Friends they'd known? Family they'd loved…and those they'd lost? No, she was right. It was better to put a lid on this before it got out of hand.

"Okay," he said, "we go with your plan. At the stroke of midnight, that's it."

She nodded, a look of relief in her eyes.

Which irked him. She didn't have to look *relieved* about it. Unless…there was something he was missing in this picture.

"Have to ask…is there a boyfriend? Don't mind making a deal, as long as it's a fair deal and we're both putting our cards, so to speak, on the table."

"No, I'm not involved with anyone. Man or woman, just to set the record straight." She smiled teasingly, then turned somewhat serious. "How about you?"

"Same. Except, well, to be honest…" He scratched his chin. "There's someone I recently dated, but it's in limbo."

She narrowed her eyes. "Define limbo."

"She, uh, wants to see if there's potential, but I'm not so sure."

"Potential? As in, meet the mother?"

He'd never taken anyone to meet his mother. "Something like that."

She mulled it over for a moment. "Okay, we stick with the midnight plan. But no sex."

"What?"

She gave him an incredulous look. "You're the one leading on Ms. Limbo."

"No, no, you're misconstruing the entire thing. Limbo means nothing's happening." He blew out a breath. "I can't believe we're having yet another weird conversation in the middle of the midway."

"But you're involved," she said, ignoring his aside.

"We *were* dating. Past tense."

She arched a brow. "Does she know you speak of her in the past tense?"

"What does it matter? We're over at midnight, anyway!" He started to scratch his chin, paused, dropped his hand. Too late. Laser-eyes had tracked the move.

"Look," he said, "as dumb as this conversation is, I'm a man of my word and I'm giving it to you here, now, straight up. Vi and I met, we dated for a few months. We both have demanding careers, the commute to each other's place is a hassle, so we're taking a break while she's in Europe. When she gets back, we're going to see where things are."

Ellie felt her world topple a little. "Vi?"

"Short for Violette."

The way he said it, made the name sound…

"She's French?"

Bill nodded.

"Accent and all that?"

"Yes, accent and—" he gave a shake of his head, a slight smile curving his lips "—all that, whatever that's supposed to mean."

It means that she's tall, lithe, makes a mouth-watering coq au vin that makes men fall to their knees, and she knows more sexual tricks than the Kama Sutra.

Rubbing her eyebrow, Ellie looked around, not wanting Bill to see the disappointment in her face. Disappointment, ha, to see the flat-out, Oz-green jealousy. She needed a moment to tame her inner beasts, rein them before they got the better of her.

Okay, there's another woman waiting in the wings. Bottom line, do you believe the limbo part?

She thought about his eyes when he'd said it. They glistened with such earnestness. A memory flashed in her mind. A sixteen-year-old Bill, going around the neighborhood looking for his kid sister.

Ellie had stood behind her mom and watched him as he paced on the porch, worried, talking about his sister, her bad report card, how she'd run away from home. He hadn't been as tall or buffed as now, but already handsome in that dark, intense way.

That day, he'd also had the same look in his eyes as he had now.

Yeah, she believed him about Vi.

"Ellie?"

She turned, met his gaze. "Okay, midnight plan is still on."

"With…or without?"

She gave a slow, teasing grin. "Bill Romero, do you think I waited this long to go without?"

6

BILL'S TEETH FLASHED white against his bronze skin. "Cool!" He grabbed Ellie into a hug, laughing. "We'll boogie down until the midnight hour, baby!"

His exuberance was infectious. Ellie laughed with him, any lingering reservations dissolving into the warm evening air. "Boogie down and up and every which other way!"

A sunburned guy in a loud Hawaiian shirt, white sunblock on his nose, stopped, his mouth agape. "Wow, dudes, what contest is that?"

Ellie and Bill turned and looked at him.

"Man, I'd like to sign up for that midnight boogie game." He took a sip from a bright red straw stuck into a coconut. "Where's it at?"

"Keep heading in the direction you're going." Ellie pointed in case he wasn't sure. "When you pass the volleyball games, take a left."

"Cool!" He teetered, caught his balance. "What's the contest name?"

Ellie and Bill looked at each other.

Bill turned back to the guy. "Twelve strokes to midnight."

Ellie, taking a sip of her lemonade, nearly choked.

"Righteous." The guy flashed them a hang ten before disappearing into the crowd.

Ellie gave Bill a look. "Twelve strokes to midnight?"

He grinned, obviously enjoying his impromptu quip. "It would have made a perfect contest name for this festival." He suddenly grew serious. "Hey, sorry about that funky mood I was in earlier."

"Like I don't have my funky moments, too."

"Yeah, you do," he teased. "I blame mine on my fiery, passionate Cuban half, what's your excuse?"

She laughed, pressed her cool lemonade container against his bare chest. He barely flinched, macho guy that he was.

"I don't have one unless I can blame it on my Irish half. The other half is very repressed, Midwestern."

"Yeah, I'd barely ever hear a peep from your house."

"How could you? The Romeros were the loudest family on the block!"

People were disembarking the Ferris wheel, couples looking flushed, their hair windblown. Some were laughing, others walking slowly with their arms wrapped around each other.

A man, dressed in denim shorts and a red-and-white striped tank top, strolled in front of the gate to the ride, calling out to the crowd. "Get your tickets to the Ferris wheel! A lucky few get a special stop at the top! Step right up, get your tickets!"

Bill dug into his pocket, pleased when he found the last few complimentary tickets. He held them up.

"C'mon, Ellie, let's go misbehave."

MINUTES LATER, a squat sixty-something man who managed to talk while chewing the butt of a cigar, admonished them not to stand up "till da ride stops" before shutting the metal bar over their laps with a heavy clang. The ride lurched, their benchlike seat jerked up several feet, then it stopped abruptly to load the next passengers.

"Don't stand up till da ride stops."

Clang.

Their seat lurched upward another few feet, stopped, swinging slightly.

Ellie, her fingers gripped around the cold metal bar, stared straight ahead, feeling slightly giddy. The ride lurched up again. Her stomach clenched.

"Nervous?" asked Bill, putting his arm around her.

"A little."

"Let's get your mind onto something else, then. Tell me about your coffee shop. What's the name of it?"

"Dark Gothic Roast."

"Gothic, huh? Why'd you pick that?"

Lurch. Her stomach rose with the chair until it jerked to another stop. They were high enough that she could see the ocean, a vast dark blue all the way to the horizon.

"Because…" She could tell him a little without giving away her secret. "…I like that era. The somber but emotional art, the great cathedrals, the stained glass."

"Sounds cool. Where is it?"

He could look it up online, or in the telephone book, so she might as well tell him. Anyway, she doubted he'd ever show up. It was in one of L.A.'s high-rise business areas—lots of tall buildings and people in suits. Anyway, unless her business loan fell through, she'd soon be moving it.

"Century City."

"So you cater to the eight-to-five types."

"Yes." The suits got a kick out of the goth theme. Some even held business meetings there. The bulk of her evening clientele came from the goth bar around the corner.

She held her breath as their bench seat rose, rose....

They stopped at the top.

"This is awesome." Cool breezes whipped her hair. Hot sun beat on her skin. She felt fantastic— more alive, more exhilarated than she had in a long time...years, actually.

He squeezed her shoulder, hugged her closer. She turned slightly and looked at him. Maybe it was the bright sun, but she felt as though she saw more in his face. A brooding restlessness, a loneliness, she hadn't noticed before. As though no place were home.

He smiled, the lines crinkling around his eyes, and the restlessness disappeared. "You okay?"

She nodded, still a bit taken aback at the glimpse she'd just seen.

"I can signal the guy to stop the ride when we're back down." His gaze dropped to her lips, slowly returned to her face.

"No," she murmured, "I'm fine."

She snuggled closer just as the ride started to descend. Wind rushed up to meet them as a thrill shimmied from her stomach all the way to the top of her head. She pressed against Bill and emitted a high, piercing shriek that she couldn't have held back if she'd tried.

Then, they swept past the ground, the blur of people and noises and smells fading away into the distance as they soared up, up, up to the blue sky and a yellow sun.

She wrapped her arms around Bill's waist, the feel of his warm skin grounding her in the dizzying rush of wind and light.

When he tightened his hold, she took advantage of it to snuggle closer. Her cheek slid down slightly, resting on his hard, molded pec. She looked into the tattooed dragon's eye, fierce and blue, the burnished green scales trailing behind. Such a big, bad dragon. She flicked out her tongue and licked it.

Salty. Warm.

Another thrill rushed through her as the ride soared skyward again. Higher, higher. She buried her head against his chest as another high-pitched shriek ripped loose from her lips.

As they crested, she felt more than heard his chuckle rumble up his chest.

"Hold on," he yelled, tightening his hold on her as they plummeted back to earth.

She didn't want to look. Didn't dare look. Instead, she hung on to Bill for dear life, clamping shut her mouth to stop further banshee screams.

Then, suddenly, they jerked to a stop.

As the bench seat swung back and forth for a moment, she kept her face buried against his chest.

"You all right?"

She raised her head. All she saw was Bill's face, creased with a wide grin.

"You're laughing at me."

"No." He tried not to grin, but his mouth refused. "Sorry, it's just…have you ever thought about doing voice-over work? Some actors actually specialize in screams."

"Very funny." She straightened a little and looked around. They were on the backside of the ride, which was a good thing because it helped center her somewhat to see all the other passengers in front and above them. "Why are we stopped?"

Bill looked down. "Nobody's getting on." He turned back to her.

When their eyes met, she was taken with how much lighter his brown eyes were than she remembered. Maybe because their faces were so close, or because of the bright light, but their color reminded her of the rich caramel she sometimes drizzled on coffee drinks.

Like caramel, the look in his eyes was sweet, too. Funny, he had more personalities than she did. The temperamental Cuban. The macho guy. And now, the sweet man with the tender, almost hopeful, look in his eyes.

Then, something odd happened as she realized that it wasn't that she was seeing something new, but that he'd let her get inside him. Not much, but enough to be vulnerable to her. Enough to trust her. Instinctively she knew he didn't give that away too often, if at all.

They sat that way for a long moment, their eyes silently probing, deeply, into the other's.

When another gust blew her hair into her eyes, he swept the strands back. But his hand remained, gently cupping her face.

"Ellie," he murmured, "you're so beautiful."

Beautiful had always seemed a word for other women, not her. Sometimes, in her goth attire and makeup, she fancied herself darkly exotic. But as a beach babe, she felt like a plastic Barbie doll.

But to hear it from Bill's lips, with that look in his eyes…she felt beautiful.

He lowered his head to kiss her and she eagerly raised her lips to meet his. And when they were so close she could almost taste him…

A cell phone rang.

Bill cursed under his breath. "With the shoot starting tomorrow, I need to be on call for any last-minute problems." Pulling back from their almost kiss, he rummaged in his shorts' pocket for the phone as it rang again. He frowned, looked up at Ellie.

"That's not my ringtone. It's some guy singing about taking a walk on the wild side."

"Oh! That's my Lou Reed ringtone." She'd been in such a fog with Bill, she hadn't recognized it. Didn't mean she wanted to answer it. But then, Candy or Sara might need her. She retrieved the phone from her purse. "Hello?"

"El, it's Tish. We've run out of Count Chocula cereal, I couldn't find any at the store, which means we're going to have a lot of pissed-off people in the morning."

She'd missed her long-dreamed-of kiss over Count Chocula? "You called me about that?"

Big sigh. "No, there's more. The moving guys dropped by, said they need a deposit to move Dark Gothic Roast to its new location. I told them it's not a done deal, but they said they need a deposit, which is refundable, to hold that time slot."

"Okay, fine, write a check."

"Where are they again?"

Tish, short for Morticia, was great with people, organized, but her memory was riddled with more holes than a body-piercing parlor.

"Office desk, third drawer down on the right."

"So, when's our big move again?"

"We'll probably be relocating in a month, tops. Just waiting for the loan approval."

"Groovy. How's it going?"

"Can't talk. I'm on a Ferris wheel."

"You? On a Ferris wheel?"

"Yeah, me. Bye." She hung up, not wanting to waste a single moment more of Bill, who was staring up at something.

"Figured out why we're stopped." He pointed upward. "It's one of the lucky couples who get extra time at the top."

Ellie looked. Over the edge of the seat at the very top, a bikini top dangled from someone's hand.

"What happens on the Ferris wheel," murmured Ellie, "stays on the Ferris wheel?"

Bill chuckled. "Not if she lets go of that top. Hey, what was that about relocating?"

"If my business loan goes through, I'll be moving the coffee business. I was waiting to hear before sharing the news with anyone. Even my brother doesn't know yet."

"To where?"

If she told him the complete truth, he'd lose it. So she fudged. "Inland."

The ride started up again. This time when Bill wrapped his arm around her, she cuddled next to him but didn't hide her eyes. Instead, every time they crested over the top of the ride, she drank in the awe-inspiring view of the coast and beach and endless ocean.

The fourth time around, as they started to crest, the ride slowed...and stopped.

She gasped, turned to Bill.

"Let's see if what happens in the Ferris wheel stays there," he murmured, wrapping his arms around her.

Up high, the blazing sun warmed her skin, but that paled compared to the heat exploding within her.

Bill smiled down at her and she responded, as best her trembling lips could. Foggily, she realized she was gripping his shoulders, as though if she didn't hold on for dear life she might float away.

He turned his head slightly, lowered it, angled his mouth to hers. She raised her mouth to his in silent compliance, moaning slightly at the pressure of his warm, firm lips. Tasting him, she leaned right into him, her body quivering with anticipation.

He didn't stop at a quick, chaste kiss, but eased her mouth open and slid his tongue inside. His tongue was smooth and nimble, flicking the corners of her mouth, sliding across her teeth, seeking and searching, an explorer claiming the new land.

Her tongue joined in, sinuously curling around, over, under his. The dance slow, inviting, gentle, its pleasurable sensations rippling through her until they pooled hot between her legs.

No big surprise. Bill Romero knew how to kiss.

Pulling back, he threaded his hand through her hair. "Like spun gold," he murmured.

For a moment she wasn't sure what he was talking about. Oh, right. The beach babe hair.

He lifted several strands and kissed them. "I feel like a miser with his fortune."

"Yeah, well, not everything that shines like gold is gold."

He blinked, let her hair slide from his fingers. "Ellie, you going heavy on me?"

She smiled. "That was my half-Irish side. It spouts heavy thoughts sometimes."

With an amused look, he cupped the side of her face, lifting her head slightly so she was looking directly at him, then let his hungry gaze travel slowly over her breasts, down her torso, settling in that region between her legs. Being up here alone, away from prying eyes, she felt aroused and bold. What happens in Malibu stays in Malibu.

She spread her legs slightly, a quiet dare. *Your move.*

He made a guttural sound that resonated down to her very nerve endings.

"Nice," he murmured. He lightly touched the fishnet stretched over where he was staring. "I have an idea."

Just imagining what he might be thinking made her go wet. "Yes?" Hardly a question. She was so hot, so worked up, she was game for anything.

He reached for her and she tensed in anticipation. "I'll take this," he said, slipping her cell phone from her hold.

"You want to *call* somebody at a time like this?"

He chuckled under his breath. "No, I want to take some photos for that Hot Shot game. My phone doesn't have a built-in camera, but I noticed yours does."

She wasn't sure whether to feel turned-on or pissed off. What happened to that great, warmer-up kiss? That boogie-till-midnight oath?

He peered at the phone. "I'd rather get down and

dirty, but it could get dangerous trying to pull our clothes back on while plummeting back to earth."

Much better. She pointed at the phone. "Press the button that says Camera, then point and shoot. Here, let me get a shot of your dragon." She took it, showed the image to Bill in the miniscreen, then handed it to him. "Your turn."

"Hmm…can you turn away just a little? Enough to get a shot of your Queen of Evil tattoo?"

She shifted, her breath catching at the expanse of sky and sea, a little afraid, a lot excited to be testing herself in more than one way. "How's that?"

"Perfect…I'll just slip your bikini bottom down a little…oh, yeah…"

She shivered as his warm fingers brushed against her tushy.

"Okay, turn back."

As she did, he rose slightly in his chair. She grabbed his leg. "Bill, you can't stand—"

"Till da ride stops, I know. I'm not standing, just hovering a little higher than usual."

"No wonder you got kicked off the ride," she whispered, not wanting to look down, see how far he could fall.

And yet, when she looked back at him…she was impressed. Not only with his gutsiness, but his obvious calling as a director. He had a way with the camera, moving just so until he framed the shot, a man with a vision that would not be denied.

Holding on to the back of their seat, he leaned

back against the bar. "Bend over a little…let me see that spiderweb tattoo through the fishnet."

She quickly did as told before her last sight of Bill Romero was him pitching into the sky.

He clicked as he talked. "Great… Lift your fishnet…fantastic…now, show me that wicked little spiderweb tattoo…good…can you take a deep breath?"

She leaned back slightly and inhaled deeply, causing the edge of the spiderweb to swell slightly over her red bikini top.

"Nice," he murmured. "A little more?"

She pulled the edge of her top down, just a little, exposing more of the tattoo.

"More," he said.

It was exciting being up here in their private little world, playing this sexy game. This was a new Ellie, not the one who put others first, but a woman putting herself first as she indulged her fantasies.

No judgments, no repercussions. Just free to enjoy and experiment and…

Be bold.

She pulled down the bikini top, showing more of the tattoo, more of her breast.

"That's good," murmured Bill, taking another photo.

She pulled it down farther.

Her nipple, hard and aroused, popped out. The impact of cool air tingled against her skin, the sensation hardening her nub.

Bill all but crashed back into his seat, his mouth

open. "Oh, yes, baby," he murmured, tracing his blunt nail around the pebbled areola, his sensual touch shooting heat straight to her groin. Holding down her top, she sucked in a shaky breath watching his dark hand against her exposed white flesh, watching his circling path tighten, draw closer to the nipple.

"Do you like that?"

"Yes," she shuddered.

He lightly flicked his finger over the nipple. She gasped with pleasure.

Suddenly, metal clanked. As the ride shuddered, began to move, she started to pull her top back up.

"Not so fast," growled Bill. He leaned down and took a gentle bite of the fullness, then trailed a sensuous path to the nipple, which he flicked, once, twice.

Wind rushed past, sounds from below sharpened.

"Bill," she murmured.

"Not yet…"

His big dark hand squeezed her breast, guided its pebbled nub into his wet, warm mouth. It felt forbidden to be doing this so exposed, in danger of being caught, which only excited her more as she watched him lap and suckle.

The sounds of the festival grew louder.

"Bill," she gasped.

He raised his head and smiled at her, a look of sleepy arousal in his eyes, before quickly pulling the bikini cup back over her breast and smoothing the fishnet covering back over her.

When the car stopped, they sat primly side by side holding hands, like two innocent schoolkids at the end of a field trip. They nodded politely to the guy, still chomping on the cigar butt, smiled to the ticket taker.

Once they were out of earshot, Bill tugged her closer.

"The Ferris wheel is not only my favorite ride," he murmured, nuzzling his chin on her head, "it's now my favorite fantasy, too."

7

SEVERAL HOURS LATER, after hooking up with Matt and Candy, and Sara and Drew, at the Hot Shot Photo contest booth, and everyone getting the text number for downloading photos, Ellie and Bill had meandered through the rest of the festival, taking photos, noshing on pretzels and later cotton candy, but mostly enjoying each other's company.

Night had fallen. Overhead, stars littered the dark sky. In the distance, lights of homes dotted the Santa Monica Mountains. Party hounds, tanned and laughing, were heading to some of the beach hot spots for drinks and more festival games.

Ellie and Bill paused in front of a fenced-in area with a dance floor. Over the gate was a sign, in bright pink and purple letters, Good Vibrations Contest, Wednesday, 7:00 p.m.

Ellie, her lips moving as she silently read the rules, suddenly laughed.

"Listen to this," she said. "'How good, good, good can you be to the tune "Good Vibrations"? You can be a dancing maniac, a juggler, a mime, just be good!

Contestants will be judged on ingenuity, creativity, and ability to keep the beat. Sexy, yes! X-rated, no! We'll play the Beach Boys hit version, or bring your own! Couples win double the points!'"

"Thinking of entering?" asked Bill.

"Maybe. I've raked in points by being hired as an extra, thank you very much, then nailed more points at Truth or Bare. Maybe some of the photos you and I downloaded from the Ferris wheel might place, but meanwhile, I should find other contests to enter, try and pull in more points for Team Java Mammas."

She was already planning how she'd spend the rest of the week without Bill, which saddened her.

"Good Vibrations, huh?" He scanned the rules. "What are you thinking of doing?"

"Have no idea."

"I have an idea. Play on your Queen of Evil tattoo."

At first she wanted to laugh, but maybe he was onto something. She thought about some of the dressier clothes she'd packed. "I have a burlesque skirt. If I give it a good tug, the Queen of Evil will show." She paused, wondering if that came out the way it was meant.

"You do burlesque?"

"No, it's a style of skirt. Although I've seen Dita Von Teese do burlesque. YouTube has videos of her performances, some Burlesque 101 stuff, too. I could watch them, copy a few moves."

"Dita Von Who?"

"Von Teese. She was married to Marilyn Manson."

"That shock-rock guy?"

She nodded.

He gave his head a disbelieving shake. "He looks like *Night of the Living Dead* who needs some serious makeup rehab. I didn't even know he dated women."

So not funny. She could take the time to explain Marilyn Manson's performances were tongue-in-cheek, but why bother? Bottom line, just as he'd never understand or appreciate Lou Reed, or the girls from the hood with their tats and makeup, he'd never accept her lifestyle, either.

All the more reason to stick with the midnight cutoff.

"Bill!" called out a male voice.

Jimmie came jogging up to them. "Glad I found you." He stopped, catching his breath. "Would've called, but my cell ran out of power." He nodded hello to Ellie, turned back to Bill. "Hey, Sullivan hates the setting for the first shoot, wants a new location."

Bill muttered an expletive.

"I know. He always does this. Figured you'd want to know before you got a big surprise tomorrow at 5:00 a.m."

"Sullivan's a micromanaging idiot."

"True. But he's our micromanaging idiot boss, unfortunately."

Bill blew out an exasperated breath. "Gordon's given me directorial power over the next few days, including final approval on all locations, to test my wings. Sullivan's last-minute bullshit could not only screw things up, but make me look bad."

Jimmie put his hand on Bill's shoulder. "I know, man. If you want to try and talk sense to Sullivan, he'll be back at his trailer in an hour."

"I'll be there."

Jimmie smiled. "That's the spirit. Hate to run, but promised the wife I'd let some guy named Majello read our brains."

"Thanks for finding me."

Jimmie smiled. "You'll handle this, Bill, just as you handle everything. You're going to be a director, whether it's on this shoot or elsewhere...." He gave his pal a knowing look. "I tell ya, indie film companies are the way to go. I'd even let you have top billing. BillJim Productions."

Bill grinned, his dark cloud lifting. "Get outta here. Bev's waiting."

With a wave, Jimmie jogged away.

Bill looked at Ellie. "Sorry."

"Work happens. I understand."

"So...where were we?"

The night air floated around them, bringing with it scents of corn dogs and the ocean. Nearby, people laughed and clapped at one of the ongoing games. It had been fun, a day to remember, but it was over.

"It's time to go home," she said softly.

"Yeah, appears that way, doesn't it?" He scratched his chin. "Your beach house is nearby?"

"Fifteen-minute walk, but you have your meeting—"

"No. A gentleman escorts his date home, and that's what I'm doing. Besides…"

"What?"

He ran his hand down her arm, looked deeply into her eyes. That's all it took, a touch and a look, and she felt her body go weak with wanting. For all her mental calculations on the pros and the cons of what they were doing, or what he'd think if he knew the truth, sometimes what was going on between them boiled down to something hot and needy that had nothing to do with the mind, and everything to do with the body.

"Like you need to ask," he murmured huskily, linking his fingers with hers. "C'mon, I'm walking you home."

ALMOST FIFTEEN MINUTES later, they stood on the porch of the beach house. Down by the shore, some diehards were boogie boarding, squeezing the very last moments out of the day. From a nearby beach house, the sultry beat of an old Doors tune, "Light My Fire," was playing.

Bill stepped closer. "Sorry."

"For?"

"Not being able to stay and light your fire."

"It's okay."

"No, it's not. I wanted to make love with you…" He trailed a finger down the side of her face, then played with her hair. "How about our moving that midnight cutoff to tomorrow night?"

His musky, cinnamon cologne was wreaking havoc with her thought processes. It was shadowy under the porch awning, although the lamp highlighted the lower half of his face. It was impossible to decipher the look in his dark eyes, although she felt him watching her, waiting for an answer.

Now was the time. Just say it.

"We're so different," she began.

He gave a so-what shrug. "But in some ways, we're the same."

She hadn't expected that. "Such as?"

"We both appreciate those classic films of Hollywood's Golden Age. We like to hang out in security guard shacks and eat their food. C'mon, how are we so different that you can't see me tomorrow night?"

"I didn't say that!"

"But you were starting to."

"Okay." She paused. "I like Marilyn Manson." She was wussing out, but considering he'd be leaving any moment, she didn't want to hit him with the fact she'd been faking the whole beach babe bit all day long. Instead, she'd test the waters, let him know that something he laughed at, she respected.

He reared back his head slightly. "You don't say."

"I say."

He lowered his head, barely suppressing a chuckle. He met her gaze. "I put my foot into it, didn't I?"

"Yes."

"He's really straight?"

"Yes."

"I shouldn't have made that comment. Sorry."

His honesty could sometimes be disarming. And charming.

"But you have to admit, Ellie, the guy can sure dress weird."

"What's weird to some might be creative and artistic to others."

He paused. "Well said. I'm sorry I said he looks like—"

"*Night of the Living Dead* who needs some serious makeup rehab."

"I'm impressed you remember verbatim." He cleared his throat, made a two-fingered Boy Scout sign. "I won't make any more disparaging remarks about Marilyn Manson, you have my word."

"Thank you."

He blew out a long breath. "Now that that's covered, what about tomorrow night?"

She smiled. "Yes, let's get together."

"Good, because if you'd said no," he warned, his husky voice tinged with mirth, "I'd have come back anyway." He checked his watch. "I need to leave in a minute. But before I go, about tomorrow on the set. It's going to be crazy busy for me because I'll be stepping into the director's seat, but I'll try to catch up with you."

"Thanks for letting me know."

He slowly fisted the fishnet material in his hand

and pulled her toward him, his eyes darkening to the shade of a moonless midnight.

She came willingly, until she stood mere inches from him, so close she could feel the heat radiating off his body.

He released his grip, dropping both hands to her hips. He kneaded them slowly as he released a strangled groan, then moved his hands around, cupping her buttocks and pulling her closer.

"Kiss me," he murmured, his words puffing warm against her mouth.

She slid her arms up his chest, around his neck, and rose up on tiptoe. Angling her head slightly, she slanted her mouth on his, their lips almost touching.

But she didn't kiss him.

She pressed her bikini top against his chest and rubbed her breasts against him, once, twice, until she felt her nipples go hard.

"Do you feel that?" she whispered against his mouth.

He released a strangled "Yes."

She liked feeling her sexual power, knowing she was exciting him, giving him something to remember until tomorrow night. Pressing her groin against his erection, she moved against him with small, tight circular motions.

"Do you like that?"

His voice cracked as he spoke. "Yes."

"I like it, too," she murmured, pressing her lips against his.

His lips were firm but full, and incredibly, deliciously soft. She moved her mouth against his in a slow, sweeping movement, her lips nibbling, sliding, pecking. She was so excited, her entire body was shaking, her breaths ragged, but she wanted more, now, because this was all she was going to get tonight.

A moan escaped her mouth as she eased her tongue between his lips. He tasted like cotton candy and lemonade, sweet and citrusy. She swept the warm, wet cavern of his mouth with slow, broad strokes, then, with a light flick, coyly teased his tongue to come play.

With a low, guttural sound, he jerked her closer, invading her mouth with his. His hard legs sandwiched on either side of hers, he ground his erection against her sex as his mouth made love to hers, his tongue tangling and sliding and licking at a frantically building pace, until, with a loud moan, he jerked back his head, ripping free from the kiss.

For a long moment, they stood stock-still except for their heaving chests, holding each other at an arm's length.

"If that's just a kiss," he muttered, "I'm dog meat."

8

ELLIE LEANED AGAINST the other side of the closed front door, her eyes closed. That was, unequivocally, the best kiss she'd ever experienced. Ever.

She ran her tongue over her lips, tasting Bill again. Warm and sweet. And the barest trace of citrus.

She opened her eyes and looked around Team Java Mamma's beach pad. "Sara? Candy?"

No answer.

She raised her voice. "I can't believe you guys! I'm ready to spill about the steamiest kiss I've ever had, and you're not here!"

Silence.

"Your loss."

She pushed off from the door and walked like a zombie toward her bedroom. What she'd planned for this vacation had turned upside down. Instead of hanging out in the beach house all day and wandering out at night, she was doing the exact opposite.

She turned a corner and shrieked.

As did the woman who faced her.

Ellie paused, her mouth still open.

As was the woman's.

"Jeez," she whispered, staring at her reflection, "you scared me." She blew out a breath. "I've got to remember this mirror is here, or I'll be shrieking all week long."

Calmer, she checked out her made-over self. Tousled, blond-streaked hair had replaced the black spikes. Tanned skin had replaced the pale look. And those pastels—light green on her lids, peach on her cheeks—had replaced the bright blues and decadent reds.

She stopped by her bedroom, looked around. Its white rattan furniture, sea-foam green walls and tropical print curtains were the antithesis of her antique furniture, Victorian wallpaper and red velvet drapes back home. Seemed everything in her immediate world had been made over. She flashed back to tonight when they'd all hooked up at the Hot Shot booth. Even her brother, Matt, had been made over!

She felt too keyed up to sleep so she decided to get ready for bed, then listen to that CD Tish gave her, a surf-goth group called Vampire Girls on the Beach. If Ellie recalled correctly, they'd done a cover of "Good Vibrations."

As she was fishing in her suitcase for her Siouxsie Sioux T-shirt, which doubled as her jammies, she ran across a girl's best friend.

Her favorite vibrator, OhMiBod, and its trusty sidekick, the wireless remote.

No more frustration for this girl!

She kicked off her shoes, whipped off her clothes and slithered into OhMiBod, adjusting its elastic bands over her hips so the butterfly-shaped vibrator sat *right there* over her clit. After slipping on her long T-shirt, she grabbed the Vampire Girls on the Beach CD, and looked around for her CD player.

Not here. She headed down the hall, checked the bathroom, finally found it in the living room. Cool. Considering she forgot to bring her headphones, she'd have to hook it up to the speakers in here.

In her West L.A. apartment, she could use her OhMiBod wherever she pleased, but the living room in this beach house was communal property.

She crossed to the front door and locked the dead bolt. Problem solved. As it could only be opened from the inside, by her, she could enjoy her OhMi-Bod without a worry.

She slipped on the CD and selected the "Good Vibrations" cut. Not bad. An interesting mix of fifties' surfer music with a dark, pulsing undertone. She preferred bands like Siouxsie & the Banshees and The Cure, although goth-surf music had its pluses. She bobbed her head in time to the music.

She fingered the remote, an ivory plastic device with three speeds and four pulsations, which made any woman a masturbation maestro. If she wanted to enjoy a classical experience, low speed with a slower pulse. Jazzy, medium speed with a higher pulse. Rock and roll? Full speed ahead and max the pulse, baby!

Surf-goth was a more classical experience, she decided. She pressed the buttons.

A light, incessant buzzing quivered against her clit. She sucked in a breath, giving herself over to the delicious sensations. She'd endured hours of fore-play today with Bill. All that teasing and taunting and touching had made her one worked-up, strapped-on, ready-for-relief woman.

She eased down onto a chair, leaned back her head and closed her eyes. She imagined herself at this morning's audition again, alone on the stage, wearing nothing but the OhMiBod and those stilet-tos. In the audience was one man, Bill, who'd paid her to pleasure herself as he watched. With one caveat. She had to share her fantasy, down to the most minute detail, as it unfolded in her mind.

She spread her legs, imagining him sitting in the very first row. His dark eyes glistened, a look of hunger on his face, as he waited to hear her innermost secrets…..

Ding dong.

She snapped open her eyes. Oh, great. Somebody was at the frickin' door.

With an exasperated huff, she punched off the remote. She stood, smoothed down her T-shirt so it hit midthigh, then shuffled to the door and peered through the peephole.

Her heart leaped into her throat.

Bill!

She hated to be caught in the act. It was an insult,

wasn't it, for a guy to find a woman he'd just left to be in the throes of masturbation?

No sweat. He didn't have to know what she'd been doing.

Opening the door slightly, holding the remote in her out-of-sight hand, she said a bit breathlessly, "Hi."

He held out her cell phone. "Figured you'd be needing this before tomorrow night. Forgot I had it on me."

"Thanks." With her free hand, she accepted it.

He cocked his head. "That's 'Good Vibrations,' isn't it?"

She nodded.

"Never heard that version before. Practicing for tomorrow night?"

She tightened her grip on the remote. "Sort of."

"Since we're getting together, how about if we both enter? Double the points for Java Mambo?"

"Java Mammas."

"Right." He flashed her a smile. "I'm feeling a little odd with a door between us."

"Oh, sorry." She opened it a bit wider, still keeping the remote out of view. "Thought you needed to leave right away again, you know, to see that producer."

"I can walk there in ten minutes, and he's not expected for at least twenty, so I have a few minutes to spare."

He leaned his head close to hers and gave her a

smile that warmed her right down to her beach babe peach-tipped toes.

She smiled back, her insides turning to mush.

He leaned closer and brushed his lips across hers, igniting a flame that spread like wildfire over her skin.

"I have a confession to make," she whispered.

"Hmm?"

She handed him the remote.

9

BILL PEERED at the remote in his hand. "What's this for?"

"How soon do you have to leave?" she whispered, opening the door a little wider.

"Five minutes?"

She smiled, excited at the thoughts searing through her wanton mind. She glanced over his shoulder, not seeing anyone for several hundred feet, either on the walkway or the beach. With Bill blocking her, no one could see her…and if she saw anyone, she could quickly duck back inside.

She lifted the end of her T-shirt, brushed her fingers across the elastic over her hip, leading his eyes down to the object positioned over her sex.

He looked down, paused. "God, you're so pretty," he murmured. "Is that what I think it is?"

"Yes."

Raising his gaze, he held up the object. "And this is…"

"A remote."

"Well, well, well…" He held it inside the door to

read the buttons. "Aren't you the electronic-age wonder."

"I'd invite you inside," she whispered, "but selfishly, I'd like to stand right here…."

His eyes glistened with lust. "I wanted to make love the first time, not just…"

She stealthily rubbed her thighs together in anticipation. "Let's call this an appetizer before the main meal."

He leaned forward, his breath warm against her neck. "Appetizer, yes…I like that." Fastening his lips on her neck, he lightly nibbled and kissed, causing her to writhe pleasurably.

Then he pulled back and looked at her. "I'm selfish, too," he said, positioning his finger on a button, "because I want to watch."

He pressed a button that brought Ellie onto her toes, the exquisite tremors zeroing right in on her sex. So intensely enjoyable, all it would take was a few more moments and she'd…

Bill stared at the hem of her T-shirt that fluttered with breezes over the firm, creamy skin of her thighs. She was rising up on her toes, pressing together her lips to suppress the needy mewling noises that lodged in her throat.

It was dark enough on the porch that it'd be difficult for someone to see unless they were standing in his shoes, plus his body blocked her….

"Lift your T-shirt," he murmured, "I want to see you."

She reached down and lifted it.

"Ellie…" He pressed another button and she gasped. "I can't wait to taste you…touch you…."

Panting, she opened her eyes and looked at him, her hips rocking slightly. "More," she said on a moan. "I want more."

Ellie felt the vibrations kick up a notch. She gasped as sheer, exacting need pooled hotly between her legs. The pleasure was so intense, so exquisite, she throbbed and ached for release from the soles of her feet to the top of her head as the tension kept building, building….

Her breath caught as her body tightened and trembled. She was hot, wet, wound so tight. Her body needed it, demanded it…so close….

For a singular moment, everything stilled…then her entire being rushed toward the point of no return….

She bit back a groan as wave after wave of release ripped through her until, too shaky to keep standing, she slumped her lax, sated body into Bill's arms.

He dropped the remote as he held her close, her breaths warm and ragged against his cheek as her body relaxed into his embrace.

Suddenly, she sputtered a soft laugh. "I think I just proved that old saying wrong."

"What saying?"

"Never come between a man and his remote? Well, I think I just did."

THE FOLLOWING MORNING, at 8:00 a.m. sharp, Ellie reported to the assistant casting director, Peter, on the set of *Sin on the Beach*. She'd met Peter the day before at her audition, so she wasn't surprised at his whirl of frenetic energy—chain-smoking, drinking coffee, ordering people around, all while talking into his cell.

She stood nearby, waiting for him to end his call. This morning, before getting ready, she'd had coffee with Sara and Candy, but despite their guy-talk tell-all, she'd stayed mum about what had happened last night with Bill. Oh, she'd said she and Bill had *kissed,* but hadn't breathed a word about the orgasm-in-the-doorway escapade. They would have loved hearing about Ellie's crazy-hot encounter, but she liked keeping it private, something shared between her and Bill only.

"You!" Peter pointed at her with his cigarette, the other hand holding his cell to his ear. "I thought I said no black bikinis!"

She started to stutter something, when he cut her off.

"Next time follow directions." He made a hold-it gesture while barking into the phone, "I don't care what he says! It's Thursday or nothing, darling." He looked up at Ellie, pointing her to a group of people in bikinis and shorts.

She headed over to the group of ten or so people, whom she assumed were her fellow extras. The girls all looked like Paris Hilton, the guys like Brad Pitt, which made the older gentleman in red shorts and a T-shirt that read Surfers Stay on Longer stand out.

Probably because she kept staring at him, he approached her with the kind of pickup line that was right up her alley.

"Want a cup of coffee?" he asked.

His long sideburns and handlebar mustache were a throwback to another era. Reminded her of herself, modeling her glam style on stars of yesteryear. The two of them obviously marched to their own stylistic drummers, which put her instantly at ease with him.

"No thanks." She smiled. "Afraid I'm picky. I run a coffee shop."

He lit up. "Well, isn't this a small world. My grandson's new friend is rooming with someone who runs a coffee shop."

A few pieces fell into place. "Your grandson wouldn't happen to run a surf shop, would he?"

"Why, yes!"

"Yes, it's a very small world." She held out her hand. "I'm Sara's friend Ellie, the one who runs a coffee shop."

He shook her hand. "Pleased to meet you. I'm Gus."

They spent the next few minutes chatting about the surf shop, her coffee shop, Gus's past surfing accomplishments. She didn't take his flirting seriously. In fact, if he were forty years younger, and she weren't besotted with Bill, she might've said yes…to a coffee date.

"Hey," said a familiar voice.

Bill.

Her heart shoved into overdrive. "Hey, yourself."

Gus gave a little salute and wandered off, leaving the two of them alone.

"Should I be jealous?" Bill teased.

Ellie looked over at Gus, who was already flirting with another extra. "No, I'm already a thing in his past."

Bill grinned. "Gotta get ready for the next take, so can't stay long, but would you like to have lunch together? Wait, let me clarify that. When the set breaks for lunch, would you like to take a walk on the beach while eating whatever I can get delivered? With my busy schedule, that's the best I can do."

"Love to," she said. "Where?"

"Just come over to my station." He pointed to an oversize blue-and-white striped umbrella, under which were several canvas-backed chairs, a portable video monitor, a small table on which sat a laptop, some papers.

She smiled. "Sounds great."

"Bill!" A red-haired kid wearing a *Sin on the Beach* T-shirt and blue baggy shorts barged in. "Video feed is having problems. Kenny needs to see you ASAP."

Bill touched her arm. "Gotta go. By the way, you look great."

"Sorry I wore black," she said, but he was already walking away. Even as he talked to the red-haired kid, others kept approaching him, vying for his attention. The boy from the hood had certainly come a long way. Even back then, he'd had that cocky, I'm-the-man way about him, which a guy had to have to stand up to, and often survive, the life on the streets. She wondered if he'd even have come this far if he hadn't had that tough background.

And yet, he seemed to despise the past that had nurtured this success. She didn't get it.

OVER THE NEXT THREE HOURS, what Ellie *did* get was that the film business was no way as glitzy behind the scenes as it was on the screen. The next several hours consisted of boredom, repetition and more boredom as the same scene—two people having a brief conversation—was shot again and again.

At eleven the assistant director instructed everyone to take thirty minutes for lunch, and she headed over to Bill's station, which was a mob scene with people demanding his time. She stood outside the umbrella while he argued with a lighting guy, gave instructions to several others, handled a call from Sullivan, all the while watching a playback on the video monitor of the scene they'd just shot.

Seemed it wasn't just Peter who multiprocessed on this set.

She was debating whether to walk away, when the crowd dispersed and Bill waved her into his inner sanctum.

"Sorry," he said, standing. "Today's been one problem after another." He picked up a sack, nudged his head toward the beach. "Let's get the hell out of Dodge."

Minutes later, they strolled along the shore, their

feet sinking into the wet sand. Overhead, seagulls squawked and circled, eager for any offerings.

"It's one of the worst shoots I've ever been on," Bill muttered, shaking his head. "Just my luck, it's also the first day with *me* in the director's chair proving myself."

She munched her sandwich, listening.

"But let's not ruin our lunch by discussing it anymore, okay?"

"It's great being on the beach," she said, watching the distant waves tumble and crash.

"Yeah, except the majestic Pacific is starting to look like the damn show to me, but you're right. It's great out here. Hey, it was also great to see your brother again last night. What's he doing these days?"

"Vice president at a software company."

Bill nodded approvingly. "Not surprised one bit. He was always a go-getter." He took a swig of his soda.

"How about your brothers and sisters?"

Bill felt that familiar nagging discomfort when people started talking about families. "They're all right."

His cell phone rang. Juggling his sandwich and drink, he retrieved it from his shirt pocket, checked the caller ID. "It can wait," he muttered, dropping the phone back into his pocket. "So where were we?"

"I was asking about your family."

He paused. "You know something, Ellie? Even though we laughed and talked about Olvera Street yesterday, the truth is, I hate East L.A. I know, you love it. Or at least like it. Why, I'll never understand, but you do." He took a bite of his sandwich, stared off at the ocean as he chewed.

"Sorry," she said softly.

He took another swig of soda, taking his time to swallow the cold, fizzy liquid. "No, I'm sorry," he said. "I meant what I said—I don't understand—but I could've been a nice guy and not a…"

She lightly touched his arm, her kindness making him feel even more like a jerk.

"Jasmine works in a hair salon," he started out, "has two kids, still lives in the hood. The next oldest, Sabrina, dropped out her sophomore year. Tried to talk her out of it, but…" He shrugged. "She's divorced, several kids, living with Mom in a condo a few blocks over from our old hood.

"My brother Jasper," he continued, staring down the beach at a couple of kids flying a bright blue and yellow kite, "is a firefighter in Eugene, Oregon."

"That's a beautiful town. Summer after high school, my girlfriends and I did a road trip to Washington state. We stopped in Eugene on the way back."

"Yeah, I visited Jasper while on a shoot there. He's happily married, *four* kids. Wife's getting her master's in psychology." He finished the last bite of his sandwich.

"And your youngest brother?"

Suddenly the breezy summer air grew hotter,

thicker. The glare of the sun on water hurt his eyes. This was the tough one, the one he never discussed.

"Wasn't his name Randall?" she asked.

"Reginald." He paused, picked up a shell embedded in the wet sand. "We called him Reggie."

"Right! Reggie." She smiled. "Once he came over to show off a mitt that'd been signed by—"

"Fernando Valenzuela. Dodgers' pitcher." Bill tossed the shell into the ocean, watched it disappear into the swirl of water and foam. "When he was eleven, all he talked about was being the next Fernando."

"What is he doing now?"

Bill watched where the shell had dropped, wondering if it had sunk to the bottom or was drifting out to sea.

"He died," he said matter-of-factly. "Gang shooting. Drive-by. Bloods and Crips, same old trash, what can I say."

He looked over at Ellie, wondering about the expression in her eyes, hidden behind those sunglasses. Did she feel pity for him? Sadness? Definitely not forgiveness because if he couldn't feel that for himself, neither could anybody else.

He looked back at the set. "We need to go. I bet twenty people are looking for me, ready to pound me with questions and problems."

"Wait a minute, Bill," she murmured, moving closer. He automatically braced himself as she wrapped her arms around him. "I'm so sorry," she whispered.

He didn't want this. Didn't want her touching

him, feeling bad for him, saying empty words that would never bring Reggie back.

But even as he thought those things, he reached for her, his hand trailing down the jut of her hip, onto the soft material of her bikini. Her warmth, her caring, even her screwed-on-wrong beliefs awakened something in him that made him want to feel again.

He held her close, feeling her soft body against his, needing that softness, craving it. The weight he'd carried for so long suddenly felt too heavy, too much to endure alone. He lowered his head, letting it sink against the cushion of her perfumed hair. He was so tired of keeping it all together, so tired of holding back.

"Ellie," he whispered hoarsely, "it's my fault he died."

10

LATER THAT AFTERNOON, what had been *one* of the worst shoots Bill had ever been on, became *the* worst.

"Have you lost your effing mind?" He paced a few feet, eyeing the video monitor. It was stifling hot, the stench of exhaust from Pacific Coast Highway overpowered the sea air, some know-nothing had just sabotaged a perfect take, and to make the day as perfect as it could possibly be, he'd lost his watch somewhere in miles of sand.

It was as though the universe was saying, "Have a crappy day."

He stopped, pointed at the monitor again. "The lighting sucked! Our star was in shadow, but the lifeguard station was lit up like Disneyland!"

The chief gaffer, a glop of sunscreen on his nose, nodded. "Yes, Bill. Sorry. Won't happen again."

Bill rubbed a spot on his chin. "Yeah, okay, I'm sorry I'm being a dick. It's just that it's—" He looked over at one of the production assistants. "What time is it?"

The girl, her pile of red hair pinned to the top of her head with a clip, glanced nervously at her watch. "It's 2:30 p.m."

"Nearly three," he sputtered under his breath. He looked back at the gaffer. "You hear that? It's nearly 3:00 p.m.! We've been shooting since 5:00 a.m., and we're *still* screwing up the *first* frickin' scene."

He stretched his neck from side to side, trying to dislodge the kink that had homesteaded between his blades, as he walked out onto the set where everyone could see him. He stopped, looked over the assembly of crew and actors.

"People," he called out, "can we pull together and finally, *finally,* get it right this next time? Otherwise, we'll have wasted an entire day with nothing to show for it."

"Yes."

"Sure thing, Bill."

"Will do."

His gaze caught Jimmie's, who stood with several of his reports. Even under a glaring sun, Bill could tell that look on his pal's face. They all needed a time-out before Bill went postal.

He signaled to the second assistant director, a quiet kid everyone called Bunker for some reason, and flashed five splayed fingers.

Bunker nodded, raised the megaphone to his lips.

"Everybody, take five. Be back in your places at exactly two-thirty-five. No excuses."

Bill grabbed his bottle of iced tea and took a long

swig as he watched Jimmie trudge through the sand toward him.

"I don't get it," Bill said when his friend arrived, glancing down at Jimmie's expensive leather huaraches. "Why do you get involved with this bullshit? Why don't you stay at home and write full-time, skip this insanity. You have the means."

"Cheap shot, Bill."

"Sorry. Maybe I should change my name to Dick so people can call me that to my face." He looked around at people adjusting lights, dragging equipment across the sand, fixing the stars' melting makeup. Typically, people would be chatting, yelling, cracking jokes.

Except for the occasional murmur of conversation, everyone was stone-cold silent.

"I'm making everybody tense."

"Yeah, you are, but it's also a tough shoot."

"Starting with Sullivan this morning." Bill was still angry at the producer's bullheadedness. "He insisted the location shot be moved, so it was moved. That cost time, money and one pissed-off star's goodwill because no one told her the site of the new location."

"Shoots happen."

"Very funny."

"C'mon, Bill, you and I both know it's a crazy business."

"But not on the first day of the most important shoot of my career."

"This is one step above a sitcom, Bill. Lots of bodies and fluff, barely enough plot to string along a story line—"

"Getting ready to hawk the indie film company again?"

"BillJim Productions? Whose first film has an award-winning script featuring a compelling and complex protagonist based on your life?" He paused. "No. That's a lost cause."

"The money would suck."

"Not if you'd stop thinking making it big equates to making big bucks. But I don't want to discuss it further."

Bill grunted. "Me, neither. Except to say, you'd be smart to contract with that financial guy who used to work for Coppola—Gary something—because he knows the business end inside and out."

"Gary Minger. Had lunch with him last week."

Bill paused. "Did you pitch him the indie film company idea?"

"Thought we weren't discussing this further."

"We're not."

"Great, let's change the subject. How's our Queen of Evil?"

A smile broke through Bill's black mood. "Fine."

"Fine?"

"Okay, extra fine. She's…good, you know?"

He thought about how his heart pounded every time she smiled. And how he'd told her about Reggie. It hadn't been easy, but he was glad now he'd done it. She was more than a lover. She'd become his friend.

Bill dragged a hand through his tangle of hair. "Have you ever listened to Marilyn Manson?"

Jimmie did a double take. "That strange guy? Never. Plan to keep it that way."

"He's okay."

"Uh, why are we talking about Marilyn Manson?"

"Oh, Ellie likes him."

"Seeing her again?"

"Tonight."

Jimmie nodded. "Give it a chance before you pull the plug. A relationship—that's dating someone for more than three months, by the way—with the right person might do you good. Help you get outside of yourself, give your life some perspective. Can't be number one all the time, Bill. Unless you like living in that small, lonely place."

"Giving me some tough love, James?"

"If I don't, who will?" He made a power sign, bumped it against Bill's fist. "Gotta check on the grips. I know how you love the details, but try not to sweat the small stuff, okay?"

"I'll try."

BUT A HALF HOUR LATER, Bill wasn't just sweating the small stuff, he was sweating the minutiae, too.

He stood, his arms crossed, staring down a group of extras. Dressed in Speedos and bikinis, their tanned bodies glistening with lotion, they stared back with wide, frightened eyes as though he was going to yell "boo!" any moment.

Except for the old guy in surfer trunks, who was taking advantage of the break to make eyes at one of the female props personnel.

"Who didn't turn off their cell phone?" Bill demanded, his voice rolling over the quiet set.

Overhead, a plane buzzed slowly through the blue, trailing an advertising sign that read Rocko's Burgers Best in Malibu 1-800-555-6609.

Peter, the assistant casting director, sat stiffly on the edge of the set, lighting another cigarette. "People," he said, half puffing the words as they escaped in a plume of smoke, "the director just asked you a question."

Not the director, yet. After this last screwup, maybe never.

An hour ago, Sullivan, who'd spent most of the day watching the taping from his producer's trailer, had taken Bill aside. In a buddy-buddy tone, he'd calmly reviewed the day. Costly. Mistakes happen. Did Bill want Gordon to take over the directing? No? Then, could Bill please get back control of the set and stop the bleeding?

That last shot hadn't just bled, it'd gushed.

In the group of extras, a woman stepped forward, her head bent. "It was me," she said meekly, lifting her gaze.

Ellie.

She nervously clasped and unclasped her hands,

the look on her face so damn remorseful, he almost felt bad. Almost. The next chat with Sullivan wasn't going to be so buddy-buddy.

Peter, taking another puff, strode up to her.

"You were explicitly told to leave your cell back at the extras' table." Although he stood right directly in front of her, he spoke loud enough so everyone could hear. "You're fired. Pick up your things and—"

"Hold it!" Bill pulled off his headset and rubbed his thumb and forefinger against his eyelids. After a moment, he lowered his hand, took a breath. "There's enough drama in front of the cameras, do we have to have it behind the cameras, too?"

Somebody snickered.

He looked at Ellie, still standing in the spot where she'd confessed, looking frightened and vulnerable.

Despite his pissed-off state, he felt for her.

"Let's not go to extremes, Peter." Bill motioned to the production assistant to hand him his tea. "She's not a professional. She's just somebody who won this job at the festival audition. Let her stay. *Minus* her cell, of course."

While Peter divested Ellie of her phone, Bill returned to his station, sipping lukewarm tea while waiting for the camera operators to give him their thumbs-up. Patience had never been one of his better traits. He liked things done fast, well and on time, but he could dream on wanting that on this set. He ticked off the seconds in his head, nudged his toe into the warm sand and waited.

Seconds became minutes.

A pair of pink polished toes entered his line of vision. He looked up.

Ellie stood there, guilt so clearly etched on her sun-pink face, she might as well carry a sign.

"I'm really, really sorry," she whispered, her voice shaking.

He watched her through slitted eyes. Over the years, he'd dealt with all kinds, from hard-assed gang-bangers to scheming studio heads. He'd been hassled and manipulated and tested by the best, but he'd usually been able to keep his attitude on cruise control.

But he was having a hell of a time doing that today. As wonderful as she was, as much as she meant to him, she'd just pricked his balloon of dreams with a very sharp needle.

He shifted in his chair, his face hot, his heart hammering, every single nerve ending raw, edgy, inflamed as years of scrambling for jobs, living on little sleep and food, fighting to prove himself rose to the surface.

He kept his eyes fixed on her face, all too aware of her plump breasts, smooth thighs and the sweet triangle nestled in between.

Part of him wanted to curse her, make her the scapegoat for this rotten day, for his rapidly down-hill-sliding career, for every single piece of malfunctioning equipment, misspoken dialogue, hell, even for the script assistant's summer cold.

The other part wanted to crush her into his arms and ride her right into the ground.

"You're making me crazy, Ellie," he muttered.

Over her shoulder he saw Ricardo, one of the continuity crew, heading his way. Ricardo was a can-do kinda guy who resolved problems before anyone else even knew they existed.

Which meant one big, hairy, unmanageable problem was heading Bill's way.

Turning to pick up his drink, he realized Ellie was still standing there, an expectant look on her face.

"What?" he barked.

She gave a little jump. "I, uh, was wondering…"

He took a sip, waited for the rest. "C'mon, I don't have time to play guess what's on my mind."

Now she looked hurt.

He squeezed his eyes shut. "Sorry, sorry, I don't mean to be an asshole. Just spit it out. Company's on its way."

"I was wondering if I could leave—"

"Bil-ly…" Phoebe strolled in, wearing a skimpy summer dress that was more skimp than dress. She deigned a glance at Ellie, then handed him a paper. "Curtiss asked if you'd read this memo. He needs an answer ASAP."

He took it, started reading.

Phoebe sidled closer. "Going to the festival tonight?"

"Huh? I don't know."

Ricardo stepped into the shade from the tent, wiping the sweat off his chin. "Hey, Bill, sorry to be the messenger, but props brought the wrong motorcycle…."

Bill's cell rang. He made a time-out gesture to Ricardo as he answered, listened to someone start explaining why one of the special effects had prematurely blown up.

"Hold on," he said into the phone. He handed back the memo to Phoebe, "Tell Curtiss the budget's too tight. And about that motorcycle..." He looked over at Ricardo but his gaze froze on Ellie.

"Thought you wanted to leave."

She flitted a glance at the others, looked back. "I, uh..."

"Look," he said, working to keep his voice even, "if you're worried about Peter, I'll talk to him."

"No, it's..."

He didn't have the time for this. "Ellie, I can't waste my time on an *extra*. Go, *leave!* The rest of us have real work to do here."

The aquamarine eyes turned glacial, giving him a look that made him wish he'd never been born.

"You said you don't mean to be," she said quietly, "but you are."

He frowned. "Don't mean to be what?"

"An asshole."

As she walked away, he felt the world pull back, the sounds of machinery and people on the set reduced to a low buzz, like a fly in another room. Even the crashing surf seemed remote, as though it'd chosen another shore.

It wasn't her words. He'd been called worse. Crazy enough, it wasn't even the job. There'd be problems, he'd be on the line, things would be fixed. Or not.

It was realizing he'd finally committed himself to something more than just him. Something better, bigger. Yet within minutes, he'd managed to slam the door and isolate himself again.

Jimmie was right. He'd made himself number one for so long, he hadn't realized what a small, lonely place it really was.

11

THIRTY MINUTES LATER, Ellie was reliving the last few days. She'd gone from glam goth to beach babe, acted and nearly been fired on a national television show….

And called the man of her dreams an asshole.

To his face.

While others were present.

Wow. Was she having fun or what?

She stopped, squiggled a pattern in the wet sand with her toe, his words replaying in her head. *I can't waste my time on an extra…. Go, leave!* She'd spent the first part of her walk furious and hurt that he'd thought she was a waste of time, feeling totally justified in her response.

Now she was blaming herself for approaching him in the first place. Peter had lectured the extras about no cell phones on the set, then the cameras were rolling, she'd belatedly realized she was holding hers, and tried to position herself so it wouldn't be seen. She'd never forget the sickening feeling when she heard the familiar "Walk on the Wild Side" ringtone jangling, realizing it was her cell….

Dumb, dumb, dumb.

She deserved to be chewed out, maybe even fired, but Bill had stood up for her. She should have left it there, but, no, she got it into her head she needed to apologize in person, which actually went okay, and would have remained okay if some anxious part of her hadn't decided she *had* to know if their date tonight was still on.

So she'd stood there—while he was being crowded with people, problems, phone calls—acting all goofy and nervous and not speaking up and he'd gotten frustrated and...

"Hey!" called out a female voice. "Gotta match?"

She looked over at a group of teens sitting and lying on multicolored beach towels, laughing and talking, a radio playing a soulful Jack Johnson tune. They looked to be fifteen, sixteen tops, most drinking from bottles in paper bags.

A girl, shiny brown hair to her waist, waved what appeared to be an unlit cigarette at Ellie.

"Got a match?"

"Sorry, no," she called back.

That's when she noticed they'd parked themselves right in front of one of the numerous No Smoking, No Drinking signs that dotted this part of the beach.

She smiled, remembering her own teenage rebellion. Except, instead of bikinis and hanging at the beach, she'd worn black and put glitter into her hair. Her glam rock phase that eventually became glam goth. Looking back, she sometimes wondered if it was an escape from her growing responsibilities at home, being an adult to her mother's child.

After chores and homework, she'd lounge in her bedroom, smoking clove cigarettes, listening to David Bowie, Bob Dylan, Lou Reed. To say she was besotted with Lou Reed was an understatement. He epitomized New York, the place Bill had gone, which was the be-all and end-all for her young heart. She'd even stenciled the lyrics to one of Reed's songs on her wall, painting the last words of the chorus—"swoop, swoop, rock, rock"—in fluorescent paint on her ceiling. The song itself was a moving tribute to a long-lost lover, yet it ended with those light, silly words—"swoop, swoop, rock, rock"—which to her had meant that no matter what happened, life was good.

Whenever she'd had a bad day, or was going through a tough time, or just needed to remember that everything would work out, she'd lie on her bed and look up at those words, and feel better.

All of which baffled her mother, and immensely amused her brother, Matt.

Matt!

That's who she needed to talk to. He knew her better than anybody. He'd known Bill in the hood, had chatted with him last night at the Hot Shot booth. Matt could give her advice on this mess she'd gotten herself into.

"What's up, El?" he answered a moment later.

"I think I screwed up. No, I know I did. It's bad."

"Oh."

Like most guys, Matt was pretty much clueless how to respond to a woman broaching an emotional topic. Like a computer, he needed to first process the data before formulating an answer.

"It's about Bill Romero."

"Okay."

"As you know, he and I are—" were? "—romantically close." She looked out at the surfers on their boards, bobbing in the ocean, waiting for a wave. Oh, if only life were so simple. "It's a temporary thing, of course."

"Of course," he said quickly. Too quickly.

Oh, right. He and Candy were doing that sensible-sex thing. Usually, Ellie would take this opportunity to play matchmaker, persuade him Candy was the best thing to ever shake up his world... But, for a change, she needed to put her problems first.

"Okay, here goes." She blew out a nervous breath. "There's a French woman named Vi who wants a more serious relationship with Bill."

"French, eh?"

"You don't have to sound so gleeful. Anyway, that's in limbo."

"What does that mean?"

"They'll be discussing their potential when she gets back from Europe in a few weeks."

He made an ominous-sounding grunt.

"However, my more immediate problem is—" she squeezed shut her eyes "—I called him an asshole."

"Were you drinking?"

Her eyes flew open. "No!"

"Did you have a reason to call him that?"

"At the time, I thought so. Now…I'm not so sure."

"Wow." Pause. "You called him that to his face?"

"Yes." She closed her eyes, envisioning it again. "Actually, I didn't call him an asshole outright. It was more of a virtual name-calling thing."

"Have you spoken since then?"

"No."

Another ominous grunt.

"I should add that right before the asshole part, I'd accidentally brought the entire production to a screeching halt."

"What happened?"

"I took my cell onto the set, after I'd been told not to, and it rang in the middle of a big scene."

"Oh."

"After that, I was almost fired, but Bill stood up for me."

"Then, something happened and you called him an asshole?"

"Yes."

"And you want me to…"

"You know me. You know Bill. Plus you're a guy. Tell me the truth. Do you think I've blown it with Bill?"

"Yes."

"Jeez, couldn't you have paused a little, made me think you needed to think it over first?"

"Sorry, sis. Look, I know you feel bad, but analytically speaking, what is he besides a childhood crush? You have your coffee shop, your friends and family, that alter-life as the mistress of the damned…what does it matter if he stays or if he goes?"

"I'm better than this," she said softly.

"In a way, yeah. On the other hand, maybe he's worth it?"

She took a deep breath of the salt-infused air. When she blew it out, she imagined all her cloudy, confused thoughts being expelled with it. She'd been so caught up in what Bill had meant to her as a girl, did she even know what he meant to her as a woman?

She did.

His strength, passion, striving for success appealed to her because those were the traits she most loved about the hood. It wasn't that others didn't have those, it was that, for too many, those characteristics had been turned inside out. She'd been thinking about what she could do to change that. They were small ideas, but everything began with a small step.

Fundamentally Bill was, in the best way, the heart of the community. Although he didn't realize it.

And until this moment, she hadn't realized she wanted to return there with him. Problem was, that would never happen.

"Thanks, Matt. I'll be going now."

"El, you sound so sad. Is there something I can do to make you feel better?"

"No, it's okay. I should be going now—"

"Wait!"

She paused. "What?"

"'Swoop, swoop, rock, rock.'"

She blinked back sudden emotion. "Matthew Rockwell," she murmured, "you're the coolest bro in the world."

AN HOUR LATER, Ellie sat at one of the stools in the kitchen, halfheartedly doodling clothes designs in her sketch pad. Upon returning to the beach house, she'd rummaged through her bag, panicked she'd forgotten to pack her favorite old Lou Reed T-shirt, which had been washed so many times it felt like a soft binky against her skin. She'd literally yelped with joy when she found it.

Wearing it, unfortunately, just wasn't the same as gazing up at "Swoop, swoop, rock, rock."

"El, what's up?" Candy traipsed in, tossed a bag onto the counter and picked up a piece of leftover rugelach.

"Sketching, making coffee."

"Coffee?" Candy laughed. "Hon, I know you miss Dark Gothic Roast, but it's eighty-something degrees outside! It's lemonade time, girl."

Ellie felt the glue holding her together start to crack. Making coffee had seemed a good way to stay busy, avoid the pity party route. But of all the crazy things, the word *lemonade* threatened to undo her.

"Bill and I—" she cleared her suddenly dry throat "—drank lemonades yesterday."

Candy's eyes filled with concern. "El? What happened?"

Ellie set down her pen. "I almost got fired from *Sin on the Beach*."

"No," Candy murmured.

Fluttering her hands in a no-big-deal gesture, she slid off the stool. "I'm going to get some coffee."

Candy followed. "El, this is a *vacation,* not a job. You can't get fired, and even if they threatened to, tell them you quit because you have better things to do, like hit the surf, catch some rays, have fun in the sun!"

"I prefer fun under the moon, but I get your drift."

"Did something happen with Bill?"

Ellie poured a cup, raised the steaming mug midair and paused. "You're right. It's too hot to drink coffee." She poured the brew down the sink. "Is it too early to have a cocktail?"

"For you, no. For me, yes. I want to be sober when I go networking with Matt."

"Networking?"

Candy picked at the piece of rugelach, avoiding Ellie's eyes. "No big deal. I'm just helping him loosen up."

The front door suddenly swung open.

"Hey, Team Java Mammas!" Sara walked in, smiling, looking relaxed. "I'm not staying long. Just a quick in-and-out to pick up some stuff before I go surfing."

Candy raised an eyebrow. "Quick in-and-out?"

Sara wagged a finger. "You know what I mean."

"Yeah, but it's fun teasing you," said Candy. "Going surfing with Drew?"

Sara nodded, her gaze drifting to Ellie. "Hey, how's our movie star?"

"She almost got fired," Candy said quietly.

Sara frowned. "What happened?"

"My cell phone went off. Brought the entire production to a screaming halt." Ellie headed for the kitchen cabinets. "Did we bring anything gooey, loaded with sugar? I know, *chocolate*. I definitely need chocolate."

"There are more Bomb Pops in the freezer," offered Candy.

"Close enough." She headed to the fridge at the back of the kitchen.

Sarah called out after her, "How're you and—"

The question cut off abruptly. No doubt Sara had just caught Candy's frantic don't-ask signals.

"It's okay, we can say the Bill-word," Ellie answered, returning with a pop and settling back onto her seat. She'd been debating whether to share this with the girls, but oh well...

"By the way, there's a French woman named Vi, short for Viaduct or something like that, in the wings." The sound of sucked-in breaths nearly drowned out the sound of distant waves. "Their relationship is in limbo—that means on hold—and they'll be reviewing it when she gets back from her European vacation." She started peeling off the wrapper.

"A French woman," muttered Candy.

Ellie rolled her eyes. "Tell me about it."

"But," said Sara, "their relationship is on hold."

"True." Like she had any room to complain, she who'd initiated the *at-midnight-our-relationship-turns-into-a-pumpkin* decree. Whatever she and Bill did, if they even got together to do it again, would be over way before Vi jet-setted in for the international liaison symposium.

She tugged off the last of the wrapper. "Supposedly we have a date tonight at seven." Their hot one-nighter that ended at twelve straight up. At some point, she'd thought that cutoff point was a logical way to protect the heart, which now seemed plain dumb. Who in their right mind even used the words *logic* and *heart* in the same sentence?

"That's good, right?" Sara looked at Candy, who shrugged.

"Well, after our tension-filled goodbye on the set…" After Matt, she'd decided not to share the asshole story with anyone else. "I'm not so sure our date's still on."

"Why the tension?" Sara looked so sad, Ellie almost wanted to comfort *her*.

"Because my rising sign doesn't like his moon?" She tossed the wrapper into the trash, missed. "Win some, lose some," she muttered. She licked the pop.

Candy gave Sara a look. "She doesn't want to talk about it."

"I know, but I'll worry about it the rest of the day

if I don't know!" Sara turned to Ellie. "Tell me this much. Did you and Bill talk after that?"

"No."

"Maybe you should call him."

"Or," chimed in Candy, "have Matt call. He knew Bill, right?"

"Don't know his cell number, and even if I did, wouldn't call. Wouldn't want Matt to, either." Ellie licked her pop for a moment, thinking about Bill. "That guy," she finally said, lowering her pop, "can be really critical, domineering, opinionated."

"Love them alpha boys," murmured Candy with a smile, which dropped instantly when she caught the looks on Ellie's and Sara's faces. "Sorry."

"Seems to me," Sara said, "those traits are excellent, if not necessary, for a directing career. Maybe he's trying so hard, it's bringing out his worst…but maybe also his best?"

Bill's face materialized in Ellie's mind, his brown eyes sparking with interest as he listened to something she said, as though nothing else in the world mattered. She loved his laugh. Deep, rich, full of enjoyment. She remembered how protected she'd felt on the Ferris wheel, the heady thrill of kissing at the top of the world, how with him she felt safe to open up, be sexually adventurous. And that wicked little soul patch…oh, mama.

In her childhood fantasies, she'd wanted him to be the first man she'd make love with. She'd grown up, there'd been other men, but deep down, that fantasy had never died. It was as though, through all these years, she'd been waiting for Bill. That their chance meeting this week was some kind of destiny.

She looked at Candy and Sara, smiling at their eager we-gotta-know-what-you're-thinking look on their faces.

Ellie took a lick, smiled. "Sara, you're right on. I was thinking about what was best about him as I walked home. He's a passionate, strong, successful guy. He's also funny, smart, *really* listens to what you have to say, has a great body—" she fanned her face with the pop, making them laugh "—and way too much sex appeal for his own good."

"So," said Sara, "what are you going to do?"

Ellie thought for a moment.

"Girls," she finally said, gesturing with the pop, "Ellie the caretaker is going to take care of herself. So I'm going to do what any smart woman should do with a man like that." She wriggled her eyebrows. "Jump his bones."

12

"SIGNIN' UP for Good Vibrations?" With a sleepy grin, the guy brushed back his long hair.

"Yes…" She squinted at his name tag, nearly lost in his bright tie-dyed shirt. "Tommy." She set the plastic bag, which held her stilettos, onto the table. Until she performed, she'd wear thongs.

"Name?" He poised his pen on the sign-up sheet.

"El—Queen of Evil."

After he wrote it down, he stared at her hair.

"It's a crown," she muttered, pulling up one of her fishnet gloves. Between learning burlesque moves, dyeing her hair black again, and getting dressed, there'd been no time to shop for a costume crown, so she'd made one out of aluminum foil.

"Your face," Tommy continued, "reminds me of a porcelain doll my mom had. White face, dark eyes, red lips. Pretty, like you."

"Thanks." She looked around for Bill. What would she see in his face? Acceptance? Amusement? Disgust?

"Performing as a single or couple?"

"Single. Maybe couple."

Tommy fidgeted with his pen for a moment. "I'm not supposed to do this, but I'll write you down as both, just in case."

"Okay."

After he finished writing, he set down the pen. "Okay, here's the part where I point out where the changing room is—" he pointed to a curtained-off changing area on the far side of the stage "—and I tell you the rules." He started reciting in a monotone. "No alcoholic beverages in the act, no X-rated movements, gestures or words, no…"

She'd already read them. Pretending to listen, she checked out the crowd. Most wore bikinis and swim trunks—spectators, she guessed, with a few who'd signed up on a whim. Some, like her, had obviously prepared. Like the couple in matching red T-shirts, holding identical back massagers. Or the surfer-dude, with Good Vibes painted onto his T-shirt, practicing on his harmonica. The guy pouring water into glasses arranged on a table didn't seem to fit, but the woman in the silver bodysuit, which seemed to vibrate with her every move, was definitely a contender.

She froze.

That vibrating silver woman was *Phoebe.* She'd piled her blond hair into some kind of cone-shaped beehive, wore a push-up bra that was more push-up-and-*out,* and those red lips were probably stopping cars a mile away. No wonder guys were craning their necks to look at her. She looked like a silver-sprayed slut.

Phoebe looked over, her gaze sliding right past Ellie. *She doesn't recognize me in my glam goth finery.*

Bill wouldn't recognize her, either, not immediately anyway. If only she'd remembered to get his cell phone number, she would have called him and bypassed all this. But she didn't have his number, didn't know anyone who did, and she wasn't dumb enough to attempt a surprise visit on the set.

Tommy finished reciting the rules.

"Thanks, I'll be sure to follow them." She glanced down at the list. "How long before I'm on?"

"You're last, number sixteen, so forty-five minutes or so."

She'd spent the afternoon watching burlesque videos on YouTube, practicing the shimmy, several struts and a move called "shakin' the front porch, shakin' the back porch." She'd always done well in dance, which she'd studied in high school and college, so she had a reasonable confidence that she'd pull this off.

Static crackled over the speakers. "Testing, testing." The woman's voice had the easy, polished tone of a radio announcer. "Can everybody hear me?"

"No!"

"Turn it down!"

"Will you marry me?"

She laughed. "Lively group! We're working on some technical issues, so bear with us. Meanwhile, my name's Didi. I'll be announcing the acts, playing the music and being the bad guy who'll yank anybody or anything that's X-rated off the stage. So keep it sexy, not X-y! Other than that, I'm here to make sure you all have a good, good, good time at our Good Vibrations contest!"

People clapped and whistled.

Ellie looked around. No Bill.

"Our contest will be starting momentarily," continued Didi. "If you brought your own version of 'Good Vibrations,' please leave it with Tommy, the cute Deadhead who's managing the sign-ups. Otherwise, I'll be playing the Beach Boys' version. Contestants will be judged on ingenuity, creativity and ability to keep the beat. Couples win double points! Have fun! Contest starts in five minutes!"

As far as Bill was concerned, there were no excuses for being late, unprepared or sloppy.

Tonight he was guilty on two counts.

He strode through the festival crowds, past flashing lights, food vendors, endless barkers' enticements—"Step right up! Everybody's a winner!" He'd left the set shortly after seven, still answering questions on his cell as he walked across the beach toward the festival where he was supposed to meet Ellie at the Good Vibrations contest, hoping she hadn't given up on him.

Although maybe she had hours ago. Problem was, he was the kind of guy who didn't take the word *no* for an answer. Or *asshole* as an ending.

He heard the Beach Boys' "Good Vibrations" song before he saw the sign. Closer, he saw dozens of people milling about, laughing, drinking, some dancing.

Through a break in the crowd, he saw a couple on the stage, both dressed in red T-shirts rubbing each other's backs in time to the music with what looked like industrial-sized vibrators.

He strolled through the crowd, looking for Ellie. Walked past a guy playing "Good Vibrations" by rubbing his fingers around water-filled glasses, another practicing the tune on his harmonica. But no Ellie.

Finishing a loop around the small stage, he approached some hippie-dude sitting with the sign-up sheet.

"Has an Ellie Rockwell signed up?"

"Ellie?" He trailed his finger down the list of names. "No Ellie. Sorry, man."

"Mind if…" He took the list, started scanning. "*El* Queen of Evil?" Couldn't be anybody else.

"She's here." He bobbed his head. "Last act."

For the first time in hours, Bill smiled. "Do acts hang out in a special place?"

"No, everybody just hangs till they hear their name."

"Well, if you see her, tell her I'll be standing—" he looked around "—next to the guy with the glasses of water." Easy landmark.

"Sure, dude."

As Bill worked his way through the crowd, a woman's voice announced over the speakers, "Let's give a hand to our next contestant, Bingo Huttner and his harmonica!"

Bill positioned himself next to the guy with the water glasses, who was creating an ethereal mix of pitches by rubbing the rims.

"You're going to play 'Good Vibrations' on those?" he asked.

The man stopped, looked up. "No, I'm going to play Rachmaninoff's Piano Concerto Number Two in C minor."

Man, he sure had a knack for pissing off people today.

"Bill?"

A woman, looking like a sexy Winona Ryder in *Beetlejuice,* stood in front of him. Her voice was familiar. That spiderweb tattoo peeking over the top of her corset was even more familiar.

"Ellie," he murmured, shaking his head from side to side in rare wonder. "What have you done…"

His gaze traveled down the long fishnet gloves, the black-and-red corset that offered up two creamy mounds, the ruffly skirt bunched high like a curtain over a show of legs in black fishnet down to her…thongs?

"Bill?"

He looked up, fighting a grin.

"Are you laughing at me?"

He scratched his chin, not wanting to put his foot into it again. She'd already walked away once today. "I was amused at the fishnet and thongs, that's all."

Her deep purple lips twitched. "I'm wearing them so I can walk, silly." She held up a plastic bag. "The stilettos are in here."

A hot thrill jagged through him as he remembered her in those shoes, quickly cooling when he caught the intensity in her eyes. Anger? Disappointment? Her makeup was like a mask, making him dependent on what he interpreted in her eyes.

"I'm sorry about what happened today," he murmured. "And being late tonight. Sullivan wanted another meeting after shooting stopped, and by the time I left the set, I had no idea how late it was." He held up his wrist. "Lost my watch today."

"Bill!" squealed a female voice. A shapely flash of silver bounced to a stop in front of him. "Remember me?"

Only a man who didn't like women wouldn't have looked at her jiggling breasts, unencumbered by a bra. If he hadn't seen the line of her sleeves, he'd swear she'd been spray painted with silver.

Obviously she'd seen what caught his eye because she gave them an extra shimmy. "It's me. Phoebe."

"Right." He started to turn back to Ellie when Phoebe tugged on his arm.

"Hey!" Locking her eyes on his, she spread her red lips into a smile that had sex written all over it. "Guess what I am?" she whispered.

"Phoebe, I don't have time for this—"

"Oh," she said, turning serious, "I almost forgot that Sullivan asked me to give you a message."

He frowned. "I just talked to him fifteen, twenty minutes ago."

"Actually, it was Curtiss who called me a few minutes ago, had a message from Sullivan."

Curtiss was her boss, so it made sense he'd call her. "So, what is it?"

She leaned forward, the movement pressing a silver-sprayed breast against his arm. Those red, wet lips whispered huskily, "He said you have to guess what I am."

"What?"

She made a *brrrr* noise with her mouth. "I'm a vibrator!"

He shook her off his arm, feeling pissed at himself for falling for such a dumb come-on. That "Sullivan asked me to give you a message" line was very good, very cunning. Everybody on the set knew Bill would say "how high?" whenever Sullivan said hop.

Those red lips moved closer. "Want to be my Good Vibrations partner?"

He stepped back. "I already have a partner."

But when he turned to Ellie, she was gone.

THE QUEEN OF EVIL was royally pissed off. And hurt. And disappointed. She regretted she'd spent all those hours this afternoon practicing and preparing for this effing contest.

And she'd never have announced her intention to jump his bones if she'd known there'd be another woman's breast planted on them.

When Phoebe lured in Bill with that line about Sullivan having a message for him, Ellie decided to book. The day Sullivan needed to call a silver-sprayed vibrator to get in touch with anybody was the day Phoebe ran her own telecommunications company.

Bill was too smart to fall for that. Or too whipped by Sullivan. Either way, Ellie hadn't wanted to waste another millisecond of her time there, so she'd wandered down the midway to this quiet picnic area next to a closed concession stand. Besides a couple making out at a far table, she was alone.

Which was good because she felt as though she was going to cry.

Blinking back tears, she set the bag next to her on the seat. "Great," she muttered to herself, fishing in the plastic bag for the hand mirror. If she cried, her face would end up looking like a Rorschach test. Finding the mirror, she squinted into it at her shadowy reflection. Too dark to really see.

She tossed the mirror back into the bag, then looked up at the man in the moon. "What do you think Bill saw when he looked at me tonight? I think he didn't like the Ellie he saw."

So, it was the cliché beach babe, blond, tanned look that he desired, not the Ellie underneath. She felt a little silly reaching that conclusion since, if she were totally honest with herself, she'd known it the moment he first talked to her after the audition. After all, when he'd seen her goth that first day in the parking lot, his only interest in her had been if she'd move her car.

He doesn't accept the real me.

For a hard moment, she hated the man she'd held in her heart all these years.

"You know you don't believe that," said a male voice.

She jumped.

A man leaned against the concession stand, puffing on a pipe. Odd to see someone at the festival dressed in a businesslike white jacket and pants, although his bald head and mustache fit right in. She guessed he owned this stand, and was probably enjoying a quiet smoke at the end of the day.

You know you don't believe that? Oh. He'd obviously overheard her self-pitying whine about Bill not liking what he saw in Ellie tonight.

He strolled to a nearby table, the thick, sweet scent of pipe tobacco in his wake, and hitched his foot onto the seat. A cloud passed over the moon, and in the milky darkness he looked almost otherworldly. Like a ghost.

She shook her head, amused at her imagination. If *he* looked otherworldly, she could only imagine what she looked like.

A roar of laughter billowed from the Good Vibrations contest.

"Sounds like they're having a good time," he said.

"Hmmph."

"But you're having a bad time."

"Yeah, well, it's been one of those days."

"Want to talk about it?"

She snorted a laugh. He probably meant well, but the last thing she wanted to do was talk about her problems to a total stranger. "Thanks, but no thanks."

She gathered her bag, stood, looked around. She didn't want to walk back down the midway, which would take her right by the Good Vibrations contest. The last people she wanted to see were the breast-slinging human vibrator and what's his name.

Unfortunately, the midway was the only way.

"You wouldn't happen to know another route out of here besides the main one, would you?"

He tapped the bowl of his pipe against the table as he shook his head. "You'll have to walk through it, can't walk around it."

Like that was a lot of help. "Okay, well, thanks." She turned to leave.

"If it's worth fighting for," he said, raising his voice, "then fight the good fight."

She looked back, frowning. "What?"

"Cinderella doesn't make it home before mid-night, but that's not the end of her story."

Somebody else had said those exact words…this man couldn't be…Magellan?

No, Magellan had that Jimmie Buffett clothes thing going. Plus, this man was too low-key. He'd probably been in the audience that day, then tonight overheard her whining to the man in the moon about Bill and he'd remembered Magellan's "message from the spirits" to her.

Although seemed odd he'd remember it word for word....

"I need to take off, too." He lowered his foot, looked up at the moon. Emitting a yawn, he stretched his arms. Something sparkled on his hand.

She recalled Magellan's pinkie ring, the blue sapphire.

As he started walking away, she called out after him.

"Wait!"

He paused, looked back.

"Your ring…is it sapphire?"

"Yes," he said, sounding pleased she'd noticed. "It's the stone of destiny."

The exact same words Magellan had whispered to her. No one else, not even Bill, could have heard that. As strange as it seemed, he *had* to be Magellan.

"You want to know your destiny, don't you?" he asked.

All she could do was stare, tongue-tied. She'd hoped that Magellan would say something to validate another dimension, that spirits really did whisper messages, yet she'd walked away disappointed.

But tonight, the way he'd seemed to read her thoughts, appear out of nowhere, even use the very word—*destiny*—that she'd thought about in conjunction with Bill just a few hours ago, well, this was it. She was open, ready for the mystery to be unveiled.

She nodded her head, her heart racing.

"Your destiny is…Gonzo."

Gonzo?

Had he said *Gonzo?*

The guy was a nut.

She watched him prop the pipe back in his mouth and stroll away.

She really didn't need any more of this beach-vacation time, thank you. Much saner to pack up and go home, get the coffee shop ready for the big move.

Another blast of applause and yells. She turned toward the Good Vibrations game, steeling herself for the walk past the activities, dreading what she might see. How she'd love not to be walking alone. What sweet revenge it'd be to have Bill see her in the company of some mammoth-sized hunk, his beefy arm wrapped protectively around her, his face darkly Byronic, his attitude edgy and wild like a Lou Reed.

She sighed, starting walking.

If only there really were a Gonzo.

13

MINUTES LATER, Ellie neared the Good Vibrations contest. She slowed down, eyeing the midway where it curved past the crowd of people. Unless she wanted to crawl behind game booths and trespass vendor stands, she had to walk the walk.

Maybe if she slouched, kept her eyes on the ground, she'd look smaller, less obvious.

She did so, staring down at sandy beach littered with cigarette butts, bottle caps, tossed ride tickets. Somebody jostled past, shoving up against her so hard, she nearly lost her balance.

She straightened, angry. "Hey, watch where you're going!" A few people looked back. Someone laughed. She suddenly felt pathetic, being angry at someone and not sure who.

Worse, she felt as though she'd given away her power.

Not just because some stranger had thrown her off balance, but from a lot of things these past few days. Because she'd changed her looks to please people, to get a job as an extra. Because she'd stayed that way to keep Bill interested, then switched back to test him. She'd spent so much energy worrying and being afraid if she'd be accepted, she'd lost her sense of self.

Ellie Rockwell was better than this.

She'd survived a father's desertion, parented a mother and prevailed as a businesswoman. It hadn't been easy, but she'd met the challenge each time, and in doing so learned power took many forms...from money to knowledge to sometimes simple charm. That's why she got the Queen of Evil tattoo, because she believed that character had been misunderstood. The Queen of Evil, she'd tell people, wasn't evil, she was powerful.

Cheers erupted from the contest.

Ellie adjusted her crown, smoothed a hand down her skirt. She'd faced worse in her life. Pulling back her shoulders, she headed down the walk.

The Queen of Evil was back.

"WE'RE HAVING A BIT of technical difficulty," announced the female voice over the speakers. "So we'll be taking a short break before our last contestant, El Queen of Evil."

Bill, standing at a taco truck across the midway, jerked his gaze toward the Good Vibrations contest. "Jimmie, she came back."

Jimmie stopped pouring hot sauce into his taco. "How do you know?"

He jabbed a thumb in the direction of the contest. "They just announced her act."

"El Queen of Evil?"

"Not sure why they added the El, but yes, that's her. How could you forget the tattoo?"

"Didn't *forget* it." Jimmie smiled. "I just don't memorize every detail about Ellie, but then I'm not the one who's in love with her." He took a bite of taco.

He thought Bill was in love with Ellie?

With a nervous laugh, he stood, fished in his pocket for change. "Hey, I talked your ear off because I've been frantic trying to find her. Doesn't mean—"

"That you love her?"

"Yeah, something like that," he muttered. He pulled out a wad of bills. "So, what do I owe you?"

"You know, when you talked my ear off, you talked about a lot more than just *looking* for her." He swiped a napkin across his mouth. "You talked about her eyes. Fishnet. Her shoes…"

Remembering those polka-dot wedges made Bill smile. Remembering those stilettos, on the other hand…

"I'm easing into this part, my friend, because I remember too well what it was like interviewing you for my screenplay. You didn't just hate talking about growing up in East L.A., you *detested* it. I had to pull the information out of you, like a dentist extracting a bad, but firmly entrenched, tooth. So when you run into me at a festival and want to talk, and a lot of that is about your past, I know how significant that is." He paused, studying Bill's face. "Hate to go poetic on you, but history binds hearts. Especially shared history."

"Being around Ellie these few days has brought some memories of the old neighborhood to the surface, that's all. Anyway—" he flipped through his money "—I'm married to my career. No time for love."

"That union you got going with *Sin on the Beach* needs some marriage counseling."

"If it's so great for you, why do you stay?" He laid a bill on the counter.

"It's only a paycheck while I plan for the real deal." He pointed at the bill. "Too much."

"Take it."

"How 'bout we place a bet?"

Bill smiled. "Double or nothing?"

"Sure."

"What're we betting on?"

"That you'll be joining the married men's club in the near future?"

Bill laughed. "Hate to see a good friend lose money, but if you must, you must." He looked over at Good Vibrations. "Gotta go. Give my best to Bev."

As he threaded his way through the hubbub of people, he heard Jim's booming voice behind him.

"So long, loser!"

ELLIE STOOD IN THE CENTER of the small stage, wishing the Queen of Evil still felt as cocky as she had a few minutes ago. It was one thing to storm the citadel. A whole other bag of beans to be inside it, dozens of eyes watching your every move.

At least she'd arrived during the break, which gave her a few minutes to check out the stage, quietly walk through her steps. She'd scanned the crowd a few times, hadn't seen Bill. Which made her feel weird. Bad. Confused. She recalled something Lou Reed was once quoted saying—"Life is like Sanskrit read to a pony." He was right.

Over the speakers, static crackled and hissed. "We're back, Good Vibers! Technical difficulties fixed. We hope." Laughter. "We've made a management decision. Another sound drop during this last act, and we call it a night. Performance will be judged on its partial. Then we'll tally up the scores, and announce the top three winners, which will also be posted on the contest sign."

Clapping, whistles.

"All right, everyone give a hand to our last contestant…El Queen of Evil!"

Whoops, yells.

Ellie frowned, looked at the announcer, who smiled back.

"Ready, your majesty?"

Her stomach did a slow-motion lurch. This was really happening. *Life is like Sanskrit read to a pony. Life is like…*

She nodded. Go, Team Java Mammas.

The music began, its moody, pulsing beat familiar and calming. Closing her eyes, she relaxed into the music, swaying slightly, feeling it as it built to a dark, rumbling sound. Like the ocean at night, churning its secrets from the deep.

Excitement tingled at the base of her spine. She stretched, releasing the thrill up her vertebrae, feeling its heat lick along her backbone, teasing and tonguing a path, the heat spreading until her entire body finally melted into the sound.

Music had always been her escape, her refuge. She'd lose herself in the sounds and words, gradually letting go of her world, immersing herself until her awareness was pure sensation and sound.

She was almost there now….

The contest, the people, the stage were slipping into another dimension…leaving her conscious of her body and its fluidity, how it felt to move and sway to the music…to be lost in sensation….

Suddenly, she recalled that feeling with Bill. The delicious feeling of being lost in his kiss, his touch….

A trickle of notes brought her back. She opened her eyes, resisting the urge to scan the crowd. Instead, she stared over the tops of their heads, focusing on the faintest threads of orange and pink in the dark blue sky.

The beat changed. She followed, rolling her shoulders side to side, gliding to the music. As the music trembled on a single note, she did a small, slow shimmy—she'd learned this years ago in dance, easily recalled it while practicing today—her movements building with the music, going faster, bigger.

A wolf whistle split the air.

She smiled, liking the encouragement. *See what you're missing, Bill?*

The tune shifted. She dropped the shimmy, slid out one stilettoed foot, the silver chain sparkling in the light. When the drum beat, once, she gave a little kick.

"Queenie, you kick, girl!" someone yelled.

The partying crowd was loose, fun, supportive. Sure, she wanted to win for the Java Mammas, but even more, she wanted to enjoy herself, get silly, have fun. She hadn't done something wild and crazy like this in years!

The beat picked up. For a moment, she forgot what she'd planned to do, but remembered in time to catch up with the beat. Fisting her hands on her hips, she bumped her hips as she strutted across the stage in a move called "you want it, you got it."

You know what, Bill? I have it, but you don't get it!

As the tempo thumped, she bumped her booty to the beat, coyly peeling off a fishnet glove. She was having so much fun, she barely flinched during a minor traffic jam of fishnet and fingers. Several tugs, and she was back to the beat.

Sort of.

She'd lost her place in the music again! As she listened, trying to remember, she waved the glove in the air, keeping time with the music. Some started clapping along. A few sang. She felt like a funky, sexy camp counselor leading everyone in a sing-along.

The music surged into a familiar cacophony of sounds.

Okay, she remembered this part! This is where she did that burlesque move called "shakin' the front door, shakin' the back door." Unlike shimmying, she'd had to practice this over and over. Well, here goes...

While her lower body sidestepped, her upper body shook. Shakin' the front door, baby, shakin' *it*. She nearly stumbled as she started back, but caught herself. After waiting a beat, she hunkered down and shook her back door so hard, it got a round of applause!

Eat your heart out, Bill!

She felt more zany, alive and boldly bodacious than she had in years. Before this vacation, if someone had told her she'd be digging being an exhibitionist, she'd have said they were crazy. But here she was, the center of everyone's attention, playing the tease, and she was loving every single moment of it.

Song was winding down. Realizing she still carried the peeled-off fishnet glove, she had an idea. A little naughty giveaway.

With a grand flourish, she made a show of tucking the glove inside her cleavage, leaving a little hanging out.

She looked around, pointed at a man in the audience.

He whooped, raised his fists in victory. "I won!" he yelled.

She laughed. Locking eyes with him, she strutted up to him, then leaned forward slightly, giving a little shimmy, letting him have a shot of her quivering breasts and cleavage…in her peripheral vision, she saw his hand reach…

Then jerk back.

A yell.

She looked up as a pair of brown hands reached out, grabbed her by the shoulders. Her breath grew ragged as she stared into a pair of dark, angry eyes set in a fierce face.

Bill!

"That's enough," he growled, muscles bunching along his jaw. "Stop."

His dark, territorial gaze should have struck terror into her heart, but only made it pound harder. A smart woman would defuse the situation with a joke, a quiet word, a passive gesture.

Not the Queen of Evil.

Her face hot, her heart racing, she squirmed, her mounds shimmying with the effort.

"Make me," she growled.

For a long, hot, suspended moment, he looked at her. Then he raised a dark, scornful eyebrow. "What?"

"I said—"

He slammed his mouth over hers, his hands gripping her arms, hers gripping back, their kiss hard, punishing, filled with dark energy and an intense, carnal rage that should have been terrifying.

But it thrilled her right down to the pointed tips of her stilettos.

He suddenly ripped free from the kiss. Still

gripping her arms, he stared down at her, his nostrils flaring with each sharp, inhaled breath.

Vaguely she realized she'd fisted his shirt in her hands, holding him in place in case he had other ideas. The music had stopped, even the crowd was quiet, the only sounds the faint clatter and shrieks of a distant ride and its occupants.

A burning urgency crackled between them, as though every teasing word, move, insinuation they'd made these last few days had coalesced into this scorching moment.

"I'll make you," he growled.

In a rush of movement, he leaned over and scooped her up, lifting her effortlessly. As he straightened, she experienced a giddy flashback of the Ferris wheel, the exhilarating assent, and then the stop at the top of the world where nothing else existed except the two of them.

She wrapped her arms around his neck, chills scattering over her body as she held on for the rest of this ride.

As he started walking across the stage, a thief with his treasure, the crowd starting whistling and clapping, the noise so loud it was impossible to hear whatever Didi was saying over the microphone.

Ellie leaned close to Bill's ear. "They think this is part of the act."

"Well, I was *supposed* to be part of it, if you'll recall."

As he carried her down the festival midway,

people flashed them looks, a few bewildered, some startled, most amused. It dawned on her she'd forgotten her thongs, could never manage the sand in these heels, but who cared? She'd crawl if she had to, but no way she was putting the brakes on this real-life fantasy. The queen was busy being abducted by a ravaging marauder intent on plundering and pillaging and she hoped a whole lot worse.

Jump his bones? She was going to pulverize them.

As a group of people parted, making way for them, a guy with a blond Mohawk winked at her, mouthing "give me your number."

"I'll give it to you," cut in Bill, pausing. "It's five-five-five in-your-dreams."

The guy's smile vanished, as did he.

If he hadn't, Ellie wouldn't have put it past Bill to take it a step further. Like a street fighter, he was savage, primal, and she'd be a liar if she said it didn't excite the hell out of her.

They were in front of some kind of giant Twister game, with couples bent and stretched all over each other. Outside, bright lights swirled to the old Chubby Checker "Let's Twist Again" classic.

Bill pressed a gentle kiss against her hairline, making her shudder. She looked up into his face, mesmerized by the reflection of red, blue, yellow lights playing on his brown skin. The vibrant colors reminded her of his dragon tattoo.

She hadn't given him enough credit. Anybody who chose a tattoo like that wouldn't be turned off by a glam goth chick. Made her feel a little dumb to have worried so much, to have even set up tonight's goth test to see his reaction. When the time was right, and there weren't so many distractions, she'd open up about her life and stop playing hide-and-seek.

After all, Ellie Rockwell was better than that.

Feeling relieved, she planted a return kiss on his cheek, tasting its salty wetness. Although she preferred to think his heavy breathing was solely due to sexual arousal, he'd obviously overexerted himself.

"You can put me down now," she murmured, "I'm too heavy."

"Too heavy?" He dipped his head again, so close she felt the warm puffs of his breath against her skin. "My Ellie is just right."

My Ellie? *Just right?*

Oh boy, now he'd done it.

If she wasn't so determined to impose some kind of logical boundary around her heart, or at least pretend to do so, she'd just open the portals to her heart and soul right now and admit she was and had always been desperately, unequivocally and completely head over heels in love with him.

Instead, she sank against him and let his words wash over her. *My Ellie is just right.* She looked up at the sky and its smattering of stars, took in the whirl of music and voices, the scents of cotton candy and corn dogs, mentally burning the imprint of it all into her brain. She wanted to remember it all, this moment, his words. Just as she used to document him in her girlish journals, she wanted him, tonight, forever branded in her woman's memories. She closed her eyes. *Remember, remember.*

Laughter jarred her back. She opened her eyes.

A couple, laughing, ran past, the girl squealing, "There it is! *Sin on the Beach* Freak Dance Fantasia!" Almost simultaneously, loud rocking music started blasting.

Ellie looked over Bill's shoulder at a dance floor packed with people gyrating, bumping and writhing all over each other.

And in the midst of it, a woman who could almost pass for Sara's twin, shimmying her body all the way down and back up some hunky surfer guy.

A twin wearing Sara's clothes.

The crowd shifted. Other writhing, grinding, dancing bodies blocked Ellie's view.

Wow. Ellie turned back, amazed. Hardworking, nose-to-the-grindstone Sara was getting into some serious mojo.

Time for Ellie to get some, too.

She put her lips against Bill's ear and whispered hotly, "How about you put down just-right Ellie and save that energy for something else." She trailed her lips to his earlobe and suckled, leaving no doubt what that something else might be.

"Okay," he said quickly, lowering her to the ground.

Their arms around each other, they gazed into each other's eyes, oblivious of the sounds and people around them.

"Your place or mine?" he murmured huskily.

"I'm within walking distance," she whispered, pressing her body against his. "Except, I don't know if my roommates are coming home." She thought of Sara. "Well, one definitely isn't, but the other—" did Candy and Matt's sensible sex agreement mean no sleepovers? "—could be home, and it'd be nice to have some privacy."

"I don't have roommates, so sounds like it's my place then." He kissed the tip of her nose. "But we'll have to drive to Venice."

She snuggled a little closer. "That's, what… thirty minutes?"

"Twenty if I'm not stopped for speeding."

She gave him a slow, mischievous grin. "Let's go, lead foot."

14

MINUTES LATER, they exited the festival and ran barefoot on the cool sandy beach, the lights from the festival offering visibility for another thirty or so feet. Beyond that, except for the lights of cars buzzing along Pacific Coast Highway, it was dark.

"My car's parked up there." Bill gestured toward the highway. "Down by the billboard."

Ellie, her stilettos dangling by their straps from her fingers, stopped. "What billboard?"

He hugged her with one arm, pointing with the other.

She groaned. "I thought that was a parked truck! It'll take us days to get there!"

"I know, parking sucks in Malibu. Everybody's stuck along the highway."

"Even if you're the director for *Sin on the Beach?*"

"First, I'm not the director, yet. And actually, it's no sweat finding a spot close to the set because we all arrive so early in the mornings."

She looked over. "Oh, I see…the billboard is about where the filming takes place."

"Tell you what. We'll take a short rest, then start walking. C'mere…" He pulled her closer and nuzzled his chin against the top of her head. "Ouch."

"What? Oh, the crown."

He pulled back, frowning at her head. "So *that's* what that is. I thought maybe you were picking up signals from outer space—"

"The queen is not amused!" she said with a smile, throwing her shoes over her shoulder for dramatic effect. Fumbling with the pins in her hair, she flashed on her odd encounter with the Magellan clone. "Who knows," she murmured, "maybe I have been picking up signals."

"I'll help." Tossing his flip-flops aside, he joined in, pulling on a strip of foil, but mostly enjoying the sensation of her silky hair, the warmth of her fingers brushing his.

"You're not helping," she teased.

"Yeah, but it feels good." He lifted strands, liking how they felt sifting through his fingers. "You look different with black hair."

She stilled for a moment. "Does that mean you like it?"

"Sure, it works on you."

"But do you *like* it?" She held out her hand with several pins. "Put these in your pocket for me?"

He didn't understand her sudden concern, but he'd learned long ago that when women asked about weight, hair or clothes, the smart man flew low under the radar.

"So, you'd like it if I kept it black?" She tugged

on a strip of foil. "I mean, is that an acceptable *Sin on the Beach* extra-in-the-background hair color?"

"Sure, it's acceptable. What's important is that *you* like it, Ellie."

He reached out, took the ball of foil, tossed it into a nearby trash can.

"Nice shot," she said admiringly.

"*You're* nice," he murmured, touching her cheek. She felt so warm, so soft…so there. So significant in the blur of his life. Everything had been moving so fast, he hadn't even realized how superficial it all felt, what poor company a film set could be, what poorer company he was as he ran from one task to the next, from one woman to the next, never stopping because to do so meant he'd have to confront his loneliness.

A loneliness that went away when he was with her.

"Tell you the truth, Ellie," he said, stroking her cheek, "you could have purple hair with green streaks, and I'd still like it."

They both laughed, growing quieter as their eyes met. He cradled her face, amazed at the connection he felt with her, wanting more of her. Not just her body, but her mind, her free spirit. What did she like to read? Did she like chocolate? Was she a morning or night person…

Did they have the potential to be more? Maybe Jimmie had been right…maybe Bill had fallen in love….

And she wondered if he liked her *hair?*

"Ellie," he murmured, his heart tumbling like the dark waves in the distance, "it's *you* I like."

He lowered his hands, his fingertips grazing the softness of her shoulder, the roughened texture of lace along the sides of her corset, the slickness of her satin skirt. Wrapping his hands around her, he cupped her bottom and pulled her gently against him.

"It's you I want."

He leaned down and pressed a kiss in her hair, drowning in the lavender scent of her shampoo, trailing his lips down her impossibly soft cheek.

"You," he whispered.

He brushed his mouth against hers, sharing her sweet breath.

"You," he murmured, "You…"

He pressed his mouth to hers, nibbling her plump top lip, tasting, teasing, before sliding his tongue between her lips. She opened her mouth for him, emitting a low, throaty sound of such pure pleasure, he felt himself get hard.

The feel of her nails scraping lightly on his neck stimulated him even more. He took the kiss deeper, invading the wet warmth with his tongue, seeking, exploring, wanting her so much his entire body ached.

With a low, prolonged shudder, Ellie gripped his shoulders, rising up and positioning herself until her pelvis pressed against his erection.

"Oh…" she whispered, "that's…so…good."

It was better than that. Holding her tightly against him, he looked around. A few couples were exiting the festival, cutting up to the highway.

"No one can see," she murmured, thrusting against him with small, controlled movements.

"Ellie…"

"Shh…oh yes, stay like that." She thrust lightly again. "They'll just think we're kissing…."

She looked up into the shadow of his face, moaning as his lips found hers.

Insinuating his body closer, feeling her flattened breasts against his chest, he groaned as their kiss picked up where they'd left off, their tongues coiling and curling and sucking, her pelvis making him crazy with those small, tight thrusts.

Cupping her bottom, he crushed her against his swollen need, growing even hotter thinking about that short, teasing front panel of her skirt. It wouldn't take much to lift it all the way and slip inside….

He yanked back his head, breaking off the kiss.

She looked at him with a stunned expression, her mouth open, those luscious mounds quivering with each breath.

"What?" she whispered shakily.

He glanced toward the billboard as he swiped a hand across his slick brow. "Okay," he said, turning back. "Now that we've rested—"

"You call that *resting*?"

"You know what I mean." He mindlessly flapped the edge of his shirt, as though that might cool him down.

"Oh, no!" she said, shaking her head vehemently. "I'm not taking a two-mile hike after *that!*"

"Ellie." He rasped a laugh. "It's not two miles—"

"I'm not through resting!" With a grin, she fisted her hands on her hips to stand her ground, teetering slightly.

He sputtered a laugh. "Okay, I get your point. I'd like a nice big rest, too, but it's time to go."

"No."

"We can't stay here."

"No?"

"No." A couple walked past, laughing, waving good-night. He nodded, waved. "See what I mean?"

"They're at least forty feet away!"

"For crissake, Ellie, you want to do it right here, in front of everyone?" He blinked at the why-not look on her face. "My God," he murmured, "you really are an exhibitionist!"

She rolled her eyes. "And this from the man who stormed the stage like King Kong."

"Like you didn't love it."

"I did," she whispered. "Every single moment."

The way she looked at him gave his heart a squeeze.

"But to go back to your question, no, I don't want to do it where people can see... I mean, that's great fantasy material, just not so hot in the real world."

"You—" He blinked. "You've done that?"

"No!" She paused. "Have you?"

"No!"

She studied his face for a moment. "Three-way?"

He cleared his throat. "Let's grab our shoes, hit the road."

She gasped. "More than once?"

"I can't believe we're—" He blew out an exasperated breath. "Once. Okay, where'd you toss your shoes?"

"*Only* once?"

"Only once."

She made a vague gesture toward the south. "Me, never. I was invited to, but I really didn't like the guy. His girlfriend was nice, but…" She scrunched her face. "Not my thing."

"Thanks for sharing," he muttered, checking the sand.

She looked out toward the black, distant waves. "Although I wouldn't want to do it where people could see, I wouldn't mind if it were darker…."

"Well, it's not darker, and your shoes aren't over here."

"Here's one…" She halted, looked over at him. "Never mind, false alarm." She picked up his thong. If he had to keep looking for it, they'd have to stay here longer….

She loved how the light played on his body. Wearing so few clothes—shorts and a shirt—there was a lot of naked to see on the man. When he crossed between her and highway lights, she caught jagged flashes of his silhouette. The outline of a muscled leg. The curve of a bicep. Even the dark, threadlike shape of his fingers.

She recalled the different ways those fingers had touched her. Feathering lightly across her back. Burrowing into her hair. Or, just moments ago, crushing her greedily against his swollen groin.

Her sex throbbed. She was so hot, so turned on….

"I'll look over here," she called out, sauntering toward the beach, looking at him over her shoulder. When his back was turned, she smiled, tossed the thong aside. It'd take a long time to find it, if it was even findable in the dark.

In a matter of steps, she'd crossed into the dusky night, where she tugged loose the satin ribbon that threaded together the front of her corset. Standing near the shoreline, she paused, listened to the distant pounding surf. A low-flying plane, its light blinking, seemed to coast in front of the moon.

She pulled apart the top of the bodice, sucking in a sharp breath at the onslaught of cool air against exposed skin. She wanted to make it as easy as possible for him to do the things she wanted to do. Fumbling in the dark with the ribbons and buttons on her corset was the last thing she wanted them to be spending their time on.

"Found one of your shoes," he called out.

She strangled back a laugh. This guy needed to be reeled in, get his priorities straight. If she wanted to go hunting for shoes, she'd go on a shopping spree with her girlfriends. Right now, all that mattered was to be together in the dark, immersing themselves with each other, feeding their hunger.

She strolled toward him, feeling bold, sexual, a predator stalking its prey. Unashamed, primed, ready to indulge her needs in the moment…not later, but here, now.

As she approached, he halted his search and straightened, watching her, a question in his eyes.

"Ellie?"

He stood on the edge of the light, not bright enough for him to see she'd loosened her top, or recognize the look in her eyes. But even a blind man in the dark could feel and hear….

She stopped inches from him, her breasts rising and falling with her needy breaths. She took his hand and pulled it to her, laid it gently on her pushed-up, swollen breast.

"Oh, yes," she said, her control growing ragged as chills rippled through her. "I love your hands on me," she whispered. "When you touch me, it's unbelievable how it makes me feel. It turns me on, makes me ache for more."

Even in this hazy light, she saw a hot, needy look flicker to life in his dark eyes.

She leaned forward and lightly touched her lips to his.

Once.

Then she pulled back and, ever so lightly, trailed his hand down over her loosened corset, letting him feel how it barely contained her spilling breasts.

"I'm so horny," she murmured, "I could probably come with a single touch."

Then she gently released his hand, turned and started walking toward the shoreline, not bothering to look back because she knew he'd follow, ready to do her bidding.

The queen had spoken.

FEW THINGS threw Bill off. He was like a bull in that way. Solid, grounded, fearless. But wave a red flag, and he'd snort and bellow and paw the ground, intent and focused on one thing and one thing only.

That is, after he regained his motor skills. For the moment, it was all he could do to remain standing. The breathy ache in her voice, the creamy plumpness of her breasts, the knowledge that she'd loosened that sexy corset had left him foggy, disoriented…and incredibly turned on.

He dropped the shoes and followed.

Stumbling across the sand, he kept his eyes on the wavering mirage of her pale back and arms. The rest of her, the black corset, black skirt, black hair, seemed to merge with the night.

The sand softened under his feet, moist from the recent tide. He paused, let his eyes adjust to the darkness. In the distance, waves sparkled under the moonlight. Somewhere out there, the noise of distant surfboards chopping and cutting the waves sounded almost like a hand stroking skin.

"Over here," whispered Ellie.

He turned, momentarily awestruck at the sight.

She looked otherworldly, a vision in black, her face hovering and faint. Like a siren in the velvet night.

Not enough light to distinguish features, but enough to grasp shapes and movements; he realized she held out her hand. She seemed so comfortable here. He smiled to himself. Perhaps because this was her realm. Yes, indeed.

The Queen of Evil.

He grasped her hand, pulled her into his arms. Lowering his head, he felt dizzy with the feel, the scent, the warmth of her. Just holding her made him crazy for relief. He gritted his teeth, fighting the need even as it spiraled higher, hotter. Burrowing his lips into her silky hair, he inhaled its rich scent like a man taking his last breath.

"Lavender," he murmured, an image flashing in his mind. Summer. Fragrant purple blossoms. "I remember now," he whispered, warming to the memory, "your mom was always watering lavender bushes along the side of your house."

"You remember the funniest things."

"It's all in the details," he murmured, burrowing a hand into the silky mass. "Lavender is like you. Vibrant and sweet."

She laughed softly. "I'm not that sweet."

"That's right." He nuzzled the sensitive patch of skin behind her ear. "Not when you're the Queen of Evil."

His hands hungrily roamed over her back, sliding over an expanse of satin, like liquid under his fingers.

"When I first saw you tonight—" he slid his hand up her back, luxuriating in the silky warmth of her skin "—your breasts pushed up like that, your legs exposed underneath that naughty skirt—" he released a ragged breath "—I thought I'd died and gone to heaven."

He slowly stroked his flattened palm along the back, up, then down.

"It opens in front," she murmured.

"Thanks for the directions," he whispered, capturing her earlobe with his teeth. He nibbled and suckled, excited by her small moan of pleasure.

She suddenly grabbed his head and pulled him into a deep kiss, teasing her tongue into his mouth with a low, needy moan that shot a blast of heat right down to his groin. She slid her tongue in and out, licking and sucking, her frenzy building.

Ellie suddenly jerked back her head, her lips leaving his with an audible pop. She stepped back, just out of reach.

He took a deep breath, confused. "You okay?"

She half laughed, the sound light, teasing. "Very okay." A moment passed. "Can you see what I'm doing?"

He blinked, straining to discern the pale movement of her hands in the dark. "No."

"Listen."

He heard a wisp of satin. A succession of light snaps.

"I'm taking off my corset."

The black peeled off, dropped. In the moonlight,

he saw her naked from the waist up, the tips of her breasts dusty against her soft, pale skin. Her lack of inhibition driving his need higher.

"Touch me," she whispered.

He closed the space between them, gently, gently reaching for her breasts, stifling a moan as his palms brushed up against her soft, full mounds.

"Yes." She shuddered.

She pressed against him, filling his hands, her nipples nestled against his palms. He brushed them lightly back and forth, back and forth, his need flaring higher as he felt the tips swell and harden, heard her whimpers and moans.

He invoked the memory of her baring her breast when they'd stopped at the top of the Ferris wheel, the jolting thrill of seeing its pebble pink tip, the creamy sheen of her mounds. "Later," he murmured, "I want to see you naked under the light… all of you…"

As she groaned her agreement, he squeezed and kneaded her breasts, then tugged and rolled her hardened nibs, watching her pale body arch with pleasure.

He lowered his head, taking one taut nib into his mouth, flicking and sucking it while stroking the lush weight of the other. When she cried out, he increased his torment, sucking and nipping the sweet puckered nipple until she lay in his arms, her back arched, her head tossed back, her breasts thrust forward as she whimpered she wanted more…more….

"Ellie," he whispered, lifting his head slightly, "you're driving me crazy."

With a needy sound, she gripped his head, holding it in place. He looked up at her pale face, the swirl of night and stars behind her head, imagining her a wanton pagan, a mysterious goddess, a demanding queen. Tightening her grip on his head, she slid and rubbed one nipple, then the other, against his lips, murmuring dark wishes which he greedily obeyed.

And then he was kissing her again, forcing her head back, his lips driving into hers, nipping, devouring, his need furious and hot and urgent...ready to spread her, take her....

Ellie leaned back, momentarily stunned at the beast that had risen in Bill's place, his mouth demanding, his tongue aggressive, his words explicit and coarse. She'd never been kissed this way, kisses that intoxicated and tormented, made her entire body ache and throb for more.

A beach babe would hate it.

This goth chick loved it.

This powerful, commanding, potent man's needs were like a searing stake to her heart, killing off all pretenses while igniting in her a lusty, unrepentant creature whose desires would not be denied. A snarl, guttural and disturbing, rolled up her throat, the primal sound lost in his ravaging mouth.

An instant later he ripped his lips away. Turning her around, panting, she faced the dark, glistening ocean. He nestled behind her, whispering into her ear.

"You hot little exhibitionist," he murmured, taking a moment to suckle her earlobe before continuing. "Let's pretend you're on stage, the wild elements your audience...."

As he spoke, he trailed one hand down to a breast, circling her aching nipple.

"Lift your skirt," he murmured, his lips moving against her neck, making her skin prickle.

She did, and he slid his fingers inside the elastic band of her fishnet stockings, inside her panties, gently separating her folds, his touch feather soft, seeking...

"Tell me where," he whispered, nuzzling her cheek.

She opened her mouth, tasted the salty air, his ministrations on her breast igniting a line of liquid heat down to her groin, where his other hand deftly, lightly circled her nub, waiting for her command.

"A little to the left," she murmured, gasping as he found the spot.

"Is that good?"

She tensed, clutching the skirt as passion whipped through her blood. "Yes," she gasped, the word dissolving into a moan as his fingers worked their magic. His lips nuzzled her neck as he dipped one finger, then two into the slick crevice.

"You're so wet," he murmured huskily.

Shuddering in her throat, she tilted her pelvis forward, rising eagerly with his building tempo.

Through slitted eyes, she looked out at the dark churning ocean, its cool breezes rushing over her, causing her skin to prickle pleasurably. She felt deliciously decadent, unabashedly wanton. Never in her life had she indulged her sexuality like this, felt safe enough, trusted enough to let her fantasy go.

She spread her legs wider to experience more sensation, her hips grinding involuntarily with the expert movements of his fingers. Her body was oh, so hot, on edge, shaking and quivering as he slipped and slid between her legs, harder and faster, driving her higher....

"Come for me," he growled.

The creature released a prolonged, needy groan.

"Yes, sweetheart," he murmured. "Give it to me, let me hear you, feel you...."

Her body shivered all over, the sensations building inside her until she didn't think she could take any more. Her entire being on edge, ready to burst, so hot, so ready.

Suddenly, release ripped through her, ecstasy so exquisite, so savage. She threw back her head and cried out, sinking against Bill's hold, riding and rubbing his hand, again and again, until the spasms gradually lessened....

She sank against him, heaving breaths, sated and sleepy, vaguely aware of his arms wrapped tightly around her waist, his chin resting on her shoulder.

They stayed that way for a quiet moment, looking out at the endless black ocean, the sparkle of moonlight, the scatter of stars.

"That's the best I've ever had," she finally whispered.

"Think so?"

"Know so."

He gently turned her around, reached into his pocket and pulled out a small square packet, held it up for her to see. "Brought it to work because I knew we had this date...."

"Even after our, uh, episode on the set, you still brought it to the Good Vibrations contest?"

"Never say never."

She smiled, taking it from him. "Me, too."

"That's what you were thinking, too?"

"Not thinking, *saying*. I made a vow this afternoon to jump your bones."

He choked back a laugh. "Before or after our, uh, misunderstanding?"

"After."

"If I'd known you were that confident, I wouldn't have worried."

"Not confident." She ripped open the packet. "Determined."

He sucked in a sharp breath as he felt her touch him, gingerly, on the outside of his shorts with her free hand. He grew instantly harder, his urgency rising like a tidal wave. "I've been so horny, so worked up," he whispered, spreading his hand around the back of her head, pulling her closer, "I could probably come with a single touch."

She laughed low in her throat, the sound incredibly seductive. "You're stealing my line."

He leaned his forehead against hers, strangling

back a groan as she caressed him. "I'd like to steal you," he murmured hoarsely. "Steal you away, keep you with me forever."

When she pulled down his shorts, he emitted a sharp hiss, biting back his need as she gently rolled the condom over his aching, swollen member.

Then she stood back, quickly removed her fishnet stockings and undies.

"Oh, yes," he whispered, tugging her to him, roaming his hands over her naked bottom, back, massaging and squeezing her breasts, finally taking her arms and wrapping them around his neck.

"Hold on," he whispered. When she did, he lifted one of her legs, hooking it around his hips.

She clung to him, teetering on her one standing leg. "I don't know if I can—"

"Just lean into me. I'm strong."

"You can say that again," she said, followed with a lusty sigh as she found her balance.

He wedged his erection up hard against her cleft, stroking it against her wet, slick opening, then rubbing it against her apex, around and around, teasing and tormenting her hot, sweet little clit.

"Right there," she suddenly gasped. "Oh, yes… there…"

She dug her nails into his shoulder, the sharp stings spiking his arousal even higher.

"Take it easy," he murmured, half meaning it. Her released inhibitions excited him, made him want her more than ever. He pressed his hips forward, while guiding himself into her stretched opening, filling her slowly, slowly.

He lowered his mouth to hers, took her deep into a hard, rough kiss. Whatever subtlety, whatever lingering finesse he'd pretended to have, shattered to pieces. He tore his mouth from hers, breathing hard, grinding his teeth as he sank into her, holding her arching body. As he seated himself fully within her, she released a deep, guttural groan.

"You…feel…so…good," he moaned.

He lightly rocked his hips, keeping his movements short, controlled, syncing his rhythm with hers. She clung to him, whimpering, begging for more. He gave it to her, thrusting as hard and deep as the position allowed him, her gasps of pleasure taking him higher, hotter, her pulsing hips pulling him in.

Need pounded through him, merging with the sounds of the distant thundering waves. He wanted to devour, ravage, plunder her sweet, ripe mouth, her hot skin…his need so hot, so raw. He spread his legs, leveraging himself as he stroked deeper, harder….

Her body tightened, tensed, then with a shriek she clawed at the air, her insides clamping down around him, squeezing, milking, driving him to that glorious point of no return….

In a mindless fever, he clutched her body tight against his, giving one last thrust.

His breath exploded as he cried out her name,

clutching her as release exploded through him, again and again, to a mind-jarring satisfaction.

For a long moment, they simply held each other, their spent bodies moist with exertion, their heaving breaths mimicking the rhythmic tumbling of the ocean.

Finally, she dropped her leg, laid her head on his chest. Bill ran his fingers up and down the bumps in her spine while she fiddled lazy fingers at the nape of his neck. Balmy breezes lifted strands of damp hair, offered cooling respite to their skin.

"Wow," Ellie finally murmured.

"You can say that again."

"So…" She pulled back, looked up into his face. "How far is it to that billboard again?"

"Not far," he murmured. He kissed the tip of her nose. "As long as we resist the urge for more rest stops."

15

FORTY MINUTES LATER, they walked into Bill's Venice apartment, located on the third floor of an old brick building on Ocean Front Walk, the famous paved beach path that ran the length of Venice Beach. The windows were open, filling the place with the scent of the ocean. The distant sounds of laughter and bongo drums could be heard from the ever-present partiers along the walk.

She looked around his perfectly ordered room, which looked more like an office than a home. Against the far wall sat a metal desk and its swivel chair, bracketed by a bookcase and a large metal file cabinet. Over the scarred wooden floor lay a faded rug, its corners at precise angles to the walls. A black leather couch sat opposite an entertainment center that looked like a guy's dream world—oversize TV, video game player, an XM radio setup.

On the clean white walls were some framed certificates, a few film posters. No photos.

Bill stood in front of the entertainment center. "What would you like to hear?"

"Got Lou?"

"Lou Reed, eh? That's right, you like his music. The former glam rocker, current rock and roller, right?"

"Close enough." She was pleased he didn't sound critical. He'd taken what she'd said to heart the other day.

He picked up the XM radio. "But you have to admit, that guy's had more styles than a Macy's department store window. Let's see what we can find."

"Lots of people go through different styles. Look at Madonna." She wandered over to one of the film posters. The background was a man's face in blue, in the foreground was a dancing woman. Frederico Fellini and *La Dolce Vita* were in big yellow letters. "Do you like Italian films?"

"Not Italian films as a genre. More I like Fellini for his inventive filmmaking."

"*La Dolce Vita.* That means—"

"The Sweet Life."

"Remember how they used to call the hood *la vida loca*—the crazy life? Now with all the new businesses and money moving in, people are calling it *la dolce vita.*"

"That'll be the day," he muttered. "Hey, can't find anything Reed-like. If you don't mind groovy beach music, how about Jack Johnson?"

"Sure." She crossed to his bookcase, checked out his collection of books on film, a shelf of bounded scripts, a slew of Kellerman, Hiaasen, Patterson novels. Funny to think of him directing a *Baywatch* clone when his tastes ran to more complex stories and characters.

The moody surf tones of Jack Johnson started playing. A song about a guy wanting to make love to his girl.

Bill's arms wrapped around her from behind, his body swaying in time to the beat. He hummed along with the tune.

She leaned against his warmth, her concerns fluttering away. Being with Bill, listening to sexy, sultry music was definitely *la dolce vita.*

"If I don't eat something soon, I might collapse before we get to the good part." He straightened, turned her around. "Like pastrami?"

"Pastrami." She gave a breathless little laugh, struggling with the quick switch from hot to mild. "I like. Yes."

"Good. Remember when I told you I make the best sandwiches this side of New York? Now I'm going to prove it to you. You can wash up while I get it ready."

"Wash up?" She touched her hand to her face, realizing what their heated beach interlude must have done to her makeup. "Please tell me I don't look like a Rorschach test."

He chuckled. "Bathroom's down the hall. There's cleanser in my medicine cabinet, hand towels underneath the sink. Dinner, my sexy lady, will be served in bed."

Moments later, she stared at herself in the mirror, groaning at the black smudges around her eyes, the smeared red on her mouth, the mottled white on her face. Fortunately, it'd been dark all the way from the beach to his building, so he'd only had a few minutes to see her like this.

She found the cleanser, wondered if it was Vi's, but so what? If she'd found other girlfriendlike stuff it would have felt weird, but the bathroom was all male—no extra toothbrush, no makeup, no tampons.

Smearing the cream over her face, thinking of all the other times she'd spent hours putting makeup on and taking it off, for the first time she wondered if she really wanted to keep doing this. Not that she wanted to stop cold turkey being a glam goth, but maybe like Lou Reed, she could shift a little, ease up on her style, on her life, on herself....

She swiped the towel across her forehead, down her cheek, her glowing tan-in-a-can skin showing through. She was starting to feel like an archaeologist, digging through the layers of Ellie. What was underneath the glam goth makeup, the fake tan, even below the pale skin, was, she realized, a mystery even to her.

SETTING THE PASTRAMI, mustard, pickles on the counter, Bill doubted she did things like this for herself. After a day of making coffee and serving food, he imagined her collapsing into a chair with a nuked meal, listening to...Lou Reed? He shook his head, smiling. Marilyn Manson, Siouxsie Sioux, Lou Reed. Other women were often too predictable, too cookie-cutter. They worked out at the same places, ate the same things, shopped for the same clothes. Eventually, predictability led to boredom and he bailed.

Unlike Ellie, who had a habit of shaking up his world, keeping him on his toes. He liked that.

Layering the meat on a slice of bread, spreading the mustard on another slice, evening it out just so, he thought she needed somebody to do this for her. Maybe she surprised him, but he surprised himself even more realizing he wanted to be that somebody. As he selected the best pickle in the jar for her because only the best would do, he finally admitted to himself how deeply his feelings for her went.

It seemed funny to have these epiphanies while making a sandwich, but on the other hand, he took great pride and care in making sandwiches. Not so odd that other things he cared deeply about would float to the surface.

He remembered a bag of chocolates he kept in the back of the cabinet. He set one, wrapped in shiny gold foil, on the edge of the plate. It stood out, nearly perfect, bringing that special extra touch to the ordinary.

Carrying the plates to the bedroom, he realized he would love Ellie Rockwell until he drew his last breath.

"DINNER'S SERVED!" he called out, rounding the corner into his bedroom. He stopped cold, his breath halting in his throat.

Ellie, naked head to toe, smiled shyly. "Hi." She looked at the plate. "That's an awesome-looking sandwich."

He looked her over, from her dark glossy hair, over her heart-shaped face, lingering a moment on her lush, pear-shaped breasts, quickly dropping over her tummy to a final stop on the curling hair at the dark apex between her thighs.

"I have legs, too," she whispered teasingly.

He ducked his head with a laugh, feeling like a schoolboy caught with mirrors on his shoes, as he scanned her legs.

"Very nice legs," he agreed. Looking back at her face, he murmured, "All in all, you're awesome-looking, too."

She laughed, pleased.

He set the plate down on his dresser. "I've suddenly lost my appetite. For food anyway."

As he approached, that simmering look in his eyes leaving no doubt what was coming next, she felt her nipples tighten as a sweet, liquid heat permeated her body.

"I thought you said if you didn't eat first," she whispered teasingly, "that you'd collapse."

"I did." He stopped right in front of her, his gaze melting into hers. "And I will."

Ellie gasped with delight as he dropped out of sight, collapsing to his knees in front of her.

He cupped his hands around her bottom, and tugged her to his mouth. Gently opening her folds, he inhaled deeply, emitting an animal sound of pure pleasure at the scent.

"You smell so sweet," he moaned, planting kisses on her mound, flicking teasing licks along her opening. He nudged her legs farther apart, his pulsating tongue slipping inside, a man on a mission, going after exactly what he wanted.

"Oh, yes!" She grabbed onto his head, teetering slightly as he delved deeper, stroking and licking. His lips were a marvel as they lapped at her tight knot, made her crazy, on fire, her hips and thighs quivering with the exquisite torment.

Just when she didn't think she could take more, he delved a thumb into her wet core, settling it masterfully alongside his relentless tongue.

The combination was like a torch to jet fuel, shooting her heat and moans sky-high.

Keeping his thumb going, he looked up at her, an unholy grin on his face. "I love seeing you like this," he murmured.

"Good," she gasped, pushing his head back into place.

The vibrations of his muffled laughter only added more exquisite sensation to his wickedly talented tongue and thumb, making her delirious with need, her body shaking like a missile on a launch pad, ready to blast off any moment. "Oh yes...right there..."

She suddenly sucked in a breath, holding it as her entire body froze, suspended, on edge....

Tears stung her eyes as the first orgasm rocked her, hard and fierce and swift, the sensations crowding each other, one hitting before another ended. She clutched his hair, back, shoulders, her body undulating, pulsing.

His thumb working her, he looked up. "Want another?"

"Are…you…crazy?" She blinked, looked down. "Yes!"

He drove her pleasure on, giving her another climax…and another…until, exhausted and spent, she grasped his hand and pulled it away, her core still spasming from his touch.

He kissed her tummy, her breasts, her cheek, then nuzzled her neck as he held her quivering body.

"Wow," she murmured, "that's the best I've ever had."

A throaty chuckle. "That's what you said the last time."

"Yeah, but this time I really mean it."

He led her to the bed, helped her lie down.

"We'll see about that," he said, positioning himself over her.

AN HOUR LATER, they sat up in bed, naked, munching on the sandwiches.

Ellie wiped her mouth, picked up a pickle. "This is the best sandwich I've ever eaten."

He nearly choked as he swallowed. "Ellie, c'mon, the best sex…but also the best sandwich? You're going to give me a big head."

She snapped a bite of pickle, giving him a lecherous look. "Speaking of which, I'd like to do that next...."

He held up his hands in a sign of surrender. "Rain check, okay? This man needs his sleep before the alarm goes off in—" he looked at the clock and groaned "—five hours."

"What time is it?"

"Midnight."

They looked at each other.

"So," he said, wiping his mouth with a paper napkin. "Is the carriage turning into a pumpkin?"

She looked intently into his eyes. "I'd almost forgotten about that. No, it's not. But maybe Cinderella's dress is turning into sackcloth."

He frowned. "What?"

She thought this would be easy. Especially after his softening on the topics of Marilyn Manson and Lou Reed, he didn't seem judgmental about how people looked. Because that's all that her confession was about, right? How she liked to dress and wear makeup differently, like the way she had tonight...no big deal, really.

But her throat had tightened, and her nerves felt hopelessly tangled. Because this was more than how she looked. On a deeper, visceral level that she didn't completely understand, she needed to know Bill accepted her no matter what she looked like.

"I'm not who I've been pretending to be."

He set down his sandwich. "You're married."

She rolled her eyes, fighting the urge to laugh. "No. As I told you, there's nobody else." She took a breath, released it. "Remember a few days ago, before the festival opened, you were at the beach trying to get a Benz moved?"

A funny look crossed his face. "Yes, but how did you know that?"

"I was the goth chick reading the *Sin on the Beach* festival poster."

He stared at her.

"You called out to me. Asked if that was my Benz."

Awareness dawned. He blinked, feigned a double take. "The spiky black hair?"

She nodded.

He looked at her black hair, which fell softly about her face. "No wonder you asked if I'd like your hair to stay black. You were…testing me."

An edge had crept into his voice. "Bill, I'm really not a manipulator, if that's what you're thinking. Yes, I tested you, but…can you cut me some slack here? Maybe I liked that you liked what you saw, and I didn't want…to lose you."

God, she felt pathetic. She felt like the twelve-year-old Ellie again, idealistic and dreamy and angst-ridden over Bill Romero, who could squash her world with just a look.

I'm better than that, dammit.

Outside on Ocean Front Walk, somebody whooped, followed by a clanging sound like a bell.

Bill glanced at the window. "That's Venice Beach for you, never a dull moment."

"Yeah, it is, isn't it?" she said sarcastically. She picked at a spot on the bedspread. "Look, as silly as it might sound, I've been freaked out ever since we got together about admitting my goth self to you, and after my confession tonight, I would have appreciated the respect of a Bill Romero truthful answer, like 'I hate glam goths so get out of my life,' or 'glam goths are better than French women' or even 'I don't care let's go to bed.'"

He grabbed her arm. "Whoa, Ellie, let's not make this bigger than it is."

She met his gaze dead-on. "Then if it isn't bigger than it is, what is it?"

He shoved aside their plates and drew her into his arms. "I want to laugh, but I'm afraid you'll take it the wrong way. The truth is, I work in a business where people look different every day. And of the women I've dated, some have changed their styles so often, they make you look like a stick in the mud."

"Like Vi?"

"Vi, yes, she changes her style. Not such a surprise as she runs a clothing shop."

Clothing shop. As though the sexually charged, overly perfect French woman wasn't perfect enough, she now had a business that rivaled Ellie's fledging clothes-design business.

"So, after this week, can I visit you at Dark Gothic Roast, see you in your element?"

Visits? Is that what their future held? She clutched at the bedspread, needing something to hold on to, forcing herself to stay cool, composed. "Sure, come visit."

"You said it's moving soon? To here?"

"Plan is to move into a storefront near Boyle Heights."

"East L.A.?" he said, incredulous. "Ellie, why in God's name would you want to return there?"

She was starting to feel as though she were on an emotional roller coaster. One moment she was tied up in knots making the big confession that she thought would be a fireworks display, but instead sizzled and sputtered into nothing but smoke.

Now she was suddenly embroiled in the topic of her upcoming business move, a discussion that for her was harmless, boring even, but it had suddenly exploded in her face.

"You sound angry," she said, surprised.

He exhaled sharply. "I don't know if *angry* is the word. Astounded, perhaps."

"Critical?"

"Critical, you bet your ass! Moving back to the hood is just plain dumb. Gangs aside, you're a businesswoman, or so you've told me, and you want to move into a region where nearly thirty percent live below the poverty level? Where the hell do you expect to get customers to buy your products?"

With a sickening jolt, she realized this issue, not the one of her looks, was the lack of acceptance she'd been so fearful about. His jaw was tight with tension, his eyes were cold with disbelief and anger.

It's none of his business, she told herself. But as soon as she thought that, her insides caved in because deep down, she'd hoped the two of them would return to their community, their roots, together.

"I don't want to explain my reasons," she said quietly, collecting the plates to give herself something to do. "I already told you and Jimmie the reasons why. Suffice to say, the neighborhood is changing for the better, and I want to be part of that change. Mom's going to be the bookkeeper for my business, hopefully for the others I rent to, as well. It's an opportunity for her, too, because she'll own stock in the business, be a part of something that's growing."

He nodded, a smirk on his face. "You should talk to Jimmie about renting some of that space for his indie company."

"The company he wants to partner with you?"

"An independent film company is a small dream, Ellie, with small returns. Just like your moving back to the hood is a small dream, Ellie, with even smaller returns. I dream big. That's the difference between you and me."

She felt raw and exposed, resentful and hurt. The plan she'd been nurturing for months—frightened but excited at the venture of expanding not only the coffee business, but other ventures—had just been unilaterally trashed.

She slid off the bed, picked up the plates. "I'll, uh, take these back into the kitchen. It's late, and you have to get up early, so why don't you get into bed."

As she left, she remembered Magellan's words that day she and Bill had been on the stage—*Cinderella didn't make it home before midnight, but the story didn't end there.*

Boy, did he have that wrong. Cinderella didn't make it home before midnight, but she should have because the story didn't just end, it had just come to a grinding halt.

AT SIX THE NEXT MORNING, Ellie slipped inside the beach house, trying not to make any sound so as not to wake anyone.

"El, is that you?" Candy, dressed in a white bikini bottom, a white shirt tied around her waist, did a double take at her hair. "You dyed it black again?"

Ellie nodded, shutting the front door behind her.

"Wearing your burlesque skirt with a *Sin on the Beach* T-shirt?"

"Yeah, it's the new goth beach look. Part Sandra Dee, part Elvira."

Candy laughed, then gave her friend a saucy look. "So if you're sneaking in, that must mean…"

Ellie wandered into the kitchen to make coffee. "Bill and I had a date, yes."

"You sound a little—"

"Just tired, that's all." She didn't want to talk about it. Not yet. As she filled the coffeepot, she glanced at Candy. "And unless you've started sleeping in your bikini bottoms, I think you just sneaked in, too."

Candy blushed. "Yeah, but it's not serious, of course. Just—"

"I know. Sensible sex." Maybe she should have tried that plan with Bill. Made a lot more sense than her midnight one, that's for sure. "How's our Sara? Did she sneak in, too?"

"Not yet." Candy sat at the kitchen counter, grinning like a kid. "Pretty good vacation, eh?"

"Sure is." Ellie busied herself pouring coffee into the filter, getting down the mugs.

"I have a business luncheon today. Do you have another call on the set?"

She did, but she didn't want to go. "Yes."

"Cool. I bet Bill drools every time he sees you in one of your killer bikinis."

"Yeah," she said softly, thinking how he was anything but drooling when he'd dropped her off. This morning they'd been pleasant to each other. Quite civil, actually, in an aren't-we-being-grown-up-despite-our-devastating-tiff kind of way.

But it had sucked all the same.

He'd given her a quick kiss on the lips goodbye, she'd said something casually cheery like "Have a great day," but her move to East L.A. had definitely built a cold wall between them.

"Well," Candy said, heading off, "gotta hit the shower, get ready for the luncheon. It's so cool you and

Bill got together after all these years. I swear, El, it's like one of those Disney movies, where despite seemingly insurmountable obstacles, true love wins out."

"Yeah," Ellie muttered, "a real Cinderella story."

She flipped on the coffeemaker, not sure whether to laugh or cry.

16

ELLIE WASN'T SURE if she was a sucker for a challenge, a fool for an insurmountable obstacle or if she had too much time on her hands. But here she was, eight hours later on the set, playing a semigoth, sorta-glam beach babe extra. Which meant she'd spent the day sashaying around in a string bikini that barely covered her goth tats, fluffing her dyed-black-over-blond hair and slathering sunblock on her fake tan.

Peter, the happy-go-lucky assistant casting director made a twirling motion, which she'd come to recognize as a time-out signal.

"Okay, people," Peter said, the lighted cigarette in his hand weaving smoke into the air every time he gestured, "take fifteen. And I don't want anyone—" he pretended to look over all of them, but let his gaze linger on Ellie so she'd get the message "—fraternizing with any of the crew, including the director. Understood?"

He'd made this speech every break, as though, given the opportunity, Ellie would break loose from the pack like some kind of rabid beachnik and make a beeline for Bill as she had yesterday.

Which she'd never do, of course.

It was bad enough she'd shown up for work.

The carriage had turned to a pumpkin, the horses to mice, but Cinderella obviously had a stubborn streak, because she'd returned to the ball minus the magic.

Ellie wandered over to a cluster of chairs and umbrellas—the extras' break area—and sank onto a white plastic chair, shielding her eyes as she looked out at the ocean, that vast blue entity that had witnessed her and Bill's heated lovemaking last night on its shore. It saddened her to realize it would never happen again.

"Hey, Ellie, what's up?" asked Gus, sitting in the chair next to her. He stretched out his long tanned legs. He wore his customary red board shorts, but today his T-shirt read Surf Shack, which Peter had fretted about and quibbled over before the shoot, citing some contract fine print about extras not wearing logos other than ones for the show's sponsors, but giving in after Gus eloquently argued that the Surf Shack, being a real Malibu hot spot, gave the show a touch of authenticity.

"Doing okay," she lied.

"Me, too." He pulled a comb out of his pocket and raked it through his white hair. "Tell you the truth, I was surprised you showed up on the set today after that little brouhaha yesterday."

The *little brouhaha* being the tension between her

and Bill when she'd been one pestering body too many at the director's station. Funny to think there was that brouhaha, then last night's brouhaha… Was the problem that she and Bill were just too passionate to be together?

Nah. Passion was one of the better things about their being together. More and more, she was realizing their problems were, oddly enough, cultural. When most people had that problem it was because of different cultures. Their problem was their common one. He hated East L.A., she dug it. His whole thing was about overcoming his past, hers was about returning to it.

"We got over that brouhaha," she said casually. But would they ever get over the culture issue? She didn't think so.

"Outside," murmured Gus, a surfer term referring to large waves building far from shore. He slipped the comb back into his pocket. "Looks like a gnarly wave headed straight for Bill."

She looked over. Sure enough, Sullivan, his face pinched, was marching across the sand toward Bill. The group hovering around him instantly scattered.

Blasts of Sullivan's words could be heard all through the set.

"Why the hell did you?…I don't care!… I told you no and you did it anyway!"

Bill's voice was low, the words unintelligible.

"Don't care!" Sullivan boomed. "And furthermore, you're fired!"

Ellie clutched the arms of her chair, watching as the two men stared each other down. She held her breath, expecting the next sound to be fists smacking.

But Sullivan abruptly turned and marched back to his trailer.

"This job meant everything to him," she whispered.

"Not that I don't feel sorry for the guy, but maybe that's part of his problem," Gus said.

An eerie silence descended over the set, the only sounds the creaking of a boom mike and the distant crashing waves.

After a moment, Bill ripped off his headset, snatched up his notebook, and without even a glance at the crew or the actors, walked away.

Ellie stood, her heart pounding, imagining his devastation. Despite what had happened between them, her heart reached out. He'd told her how, starting with film school, he'd spent years honing his skills and working toward a job such as this one where he'd finally have the opportunity to prove himself as a director.

And now that opportunity had been torn away from him.

She disagreed with his need to dream so big, but she wasn't so small as to abandon a friend.

"Tell Peter I'm leaving," she said to Gus.

"You coming back?"

"Nope." She started walking after Bill. "My beach babe days are over."

BILL HEARD Ellie's urgent pleadings behind him, but he kept walking. He didn't want to talk to anybody, deal with anything. His throat scalded with the words he'd held back, the accusations he'd wanted to scream at Sullivan. The guy was a *line* producer, not a creative producer. Which meant he was the bean counter, the budget-meister, the money cop who watched the bottom line and never had anything, *anything,* to do with the artistic aspects.

Unfortunately, the invisible executive producer had given Sullivan free rein to be whatever he wanted to be.

Bill cursed, pissed at the entire film industry that broke people's souls, pissed at Sullivan who'd micromanaged the shoot to failure, but mostly pissed with himself because he'd gambled his career on this gig and lost.

"Bill, please wait!"

"No, Ellie!"

"C'mon, I'm your friend." A short yelp. "Ow, ow, ow!"

Blowing out an exasperated breath, he turned, glowering at her. Ellie, black hair flopping in her eyes, was jogging in place, her face tight with pain.

"What the hell—" He looked down at her bare feet, his frown deepening. "What is it with you and shoes? Either you're wearing heels too high, wedgies too unmanageable or you're barefoot on hot sand. Are you crazy?"

She winced, blinking back the pain. "Probably,

but that's beside the point. I was worried about you. Didn't want you to go."

He saw the twelve-year-old girl again, who'd run out barefoot in the middle of the night, desperate to know if it was really true, was he leaving....

Shaking his head, he walked back to her. "C'mon," he said, opening his arms, "I'll carry you."

"No! That's not why I followed. I wanted to be here for you, not—"

He lifted her into his arms, shifting her weight to get comfortable, then turned and continued walking, this time more slowly, across the sand. Sunbathers looked up. A guy with a boogie board cut in front of them, grinning.

"Bill, please, put me down."

"No."

"You're under enough stress, you don't need to be carrying me."

"Yeah, well, you don't need to be searing the skin off the bottom of your feet, either." He blew a drip of sweat off his lip, tightening his grip on her.

He walked in a straight line across the beach as though he had a purpose, as though he knew his goal. But in truth he was lost, more lost than he'd ever been. But he kept moving forward because it's all he knew to do, aware only of the hot sun on his skin, the salt in the air, the feel of Ellie in his arms.

Ellie.

He tightened his hold on her, holding her closer, needing her as he never had before.

"Ellie," he whispered, his voice fractured, "I'm nothing."

"No!" She cradled his face with her hand. "You lost an opportunity, but you didn't lose yourself."

He snorted a laugh. "You don't understand Hollywood. Newbie director gets fired from first gig? It's like a death sentence. Nobody will hire me now. Nobody."

A couple of kids, carrying bright plastic buckets and shovels, screamed and laughed as they waddled in front of their parents toward the shore.

"Maybe," she said, treading carefully, "this is a sign for you and Jimmie to start your company."

He walked a few moments in silence. "Never did like Sullivan. The man has an ego the size of Manhattan."

If Sullivan's ego was Manhattan, thought Ellie, Bill's was Texas.

That's when it hit her. This wasn't just about losing a job, an opportunity. It was about being big, which to Bill was synonymous with success. Directing a big film, being an A-list Hollywood power player, being a big name…because anything less— such as running an indie company—was too small to be significant.

As sad as she was for him, she was suddenly irritated, too. The kind of irritation that comes from caring and having your hands tied behind your back. She'd thought earlier how Bill was driven to overcome his past. At some point he'd decided, unconsciously or not, that he couldn't do that unless he was bigger, better than the next guy.

No wonder he felt like nothing. In his mind, he'd lost all his power.

MINUTES LATER, they reached the entrance to the festival. Bill, flushed and breathing hard, set her down on a shady patch of sand underneath an awning. "Let's go in. I'm parched, need something to drink." He looked at her feet. "And we need to get you some thongs."

"Thanks."

Catching his breath, his gaze traveled up her legs, lingering on the snug bit of material between her legs, his problems pushed aside enough to remember her taste, her cries of pleasure, the way her body trembled just before she came.

"Look," he said, meeting her eyes, "about this morning…"

She shrugged. "It's okay."

"It's just that…where we grew up…"

She quietly nodded, took his hand. "Bill, I think I understand more than you know. Let's get that cold drink."

THEY MADE A PACT to avoid reality.

For as long as they were inside the festival, they were not allowed to discuss or worry about Sullivan or *Sin on the Beach*. Comments about goths or anything gothic were fine as long as a certain someone didn't start obsessing whether she was acceptable as one. To ensure they didn't stumble into a tension-fraught conversation, neither was allowed to say the words "director" or "East L.A."

That settled, fifteen minutes later they meandered down the midway sipping their drinks, Ellie in a pair of new black thongs, two people who for all appearances didn't have a care in the world.

Suddenly Bill halted, tugging her to his side. "Ellie, look!"

He pointed to the three screens outside the Hot Shot Photo Contest, each displaying photos that randomly changed every few minutes.

Ellie nearly choked on her drink. "Oh, no."

Bill grinned. "Oh, *yes*."

Ellie's face filled one of the screens, looking shy but obviously excited. Or maybe she just remembered how excited she'd been.

"Please tell me you only downloaded the G-rated photos," she murmured.

"I only downloaded G-rated, promise. This is great. They're showing all the downloaded entries until the winners are announced at the end of the festival."

He stood behind her, his arms encircling hers. The way he cradled her, she felt incredibly close to him.

"I remember that ride so well," he said in a low voice. "The sweet scent of your skin, our first kiss… You tasted like lemonade and sunshine."

The photo dissolved as another one displayed.

"Wow!" She stared at the crisscross of her fishnet cover-up transposed over the lines of the spiderweb. "Bill, you're a good photographer!"

"That's because…"

She knew the rest of it without his saying. Because of his training as a director.

"Because I'm visual," he finally said.

"More than visual," she said gently, "you're talented, too. Look how others are stopping to look at the photo."

He nuzzled the soft pink shell of her ear, then nibbled on the lobe. "Maybe that's because of the beautiful woman in the picture."

When a close-up of a dragon head flashed on another screen, the gathering crowd oohed and ahed.

"You're a good photographer, too," he whispered into her ear.

Gasping softly, she reached up and stroked his face while continuing to watch the photos of themselves.

"It's exciting to watch us," he murmured, trailing his fingers around her waist. "We're good together, Ellie."

She held her breath, as though to release it might release the magic of what he'd said. Silly, and yet when she finally exhaled, she did it slowly, as though testing the magic of his words.

Nothing changed. He still cradled her from behind, they still stared at the photos although theirs were no longer flashing on the screens.

We're good together, Ellie.

So what if they'd had a few bumps in the road, they kept coming back together, kept reconnecting, kept digging deeper and finding new meaning in their relationship. Yes, relationship. She knew as certainly as her heart was beating that this would go on.

Maybe for the long haul?

They were at a point in their lives where they were both starting new careers. Hers with the expanded coffee shop, clothing-design business, not to mention overseeing other commercial rental spaces. His with whatever he wanted to pursue next. Starting out together, they could give each other a lot of support and encouragement, be each other's cheering sections.

Of course, he'd refuse to move to East L.A., would probably refuse to even visit her there. Which meant the commuting would be up to her, which would be stressful and difficult. A normal twenty-minute drive on the 405 could take up to three hours during peak times. No way she could handle hours-long commutes and kick off several businesses, which meant this whole damn thing was doomed before it got off the ground so why even care?

"All that stands between fear and outcome is courage, my friends, courage!"

"Hear that?" Bill chuckled. "Sounds like our friend Magellan is nearby."

"He's a nut."

"So we all are, I say." Bill pulled her around, kissed her on the tip of her nose. "The guy's funny, and laughter is the best medicine, so I say let's join the audience and enjoy ourselves."

She gave in, wanting to shake her thoughts. Bill was right. Laughter was a good thing.

A few minutes later, they stood in the crowd, watching Magellan lure a young couple onto the stage.

"Come, come," Magellan said to the guy and girl heading up the stairs to the stage. "I have no tricks up my sleeves, just the insights of my mind into your lives, and the mysteries I will foretell!"

"Do you think he'd bald underneath that turban?" asked Ellie.

"Bald?" asked Bill. "Could be. That turban fits pretty snugly."

Magellan suddenly stopped talking. Turning to the audience, he scanned the crowd.

"Ah," he said, his gaze falling on Bill, "have you learned what has roots nobody sees, is taller than trees?"

The first lines of the riddle. Bill smiled, shook his head.

Magellan nodded knowingly, his gaze drifting to Ellie. He gave her a wink before turning back to his act. "Everyone," he said, sweeping his hand to the young couple on stage, "give these brave people a hand."

Someone touched Ellie's shoulder and she jumped.

17

ELLIE GASPED, jerked her head around.

"Sis!"

"Matt!" She looked him up and down. "Wow, look at you! Brad Pitt, step aside."

Her brother actually blushed. "I'm a made-over man, what can I say?" He nodded to Bill. "We meet again, neighbor."

"How's it goin', Matt?"

"Great. Hey, El, I just saw the Queen of Evil's name posted outside the contest area as one of the winners for the Good Vibrations contest. Congratulations!"

"Cool!" Ellie gave Bill a high five.

"So, why aren't you two on the set? I didn't know Hollywood directors got to play hooky."

"Yeah, they do," chimed in Ellie. "It's one of the perks. So how's Candy? Wasn't today some kind of important business luncheon?" If she kept talking about Candy, the conversation wouldn't return to Bill's directing career. "Yes, it was. She told me this morning. Duh. I should've remembered that. That Candy, wow, is she a marketing powerhouse or what?"

Matt started to speak.

Ellie cut him off. "She deserves recognition for that, too. Which will happen of course when she gets that team leader thing at SyncUp."

"What?" asked Matt.

"You know, that team leader position—"

"Candy *knew* about that?"

"Sure! That's Candy for you. A mover and shaker, her finger always on the pulse of what's happening."

"I, uh, need to go." Matt started to leave, stopped, turned back. "Good seeing you again, Bill."

"Same here, Matt."

With a halfhearted salute, her brother disappeared into the crowd.

"He seems to have a lot on his mind," said Bill.

"Don't we all."

Bill gave her an approving look. "So the Queen of Evil is a winner, eh? Let's go check that out, see how she, I mean you, did."

She smiled. "I've been pretty silly...."

"Silly's good. Worrying's bad." He put his arm around her as they started walking toward the Good Vibrations stage. "Would've been nice if you'd let me in on your internal angst so I could have put your mind to rest."

"I'm not always so good about speaking up."

"Coulda fooled me."

She laughed, playfully punched him. "Bill Romero, you should know better than to mess with the Queen of Evil!"

A FEW MINUTES LATER, they stood in front of the Good Vibrations stage, now empty, where it had all happened the night before.

"Here it is!" Bill leaned closer to the sign. "Queen of Evil, you came in second place."

"Second?" She peered up at the sign. "Who knocked the queen out of first place?"

"Keep in mind, queenie, it was a tough competition. Ready to hear?"

She nodded, liking how they were playing with each other.

"First place went to...Danny Gerash and his singing water glasses."

She feigned disappointment. "If only I'd brought more water into my act."

"Obviously, that was the key." They shared a smile. "But they gave you, I mean us, *couple* points, queenie!"

"Team Java Mammas will be proud."

They stood, their arms around each other as they looked out at the empty stage.

"I have good memories of that," whispered Ellie.

"Me, too. After I got over my jealousy."

She gave him a squeeze. "The Queen of Evil got you that worked up, huh?"

"No," he breathed, stroking his hand along her arm, "Ellie Rockwell got me that worked up." He slid his hand down to hers, lacing their fingers, his warm fingers lazily stroking and rubbing hers.

"Come on," Bill said, leading her toward the stage, "I want to be a couple again."

They left their drinks on the edge of the small stage, then walked to the center where he gathered her into his arms, swaying slightly to an unheard tune.

She linked her hands together around his neck, laid her head on his chest, heady with his scent, his strength, the sweetness of the moment. The festival receded like the waves, pulling far back to the sea, leaving the two of them here in their own private world.

His hands moved down her back, settling momentarily on her hips where he pressed her against him, showing her how she made him feel. Then he skimmed his fingers back up, feathering lightly across her bare skin, up to the sensitive area of her neck.

She shuddered, looked up into his face, saw in his eyes that he hid nothing from her. Neither the pain of his dismissal…nor the intensity of his desire. He was a strong man, probably the strongest she'd ever known, which made his willingness to let down his guard and be vulnerable all the more precious to her.

He was showing her that he trusted her.

He slipped his fingers up her neck, cupping her head with his hold, his other hand gliding up her rib cage, up to the swell of her breast which he gently massaged, his body turned so it shielded his movements from others.

He leaned close, his stubble rough against her

cheek. "I want you," he murmured, his mouth nibbling seductively at hers. "I need you."

Fire leaped in her belly as he pulled her tightly
against him, his hard male body against hers. Over
his shoulder, she saw the curtained-off changing
area still standing, hidden behind some stacked
chairs and equipment. The sight was dangerous,
made her think of things she shouldn't be thinking,
not in broad daylight....

Another part of her said *screw it*. This man needed
her, she needed him, and after what they'd been
through, maybe this was all they had. Now. Here.

Not wanting to think or question, she took his
hand and led him off the stage.

Moments later, after peering outside to ensure no
one had seen their escape, she slid the curtain closed.

Sunlight filtered through the blue material that
fluttered with the ocean breezes, the rippling light
creating an underwater effect.

She looked at him, her heart hammering, her
breaths suddenly shaky. All the tension, passion, heat
of the day welled up inside her, burning off every last
coherent thought. All she wanted was to touch him,
feel him, taste him.

He slid down her bikini bottom, inched his hand
into her wet curls, zeroing in on her core. Stifling a
cry, she fumbled with his shorts, managed to pull
them down far enough to free his stiff cock.

"No," he growled, working her harder, "you first."

She sputtered a contradiction that ended in a hiss

as she widened her thighs, her sex throbbing with his probing, circling fingers, her hand mindlessly squeezing his sex, her mouth blindly streaking his face, his lips, finally latching onto that bushy little soul patch, suckling as though her very life depended on it. A hot, bold quickie. She'd never done this before, but then, no man had ever been Bill. With him, she felt unabashedly wild, exquisitely free, incorrigibly wanton.

Panting, rubbing, licking, she suddenly rose onto her toes and arched her back, foggily realizing those depraved, needy grunts were hers.

She clutched his shirt for balance, clenching her teeth as the first climax hit, stifling her panting squeals as she rode his hand, thrusting her hips hard and tight, over and over to completion until, with a final whimper, she settled back onto her feet. Lazily opening her eyes, she pulled out his hand and, while holding his gaze, lightly flicked her tongue over the tips of his fingers.

His eyes glinted with heat and surprise.

With a wicked grin, she sank to her knees onto the sandy floor.

She took him into her mouth, his shaft so smooth and hard, his taste salty, musky. Still throbbing from her own orgasm, she groaned as she drew him into her mouth, loving his deep shudder of pleasure.

Sea breezes swept underneath the curtains, stroking and cooling her heated flesh. Cradling his balls with one hand, she juggled them softly as she twirled her tongue around the hardened ridge, a teaser before taking him in with a long, wet suck.

Tightening her lips, she pulled her mouth back up his rigid sex, stroking in tandem with her hand, repeating the movement slowly back down, up, down….

His hands tangled in her hair as his hips twitched. "Look at me," he whispered hoarsely, "Ellie, please…"

She held his dark gaze as she licked and stroked and sucked, her hands working with her tongue, her eyes telling him everything she'd never said in words.

"Ellie…" He blinked, his voice racked with emotion. "Ellie, I…"

As his release came, she took him in, coddling him with her mouth and hands, savoring his pleasure, knowing that what'd they done had been more, much more than a hot quickie. Hot and quick, yes, but they'd also made love.

Love.

Which he'd known, too, even though that was the word he'd left unsaid.

Soon after, they continued their stroll down the midway, sipping their melted-down lemonades, occasionally sharing a secret smile.

If there was ever a moment in her life that felt perfect, this was it. The swirl of ocean air, the happy energy of the festivalgoers, the quiet, unspoken connection between her and Bill. For a crazy moment, she felt as though she didn't deserve this, that maybe their pact to stave off reality meant this was a dream and nothing more, that it would end after they passed through the festival gates and returned to the real world.

A cell phone rang.

"Not mine because I left it at the set," Ellie said with a shrug. "Plus I have the Lou Reed ringtone."

"How could I forget," teased Bill, flicking her an amused look as he fished in his shorts' pocket. He retrieved his phone, answered it.

"Bill here."

He listened, his face growing tight, angry. He looked at Ellie, mouthed "Sullivan."

Sullivan.

She felt an ugly foreboding, wondered if the producer was blaming Bill for more problems, maybe threatening legal action. What a mess. So much for their escape from reality.

Then, a look of surprise came over Bill's face. He glanced at Ellie, his eyes sparkling.

"No need to," he said into the phone. "Okay, go ahead… Yes… All right… Fine… Thanks, bye." He flipped it shut, dropped it back into his pocket, then flashed her a big, guess-what grin.

She returned the smile, but inside she felt chilled, afraid.

"Sullivan apologized. Asked me to come back as director."

Down the midway, the merry-go-round started, the calliope playing a lighthearted, airy children's tune. In the distance, Magellan called out for people to be brave, to have courage.

"That's great," she said cautiously, "if that's what you want."

He sputtered a laugh. "Are you kidding? Of course I want it! But that's not the best part. He's asked me to be the next director. No more tryouts, no more filling in. I'm number one, Ellie!"

He pulled her into a bear hug, squeezing her so hard, she could scarcely breathe. "That's great," she heard herself saying in a voice she didn't recognize, "just great."

He pulled back, his smile fading as he caught the look in her eyes.

"What is it?"

She swallowed, wondering if she should say what was weighing on her heart. But if she didn't, she was no better than the Ellie who'd stuffed down the truth about herself, imagining it to be worse than it really was. Maybe that was true here, too. What she imagined wasn't as bad as she thought.

"Bill," she said softly, "you're not happy in that job."

"Says who?"

Now that she'd said it, she realized her words were dead-on right. He'd have the job, the title, but he'd lose his self-respect.

"Me. Sullivan won't change. Like you said, he's a line producer trying to take artistic control. You'll live under his thumb, under his public humiliations day after day. You're better than that job."

"Better?" One black eyebrow shot up. "Look, Sullivan's an asshole, I'll grant you that. But sometimes that's what it takes to run a big, successful project." He half smiled, made a dismissive gesture. "Forget all that. The fact is, it's the kind of big break I've spent my entire career going after, and if it means I have to deal with an asshole on a daily basis, so be it."

The calliope sounded so loud, the organ music jarring. She touched her fingers to her brow, trying to shut out the chaos of people and noises around them. She lowered her hand, suddenly feeling tired and drained from the intensity of the day. "I just think you'd be happier at the independent film company—"

Bill tried to bite back the expletive, but it shot out anyway. "Sorry," he muttered, raking his hand through his hair. "You and I have a bad habit of having these arguments in the middle of the damn midway."

She twisted her mouth. "Maybe we should have made a pact about not doing that, too."

They stared each other down for a long moment.

"I think our problem," he said quietly, "is that you dream small, Ellie, and I dream big."

"*Our* problem?" She laughed. "I think *your* problem is you're so caught up in being a big man with a big career you've lost all perspective."

People were gawking, craning their necks as they walked by.

"Ellie, just because you're settling for a small dream doesn't mean I have to."

He saw the hurt in her eyes, and hated himself for

putting it there. It was inevitable, he now realized, that they'd reach this point. He could never go back, and she could never not.

"By *small*," she said, "you mean the hood."

He nodded.

"Have you ever thought that no matter how big you think you are," she murmured, "your prejudice will always make you small? You're ashamed of your roots, and until that changes, you'll be ashamed of yourself."

His face turned hard, dangerous, as his gaze delved into hers. "Let me get this straight. Just because you're going back, it's going to get better? Like, all those poor kids who think being successful is growing up to be a drug dealer and driving a Range Rover…*you're* gonna change that?"

"You're changing the subject."

"You brought up the hood, sister. Seems you think throwin' lattes at the homies will cover up all the neighborhood's problems." He held up a strand of her hair. "Let's see…this is black over blond over black…but I recall you had penny-colored hair that matched your freckles when you were a little girl. Where'd they go? In my book, people cover up the things they're ashamed of."

If he'd stuck a knife into her, it would've hurt less than his slicing words. Maybe because what he said resonated deeply within her.

The way he looked right now—his tough-guy body language, the pitch of his shoulder, the way he'd flung out his hand behind his back—brought back memories of the boy from years ago. His back up, watching out for his family. Tougher than the next guy. Not taking it off nobody.

"Doesn't take a genius," she said softly, "to figure out that someone who slathers on makeup and clothes might be covering up something, even from themselves. What's sad is the person who thinks the glitzy job, the big bucks, the fancy title disguises who he really is—a punk kid on a street corner, angry at the world for the burden and hurt it placed on his shoulders."

She watched him walk away, barely aware she'd dropped her drink, its cold liquid pooling around her feet.

In the distance, Magellan cajoled his audience. "I have no tricks up my sleeves, just the insights of my mind into your lives, and the mysteries I will foretell!"

She'd been conned by the festival and its smoke and mirrors, by the carnies and their tricks, even by the games and their promises.

But most of all, she'd been conned by love. Everything she'd felt and believed and desired had been nothing but an illusion. Had been nothing but a trick of light in her heart.

18

THE NEXT MORNING, after Ellie had helped convince a disheartened Sara not to give up on Drew and helped a mortified Candy recover from yet another of her festival escapades, Ellie lied to both her pals and said she was spending the day being an extra on the set.

Then, after they'd left the beach house, Ellie returned to pack up and leave.

Gus, bless his heart, had dropped off her purse, so she didn't have to go back to the set to pick it up. After she got her things together, she'd leave a note that there was a crisis at Dark Gothic Roast and leave.

Inside, she headed to her room, started tossing her stuff into her bag. Holding up her burlesque skirt, she smiled at its wet, bedraggled appearance—the result of that lusty night at the beach with Bill—before tossing it into the trash can.

What happened in Malibu could sure as hell stay in Malibu.

Cinderella was finally leaving the ball. A bit worse for wear, but that's what happened when you overstayed your welcome.

She headed into the bathroom to wash her face. Looking into the mirror, she heard Bill's words—*In my book, people cover up the things they're ashamed of.* Was that it? She was ashamed?

Of what?

She'd certainly put a lot of time and effort into covering up parts of herself. She'd dyed her hair so much, even she couldn't remember its natural color. Her tan face was part fake, part natural, but give her a few goth minutes and it'd be artificially snow-white again.

She squinted, leaned forward. Well, surprise, surprise. There were a few freckles over the bridge of her nose, just like when she was a kid.

Made her think of her dad…he'd touch her freckles, giving each one a name…silly names, always different…Tina, Teeny, Itty, Bitty….

When he'd left, she'd blamed herself. Didn't matter if her teacher, her mother, even Matt said no, that's not the case, she did. If only she'd been better, nicer, sweeter, she'd have been more acceptable and he wouldn't have left.

She opened the medicine cabinet and collected her pancake makeup, the blood-red lipsticks, the dark pencil sticks…and tossed them into the trash. She could always buy more, but for the time being, she had the urge to let those freckles get some fresh air again.

Heading back to her bedroom, she heard someone knocking at the door. Maybe one of the girls had forgotten their keys. Or Matt had heard about the guy

Candy had dragged home last night. Well, Ellie wasn't going to give him her sisterly matchmaking caretaking advice. No, not this girl. She'd tell him that any guy who agreed to something called *sensible sex* needed to look up the word *oxymoron* in the dictionary.

She opened the door, ready to say just that, and froze.

Bill, looking sheepish and too handsome for his own good, leaned against the doorjamb. She wrapped her arms around herself as though that could contain the breathless emotion that clutched at her heart.

"Hi," he murmured. When he dipped his head, sun glinted off a gold earring.

"Hi."

He glanced at her nose, smiled. "I see your freckles."

She shrugged, checked out the smooth planes of his cheeks and jaw. "I see you shaved."

"Kept the soul patch, though." He tickled it with his finger.

"Good," she whispered, remembering it all too well.

"May I come in?"

She hesitated, dreading the inevitable sorry-let's-be-friends talk. "Shouldn't you be on the set?" she said oh-so-nonchalantly, stepping back to let him inside.

"I was."

"You're on a break?"

"Sort of."

"Well, glad things are working out." So cavalier, so together, as though her heart was still in one piece. Really, Ellie should win an Academy Award. "I'm packing, getting ready to go home."

"Oh, I'd hoped— Well, I brought good news."

"*Sin on the Beach* has a plotline?"

He flashed her an amused look. She'd miss that look.

"No." He pulled an envelope from his pocket. "We won a Hot Shot prize. Not one of the *top* prizes, but a fun one nevertheless—the Dishonorable Mention award." He handed the envelope to her.

She opened it, read the coupon for a free weekend at a five-star hotel, including meals. "Guess it pays to be dishonorable," she said a little too lightly, handing it back.

He held up his hands. "No, it's yours."

"I'd feel a little silly going alone. Maybe you and Vi?"

"You know," he said, growing serious, "that Dishonorable Mention award made me think of things in my life that were so intolerable, they'd become dishonorable. So I made a few calls this morning to fix that. First one was to Vi. Told her we're not going to have that talk."

Vi the *Kama Sutra* Wonder with the French accent was no more? Before Ellie gave in to the cheap thrill of success, she reminded herself she and Bill were no more, either.

"Made another call after that," he continued, his

brown eyes solemn. "Remember how Magellan said the bridge between fear and outcome is courage? I called Sullivan, told him I was staying only out of fear and quit. He wanted me to elaborate, so I told him sometimes big isn't better. I'm sure he'll be pondering that for days."

She let the words sink in. "You *quit?*"

He nodded. "Made another call right after that to Jimmie, asked if he'd still like me as a partner in JimBill Productions."

"I thought it was—" She smiled. "After what you put him through, he should get top billing."

"That's what I thought. He's already pulling his script from consideration at another studio—I told you he wrote that protagonist based on my life growing up?"

"I recall hearing something about that."

"Yeah…character's name is Gonzo."

For a moment she couldn't breathe.

Bill stepped closer, a worried look on his face. "Ellie, you okay?"

"Yes, I think…I need to sit down."

He followed her to the couch, sat next to her. "You're shaking."

She waved off his worry. "I'm okay, it's… Magellan."

"What about him?"

She dropped her hand back into her lap, realizing she'd finally had her first real supernatural experience. "He's the real deal," she whispered.

"You think?"

She nodded. "I know he is. It's just...I learned something too late."

Taking a deep breath, she rolled back her shoulders. "I was next on your list of things to fix, so let's get it over with."

"Over with?" Bill knew he'd been a jerk yesterday, but he'd hoped this would turn out differently. That's what he got for being a cocky, temperamental, bullheaded man. He believed his own stories, especially the ones he made up in his mind.

"Speaking of intolerable and dishonorable," he said solemnly, "I'm sorry for the things I said yesterday. You were right when you said I was ashamed of my roots, and until that changes, I'll be ashamed of myself."

This was harder than he thought, but he had to say it. "You know, it wasn't me who was the golden boy of my family. It was Reggie. He was smarter, kinder, better than all of us put together. I was busy with my studies in New York when Mom called to say he'd fallen in with a gang. She wanted me to come home, talk sense into him, but I was too caught up in myself." His voice dropped. "Sometimes in life, it's not what you do, but what you don't do."

He suddenly felt as though the facade he'd held together all these years cracked, and the loss, the overwhelming loss rose to the surface, seeped through the breaks, wiping out the years of control, but not the guilt...the horrible guilt....

"Oh, Bill," Ellie murmured, wrapping her arms around him, holding him tightly against her. "It wasn't your fault."

He laid his cheek against hers, giving in to her softness. Neither spoke for a long moment.

"I've been thinking about that riddle," he finally murmured. "What has roots nobody sees, is taller than trees, its virtues it sows, and yet never grows?"

She shook her head. "I don't know the answer."

He pulled back and looked into her eyes. "Yes, Ellie, you do. You always have. The answer is home. Roots. I want to return there, do the right thing in honor of my kid brother. You set up your coffee shop and clothing designs, Jim and I will set up our indie company. And let's make a place other than the streets for kids like Reggie."

She nodded, blinked. "Sure."

He sat up, a funny smile on his face. "Me, a guy who loves details, and I forgot the most important part." Cradling her face with his hands, he let out a long, slow breath as he looked into her bright, questioning eyes.

"I love you, Ellie Rockwell. I think I've loved you ever since that night years ago, when you asked if I was going away. I should have known then no matter where I traveled or what I did, the place I belonged was there, with you."

"Seventeen."

"What?"

She looped her arms around his neck and smiled. "That night was seventeen years ago."

He quirked a smile. "You have a good memory."

"It's not just my memory." She leaned closer, whispering against his lips. "I know because in my heart, I've loved you every single day, hour and minute of those seventeen years, Bill Romero."

And Cinderella, no longer worried about curfews or hair color or even the misunderstood Queen of Evil, kissed her prince.

Swoop, swoop, rock, rock.

* * * * *

Don't miss the conclusion to the
SEX ON THE BEACH *mini-series!*
Look for Wild Child *by Cindi Myers, coming August 2008 from Mills & Boon® Blaze®.*

Cool drinks, warm sand and sexy guys!
Everything a girl needs for the perfect holiday.

Wild Child *by Cindi Myers*

Sara Montgomery needs this vacation in the biggest way. But getting unplugged from the mobile phone and laptop is proving tricky. Luckily for her, Drew Jamison arrives as the perfect distraction…

Turn the page for a sneak preview of Wild Child *by Cindi Myers*

The sensational conclusion to the SEX ON THE BEACH *mini-series available from Mills & Boon® Blaze® in August 2008.*

Wild Child

by

Cindi Myers

THE COOL firmness of sand between her toes, the smell of salt and suntan oil, the thunder of waves and the shrill cries of seagulls transported Sara to her girlhood. Walking alongside Drew, she felt that same sense of possibility to the afternoon—that wonderful anticipation she'd come to Malibu to rediscover. With a surfboard tucked under one arm, he even *looked* like the idols of her youth. Anything could happen as long as the sun shone and her companion kept smiling at her.

She glanced at him and he winked. Now she *really* felt like a girl again; it was all she could do not to giggle. She was glad she'd agreed to come with him. He was easy to be with, and he'd given her the perfect excuse to get away, though her phone was in the beach bag she'd grabbed to bring along.

Whether she could go through with her original plan to seduce this hottie was debatable. Her seduction skills were definitely rusty.

Ellie would probably say that was all the more reason for her to practice.

They passed a carnival laid out on the sand—

Ferris wheel, arcade games, a stage and volleyball nets. A man in a lime-green turban and a Hawaiian shirt stood at a booth near a sign that read Magellan the All-Knowing. "What's all this?" Sara asked.

"It's all part of the big *Sin on the Beach* party." Drew raised one eyebrow. "I figured that was what brought you here this week."

She shrugged. "My friends said something about it, but I never realized it was so…elaborate."

He nodded. "They're hosting a week-long bash— games, dancing, contests, prizes. It's bigger than spring break."

A week-long bash? "Guess we lucked out." She grinned at him. Talk about the perfect setting for a wild fling.

"My shop is just a little ways up the beach," Drew said. "My grandparents started it almost forty years ago."

"It's hard to imagine having a grandfather who surfs," she said. "It seems like such a hip, young thing to do." Her own mother—like her father before he'd died—was a serious, hard-working person. Even after they'd moved to L.A., her mom had never acclimated to the west-coast lifestyle. She complained that the sun shone too much.

"Grandpa Gus definitely isn't an old fogey," Drew said. "If anything, he acts too young. He forgets he can't do everything he could as a young man and it gets him into trouble."

"And you worry about him," she said.

He gave her a sharp look. "Does it show that much?"

"Not really. But I can relate. I'm the same way with my Uncle Spence. He's younger than your grandfather, but he works so hard. He never lets himself relax, and he worries about everything. He depends on me a lot to help with his business and I hate to let him down."

Drew nodded. "I love Grandpa, and I don't really mind, but sometimes…" His voice trailed away.

"Yeah, sometimes." She knew exactly how Drew felt. Could it be she wasn't the only young adult in the world with too many responsibilities and too much guilt?

"Would you like to see the shop?" Drew asked. "Then maybe we could do something together."

She could think of any number of things she would like to do with him—some of which involved wearing no clothes. Obviously her libido was taking the idea of a no-holds-barred vacation seriously. But even the more sensible part of her liked the idea of getting to know this man better. "That would be great," she said.

Like a bad-tempered chaperone determined to cramp her style, her phone started vibrating, rattling against the keys in the bottom of her bag.

"What is that?" Drew asked.

"Nothing." She groped in her bag, trying to locate the off button for the phone, but only succeeded in getting the strap wrapped around her sunglasses case.

"Seriously, what's that buzzing noise?" Drew moved closer. "Do you have something in there?"

"No, really, it's fine." If she broke off yet another conversation with him to take a call, he was going to think she was a complete workaholic.

He stepped back, grinning. "I've heard about those things, but I never knew a woman who carried one with her to the beach."

"It's not… You don't think—" Her face probably came close to matching the color of her swimsuit. She jerked the cell out of her bag. "It's a phone!"

He laughed. "Hey, did I say it wasn't?" He shook his head. "Go ahead and answer it. Maybe it's your roommate again."

She should be so lucky. She checked the caller ID. "No, it's my uncle."

"Then you'd better answer it."

"Yeah, guess I'd better." She flipped open the phone as she moved a few steps away.

"Sara, why haven't you called the title company?" With those words, Uncle Spence made her magical mood vanish.

The title company! She groaned. "I'm sorry. I got busy and it slipped my mind. I'll call in the morning."

"You need to call now. Granger's been asking me about the closing." She pictured him standing in the clubhouse, sweat pouring down his red face, working himself into a lather over his imagined failure to make a good impression on his top client. "We're having dinner later and I'd like to be able to tell him something specific," he said.

"Just tell Mr. Granger that everything's on schedule and he doesn't need to worry."

"Do you have that flow chart you made up that shows the closing process and everything that happens?"

"*Ye-es.*" She glanced at Drew. He was leaning on his board, looking out at the ocean. She hoped he wasn't getting impatient.

"I'll give you a number to fax it to," Spence said. "I'll give it to Granger at dinner. He's wild for any kind of chart or graph."

"I don't have a fax machine right here."

"Then e-mail it to the office. I'll have Tabitha print it out and fax it."

Drew glanced over at her. She waved. "Uncle Spence, can't this wait?" she asked. "I'm really busy with something else right now."

"How long will it take you to e-mail that chart? And one call to the title company isn't so much to ask." He sighed, sounding sad. "I'm really counting on you, Sara. It's not like you to let me down."

Every word was like another bucketful of sand being poured over her, burying her in guilt. She swallowed hard. "Okay. I'll see what I can do."

She hung up. So much for a carefree afternoon of romance. "Is something wrong?" Drew returned to her side. "You look upset."

"I'm sorry, I have to go," she said. She replaced the phone in her bag, avoiding his eyes. "Something's come up at the office...I'm sorry."

"You can't let someone else take care of it?" he asked.

She shook her head. "No. I'd better go."

She could feel his gaze on her, intense and probing, and disappointment dragged at her. He was such a great guy. They could have had fun together…. She shook her head. "It was great meeting you," she said. Lame words, full of regret for what might have been.

"Yeah. Maybe I'll see you around."

"Yeah." Except she'd be too mortified to go anywhere near him again.

Surfboard tucked under his arm, he strode across the sand. She watched him go, suppressing a sigh. Drew was just too perfect. She'd blown it. Lost her chance. She was doomed to a life chained to her computer.

Celebrate 100 years of pure reading pleasure with Mills & Boon®

To mark our centenary, each month we're publishing a special 100th Birthday Edition. These celebratory editions are packed with extra features and include a FREE bonus story.

Plus, you have the chance to enter a fabulous monthly prize draw. See 100th Birthday Edition books for details.

Now that's worth celebrating!

July 2008

**The Man Who Had Everything
by Christine Rimmer**
Includes FREE bonus story *Marrying Molly*

August 2008

Their Miracle Baby by Caroline Anderson
Includes FREE bonus story *Making Memories*

September 2008

Crazy About Her Spanish Boss by Rebecca Winters
Includes FREE bonus story
Rafael's Convenient Proposal

Look for Mills & Boon® 100th Birthday Editions at your favourite bookseller or visit
www.millsandboon.co.uk

2 FREE

BOOKS AND A SURPRISE GIFT!

We would like to take this opportunity to thank you for reading this Mills & Boon® book by offering you the chance to take TWO more specially selected titles from the Blaze® series absolutely FREE! We're also making this offer to introduce you to the benefits of the Mills & Boon® Reader Service™—

- ★ FREE home delivery
- ★ FREE gifts and competitions
- ★ FREE monthly Newsletter
- ★ Exclusive Reader Service offers
- ★ Books available before they're in the shops

Accepting these FREE books and gift places you under no obligation to buy, you may cancel at any time, even after receiving your free shipment. Simply complete your details below and return the entire page to the address below. You don't even need a stamp!

YES! Please send me 2 free Blaze books and a surprise gift. I understand that unless you hear from me, I will receive 4 superb new titles every month for just £3.15 each, postage and packing free. I am under no obligation to purchase any books and may cancel my subscription at any time. The free books and gift will be mine to keep in any case.

K8ZED

Ms/Mrs/Miss/Mr ....Initials ....
BLOCK CAPITALS PLEASE

Surname ....

Address ....

....

....Postcode.....................................

Send this whole page to:
UK: FREEPOST CN81, Croydon, CR9 3WZ